W9-ARE-629

Praise for *The Crimson Cord*

"Impeccable research and vivid prose from Smith bring the ancient city of Jericho to life."

—*Library Journal*

"Smith, the author of the bestselling Wives of King David and Wives of the Patriarchs series, has made Rahab's dramatic tale newly affecting and vivid."

—*Booklist*

"Don't hesitate to recommend this first book in the Daughters of the Promised Land series to lovers of biblical fiction."

—*CBA Retailers+Resources*

Praise for *The Prophetess*

"This is both a well-drawn love story as well as the wistful imaginings of early Israel."

—*Publishers Weekly*

"Deborah is portrayed as a strong leader and a sensitive, protective mother, making this powerful biblical figure accessible to readers."

—*RT Book Reviews*

"At last, the mystical figure of Deborah comes to life! With obvious research and attention to detail, Jill Eileen Smith gives vivid voice to the women at the center of Israel's victory over Canaan. A tale of strength and faith that bears relevance even today. Not to be missed!"

—**Tosca Lee**, author of *The Legend of Sheba* and multiple *New York Times* bestsellers

REDEEMING GRACE

Books by Jill Eileen Smith

THE WIVES OF KING DAVID
Michal

Abigail

Bathsheba

WIVES OF THE PATRIARCHS
Sarai

Rebekah

Rachel

THE LOVES OF KING SOLOMON (ebook series)
The Desert Princess

The Shepherdess

Daughter of the Nile

DAUGHTERS OF THE PROMISED LAND
The Crimson Cord

The Prophetess

Redeeming Grace

REDEEMING GRACE

RUTH'S STORY

JILL EILEEN SMITH

Revell

a division of Baker Publishing Group
Grand Rapids, Michigan

© 2017 by Jill Eileen Smith

Published by Revell
a division of Baker Publishing Group
P.O. Box 6287, Grand Rapids, MI 49516-6287
www.revellbooks.com

Printed in the United States of America

All rights reserved. No part of this publication may be reproduced, stored in a retrieval system, or transmitted in any form or by any means—for example, electronic, photocopy, recording—without the prior written permission of the publisher. The only exception is brief quotations in printed reviews.

Library of Congress Cataloging-in-Publication Data
Names: Smith, Jill Eileen, 1958– author.
Title: Redeeming grace : Ruth's story / Jill Eileen Smith.
Description: Grand Rapids, MI : Published by Revell, a division of Baker Publishing Group, [2017] | Series: Daughters of the promised land ; #3
Identifiers: LCCN 2016040820| ISBN 9780800720360 (paper) | ISBN 9780800728533 (print on demand)
Subjects: LCSH: Bible. Old Testament—History of Biblical events—Fiction. | Ruth (Biblical figure)—Fiction. | Women in the Bible—Fiction. | GSAFD: Bible fiction. | Christian fiction.
Classification: LCC PS3619.M58838 R45 2017 | DDC 813/.6—dc23
LC record available at https://lccn.loc.gov/2016040820

Most Scripture quotations, whether quoted or paraphrased by the characters, are from The Holy Bible, English Standard Version® (ESV®), copyright © 2001 by Crossway, a publishing ministry of Good News Publishers. Used by permission. All rights reserved. ESV Text Edition: 2011

Some Scripture quotations are from the Holy Bible, New International Version®. NIV®. Copyright © 1973, 1978, 1984, 2011 by Biblica, Inc.™ Used by permission of Zondervan. All rights reserved worldwide. www.zondervan.com

This is a work of historical reconstruction; the appearances of certain historical figures are therefore inevitable. All other characters, however, are products of the author's imagination, and any resemblance to actual persons, living or dead, is coincidental.

Published in association with the Books & Such Literary Agency.

17 18 19 20 21 22 23   7 6 5 4 3 2 1

In loving memory of my mother-in-law,
Evelyn Smith (1912–2000).

In honor of my mom, Shirley Ruth,
who shares Ruth's name and giving spirit.

And for my two daughters-in-law, Carissa and Molly,
because you are loved like Naomi loved Ruth.

PART 1

In the days when the judges ruled there was a famine in the land, and a man of Bethlehem in Judah went to sojourn in the country of Moab, he and his wife and his two sons. The name of the man was Elimelech and the name of his wife Naomi, and the names of his two sons were Mahlon and Chilion. They were Ephrathites from Bethlehem in Judah. They went into the country of Moab and remained there.

Ruth 1:1–2

1

1297 BC

Naomi lifted the hem of her robe as her feet fairly flew down Bethlehem's streets toward the outskirts of town. Neta, second wife of her brother-in-law Melek, trailed two steps behind. The sun beat high overhead, its rays licking the sweat along her brow. Some of the townswomen who were not inside their homes resting at this hour hurried to catch up with her.

"What is it?" one of them shouted, breathless.

"Please, Naomi, slow down." The voices included Neta's, and Naomi realized the woman could not run nearly as fast as she, especially when something urgent beckoned. Memories of childhood races with her brothers surfaced, but she stopped the smile such thoughts always evoked. This was not a time to smile.

She slowed her steps and glanced behind her. "Boaz's wife Adi is in trouble." She turned and kept running, shouting as she went. "I'm going to see if I can help."

The heat made breathing difficult but she pressed on.

Surely Gilah and Liora and the midwife should have delivered Adi of the child by now. Surely Neta was wrong.

But the fear in her gut would not abate.

She came to the edge of the village where Boaz's house spread along the wall that bordered his vast fields—fields inherited from his highly respected father, Salmon, the spy who had helped capture Jericho.

As Naomi stopped before the great doors and rapped on the wood, memory surfaced again of Boaz's parents, Salmon and Rahab. Neta drew up beside her, her breath coming fast.

Please, Adonai, blessed be Your name. Let Adi live. How Boaz doted on this wife who had remained barren for so long, had waited even when his sisters Gilah and Liora suggested he take a second wife. And now . . . surely the Creator would not give the woman life in her womb only to steal hers in return?

The door opened before Naomi could ponder that thought, and the two women were ushered into the cool interior of the limestone house. She wiped the sweat from her brow, not allowing the servant even a moment to wash their feet.

"Take me to her," she commanded, forcing the rising panic to remain hidden. The servant led them down a long hallway to a room Naomi recognized as having once belonged to Rahab. The memories rushed through her again—so many days of helping care for Rahab during her failing health and so soon after Boaz had lost his father . . . *Please, Adonai, don't put Boaz through such grief again.* Though she had been a young, inexperienced bride herself at the time, she came. Elimelech was Salmon's cousin, after all, and family came first, no matter how awkward she felt or how useless she seemed. Anyone could carry water or grind flour or bake bread.

Perhaps she would find that was all she could do now for Adi or her child, but one look into the darkened room stopped her short. The acrid scent of blood and sweat assaulted her. Female servants stood immobile along the wall while Gilah and Liora helped a weak, fragile Adi to her bed. The midwife stood in a corner, holding an unmoving bundle.

Naomi blinked, adjusting to the lack of bright sunlight, her heart constricting, blood draining from her limbs. Neta touched her arm as the two took in the scene. Adi's body grew limp, and it took both of Boaz's sisters to settle her among the cushions.

"It's all right, Adi," Gilah said softly. "Come. Let us clean you up and you can rest."

Naomi glanced at the midwife, then grabbed a stack of blankets and carried them to the courtyard to heat them over the fire. Once the blankets were warmed, she hurried into the room again and handed them to Neta. "Make sure she is warm enough." She whirled about and faced the useless servants. "Find some broth—surely there is some left from last night's stew—and bring it quickly." They hurried to obey while she turned her attention to Adi. She touched Gilah's arm. "Was it a hard labor?"

Gilah nodded but did not speak. One look at the woman told Naomi all she needed to know. She motioned Gilah out of the way and quickly examined Adi. She had been through this with several of the women of the village, some of whom had died in childbirth. She could not let that happen to her husband's cousin's wife.

"There now, my child. Rest. All will be well." Naomi accepted a warm compress from Liora and put it on Adi's forehead. Suddenly, she could take the dark no longer. "Pull the curtains aside," she demanded as she continued to press the cloth over Adi's face, gently smoothing it. The light would encourage the woman to live, whereas the darkness tended to pull the soul toward despair. Adi did not need to add darkness to her loss.

Moments later servants entered with the broth. Naomi took the piece of flatbread and dipped it in the bowl. "Open your mouth, Adi. You must eat, even if it is only a few drops." She coaxed the slight girl, who obeyed in silence, until at last Adi shook her head, unwilling to open her mouth anymore.

"My baby," she whispered, her eyes turned toward the window where the midwife bent over the child, wrapping him for burial.

"A boy," Naomi said, cupping Adi's face. "Adonai Elohim, blessed be He, has taken him to Himself." It was not something a woman in such a weakened condition should have to hear, but the truth could not be avoided.

Tears slipped over Adi's cheeks, wetting Naomi's hand. "I want to hold him."

"You will be unclean." Gilah, always one to pick at every letter of the law, spoke from the foot of the bed.

"She is already unclean with the birth." Naomi forced back the irritation Gilah's words evoked. "Bring the child here."

The midwife gave Naomi a quizzical look, but she brought the wrapped babe to Adi and lowered her arms to show the mother a perfectly shaped infant.

Adi lifted weak hands, and Naomi helped her settle the child against her chest. Weeping filled the room, Adi's voice a deep, guttural sound.

"It is time to send for Boaz," Naomi said to a servant standing idle. "Tell Reuven to find him. He will want to see his son, and we must prepare for the burial before nightfall, which will come too soon." She faced Liora. "Where are the ointments to treat the cloths?"

"They are in the cooking rooms." Liora slipped away while Adi rocked back and forth, her groans turning to deep sobs.

"Should I get Melek?" Neta leaned close to Naomi, her eyes wide with near terror at the utter sorrow coming from Adi. She looked like a bird about to give flight.

"You!" Naomi called to the departing servant. "When you have found Reuven, go yourself and get Elimelech and Melek." She patted Neta's arm. "The men will come." Despite her relation to Melek, she had never cared for Elimelech's brother, but his presence at the burial could not be helped. "In the meantime," she said, facing Neta, "go and gather the women of the town. They will want to organize the trip to the cave."

Naomi glanced back at Adi, who clutched the child to her chest, eyes closed, her cries filling the bedchamber.

Naomi stood and backed away. She leaned close to Gilah's ear. "She is not strong enough to walk to the cave. How will we get her to release the child?"

"Boaz will be able to convince her," Gilah whispered. "She always listens to him." An action Naomi knew Gilah scorned, for everyone was aware that Boaz's older sister controlled her husband at every turn.

"Let us hope so." Naomi did not doubt Adi's submission, but where this long-awaited child was concerned, she had her doubts that even Boaz would be able to convince Adi to let them lay the boy to rest without his mother.

The afternoon sun warmed the soles of Boaz's feet, and the rocky terrain dug into his knees as he knelt, face to the earth, in the fields beyond his house and the walled village of Bethlehem. He should go home, stand at her side whether the midwife wanted him there or not, but ever mindful of the law and the embarrassment to Adi, he had fled when they shooed him away. He told himself this was just the way of women, and men had no part in such things as birth. Hadn't his own father told stories of how he had paced Joshua's tent during his mother's labor with him?

Adi would be no different. *Please, Adonai, give her peace. Let the child be safely born and my Adi's pain leave.* Her screams as he'd reached the edge of the outer court had nearly made him turn back. His gut clenched with the sound of it still ringing in his ears.

Tears filled his eyes, trickled into his mouth. She had wanted a child so badly. He had done all in his power to make her happy through the barrenness and miscarriages, and still they waited. Why had the Creator caused the wait to be so long? Yet he had refused to question the Lord in an actual prayer, lest he accuse the Almighty somehow of wrongdoing. He understood waiting, so he assured his beloved that they would wait. Hadn't his own birth been something of a miracle? His mother had considered herself incapable of begetting and bearing children—and yet God had stepped in. As God had finally stepped in for Adi.

He wiped the sweat from his brow and glanced toward the distant town. How much longer should he stay away? He slowly stood and brushed the dirt from his robe, donned his sandals once more, and walked the edges of his fields. Planting season was still a few months away. By then Adi would have gone through her purification and the child might be old enough to take with him on a short walk in the sunshine while the sowers sowed the wheat and barley.

The sun had passed its midpoint now, a time when the workers would have returned to harvesting the grapes in his nearby vineyards. He should ride out and see how things were getting on, but could not bring himself to go too far, in case . . .

His overseer Ezra would make sure all went well.

The assurance comforted him a brief moment, quickly replaced by the nagging fear he could not shake. His pacing accomplished nothing except to exacerbate the agonizing pain of not knowing.

He turned back toward the town, where his estate sprawled on the north ridge, and squinted against the sun's bright glare. Was that Reuven, his manservant? He shaded his eyes and peered intently. At the sight of old Reuven running, robe girded into his belt, Boaz's heart melted and his knees nearly gave way. His stomach soured as it had the moment he'd first heard Adi's screams.

Reuven never ran.

Boaz stared, his feet rooted to the earth, his mind whirling. *Adi.* Something was terribly wrong. The thought jolted his deadened limbs and forced him to move. In one fluid motion, he tucked his own robe into his belt and bolted forward to meet his servant. They both stopped several cubits from the city gates, chests heaving.

"What has happened?" Boaz placed a hand on the servant's shoulder. "Tell me."

Reuven drew in a few short, gasping breaths. "Adi . . ." His wife's name on the servant's lips, so choked, so anguished, sucked even the mild hint of breeze from the air around them.

Boaz fought the urge to drag the words from the man. "I must go to her. Is the child safely born?" He turned to run, but Reuven stayed him with his hand. The fear that had wakened Boaz every night this past week returned with too-certain clarity. "Don't tell me," he whispered.

But Reuven spoke at the same moment. "Adi has birthed a stillborn child, my lord." The words were a double-edged sword, sinking deep into his gut.

"And Adi?" His tongue felt thick, the sound gravel. His arms were weighted, lifeless.

"She lives." Reuven grasped Boaz by the arm and guided his feet forward. "But she is very weak. Naomi begged you to hurry. We must build a bier for the babe and gather men to open the cave. Of course, the child must be buried by nightfall."

Boaz nodded numbly, his world a sudden whirl of impossible images, his body moving with Reuven's aid to the city gate.

"Naomi has taken charge," Reuven said as they stepped under the stone arch. "She fears Adi will not release the child, and Adi is too weak to walk to the cave."

"Adi will live then?" He barely heard the rest of Reuven's words. He had heard the tales of women who lost their senses after the loss of a child, and of those who died soon after when the grief grew too great.

"Naomi is doing all in her power to help Adi do just that, my lord."

Boaz blinked, all at once aware of his surroundings. "The child . . . was it . . . ?"

"A boy, my lord."

A boy. The sword twisted deeper. His firstborn—a son at last—lost to Sheol.

"Come, my lord, we must hurry." Reuven tugged his sleeve, and Boaz moved as one in a dream. Of course they must. Tradition required the dead be buried within a day or by nightfall, whichever came first, as they did not embalm bodies as the Egyptians did.

He looked up and saw the elders sitting beneath wide awnings on the roof of the gate. "I need men to help me bury my dead," he called up to them. "Send them at once." Though truly, if it was just the infant, did he really need the whole town to follow, to watch his grief?

He did not wait for a response. He knew the men well enough to know they would find out and come regardless. News traveled fast in Bethlehem.

And suddenly, he could no longer move as one in a dream. He rushed ahead of Reuven until he thought his lungs would burst. Sweat coated his back. In the distance, the sound of men's voices told him Reuven had stayed behind to answer questions. Boaz could not bring himself to face words of sympathy.

He opened the door and slipped into the cool halls, stopping suddenly at the nearly complete absence of sound. No more grunts or cries or commands coming from the birthing room. Even the servants, if they were still about their work, seemed to be walking on tiptoe or bare feet lest they disturb the sacred silence.

A new fear drew him up short. Had something happened to Adi while Reuven was out fetching him from the fields?

"Adi?" He called her name as he always did and tilted his head to listen. The indistinct sounds of women's voices drew him closer to the birthing room.

"I'm here." Her voice was so faint. He forced back a sob

and hurried into the room. He stopped at the threshold. Adi's gaze met his, but in an instant his eyes traveled to the unmoving wrapped bundle in her arms. *Oh, Adi!* This time a sob did escape him, but he swallowed hard, forcing his emotions under control. He would not weep. Not in front of her, lest she be driven to despair.

He dragged himself into the room. Naomi stood from where she'd been kneeling at Adi's side and allowed him to come forward. He knelt beside his wife and cupped her cheek. "You are well?"

She shook her head, tears filling her eyes. She turned the babe so he could see the face of his son. "He's so perfect."

He searched her face for some sign that she understood that the child's gray pallor was not perfect at all. She held him up but did not release him.

Boaz stared at her, uncertain. He glanced at Naomi, who motioned for him to take the child. He looked into his wife's eyes, saw the expression of sadness, the love. He swallowed hard, then slowly placed a hand on the child's wrapped body. "Let me hold him?" The fragile look in her eyes sent a stab of fear to his heart.

She nodded but would not release her hold until his third attempt to take the boy. He breathed a sigh when at last he held the unmoving bundle, but as he turned to hand the child to Naomi, Adi clutched his arm with strength he did not think she possessed.

"Don't take him!" Her voice rose with her weeping. Adi leaned her head against his arm.

He looked at Naomi, his thoughts churning. "We cannot keep him, beloved," he soothed. "He needs the midwife to clean him for you." God forgive him. He had lied to his own wife!

"No! She will hurt him. I will do it."

Naomi came up beside him and managed to grab the child from his arms, but the action brought on more screams from Adi. "Don't take him!" She turned on him, her gaze wild like that of a she-bear. "They won't bring him back, Boaz. You must go and get him."

It took all of his strength to hold her down. Somehow in the chaos he sensed his sister Liora put cloths on Adi's forehead and heard Naomi call for the town physician. Adi needed herbs for calming, Naomi said in the distance, but Boaz could barely hear her above his wife's screams.

"It's all right, Adi. There will be more sons." He heard his voice calming, soothing her, but her normal willingness to listen to him had fled.

His thoughts churned, his prayers silent, desperate. *Adonai, my Elohim, what can I do? How do I help her? Where, how, do we go on from here?*

He could not bear to consider why this had happened. Did not the Creator have the right to give and take away? And yet, had Boaz not been righteous? Had he not kept the laws? What possible good could there be in denying them this child? In denying Adi, whose screams made him want to flee but for his need to hold her, to console her, until someone could help.

Please send help.

2

The wind whipped Naomi's headscarf as she walked with her family to the outskirts of Bethlehem. Gilah, Liora, Neta, and the other women in Boaz's family surrounded her, scarves pulled low, weeping as they went. Mahlon and Chilion, two of the six men barely able to fit around the tiny bier, led the group, while Boaz supported Adi, nearly carrying her most of the way.

Adi had refused the herbs and insisted that Boaz allow her to come, but Naomi worried. Something was strangely different in Adi's sudden silence, a malady Naomi had heard the town's gossips talk of in hushed tones regarding other women who had lost children. Had Adi's mind altered with such terrible grief? Surely not. Adi would recover as she had with each miscarriage, with each year of barrenness.

Oh Adonai, why should one woman suffer so much loss?

She glanced at Elimelech, overcome with a sudden wave of gratitude for him, for their two sons. The sun glowed nearly red behind them in the west, as though God's heart bled with

Boaz and Adi's grief. The hills with the line of caves drew closer, the ground barren and dusty and hot beneath Naomi's sandals. She would welcome the early rains next month and the relief they would bring from the unbearable heat.

She tasted the salt from her tears, her gaze settling again on her own precious family. Elimelech was not much older than Boaz, and Mahlon and Chilion had their whole lives ahead of them. Soon she would have to seek wives for them, and then grandchildren would fill their home.

She stopped as the small crowd came to a halt. Most of the town stayed behind for an infant burial, and many times only the parents' relatives buried the child in an obscure tomb. But Boaz and Adi were well loved and had lost so much. The family had rallied to support them.

The sun dipped lower, now ablaze over the rise, illuminating the caves. The men carrying the bier laid it on the ground and rolled the heavy stone aside, then lifted the bier again and carried it into the cool interior. Naomi moved closer, peering into the cave. How strange to return to the dust from which they came. Stranger still to never have seen the light of a single day. And yet many women lost infants in such a way. It was common. Accepted.

But one glance at Boaz and Adi made her rethink that acceptance. Adi had always smiled and told Boaz the next one would live. But how much loss could a woman bear?

Melek cleared his throat and faced the small gathering. "May the God who gives life take the life of this child—Menahem, a name Boaz has chosen to comfort them—and give him a place in the kingdom of God. And may the Creator grant another to take this child's place."

Soft murmurs of agreement filtered through the family

until silence settled once more. Everyone knew that Melek himself had taken two wives in an attempt to bear a son, a competition he'd held with Boaz, though after Adi's second miscarriage, the teasing and competitiveness had stopped. Melek at least had daughters, and his wives were healthy.

The sound of the stone grating and coming to rest with a thud as it fell into place jolted Naomi. She would never grow used to such a sound, such finality.

She looked at Boaz and Adi, their arms wrapped about each other, their weeping filling the silence. Naomi lifted her voice with the rest of the women, wailing and crying over the loss, then moved as one with her husband's family and surrounded Boaz and Adi to return to the village.

Six Months Later
1296 BC

Boaz led his donkey over the flat terrain bordering his fields, with Ezra, his overseer, at his side. Though Ezra was not of Israel, he had changed his name and accepted their faith long ago when he came from Egypt as a discarded slave. They had much history in common with Egypt and slavery, and Boaz had found the man to be a good leader and an even better friend.

He caught Ezra's concerned gaze as they looked out over fields that should be flourishing with wheat and barley. But the rains of Tebet, Shebat, and Adar had failed to come these past three months, leaving a winter that was too mild and devastating for both crops.

"As you can see, my lord, even with the servants carting

water from the well near Bethlehem's gate, the plants are stunted and half are wilted. There will be little harvest this year." Ezra turned in his saddle to meet Boaz's gaze. "Shall we go to the next field? It is much the same."

Boaz stroked his beard, his gaze roaming east to west. Everywhere he looked the land showed mostly dried and brown stalks half their normal size.

"I have seen enough," he said, shaking his head. Why had Adonai stopped up the heavens? Had the people sinned in some way? Had he?

"What would you have us do, my lord? At this rate there will be little to harvest." Ezra's donkey moved to munch on a small patch of grass that clung to the edges of the field. "I could send the workers home. We could just let it go and count our losses."

Boaz looked over the fields again, his gaze slanting heavenward. He had barely prayed since the child's loss, except in Adi's presence to bless a meal. She knew he was praying by rote, but she seemed as lifeless as he at times, neither one able to force themselves from their stupor. In truth, he worried about her more than he prayed. She was not the same, and he wondered if he would ever have his wife back again. Even her normal reminders to help the poor had stopped.

"You will help them, won't you, Boaz? We can't disobey the Lord and greedily glean to the edges of our fields." She'd been the one to hold a sack of grain out to him for the workers. Until this last babe. Now she moved about the house as one with no purpose. He shivered despite the heat bearing down on his head from a sun too bright.

"We can't send them home," he said at last, meeting Ezra's gaze. "We will double the workforce, draw more water from the well, and pray it does some good." Adi would be pleased with his decision. Perhaps it would even bring that smile to her face once more, the smile that lingered in his memory but rarely surfaced now.

Ezra kicked his donkey's sides and followed Boaz as they made their way back to Bethlehem. "What if the well runs dry, my lord?"

Ezra's words brought him up short. He hadn't thought of that. The well of Bethlehem had been there for so long, drawing on some underground source. Surely it would last. He glanced heavenward again. If it didn't rain . . .

"I don't know what we will do if this turns into a long famine." Such a thing would be almost worse than his recent loss, for they could lose many people in a famine. Children could die of starvation.

"Let us pray that doesn't happen," Ezra said. But his dark brows knit, a sure sign of worry.

He shook himself. "Yes . . . pray." Would God even hear their prayers? He often sent famine for a reason. And so many were not following the Law of Moses as they had during his father's lifetime when Joshua led the people. Now, under the judges' rule, everyone did what they thought was right.

"In the meantime, let us get to work securing those workers and watering these fields." He glanced at Ezra. "And hope God hears us."

3

Boaz coaxed his donkey into a fast trot through the gates of the city until he came to the courtyard of his estate. Ezra would follow his command to water the fields and work to save the crop. Boaz would join him later, but for now, he needed to speak to Adi. To reassure himself that she was all right.

Why did such fears for her welfare continually rear up in his thoughts?

A deep sigh lifted his chest, and he heaved the air from his lungs in an effort to calm his emotions. Adi was fine. She was simply grieving. He had nothing to fear. She would conceive again and they would raise a fine family. He had to stop thinking the worst. Surely his mind would be lost like the foolish ones if he did not return to some type of normal life.

Another sigh escaped, less distressed this time, as he stopped the beast at the edge of his outer court, dismounted, and allowed a servant to take the animal to the feeding trough and the stalls beside the house. Reuven met him as he stepped into the entryway, while another servant hurried to take his sandals and wash his feet.

"Are things as bad as you feared, my lord?" Reuven need not ask the question, for they both knew the answer was an obvious one.

Boaz shook his head, willing, forcing, the brooding thoughts aside. He had no right to his anger. Grief had already lingered for six months. They must get on with life despite their loss.

"My lord?"

"Yes," he said, forcing civility into his tone. "Worse, perhaps." He barely felt the warmed water or the towel the servant used to dry his feet. "I should meet with the elders," he said, more to himself than to Reuven. "I sent Ezra to try to salvage our harvest, but the townspeople are going to need to help."

He stood and walked barefoot over soft rugs Adi had so lovingly placed over the stone floors. She had not worked on such projects since the babe. He stopped, glanced down, struck by the sudden knowledge that Adi had grown more listless than he cared to admit. Servants had taken to doing the things she had once enjoyed, and he saw now why he always felt an urgency to come home during the middle of the day.

"Are you all right, my lord?" Reuven touched his shoulder, and Boaz lifted his head, allowing this one trusted servant a brief glimpse of his pain.

"I fear for her, Reuven. She is thin and pale and the smile no longer reaches her eyes. I don't know what to do for her." He heard the despair in his tone, feeling his weakness.

Reuven studied him a long moment, his look thoughtful, not pitying but genuine and kind. "She needs time, my lord," he said.

Boaz faced Reuven, slowly nodding. "Yes. Time. But how much time is enough? I fear . . ." He looked away. "I fear she will never be the same, never be the joyful Adi I've always known."

"You don't know that." Reuven pointed beyond the house to the wide-open spaces. "Perhaps if you took her to the fields or went with her to visit the poor. She has always enjoyed helping others."

Boaz glanced over the room, and his words stuck in his throat. There Adi stood in the archway, listening. Their gazes met.

Boaz went to her. "Adi." He cupped her arm.

She shook off his touch. "You think something is wrong with me."

"No. You are just grieving, and I want to help you." Boaz lifted his hands in a gesture of entreaty. "Please, Adi. I just want to see the joy in your life again."

She stared at him. "How is it that you can have joy when our son lies in Sheol? We waited so long . . ." Her voice dropped to a whisper, and Boaz leaned close, attempting to hear, but her words were lost.

"And there will be another. As God gave Seth to Eve in place of Abel, He will give us another, Adi. We just must be patient." His voice carried a pleading tone, and helplessness crept into his heart once more.

"You can't be sure of such a thing. Abel lived long before Cain killed him. And that was an entirely different time." Adi crossed her thin arms and looked at him through hollow eyes.

Boaz longed to pull her close, but she seemed to shrivel into herself and backed away from him. She turned and rushed down the hall toward her room.

"Adi! Wait!" He started after her, but Reuven stopped him.

"My lord, give her a moment, then go to her."

Boaz paused, turned, and faced his servant. Another deep sigh lifted his chest. "Reuven, I have spent my life doing all God wanted. I have followed the law, have been kind to my neighbors, have given to the poor and helped the orphans and widows. I have done my best not to question the ways of the Almighty, nor charge Him with wrongdoing, and yet here I stand longing to do that very thing." A shiver worked through him, and he could not stop his hands from shaking. He clenched them and stiffened his spine. "What more could I have done?"

Reuven tilted his head and looked deeply into Boaz's eyes. "God did not take your son because of some sin you or Adi committed. Our God is not evil, like the gods of the nations around us, nor does He plan to do us harm."

"Chemosh requires human sacrifice, Reuven. How is the death of an innocent any different? Does not our God control life and death?" The question had haunted him since he'd seen the gray pallor of his only son's face.

Why, Adonai? The question slipped from his heart unbidden.

"All men die, my lord. It has been the same since the curse of Eden."

"And yet his time had not even begun." He almost added, "And God could have prevented it," but stopped the seemingly blasphemous words.

"No one chooses his time. That is up to God." Reuven moved to retrieve a flask of water from a nearby urn Adi had made. He poured some into a cup and handed it to Boaz.

Boaz took the cup but did not drink. He would have smashed it against the wall and stormed from the house but for the staunch sense of self-control that held him in a tight grip.

"I do not understand our God," he said at last, turning away from his faithful servant. He had never doubted. All his life he had believed what his parents had taught him of the miracles Adonai Elohim had done for Israel. But this . . . this loss was beyond his understanding, and he could not reconcile the God of miracles with one who would let his innocent son die. Not after they had waited so long.

He walked toward Adi's bedchamber, but called back over his shoulder when he realized the famine still needed to be addressed. He had no strength to deal with another devastating loss alone.

"Send for Elimelech and Melek," he called to Reuven. "We need to discuss how to save the people from starving since it appears our God has no intention of doing so."

Naomi stopped turning the grinding stone and looked up at the sound of male voices. Elimelech's shadow fell across the court's tiles, and she squinted against the sun's glare at his approach. Mahlon and Chilion moved to the bench, where a servant quickly met them to wash their feet. Elimelech stroked his graying beard, glanced at both of his strapping sons. The boys were so much healthier now than they had been that long-ago day when the town physician had thought nothing could be done for them. Naomi closed her eyes against the memory of the physician's shaking gray head and the sorrow in his deep-set gaze.

A brief prayer flew from her heart to the heavens. *Thank You, Adonai, that they still live.* Both Mahlon and Chilion had contracted some strange malady that made them feverish, with burning throats, red spots over their chests, and such weakness . . .

Naomi drew a breath. It was only a memory now. She shook herself as she turned from gazing on these beloved sons to her husband, who stood before her unmoving.

"How did it go?" Naomi saw his brows dip, his lips curve in a telltale frown. Of late, Elimelech's mood had often been sour.

He sat on a bench opposite her. Naomi stood. She could spare a few moments before baking the bread for the evening's meal. She sat beside him and took his hand. "You are troubled."

He nodded, then pulled the dusty turban from his head. "Boaz is ever the dreamer. Even dealing with a grieving wife he thinks we can somehow save all of the crops, despite the drought." He looked at her. "He is not thinking clearly or wisely."

Naomi searched her husband's gaze. He was a practical man, but also one who carefully watched what belonged to him. Where Naomi would give to the poor, Elimelech would warn her not to give too much. It had been a point of contention between them on and off for years.

"Tell me what he said." She knew Boaz had not been himself since Adi had lost the child because Adi had not been herself either. He had tried to coax her out of her sadness, but nothing he did seemed to help, and Naomi found herself trying to come up with ways to make the girl smile again. Still, she had faith in Boaz. Surely his plan was not so strange as to prove impossible.

"He wants to hire every able man and woman, citizen and alien, to draw water from the well near the gate and water every wheat and barley field throughout our territory." He looked into her eyes. "Can you imagine the cost of such a project? Who does he think is going to pay these workers? And with no rain, the well will run dry. We should be preserving the water we have, not foolishly pouring it on dry ground that will yield little."

"Father is right," Mahlon said, coming closer to join the conversation. "He told us of Boaz's plan when we met him coming from the fields. The crops are already dying of thirst."

"But perhaps Boaz has a point," she said, wanting to defend him, even if it meant disagreeing with her men. "If we don't try to save what is left, what will we eat? The whole town cannot survive on water alone." How would she help the widows and orphans that so often depended on her for care?

Elimelech studied his hands, and she noticed how worn they seemed. This drought worried him, and as he was ten years her senior, she wondered if the added burden was taking a toll.

"Perhaps the people would work for the food we would save," she said, longing to give him hope. "Surely the famine will not last another season."

"I suppose you have a point," Elimelech conceded, looking at her once more. "We will do it Boaz's way this time." But she could see the furrowed brow, the doubt in his gaze.

She patted his knee. "Adonai has been gracious to us. Until now we have had more than enough. It only seems right to encourage those without to help us help them. Do you not think so?" She smiled into his eyes, saw the way they softened at the edges. She breathed a soft sigh. He would listen to her. This time.

"You sound exactly like Boaz. Though Melek agreed with me, and we both have the wisdom of years on our side, dear wife. Boaz speaks rationally, but one look at the man will tell you that he is only half listening when people speak. Melek and I only half agreed because Boaz seemed to need us to do so. But I warn you, Naomi. His grief or the grief of his wife will not be a good enough excuse next time." He paused, looking around at their small family, and cleared his throat. "If our God withholds rain from us next year as well, I will not stand by and waste our precious seed on ground that will not grow it." He crossed his arms as though his mind had been made up long ago, a sign of his stubbornness.

Naomi stared at him, eyes narrowed, a sense of dread rising within her. "What exactly will you do if not plant and hope and pray for rain? We must plant before the rains come. You cannot know whether God will grant the rain or not. That's why we plant in faith."

But Elimelech was already scowling. "We will still have grain, even if I save the seed."

"What are you talking about?" Naomi looked from her husband to her sons, but Mahlon and Chilion seemed equally curious. Clearly Elimelech had told them nothing.

"I am talking about working the harvest of others. Of gleaning and helping to bring in the crop."

"And where do you expect to go that the drought would not reach?" She heard the rising anxiety in her tone and silently told herself to relax. There was nothing to worry about yet.

"Moab has need of workers, and the land near the Dead Sea gets steady rainfall even if we don't." Elimelech stretched out his hand to her and grasped her cold fingers. "Do not fear, my love. I will take the boys and go there and work their fields—once Boaz sees that we will harvest very little here. At least then we will be assured of enough to last us until the next season."

She felt his grip, but the warmth of his hand would not penetrate the sudden chill working through her whole body. "Moab?" He would take her sons to work among their enemies? A people who not so long ago had oppressed Israel for eighteen years?

Elimelech nodded. "Since we defeated their king and their men, I have heard from traveling merchants that attitudes toward Israel have changed. I am sure they would welcome our able help."

"This year?" She could not wrap her mind around his words. "You would leave me alone and travel to a foreign land?"

"We would not be gone long." He patted her arm. "Do not fret about it now, my love. If things turn out better than I expect here, then we will go next year. If the need arises." He moved to the bench along the wall near the door of the house. A servant came to wash his feet.

Naomi stayed where he'd left her, staring into the distance.

"Just think about it, Naomi."

She shook herself, resolve stiffening her back. "If it comes time that the famine grows so bad we must seek food elsewhere, you will not go without me."

He met her gaze across the court, and for a moment she thought he would object. "Very well," he said at last. "When the time comes, we will go together."

If the time comes, Naomi amended, but did not voice the words. Pray God that time never came.

4

SPRING 1296 BC

Ruth lifted the water jar to her shoulder and fell into step with Orpah, the breeze gentle against their faces. The winter rains had filled the large jars near their homes, but they were nearly depleted now and must be restored. Ruth was glad for the chance to walk to the Arnon and slip away from the squabbling of her mother, Shiphrah, and younger sister, Susannah.

"You seem rather pensive today," Orpah said, glancing her way. She looked up at the bright blue skies. "How can you possibly have any reason not to smile on such a gorgeous day?"

Ruth looked at her friend and gave her the smile she craved. "Is that better?"

Orpah laughed. "Only if you tell me why you are not skipping for joy to leave the village. We've been cooped up during most of the rainy season. I've hardly seen you." She kicked a stone and laughed again. "Tell me you've missed me. You know you have."

"All right. I've missed you. I am glad to get out of the house." Ruth chuckled, but the effort felt forced.

Orpah looked at her and lifted a curious brow. "Trouble at home again?"

"Isn't there always?"

Orpah gave Ruth a knowing look. "Is your mother back to pushing Te'oma on you?"

Ruth nodded, her mind drifting to times long past, to places she did not wish to go.

The war of her childhood had gone on for weeks, and her father had assured her one morning that things were turning in Moab's favor. "I'll be back before nightfall," he'd said, then kissed her cheek and slipped out of the house that was one of many noblemen's homes on the main streets of Kir-Hareseth.

But hours later, before the sun had crested the horizon, one of the lesser nobles, a man Ruth had never met though she had played with his children, entered their home and convinced her mother to follow him. Ima did so and ordered five-year-old Ruth to follow.

When she couldn't move for the fear that still woke her at times in the night, the man's son grabbed her hand.

"Come on, Ruth," Te'oma had said as a volley of arrows hit the side of one of the palace outbuildings. "We have to follow my father."

"Do you ever think back to that day?" Ruth glanced at Orpah, who had lived on that same nobleman's street and also lost her father in the fight.

Orpah stopped walking, though the Arnon was just over

the next rise. "I dream of it sometimes. But I don't have the constant reminder of it that you do."

"I wish Aali had never become governor. I wish my mother had never followed him even if we did escape to Dibon." Ruth looked beyond Orpah to a copse of trees lining the banks. "I wish I had never met Te'oma." A sigh escaped and she sought her friend's gaze. "Susannah is barely six, yet she already plays as though she is a mother and begs a neighbor boy to be the father. My mother stops the play, not even allowing the child to pretend to marry until I agree to wed Te'oma. Of course she thinks the match is a good one." She turned and began walking again toward the river. "Why couldn't my mother have remarried someone worthy of her and not given herself as mistress to that man?"

"He saved your lives. Your mother had no other way to repay him." Orpah shrugged as if the idea was of no consequence, for her mother had done the same with a different elder in Dibon. "You could do worse, you know." Orpah fell into step with Ruth as they began walking again. "If you don't want to wed Te'oma, say the word. Maybe he'd give me a second look." She laughed. "I'd be happy to live in a wealthy household with servants to do all of the work."

"He might have been a fun playmate as a child, but he has grown into an arrogant and foolish man," Ruth said, shaking her head. "He frightens me with some of the cruel things he says. I could never marry him."

Orpah met her gaze. "Most men are arrogant and all men are foolish. That's why it's up to us to train them." Her expression turned dreamy. "You have to admit he's comely to look upon. And I daresay he would be like clay in your hands."

Ruth laughed, a cheerless sound. "Oh, stop it. If his mother hasn't taught him better manners than he displayed last year at the olive harvest, nothing I can say will improve his character." She looked deeply into her friend's dark eyes, knowing Orpah would regret this, but Ruth could not deny her—not if she truly wanted Te'oma. "If you want him so badly, ask your mother to arrange it. I will not stand in your way." She turned and hurried down the bank to the river's edge.

Orpah quickly caught up with her. "You seriously don't care? Everyone expects you to wed him by next summer."

Ruth stood watching the water rush past on its way toward the sea. She loved this spot, especially during the festivals to Chemosh. The rush of water helped drown out the music that never quite hid the screams of those meant for sacrifice. Or of the mothers whose babies were taken. She shuddered at the memories. So many women never recovered even if they went on to have other children. Others acted as though all was well, but they grew bitter and snapped at everyone when they grew old.

"I don't care what everyone expects, Orpah. My mother is not married to Governor Aali, and I do not have to accept her choice. At least not for another year." By twenty she would have to choose someone, for she could not stay in her mother's house forever. Everyone knew women were meant to marry, like it or not. Or live with a man willing to support her. Her mother had been a concubine to her real father, with little of the benefits of a true wife, but since his death she had been in the even worse position of mistress to the governor—belonging but not belonging. All that remained of her father was that last kiss on her cheek and his promised return. So much had faded with time.

"If not Te'oma, then who would you have your mother pick?" Orpah dipped her jar into the water, allowing it to fill, as Ruth did the same.

Ruth pulled the jug onto the grassy spot on the bank and sat for a moment, letting the damp breeze tickle her face. "I don't know. There are so few honorable men in this village. Every man lies to his neighbor. The governor"—she lowered her voice and looked quickly about—"and those who work under him would take a man's hard-earned grain or seed or gold when his back is turned."

Orpah gave her a strange look. "But it has always been this way. Would you remain unmarried?"

Ruth studied the grasses beneath her feet, then pulled one from its roots. "I don't know why these things trouble me, Orpah. Truly, I don't. It is the way of our village, and my mother agrees with it all. But something inside of me keeps hoping that someone will come to town, perhaps with the next caravan, and take me away from all of this." She swept her hand in an arc toward the town. "Is there no place on earth where men respect each other's work, each other's things, each other's women?" She glanced at her friend. "I know, it sounds foolish to dream such things. But while I love the beauty of this land and I would miss my sister—and perhaps my mother—I would not miss Moab or its festivals or its arrogant men."

Orpah looked out over the water. The Arnon was too wide to cross without knowing how to keep afloat as one could do easily in the Dead Sea. Many a mother whose child Chemosh had claimed had thrown herself into these very waters.

"Do you fear you will be one of those women?" Orpah settled beside her and played with a blade of grass. "I think about that often. I know you think me flighty and never serious, but I fear that if I marry the wrong man, we will be chosen—I will be chosen—to give up my first child." She met Ruth's gaze. "I don't think I could do it."

Ruth studied her friend in silence. "It is exactly why I cannot marry Te'oma."

"But with all of their wealth—and with the priest's ear—aren't they the ones who do the choosing? The governor would not allow his grandchild to be offered. It is the poor, like us, who are chosen." Orpah's voice had risen in pitch, though her words were just above a whisper.

"But can the priests be trusted? Even with all Governor Aali's gold, if the priests choose . . . they say Chemosh plays no favorites. Even King Eglon, when he lived, offered the son of a concubine on that brazen altar." Ruth shuddered at the very thought. The tale had been passed down—something that had happened long before she was born—but it troubled her just the same. "I would run away the moment my son was born. I would not even wait until he was named." Ruth said it to make it so. But she wondered, if the time came, whether she would be allowed to do as she pleased.

"It would be better if we had girls," Orpah said, her tone sardonic. "At least we are spared such fate most of the time."

"Unless the gods randomly choose differently than we are used to." Ruth leaned close. "It is why I fear the gods of our people. I fear them and I despise them. But I dare not say so to another soul." She touched Orpah's arm. "Promise me you will not repeat our words."

Orpah nodded, though her eyes grew wide. "Do you think the gods know? Would they hold it against us for saying such things?"

The fear Ruth often fought slithered through her as the two of them gripped each other's hands, gazes locked. "I don't know. Perhaps the river has masked our voices and the gods cannot hear," she said, hopeful.

Orpah nodded. "Perhaps Chemosh is sleeping." She leaned in and hugged Ruth. "But to be safe, let us speak no more of this. We do not want to awaken his wrath."

Ruth returned her friend's embrace, and the two stood in silence. "Yes, let us talk of other things." They lifted the jars to their shoulders and returned home.

5

Two Years Later
1294 BC

So it had finally come to this. Naomi turned in a circle, taking in the brightly embroidered cushions, the woven rugs, the clay jars, and the low table where she had placed food for more than twenty years. How could she possibly leave this place? What should they take with them?

Ziva, an old widowed servant whom Naomi had hired to help with chores, entered the room. What would the woman do now without Naomi to help her?

"The men have loaded the cart with all of the cooking utensils I gave them, mistress. Do you want me to roll up this rug or just the bed cushions?"

Naomi looked again at all of the items that held so many memories. So few would fit in the cart.

She shook her head. "No, nothing from this room. We will take the bedrolls and the water jars. Did you pack the spindle and distaff and the small loom?" The big loom would have to stay. If they were in Moab long, Elimelech could build her a new one. But if she had any say in the matter, they would only be there a season.

"Yes, mistress. I packed all that and more. The smaller grinding stone and the three-pronged griddle, the jars of barley and wheat and olives and dates, and the skins of wine."

Naomi faced the woman, saw the lines of sorrow along her brow. How could she leave such a faithful servant? "I want you to stay here while we are away. Use the things that are left. Plant what you can in the small garden area, eat the food, and if you have any left, help those in need." She touched Ziva's arm. "When I return, I will replenish whatever you have used." The garden and house were the only part of their land Elimelech had not sold to their closest neighbor to fund their trip. He knew, as did everyone else, that the land could not be permanently sold, and planned to reclaim it in seven years.

Would they really be gone so long? A knot twisted in Naomi's stomach at the very thought, but her attention turned back to the woman whose eyes now filled with tears.

"You are sure, mistress?"

Naomi swallowed back her own emotion and held her close. "Very sure. I would not leave you homeless."

She turned away and walked through the courtyard toward the street, where Elimelech and her sons waited with a donkey hitched to a cart and a small flock of goats following. The old woman came through the house a few moments later and lifted the bedrolls onto the back of the cart.

"Are we ready?" Elimelech looked at her, then glanced at the lightening sky. Dawn had barely crested the horizon, but they had packed much the night before. The sacks of dates and jars of olives, the harvesting equipment, and the few extra clothes they owned were tucked into the corners of the cart.

"As ready as we can be, I suppose." She saw his foot tap and the anxious way he kept glancing toward the city gate.

"Then let's go. We said our goodbyes this whole past week. We must get started or it will take us longer than the five days I've planned for this trip." He turned away from her and took hold of the donkey's reins, tugging the animal forward.

Mahlon and Chilion walked beside the cart while Naomi followed on the opposite side behind her husband. Why did it have to come to this? The famine had taken its toll. She understood that. But she still agreed with Boaz. The land had produced some grain. Enough to survive, though not enough to rejoice in. Still, no one else felt the need to abandon his or her home. Why did Elimelech think it so necessary to flee the land God had given to them and go to a foreign place they did not know?

The sun crested the rise now, its morning hues of pink and pale yellow amidst a cloudless sky promising a warm day, probably steaming hot by the time it reached the midpoint. They were right to get an early start and walk as far as they could.

But as they passed the merchants who were just now beginning to open their shops, and the women moving ahead of them through the open gate to gather water from the well, Naomi fought the sting of tears.

She lifted her head and smiled and waved at the women. "Peace be with you," she called to those closest.

"God be with you," they returned in kind.

"Return to us safely and soon," another said.

Naomi nodded, smiling still, though the expression felt

frozen in place. The gates loomed ahead, and she caught sight of Melek and his wives and Boaz and Adi waiting. In the three years since their son's loss, Adi had not conceived, but she did not look as wan and weak as she had back then. In time she would be the Adi Naomi had known so well. If only Naomi could stay to see the changes, to give Adi continued hope.

Elimelech stopped the donkey and embraced each man one last time, while Naomi clung to each sister-in-law.

"We will miss you," Neta said softly against her ear.

"Hurry back," Boaz's sisters said, hurrying to join them, weeping.

"I wish you wouldn't go," Adi said, coming last. "Boaz is sure the famine will lift soon." She held Naomi in a warm embrace as though she had no desire to release her.

"I hope he is right." Naomi longed to reassure her, unwilling to repeat Elimelech's comments of the night before against that very thought. Of course Boaz couldn't know for sure, but he could hope. Only God could control the way the wind blew or when the rains fell—even in Moab. But God had been silent during their many prayers, and still the rains remained in the clouds.

Elimelech moved into her line of sight and motioned for her to come. She nodded and gave Adi one last reassuring squeeze, then turned to follow her small family through the gates of Bethlehem and into a world she did not know.

6

Five Days Later

The marketplace in Dibon teemed with people, not just those from the city and surrounding homes, but travelers—a caravan that had come a great distance.

Ruth met Orpah at the designated spot near the old weaver's tent where a toothless, plump woman sat at a loom from the break of dawn until the sun dipped out of sight. At times, when Ruth had left to escape the stifling atmosphere of her mother's house, she had wandered near enough to this booth to hear the loom still at work, dark though it was. Once, she had risked speaking to the woman and discovered she was nearly blind and wove her beautiful patterns by the feel of the threads. It was a skill Ruth thought impossible to master, but somehow the old woman knew. Even when unkind boys tried to switch the baskets on her, she still knew.

"There you are." Orpah sidled up to her, pulling her from the memories. "Have you ever seen the town so full of people?" She glanced around, her gaze resting on the foreign caravan. "They say they have come from Bashan. Do you know how far that is?"

Ruth shook her head. "I know it's beyond Ammon to the north, as far as birds fly in a day."

"Longer than a day. It took weeks for them to weave through the foothills." Orpah drew in a quick breath. "There are some Israelites among them," she whispered, leaning close to Ruth's ear.

"Israelites? What would they want with Moab? We have been enemies for years." She followed Orpah's gaze, searching. At last she spotted them. Three men noticeably stood out with their long beards and the tassels with one blue thread on each corner of their garments. One woman kept close to them, her head covered in a simple scarf, her striped robe dusty from travel.

"We should offer them shelter." Ruth spoke before thinking through her words.

Orpah looked at her, aghast. "You can't be serious. Where exactly would you put them? In the room with your mother or sister? Or would you share your bed with the whole lot of them?" She gave Ruth a look that revealed how ridiculous her thoughts were.

"No, of course we can't do such a thing." She sighed, longing to do something. "The woman looks so lost and tired." Empathy filled her, despite the fact that they were from Israel. "Surely someone in town has enough room for them."

"How do you know they are even here to stay? If they are passing through, let them sleep in tents outside the village walls, as their people have done for generations." Orpah crossed her arms over her chest and glanced from the Israelites to Ruth. A moment passed between them in silence, then Orpah turned back and took a longer look at the small group. "The younger men are good to look upon," she said softly. "They appear to be a single family."

She took Ruth's hand and dragged her slowly closer to the caravan. Donkeys pulling carts and camels piled high with wares filled the narrow streets. "The Bashanites are apparently here to trade," Orpah said, looking on some of those wares with appreciation.

Ruth pulled Orpah to a stop several paces from the Israelite family. She leaned close to her friend. "We can't just go and speak to them."

"Why not?"

"It would be unseemly."

"We could talk to the woman." Orpah tugged her closer again, but Ruth refused to budge.

"What are we supposed to say?" She had never spoken to an Israelite, but she had heard of the way their judge Ehud had killed Moab's King Eglon. She remembered enough of the loss of her father to have a sound dislike for the whole lot of them.

"We will ask them why they are here," Orpah said in a matter-of-fact tone. "They are probably just passing through, but don't you find it curious that they have the courage to come here at all?" She glanced at one of the young men. "Isn't he handsome?" She released a sigh, which made Ruth laugh.

"You are impossible." Ruth sized up the small group, saw the older man look over the town as if he were seeking something in particular—or someone. Moments later, Governor Aali himself entered the square and came up to the man.

Ruth glanced at Orpah and the two moved closer. It was impolite to listen in, but perhaps Orpah was right—it would be a good thing to welcome the woman. Ruth led the way, slowly at first, then lifted her head in confidence.

She stopped an arm's length from the woman. "Peace be with you," she said, catching the woman's eye. "I am Ruth and this is Orpah. Welcome to Dibon."

The woman looked at Ruth first, then met Orpah's gaze and offered them a genuine, relieved smile. "Thank you," she said, her voice soft, kind. "I am Naomi from Bethlehem Ephrathah." She raised a hand toward the men, who were caught up in a serious conversation with the governor. "These are my sons and my husband."

Ruth nodded, searching her mind for something more to say, for she was suddenly at a loss for words. One of Naomi's sons glanced her way in that moment, and his smile caused a hitch in her breath. Orpah was right. They were comely men.

Her cheeks heated at that thought. She turned her attention back to Naomi. "Are you here to visit someone?"

Naomi's slight grimace made Ruth wonder if their reasons for being here were painful.

"We have come to escape the famine in Israel, and we hope to work the land as gleaners and perhaps rent land to plant crops of our own. My husband sent ahead to your governor and has met him a few times in years past when he came to glean with my oldest son." She spoke quickly, and Ruth thought again that the woman must harbor painful reminders of some great loss. But then, leaving your home for a foreign land would be loss enough.

"So you plan to stay awhile," Orpah said, extending an arm in an encompassing gesture. "Our town will surely be happy to have you." She smiled at Naomi, as did Ruth, trying to put the woman at ease, though she doubted the truth of Orpah's words.

"I plan to stay only as long as my husband fears the famine in Bethlehem," Naomi said softly. "But I thank you for your kindness. I feared you would not welcome strangers such as us." She glanced toward the merchants' shops, and her gaze turned the length of the town square. "I know Moab and Israel have not always been on friendly terms."

Ruth nodded, then placed a comforting hand on the woman's shoulder. "And yet we are related, are we not? For Abraham is your father and Lot is ours, and they were uncle and nephew. Surely we can overlook any past differences." But the words sounded false to her own ears even as she said them. Could she forget the war enough to welcome the very foreigners who had changed her life forever? Could the town as easily forget?

"Yes. We are related," Naomi said, her eyes brightening. "I do hope the women of your village are as kind as both of you." She smiled at each of them, and in that moment Ruth thought her beautiful. Perhaps she could overlook the past for one lonely family.

"We will be happy to go with you to make the acquaintance of the other women," Ruth promised, glancing at Orpah, who confirmed her words with a firm nod. "When your husband has finished his business with the governor and you are settled, we will show you around."

Naomi's husband called her away then, and they parted soon after with the promise to meet again the following day.

"I hope she brings those two sons of hers with her," Orpah whispered once the woman was out of their hearing. She giggled, and Ruth rolled her eyes as they walked along the path where the caravan masters were unloading their wares.

"You're impossible." But Ruth could not help wondering if the son she had noticed was as kind as the mother.

Naomi slammed the last tent peg into the earth, straightened, and rubbed the small of her back. They had brought only two tents with them, one for her sons and one for herself and Elimelech. She had dearly hoped they would not have need of more, as they would if her sons married—*Oh Adonai, please don't let it be so in this foreign place*—for if she had her way they would soon return to Bethlehem, despite their currently landless state.

Why had they come?

A sigh escaped her as she surveyed the field outside of Dibon where the governor of the town had given them leave to set up camp. Elimelech would work out the details of their stay over the next week, but in the meantime, the governor seemed hospitable enough. At least enough to please Elimelech.

She carried the mallet into the tent and set it in a basket that held a few extra wooden pegs, then surveyed the small room. One partition separated their sleeping area from a sitting area. She set about placing a few rugs and cushions on the floor and carried their bedrolls to the other side of the curtain. How she missed Ziva and Adi and Neta! To have other women to help, to talk to . . . but no. She had her family, and that was all that mattered. And they would want to eat soon.

She picked up one of the water jars and left the tent. The city was fortified and had cisterns attached to many homes within its walls. Only when the cisterns ran dry would the women travel to the Arnon or one of the tributaries to draw water. Naomi sighed. It would be difficult to make the acquaintance of these foreign women, despite the friendliness of the two young women at the market yesterday.

It doesn't matter, she told herself for the tenth time that morning. She would adjust. That's what women did. They accepted the changes life brought their way and continued on as they'd always done.

The thought did little to comfort, but she stiffened her back and walked, head held high, toward the Arnon.

"Do you want me to go with you, Ima?" Chilion's voice from behind caused her to turn and smile at her youngest son. "I can carry another jar so you don't have to make the trip twice."

She nearly scoffed at the thought of a man carrying water, then paused. "I would enjoy your company, if your father doesn't have need of you."

"Father returned to town with Mahlon." He shrugged when she lifted a brow and gave him a scrutinizing look.

"He said nothing to me of this." But Elimelech often did things without telling her. Perhaps he did not wish to endure her questions or disagreements with his choices. Lately, the slightest question sparked the greatest irritation in him.

"He returned to have a look around the town, meet the merchants, reacquaint himself with some of the men whose fields he worked last year." Chilion lifted the jar from outside his mother's tent and carried it between both arms.

Naomi nearly laughed at the sight he made with the large jug sticking out in front of him. She lifted hers to her shoulder and held it with one hand, but Chilion did not follow her lead.

"What else has your father told you?" *That he has failed to tell me.* But she held her tongue. Better not to antagonize the boy. Her sons had enough trouble with their father without her adding to their misery.

Chilion fell into step with her, eventually shifting the jug to his shoulder as she had done once they were out of sight of the city walls. "He is anxious to start planting our own crop of barley and then wheat, but he has to purchase some land from a willing landowner. The governor was little help, so Father is seeking some of the men in town to see if those he helped with their harvests last year are willing to part with a field or two."

"He wants to purchase the land? I thought he intended to only rent the use of it for a season." Her stomach did an uncomfortable turn at this news. To purchase land . . . Elimelech had received a goodly sum for the land they sold in Bethlehem, but he only did that knowing it would return to him in seven years. But land purchased in Moab didn't work the same way. Did that mean he planned to stay permanently or at least the seven years? What of wives for their sons?

"He wants to build a real house here. He said more than once that he has no intention of living in tents." Chilion glanced at her. "Surely you knew this, Ima."

She looked beyond him. "He did not say such things to me. You remember I did not walk beside him as you did on the journey here. We did not speak of such things when we stopped each night." No, Elimelech had joined them to a caravan and spent the evenings talking with the men of Bashan, while she had huddled in their tent alone. By the third day, she had attempted conversation with a few of the women, but they did not seem interested in talking to an

Israelite. And most of the people in the caravan were men. So Naomi had walked alone.

"Well, he spoke of it often enough," Chilion said, his voice taut with a hint of disdain. "He did not bother to ask Mahlon or me if we liked his idea, Ima. He just told us what we were going to do. And he asked the men of Bashan for the best way to speak to the governor of Moab."

"It sounds like your father was simply trying to be wise in our dealings with the Moabites. I suppose the caravan drivers had plenty they could tell him about the men of Dibon." Why had Elimelech kept this news from her?

"Yes, they had much to say." Chilion grew silent as they neared the Arnon. Naomi followed his gaze to the brush lining the bank, where two young women stood deep in conversation.

She glanced at her son, whose wide smile told her that he had seen their profile. Even from a distance, the women were lovely . . . and familiar. What were they doing here? But it was obvious, for they carried weeping jugs of water on their shoulders.

The women turned to make their way up the bank and caught sight of Naomi and Chilion. They moved closer.

"Naomi?" The one called Ruth spoke first, but it was the other who could not seem to take her gaze from Chilion's.

"I did not expect to see Moabite women drawing water at the Arnon," Naomi said, feeling the heat of embarrassment warm her cheeks. "That is, I saw the cisterns attached to your homes and did not think . . ."

Ruth laughed, a delightful sound. "I completely understand. But Orpah and I love the river, so we make every excuse to come here to draw water, which is so fresh compared to the standing water in the cisterns." Her smile put Naomi at ease.

"May we help you?" Chilion said, speaking obviously to Orpah, though he glanced briefly at Ruth. "I can carry that for you."

Orpah's face became a lovely shade of crimson, and shyness crept into her gaze. "Oh no, my lord, we are fully able to draw the water." She dipped her head slightly in respect. "But thank you for the offer."

She smiled at him, then slowly took a step back. Ruth seemed to sense her friend's unease and bid them, "Peace be with you," and the two moved on.

Chilion stood at Naomi's side, watching the young women until they were out of their hearing, then faced his mother.

"I'm going to marry that girl," he announced, smiling. He moved swiftly down the embankment to the river before Naomi could chide or challenge him.

7

Six Months Later
1293 BC

"Now that the house is built and the crop is in and growing, I want to start building a silo or two to store the grain." Elimelech sipped from a clay cup of wine leftover from Bethlehem's wine pressing the season before. "From the look of things, I expect a good yield."

Naomi glanced up from the corner where she sat spinning goat's hair to make into fabric for an awning. "Whatever will we do with so much grain, my husband? Would it not be better to send some to our brethren back home?" She often spoke of home, though Elimelech did not seem overly pleased to hear it. She could not let him forget.

Elimelech lifted his gaze to hers, the slightest scowl between his dark brows, though he seemed to be considering her words. "Our people could have moved here as easily as we did, Naomi. Though I might consider selling a small amount . . ." He paused and shook his head. "I still want to build the silos." He set the cup on the floor beside him. "And I have agreed to help our neighbor tend his vineyards for a share of the profit and the right to take clippings from his best vines and plant a vineyard of our own."

Naomi let the spindle stop, stunned at his comment. First the fields that he had finally convinced the governor to sell to him, then vineyards from this neighbor? What next? Did he have his eye on an olive grove somewhere nearby? Her stomach did an uncomfortable dip. *Oh Adonai . . .*

"Perhaps we will harvest enough for the sacrifice and for giving some to the poor and still have plenty for your storage." She held his gaze, silently pleading with him to see things her way. "It would please Adonai for us to be generous, would it not, my lord?"

He rubbed his bearded chin, then abruptly stood. "You would give everything we own away, Naomi. Yes, of course we will offer the sacrifice and give some to the poor. I am not completely heartless." He left the house without a backward glance.

She had not said he was heartless. But her heart felt distant and abandoned by his actions and his words.

The following night Elimelech left their house again immediately after the evening meal, Chilion in tow. Naomi glanced at Mahlon, who remained seated in the courtyard. Stars glittered above them, bright gems beckoning.

"I haven't seen the stars this brilliant since Bethlehem," Mahlon said, glancing her way. "Does it make you long for home, Ima?"

She drew a steadying breath, not wanting to give away her truest emotions. The fact that Elimelech considered the town's evening festivities worth his time troubled her more than where they were living. Though if they had never left Bethlehem, he would not be faced with such temptations.

"Many things make me long for home, my son." She met his gaze and forced a smile. "But I am here with all of you, and where you are, that is where I make my home."

He nodded, but his thoughts seemed distant. "I like it here," he said at last. "That is, I like what I have found here." He looked at her then, giving her that mischievous grin she loved so much.

"And what have you found so appealing?" She feared she already knew, given Chilion's continual comments about Orpah. How long could she keep him from asking Elimelech to seek the woman's hand in marriage?

"I find the Moabitess Ruth a very kind woman." He stood and came closer to her, taking her hand in his. "I think Ruth would make a fine wife, Ima. I know you have your heart set on me sending to Bethlehem for a wife, but . . ." He glanced away for a moment and she saw his Adam's apple move. A deep sigh escaped him. "I don't think there is a more beautiful woman in all of Israel."

She faced him and waited until he looked at her once more, saw the intensity in his gaze. How could she say the words she knew would turn that intense passion into anger? She could lose him to a foreign woman.

"Give it time, my son," she said, doing all in her power to keep her voice calm. "If we return to Bethlehem in a year or two, would Ruth follow you? What if you wed her and she decides she prefers her foreign ways? She could return to her father, or her father could refuse to let her go. To marry one who is not of us . . . you take too big a risk."

"Her father is dead, Ima. And the man her mother entertains is not her husband. Ruth is of age to decide for herself, though I am sure she would seek her mother's approval." Mahlon gave Naomi's hand a gentle squeeze. "Chilion also wants to marry a Moabite, Ima. Ruth's friend Orpah."

Of course he did. He had told her so the first day he met the woman six months before. "I am aware."

"But you do not approve." Mahlon released his grip and leaned away from her. "Why do you find these women so repulsive?"

Naomi scoffed. "I do not consider them repulsive, my son. I only wish for you to keep our bloodlines true and pure—we are of Bethlehem Ephrathah, and you should both marry women from our city and our tribe." She held his gaze. "You know I do not say so lightly. I say so out of a desire to please Adonai. And I do not think we are right to be living among our enemies and considering them as possible kinsmen."

Mahlon glanced beyond her, but she could fairly see the thoughts turning in his mind. He stood and walked to the edge of the courtyard and stopped to stare out at the fields beyond.

Naomi watched his back for the space of many heartbeats, counting her breaths. She had hurt him or angered him, but with Mahlon it was always so hard to tell. She looked heavenward, wishing she could pull wisdom from the stars. The thought to pray crossed her mind, but the words would not come.

At last Mahlon turned to look at her. "I do not understand

you, Mother. There is no good reason not to marry Ruth and Orpah. There is no good reason that I can see to marry women from Israel. Surely our God accepts foreigners. Did he not accept Boaz's mother Rahab? What possible wrong could there be in accepting these Moabites, especially if they will embrace our ways?" His glare bored into her. "You know I am right."

Naomi searched his hardened gaze. She knew that look, the one of anger barely concealed, the look he carried when he could not win his father's approval. "Has your father already given you his blessing?" The thought dawned on her suddenly and caused a deep ache in her gut.

Mahlon shook his head. "I have not asked him yet." He knelt at her side and took her hand in his again. "He would only seek your approval, Ima. So I wanted you to know my feelings first."

"You are not asking my approval then, only that I convince your father." She knew the truth of her words by the gleam in her son's eyes.

"It is a decision I hope you will accept," he said, his voice gentle.

"That you have already made, my son?" Naomi's mother heart hurt that she had so little influence, so little say, in her son's choices. Weren't his parents supposed to be the ones to arrange such a thing? And yet in this foreign land, who knew what kinds of things Mahlon had heard from the foreign men he spent time with when the sun went down? Perhaps Moab's customs were far different, and Mahlon seemed to find them agreeable, at least in this case.

"I would like your blessing, Ima, but I will marry Ruth with or without it." Mahlon stood, his jaw set, his gaze penetrating.

"If she will have you." Naomi could not resist the reminder. "Or are you telling me she already has?"

He shook his head. "I have not asked her yet. So will you speak to my father? Will you accept my choice?"

Naomi released a sigh held too long. She searched this son's gaze once more, wondering how he had grown into such a determined man without her notice. "I will think on it," she said, unable to bring herself to promise more.

He nodded, turned away, and left her sitting alone staring after him.

Naomi turned over in her sleep and immediately awoke when she felt the empty mat beside her. Darkness bathed the room, with only a swatch of light coming from a small lamp—just enough to see should she need to leave Elimelech's side before he awoke.

But one look told Naomi what her heart continually feared. Elimelech was not in their bed yet. He had taken to keeping their sons in town later and later, leaving Naomi alone in this house outside the city walls. Though she barred the door and Elimelech had built a stout wall around their little sanctuary, Naomi could never quite shake the fear his absence evoked.

Where was he?

She let her eyes adjust to the light flickering from the hall and glanced about the room. No sign of her husband. She jumped up, snatched her robe from the peg on the wall, and grabbed the lamp from its niche. She walked quickly, her bare feet padding the stone floor Elimelech had so proudly built for them. She stopped at the room Mahlon and Chilion shared. Their bodies were stretched out, their even breathing telling her they were well.

She heaved a grateful sigh. But . . . they never left town without their father.

Where are you?

Her heart beat faster as she hurried to the sitting room. Surely Elimelech had simply fallen onto the cushions in the main room and slept, not wanting to disturb her. Even in a drunken state, which had grown more frequent in the months since coming to this foreign place, he could be considerate of her need to sleep undisturbed.

The air in the room smelled foul, and a prickly fear crept up her spine as she passed the empty sitting room and moved to the courtyard door. High windows allowed air and the moon's glow into the main room of the house, adding to the light from her lamp. She turned again, searching where her eyes could see. Still no sign of Elimelech.

Heart pounding harder now, she lifted the heavy board, pulled the latch, heard the familiar creak of the leather hinges, and paused. Her stomach knotted, and a feeling she had not known since her father had passed into Sheol rose within her.

The smell, stronger here, carried the unmistakable stench of death. She choked back a sob. Surely some wild animal had left a carcass nearby, something she would insist Mahlon and Chilion remove and bury at the first hint of dawn. But as she took one step into the courtyard, she could not miss the form of a man lying prone in the dirt just beyond the wide stone enclosure. The gate to the outer court remained closed, but she could see his feet through the slats in the wood.

"Elimelech?"

She set the lamp on the stone ledge and fought with yet another board and latch, finally pulling them free. She burst through the gate. Rushed to her husband's side and fell to her knees. But one touch of his cloak made her fingers recoil. The sticky feel of blood coated them. Her pulse jumped. But she ignored the desire to stay back, to not look.

She must help him.

Using both hands this time, she rolled him from his stomach to his back. He landed with a thud against the dirt, and Naomi could not force back a startled cry at the sight of him. Claw marks had drawn deep lines down his chest and slashed across his once handsome face, taking most of his beard off. His robe was torn as though it had no substance, and blood coated the front of his tunic so fully that it had dripped all the way to his knees.

Oh God, what happened to him?

She stared, unable to move, to breathe, until she thought she might faint. She rocked back and forth, moaning, the jolt of realization hitting her. She dragged in a breath. Choked on the stench. She scooted away from him, scrambled to her feet. An animal must have attacked him on his way home from the town. A bear? A lion? Mahlon would recognize the claw marks.

Her feet fairly flew back into the house toward her boys' room. "Mahlon! Chilion!" she cried out, startled by the loud sound in the darkness. How did they not know this had happened? Why had they not stayed with their father?

The vision of Elimelech rose in her mind's eye, bringing her bile with it. She pressed bloodied hands to her middle and forced herself to calm for a moment. She swallowed once, twice, then drew another breath. At last she turned and ran down the hall, shouting for her sleeping sons with every step.

"Bears roam these hills," the governor said to Mahlon and Chilion as townsmen came shortly after dawn to help her sons prepare their father for burial. "Though they usually do not attack men unless the she-bear feels threatened about her cubs. They live in the caves not far from the town gates. It is why we do not travel outside the city at night. Surely your father knew this."

"What I want to know is why he went into the city night after night in the first place. A bear never bothered him all these past months." Naomi turned on her sons. "And why were you not with him?" She looked from Mahlon to Chilion. "What was so important that he couldn't conduct his business there in the daytime?"

Chilion simply shrugged, but Mahlon's dark brows drew into a deep frown. "He enjoyed the gaming houses, Ima. He didn't gamble, but he found the men of the city more amiable after a few cups of barley beer than when they were working under the hot sun." He said it as though he agreed with his father, and the thought chilled her. She leveled him with a disapproving look.

"I assure you, Naomi, your husband did nothing dishonorable. All of the men of the city congregate in the evenings. It is a time to relax and to strategize better ways to increase the land's yield." The governor smiled at her in his disarming way, but she could only nod. She did not like this man or his city. And now, without a husband to protect her, she was even more vulnerable to men of his ilk than she had ever been in her life.

"Father was trying to secure a vineyard, Ima. I believe he had just placed his seal on the contract when Mahlon and I left to return home," Chilion said. "He had decided to stay to celebrate with one more drink."

"He should have hired an escort to see him home. Plenty of our guards are willing to do the task for a small fee," the governor said. "Our guards are well trained in keeping the wild animals at bay."

"At the very least, he should have carried a torch." Naomi spoke to hear herself talk, to make sense of Elimelech's unreasonable actions. Surely he'd carried a torch, hadn't he? But there had been no sign of one. And Elimelech was adept with the bow, which he also usually carried on his back for protection. Where was it now? But she did not voice the questions, for the men suddenly came to declare the body wrapped and placed on a bier, ready for the trek to the town's common burial cave, where the poor and unknown foreigners were laid to rest.

She bit back the urge to weep as they neared the place, outside of Bethlehem, outside of Israel. This should not be. Elimelech was part of a princely line that deserved better. He should be buried with honor in Bethlehem. But he had led them away from the safety of Bethlehem. Away from everything familiar. And Mahlon would not agree to use their reserves to pay for his father's return to his homeland.

She could not go against her firstborn's choice without a husband to force him to carry out her wishes.

8

Three Months Later
1293 BC

Ruth looked up from the loom where it stood in a corner of her mother's courtyard. Male voices drew her attention to the street, toward the avenue leading to the marketplace. She stood and took a step back into the shadows. If Te'oma was among the men, she did not wish to be seen.

A moment passed, the wind carrying the voices along with the scent of the almond trees just beginning to blossom in this month of Adar, when the days in their valley alternated between sunny and wet. Definitely not Te'oma's voice. But there was familiarity in the sound. The men approached, and her heart beat a little faster, her attention fully drawn away from the tunic she was weaving.

The foreigners, Mahlon and Chilion, stopped at her courtyard gate, clearly seeking someone from her home. She rose slowly, debating whether to call her mother to come or to greet them herself. She paused, realizing they had seen her.

"Welcome, my lords," she called loud enough for her mother to hear. "How can we help you today?"

Ruth had not had many occasions to seek out Naomi since her husband's passing three months before. The woman rarely left her house on the outskirts of town except to draw water from the Arnon, and Ruth seemed to continually mistime a meeting with her there. How was it then that both of her sons stood before Ruth's gate?

"I do hope your mother is well?" The thought that she might not be troubled her.

Mahlon took a step closer to the gate but did not enter the court. "Is your mother about?"

She tilted her head, giving him a curious look. Why didn't he answer her question? "She is in the garden at the back of the house. Shall I get her for you?"

She glanced at both men and caught Mahlon's nod. She took two steps toward the door to do their bidding, but paused as Mahlon spoke again.

"Yes, please. That is—" He stopped midsentence as if uncertain. "I'm afraid I am not well versed in these things."

His confusion made her turn. She glanced into his handsome face, saw the slight clenching of his chiseled jaw. She moved a few steps closer. "I'm afraid I don't understand, my lord. Has something happened to your mother?" A protective feeling for this man's grieving mother rose within her. She understood what it was like to live in a house with only one parent and a younger sister—without a father's protection.

"My mother?" Mahlon shook himself as if he just now realized her words. "My mother is well, thank you. And she would be here handling this for me except for her grief . . ." His words trailed off.

Chilion placed a hand on his brother's shoulder as if to offer him reassurance. He said something Ruth could not hear and then stepped back, leaning against the brick of the court.

Mahlon looked at his younger brother, then faced Ruth once more. "May I speak plainly?" He indicated the gate between them, and she realized that she had not even had the decency to invite the men into the court.

She hurried to the gate and unlatched it, then moved quickly to the door and called for her mother. She returned to face Mahlon. "Shiphrah, my mother, will join us shortly."

"I wonder," Mahlon said softly, "is it you who chooses the man you are to wed? Or is your mother the one I should approach with such a question since you have no father?" His earnest, intense gaze followed his tentative smile.

Ruth swallowed, and her heart skipped a beat. He wanted to marry her? A stirring grew in her middle as his dark eyes held hers. Such a handsome man. *A foreign man, whom you barely know.* Her heart beat faster with that thought.

Her mother and Governor Aali expected her to wed Te'oma—soon. Her mother had continually worn Ruth down with her insistent comments about the young man since before Naomi and her family had come to town. "He would give you more than you could ever want, my daughter. Why would you consider anyone else when Te'oma will inherit all that his father owns? Aali is the wealthiest man in Dibon."

But the governor's son did not compare in manners or good looks with this Israelite, and Ruth had grown weary of Te'oma long ago. Was Mahlon an answer to her prayers— the repeated mantras she had spoken each night? Would Chemosh answer such a prayer when Ruth wanted no part of the ceremonies that accompanied his worship?

"Have I said something to offend you?" Mahlon's voice brought her up short, and she realized she had been staring at him, mouth hanging slightly open. Words failed her. She clamped her mouth shut and forced her gaze from his, glancing behind her at the sound of her mother's footsteps.

"No. Yes. That is . . . here is my mother." Heat crept up her neck as she turned and waved a hand toward her mother, who was walking toward them, wiping the dirt from her hands onto a piece of scrap linen. "She is the one you should ask."

In truth, Ruth would be the one to make the decision. If her mother could force her, Ruth would have been sent from the house long ago.

"Orpah has agreed to wed Chilion," Mahlon said before her mother reached them, as if for Ruth's ears only.

Her eyes widened. She glanced at Chilion, whose smile confirmed Mahlon's words.

"My dear girl—entertaining men without my approval?" Sarcasm tipped the edges of her mother's tone as the woman placed a hand on Ruth's shoulder.

"We were merely talking, Mother. Nothing more. This man"—she pointed at Mahlon—"wishes to speak with you." She moved back several paces and allowed her mother to take her place.

Her mother held the towel like a shield in her hands and narrowed her catlike eyes at Mahlon. "You are that young man whose father came from Bethlehem. Such a tragic loss." She shook her head. "Do give my regards to your mother."

Mahlon shifted from foot to foot and barely met Shiphrah's gaze. "Thank you. I will tell her." His voice held its own trace of grief, but a moment later he lifted his head again and sought her mother's gaze. "I have come not to grieve my father, my lady, but to seek your daughter's hand in marriage. The three months of mourning have passed, and I wish to wed Ruth."

Hearing the words said like that caused a flutter in Ruth's middle. Had Orpah truly agreed to marry Chilion? She glanced at the man again, his gaze more sober now, though he still carried that self-assured stance. His brother seemed not quite so confident. But perhaps it was because Chilion already had his answer.

Mahlon and her mother continued to speak, but Ruth barely heard the words. She had already heard the question, already knew how her mother would haggle and put him off, and the arguments over Te'oma that would ensue this night. Arguments she wanted no part of.

She stepped closer to her mother, who said, "I'm afraid my daughter is already spoken for. The governor's son has long had his eye on my Ruth. Can you pay such a price for her as he is able to pay?"

Mahlon nodded without hesitation. "My father left me a goodly inheritance. Name the price and I will pay it."

Her mother glanced her way. Ruth caught the calculating look in her eyes. "Ten pieces of gold," Shiphrah said, her smile beguiling.

Ruth's breath caught. So much. Te'oma could pay it, of course, but could Mahlon?

Mahlon reached into the pouch at his waist. He counted out ten golden nuggets, each large and weighty. Ruth swallowed. To ask so much was unreasonable.

"I see you are not a poor Israelite as some have claimed," her mother said. No doubt Aali had been the one to say it of Mahlon's father. And suddenly, Ruth wondered how long

Aali would tolerate the Israelites in their midst. Might this be her chance to leave Moab, to find rescue from the miserable ways of her people?

"I will marry him," Ruth said before her mother could bargain further. She extended her hand to accept the gold and placed half of it in her mother's hand. "The rest is mine," she said, knowing full well that she was entitled to part of the bride-price, and also knowing that Aali would try to take it from her. She looked at Mahlon. "Come for me at week's end."

Appearing dumbfounded, Mahlon looked from Ruth to her mother. When neither woman said anything more, he nodded and smiled.

"At week's end then." He turned with his brother and left the house.

"What did you do?" Shiphrah waited until Mahlon and Chilion were out of sight before she turned on her daughter and poked a finger at her chest. "You can't just tell a man to come for you in a week! A wedding takes time to plan, months of waiting and preparing."

"It will cost you less to just let me go with him." Ruth glanced at her mother's hand that still held the gold nuggets. "And it will keep you from trying to dissuade me." She lifted her chin, her determination rising with it. "I have never had any intention of marrying Te'oma, Mother. Yet you could speak of no one else. Now we have a choice, and I choose the Israelite." She brushed past her mother and returned to the loom. She should grab the water jug, beg Orpah to join her, and hurry to the Arnon, but the tunic needed a few more rows completed.

"How dare you speak to me like that." Her mother moved

closer, her voice low, almost menacing. "You know I have only had your best interest at heart. You should have listened to me and married Te'oma long ago." She fingered the five nuggets. "He would have paid far more than this."

Ruth glanced beyond her mother toward the gate that needed to be latched. And suddenly, the need to leave, to escape this discussion, overpowered her. She picked up the loom and moved it into the house, the rows unfinished.

"Have you nothing to say to me? Ungrateful child!" Her mother tromped after her and flung the gold to the floor. But a moment later she realized the mistake of her outburst and scrambled on hands and knees to recover the valuable pieces before one rolled into a crevice between the stones, out of sight.

Ruth set the loom in its corner near the window and bent to help her mother find her gold. When the last piece was firmly in the pouch of her mother's robe, Ruth stood and grabbed the jar near the door.

"I've made my decision, Mother. Do not hold it against me or think me ungrateful. I am merely choosing one man over another. I believe I will be happier in the home of the Israelite than I would be as second or third wife to Te'oma." She lifted the jar and strode to the door.

"Te'oma has not wed. You would be his first." Her mother stood, arms akimbo.

"There are two or three other young women whose fathers are in negotiations with Aali. Did he not tell you this?" Surely her mother knew more than Ruth had heard from the gossips at the marketplace.

"You would have been first," her mother insisted. "Aali gave his word."

His word is of little value. But she only said, "I'll be back," then hurried from the house in search of Orpah.

Naomi placed platters of goat cheese, greens from the small garden that had begun to ripen, dilled cucumbers, and a mixture of almonds and pistachios on the low table set before Mahlon and Chilion. They could not afford to kill a goat, there had been no fish from the Arnon in days now, and she would not shop for meat in the markets of Dibon—meat that was surely sacrificed to the gods of the Moabites before it was sold to the common people.

The thought troubled her, yet again bringing to mind the desire to leave this place. The time of mourning had passed, but the grief lingered. She would never remarry, but her boys needed wives. She must make them see that they should return home now.

"We went into Dibon today, Ima," Mahlon said, interrupting her longings. "We have news for you."

She looked up from the flask of goat's milk she had just finished pouring into a clay cup for Chilion. She capped the flask before pouring her own to listen. "What sort of news?"

Chilion's smile caused a lump to form in her middle. She knew that calculated look, the overconfident tilt of his chin. "We went to seek our brides, Ima," he said, speaking for Mahlon too. He glanced his brother's way and shrugged as if to say, "You continue."

Mahlon cleared his throat. "Chilion has secured Orpah to be his bride, and I have paid the price to gain Ruth as my wife. She said to come for her at week's end."

Naomi swayed and nearly dropped the flask. She stared

at Mahlon, then slowly aimed her gaze at Chilion. "Week's end? No bride marries so quickly."

"It was Ruth's idea, Ima. I fully expected to wait a year, though I had hoped it could be shortened to a few months." She heard the awe in Mahlon's voice, as though it surprised him that the girl should want him at all. Ruth did not know her son or his temper when things did not go his way. Why would the woman agree to hastily wed a foreigner . . . unless she was seeking to escape a situation she considered worse?

Naomi regained a bit of her poise, the shock slowly wearing off. "I suppose Orpah has agreed to an equally quick marriage?"

Chilion frowned at that, his normally cheerful countenance losing some of its joy. "I am afraid we did not discuss the timing. That is, her mother suggested six months, and Orpah did not disagree."

Naomi released a breath. "Good. That will give your brother's wife time to settle with us before we add another."

"Unless Orpah could be persuaded to come sooner." Chilion sounded so hopeful.

Naomi looked at her youngest. She had found it difficult to ever deny him anything. Perhaps she had failed him because of it. He wouldn't be so anxious to get his way now if she had more often told him no.

"I'm told Ruth and Orpah are friends. It would seem right to bring them home together."

Mahlon held up a hand. "One at a time, my brother. As I'm the firstborn, give me the right to wed before you." He smiled as he spoke, but his words were firm.

Chilion laughed, and Naomi knew it was to dispel the tension just beginning to arise. "Never fear, brother. You can keep your right of firstborn. I am no Jacob." He winked as he smiled. "I'll bring Orpah home after your wedding week is completed."

Naomi looked from one to the other. Two new women in two weeks? The house was too small. Up until this moment Mahlon and Chilion had shared a bedchamber.

"I suggest you two get busy and add a room to your father's house, unless you want to squeeze four people into one small space." She set the flask into a crevice in the stone floor, ignoring her thirst. She was not looking forward to such change so quickly. She did not want her sons to marry foreign women. But without Elimelech here to guide them, there was nothing she could do to stop them.

9

Are we really going to be sisters?" Orpah laughed, a delightful sound, as she dipped her jar into the waters of the Arnon. "I knew Mahlon favored you, but I wasn't sure he had the courage to ask."

Ruth dipped her own jar into the river and hefted it to the grassy knoll above the rushing current. She sank onto the bank beside Orpah. "I can't believe he asked or that I accepted. And so quickly!" She offered Orpah a tentative smile. "The idea seemed like my perfect way out."

"From marrying Te'oma." Orpah's look held sympathy. "I hope we don't regret these choices." Uncertainty flickered in her dark eyes.

"Naomi's household has to be better than my mother's." Ruth said it to make it so. But what did she really know of these Israelites? Of any Israelites?

"I know things have been hard for you lately." Orpah placed a comforting hand on Ruth's arm. "Perhaps Mahlon's home will offer us more peace."

Ruth nodded. "Our home has not known peace since my father was killed in the war."

Silence settled between them. At last Orpah spoke. "Why are we marrying Israelites when it is the Israelites who killed our fathers?" Her brow furrowed as though the thought had just now occurred to her.

"If King Eglon had not oppressed them for so many years, Israel would not have gone to war with us," Ruth said, trying to justify the past. "We can hardly blame them for wanting out from under Eglon's thumb."

Orpah looked into the distance, the water from the river a steady lap against the rocks along the shore. "It is still going to be strange, I think. I know Chilion is good to look upon, and he is one I cannot stop thinking about." She laughed. "But their ways are so different from ours. Our people have been fearful of Israel one moment and oppressors of them the next."

"We are not considered clean in their eyes. Foreigners," Ruth admitted. "But why would Elimelech have come to our land if he was not trying to bring about change, seek peace? I think our peoples could get along if we but put forth the effort. Why can't we live as one?" The idea had been growing in her since she had accepted Mahlon's request. Surely their god was not so selective as to call only those born of Jacob's blood his own. Abraham shared Lot's blood, so the peoples were kin.

"I doubt very much that your wishful thinking will bring peace between our nations for any lasting time. But perhaps we can at least attain peace under Naomi's roof." Orpah stood and grabbed her water jar. Ruth did the same. "I best get home. I have much to do if Chilion is going to come for me soon."

"I have five days left," Ruth said, the realization making her suddenly think through the many things she had yet to accomplish. "I have a tunic I need to finish weaving."

They hurried their steps toward Dibon, urgency overtaking them. Ruth was not sure if she was rushing to Dibon or away from all it represented.

The sound of the hammer and chisel grew to be a constant thudding in Naomi's ear as she worked the grindstone for the evening meal. Her boys would be ravenous after working so hard to add two extra rooms onto the house. They had spent days dragging stones from the river to build the walls that would extend the house. The room her boys used to share would become a place for the girls to set their looms and mats during the time of their uncleanness. The two new rooms would give each couple the privacy they needed.

Naomi almost smiled at that thought, remembering the hope and joy she had experienced as a young bride. Elimelech had been older than she, but from a young age she had expected to marry him, this cousin who had always treated her with such kindness. And when the boys came along . . . This time a smile did curve her lips. Elimelech would not hold a grandson on his knees, but perhaps these two Moabite women would bring the joy and laughter of children into her home once more.

She stopped the turn of the stone as she caught sight of Mahlon approaching. He wiped sweat from his brow, his face flushed with the exertion of the past few days.

"You are working too hard, my son." She tsked. "This is why parents usually negotiate a year for a marriage to take place." She lifted her hands and shook her head. "Ach! But do you listen to me? You will wear yourself out and have nothing left to give your bride." She stood and brushed the flour from her skirt and went to retrieve water from the jar.

She carried a clay cup to him. "Sit," she ordered, motioning to the stone bench. "Rest a moment."

Mahlon obeyed. "It seemed much easier when Father was with us."

His comment caused Naomi's eyes to brim, but she would not cry. She could not bring herself to cloud this hopeful moment with sorrow, even if she was not getting the daughters-in-law she wanted.

"We are nearly finished," Mahlon went on as Naomi poured him another cup. "Chilion is working to build the stairs to the roof."

"Tell me you put in the parapet." The law required a border on house roofs so that no one accidentally fell to their deaths.

"Yes, Ima, we added the parapet before we started on the stairs. Can I ask you to help fix the inside of the rooms once we finish? I will go to market to purchase whatever you think we need, but the floor needs sweeping and there are pieces of debris that must be tossed into the ravine."

Naomi nodded. "Of course, my son. I would have helped you build if you had but asked." Though she knew she didn't have the strength to lift the heavy boulders, she could have filled the spaces with mud.

"We wanted it to be the work of our own hands, Ima." Mahlon set the cup on the bench and leaned back, taking in a deep, slow breath. He coughed with the action, something he often did when he exerted himself, but whenever Naomi spoke of it, he simply waved her concerns away. He would put her in the grave for sure with his determined foolishness. "Now tell me, what should I purchase to fill the rooms?"

Naomi looked him over. "Give me the coins and I will go to market for you. How can a man pick out things a woman will need? Plus Ruth will bring many things of her own, so you don't want to fill the room with more than you should. Get your brother and I will do the same for him."

It was ridiculous to feel almost happy at the prospect of doing this for her sons, especially when the girls were Moabites. But whether they were foreign or familiar, Naomi could not deny the fact that she was glad to see her family expand. Glad to know that she would soon carry a future and the hope of grandchildren. Glad that she had a purpose and girls to teach the laws of their God, to work beside for the good of the family, and to love, because Naomi's heart desperately needed someone besides herself to lavish love upon.

And glad that though God had taken away, He had also seemingly given—just not in the way she expected.

10

Ruth turned in a circle in front of Shiphrah, her sister Susannah, and Orpah to allow them to examine her wedding garments. They were woven of the finest material her mother could afford, multicolored in red and black and a few gold threads here and there. A headscarf of matching reds and blacks covered her hair, and the veil provided a thin layer just over her nose.

"Do I look exotic?" She laughed at herself for even asking such a question. But a part of her wanted to impress Mahlon. What better way than to dress the part of a nearly royal bride?

"Your father would have been proud," her mother said, a catch in her voice. "He was one of the king's advisors, so the colors and jewels suit you well, my daughter." In a moment of charity, Shiphrah had given Ruth earrings that had belonged to her great-grandmother, golden orbs with blue jewels set in delicate filigree. Ruth touched them now and looked at her feet. She did not need to be reminded of her father on such a day. It only brought the familiar ache of missing him to mind.

She looked briefly at her mother and offered a smile. "I wish he could be here to see me off." She spoke quickly. Swallowed hard. The memories should not bring such pain now. But the years since his loss could not separate the desire to have her father here on this of all days in her life.

"Well, we are here," Orpah said, her voice cheerful. "And Mahlon will be here very soon." She giggled, then took Ruth's hands in hers. "You will make him very happy."

"Well, I hope you know what you are doing." Her mother's caustic comment sent a barb to Ruth's heart. Why did she always ruin the moment?

"I will miss you," Susannah said softly.

Ruth released Orpah's grip and took her sister into her arms.

"Be careful, Susannah. Don't wrinkle her robe."

"I won't, Ima," Susannah said. She moved back to gaze at Ruth once more. "You are the prettiest of brides."

Ruth kissed her sister's forehead and placed both hands on her shoulders. "And you will be even prettier when your time comes."

A commotion in the street caused them to pull apart. Ruth's heart skipped, anticipation growing along with the slightest sense of fear. Was she doing the right thing? She didn't know Mahlon well at all. She had only spoken a few times to Naomi. Oh, but he was so handsome with that dark hair and partial beard covering only his chin, something common in Moab but not Israel. The first time she had seen him his beard had been long, the way the men of Israel wore it. When had he changed?

She pushed the question aside, aware of the flutter in her middle at the very memory of the way those deep-set eyes had nearly seen through her the day he asked for her hand. Would she eventually be able to read his thoughts? She did not even know the things he liked or didn't like. What if she made food he detested? What if he found her displeasing? She could be divorced as fast as she was wed!

Orpah touched her shoulder. "They are coming," she whispered. "Do not fear. All will be well."

The words calmed Ruth but a little. She nodded in spite of her uncertainty.

"Look!" Susannah cried out. "There he is!"

Ruth peeked through the window of the house. Sure enough, Mahlon strode at the head of a crowd of men from Dibon, his brother at his right hand. His clothing was that of Moab, not Israel—his garb princely. For the briefest moment she wondered how he had come upon the clothing, for Te'oma's father had been none too happy about the match from the start, and her mother had warned that Mahlon could have trouble getting the things he needed for their wedding day.

Obviously not. She breathed a little easier. Te'oma's father must have seen reason somehow. Appeasing a foreigner must have held some appeal for such a politician.

The men reached the gate and pushed it open, its creaking sound breaking the silence that had descended upon the house. Mahlon entered first, took several steps across the large court, and knocked twice on the closed door. "Behold, the bridegroom comes," he called, his voice steady, self-assured. "Allow me to welcome my bride to her new home."

Ruth's heart beat fast and her stomach quivered as her

mother walked slowly to the door. "Who is this that knocks on my door?"

She held her breath, anticipation racing through her.

"Your daughter's beloved, my mother." Mahlon's voice echoed through the house despite the closed door. "Is my bride ready?"

Ruth stood, hands shaking, and smoothed them along her gown. She strode quickly and had to remind herself to slow her steps as she walked toward her new role as wife to an Israelite. At last she reached her mother, whose hand held the latch. At a nod from Ruth, her mother opened the door.

Mahlon stood before her, tall, stately, with the light from the setting sun and a few torches framing him in princely shadow. She drew in a sharp breath, taken away by the scent of sweet spikenard and the deep smile that broadened his lips. His dark eyes twinkled as though they held a secret, and she found herself longing to share in it.

"Will you come?" he asked, holding a hand out to her.

She placed her smaller one in his, feeling the strength of his hold. "I will come," she said, offering him a shy smile.

He kissed the back of her hand, bending close enough for her to get a greater whiff of the spikenard. "Much joy awaits us," he whispered for her ears alone.

He straightened and pulled her to him. A procession followed both of them through jubilant streets, and musical well-wishers all across Dibon trailed behind them, through the gates and across the field to the groom's house.

Ruth had come home.

11

The party lasted long into the night. Naomi's household overflowed with wine and food and laughter. Neighbors Ruth barely knew had come, anything to give excuse for free food and flowing wine. Though most brought a gift of some sort for the newly married couple, Ruth couldn't imagine how Mahlon could afford to pay for such a large gathering.

"Did you invite the whole town?" she asked when they were at last alone in the rooms he had built for her.

He quirked a brow. "Does that surprise you? I thought this was the way weddings are done in your town."

Ruth stood before him, heart pounding, as he gently touched the veil at her temple and pulled the comb free that held it in place. "Who told you such a thing?" She kept her voice gentle, lighthearted.

"The governor, the men at the market, several people." He gave her a quizzical look. "You seem surprised by this."

Ruth's pulse jumped as his fingers touched her neck and flipped a piece of hair behind her back. "I see."

"What do you see?" He had the veil removed now, and she saw passion light fire in his gaze. If she said something to anger him, she would lose the moment. "Perhaps we could speak of this another time." She reached for the strings that tied the robe at his neck, hoping to distract him.

"Another time, yes." He bent closer then and kissed her neck. "You are most beautiful, my bride." His hands moved to the belt of her carefully woven robe and wasted no time in removing it.

She briefly realized that it would be just like the governor to encourage Mahlon to invite every man in town to this wedding, just to take some of the money from Mahlon's pockets. Most weddings did not host such elaborate feasts and were not expected to provide so much drink. They would make her husband a poor man before he had a chance to establish himself. Was this her fault because she had refused to marry the governor's spoiled son?

The thought flitted through her mind, but she quickly lost her focus to the man lifting her into his arms and carrying her to the thick mat in the center of the room. The scent of sweet frankincense rose from the candles placed in niches in the walls, and as Mahlon knelt beside her, his lips covered hers so completely that she forgot everything except her husband's love.

The wedding week passed in a blur for Ruth, and before she had barely taken her place beside Naomi, Orpah was ushered into the family home with as big and long a feast as Ruth and Mahlon had celebrated—a full seven days.

"I would not begrudge my sons their wedding feasts," Naomi confided to Ruth one day, "but the cost of the wine and just trying to keep up with the food is taking more funds than I expected." She swiped dust off her hands from the grain she'd been grinding and met Ruth's gaze. "I fear Mahlon and Chilion will find it difficult to meet our basic needs once this final feast ends."

Ruth did not flinch, though inside she was struggling to accept this sudden piece of information. This was her fault. If she had suspected even in the slightest, she would have warned Mahlon and Naomi not to include the whole town. All they needed to do was have Mahlon come for her, whisk her away, and wed her. A feast was a nicety, but it was not necessary in Dibon. Weren't the roots of Moab settled in unconventional "marriage"? Though no one truly considered their father Lot "married" to either of his daughters, it had affected the way the people viewed marriage, viewed the ceremonies surrounding marriage. The governor must have heard of the way the Israelites handled the arrangements and convinced the men of the town to play along. All to take money from these unsuspecting Israelites.

A burning knot formed in Ruth's middle, and she covered the spot with her hand.

Naomi lifted a quizzical brow. "Are you all right, my daughter? You look pale. Please, come sit down." She led Ruth to the bench in the courtyard and quickly retrieved a cup of water. "It is too soon to know if you are already carrying a child, but it is possible . . ." Her voice trailed off and a dreamy expression overtook her. "How wonderful that would be."

"It is not that," Ruth said quickly. "I fear I am just worried at the expense you are all going to on our behalf. I fear . . ." She paused, unsure how much to reveal to this new mother-in-law. Would the woman tell Mahlon? What would Mahlon's reaction be?

"You fear what?" Naomi's voice softened, but her eyes narrowed the slightest bit. "What are you not saying?"

Ruth swallowed a sip of water and gripped the cup with both hands. "Only that my people do not normally put on such an elaborate wedding affair. And I fear that the governor has misled my husband to use his gold to pay for things he had no need to purchase." She released a sigh, certain she had said the wrong thing.

But Naomi only nodded and sank down beside her on the bench, her sigh one of defeat. "I have sensed it all along. When I purchased the items for your rooms at market, the women seemed surprised that we would expect a crowd of well-wishers." She looked Ruth's way. "I should have come and asked you right then. I should have confronted Mahlon. We will be ruined when all along I knew better."

Ruth touched Naomi's hand. "No, Mother Naomi, it is not your fault. If anyone is to blame, it is I."

Naomi stilled but covered Ruth's hand with her own. "That is not possible, my dear girl."

Ruth shook her head. "No, it is true. The governor keeps my mother as his mistress, and for years the two of them have tried to wed me to the governor's son. But the young man is spoiled and selfish, and I refused. I think my acceptance of Mahlon made them angry enough to seek Mahlon's and Chilion's ruin."

Naomi sat in silence, seeming to process Ruth's words. Ruth looked across the plains to the gates of the city where the shadow of the sun's descent spread across the stones. Men began to emerge, headed their way.

Naomi followed her gaze and abruptly stood. "Well, there is nothing to be done about it now. We will continue this feast for the rest of the week and then do our best to make up our losses." She moved to gather the ground wheat and added water to make the flatbread.

Ruth stood to help her, wondering, given the governor's obvious hostility, if making up their losses would be even remotely possible.

12

HESHVAN (OCTOBER) 1288 BC

Orpah lifted the heavy water jar and placed it upon her shoulder while Ruth waited for her sister-in-law to catch up to her. Normally, they would sit awhile and talk by the river, but Naomi waited on them to bring the water and then hurry off to tend the gardens. The winter rains had produced a good crop, and it was going to take many hands to bring in the produce. Ruth had even hired her sister and some of their friends to help them.

"Your pace is slow this morning," Ruth said as Orpah finally fell into step beside her. "Does something trouble you?" She glanced Orpah's way, her gaze narrowed.

Orpah shook her head. "No. Only that the way of women is upon me again." A deep sigh escaped. "It has been five years, Ruth, and yet neither one of us has borne a child." She met Ruth's gaze. "Chilion grows angry every time I am forced to tell him it will not happen this month. Does Mahlon have the same reaction?"

Ruth looked into the distance. How to explain Mahlon's moods? She had kept his temper to herself, not even confiding in Naomi. "He does not say so," she said at last, "but he grows silent and his moods change with the wind." She slowed her step, suddenly in no hurry to return to the house. "Do you think their god is punishing them for marrying us?"

Orpah's eyes grew wide. "Why would a god do such a thing? You think they were wrong to take Moabite brides." It wasn't a question, and Ruth knew Orpah could read the worry in her expression.

"I do wonder sometimes. Perhaps if we offered a sacrifice to their god . . ." Her voice trailed off as she felt Orpah bristle beside her.

"Perhaps the real problem is that Chemosh knows we will not be willing to sacrifice all to him once a child is born to this family. Why would Chemosh give a child to one of us if we are not willing to give that child back to him? What if one of us is chosen to sacrifice our own?" She said the words as though they mattered little to her.

"What are you saying?" Ruth stopped. Lowered her voice to a hoarse whisper. "You've always feared such a thing. How could you even consider it now—to your own offspring?" She met Orpah's narrowed gaze. "I could *never* do such a thing. Ever."

Orpah did not blink, and Ruth felt a sinking feeling settle inside of her. Had her friend changed so much in such a short time?

She moved on again, picking her pace more quickly over the dirt path.

"You don't have to rush away from me." Orpah hurried to catch up. "I don't know what I would do." Did she say the words to appease? "I just think we have ignored Chemosh since we came to this place, and perhaps it is time we change that. There is a festival to him in a few days. I've asked Chilion to take me." She let the words stand in the air between them. "You should ask Mahlon to come with you as well."

"I don't want to go." Ruth stopped again and studied this friend she felt she suddenly did not know. "I have never agreed with the festivals. You know this." She turned and walked on. "I will not ask Mahlon to take me. I think it is a mistake for our husbands to participate in a ceremony that could anger their god."

Silence fell like a weighty thing for many steps until at last Orpah spoke. "Not every festival involves sacrifice. This one is simply the new moon feast of the fruit and olive harvest. What could be so wrong about that?"

Ruth clung a little tighter to the jar she held.

"Do not even the Israelites celebrate the new moon and offer the firstfruits of their harvest?"

"Yes," she said in a mere whisper. "But somehow I don't think it is the same."

"Well, it is not so very different. Besides, Chilion has already asked his brother."

Ruth's stomach knotted in that painful sense she always felt when Mahlon wanted something she did not agree with. "What did Mahlon say?" She should already know this answer, and it galled her to have to ask someone else what her husband was thinking.

"He said he would talk to you." Orpah did not smile, and her gaze was penetrating. "If you want to keep peace between the brothers and with your husband, I suggest you come along. You can explain the festival to Mahlon. Point out the things you don't like. But I daresay this festival is harmless."

"Perhaps," Ruth conceded, "but it is the others it will lead to that worry me." She drew in a breath, knowing her words were not penetrating Orpah's determined beliefs. "Why did you convince Chilion to take you?"

Orpah shrugged. "I miss the life of the village. I miss the cultural dances and the gaiety of the festivals. I thought it would be fun."

"So when the next festival comes along, the one that *does* require blood sacrifice, how will you blot out the screams of the chosen one? Or will you convince Chilion to leave by then? That is, *if* the townspeople will allow you through the gate." Ruth was shaking now, her anger rising. She would not only have her husband to battle but her sister-in-law and brother-in-law as well.

Orpah huffed a frustrated sigh. "You worry too much, Ruth." She walked on ahead but tossed one last barb over her shoulder. "Don't ruin this for your husband. Chilion is sure he will want to go, and we both want to have a good time. If you fight all of us on this, the future won't be pleasant and you know it."

Ruth stared after her as Orpah lifted her chin and walked in defiance through the gate of Naomi's courtyard.

13

"Are you coming or not?" Mahlon stood at the threshold of their room, dressed for the new moon festival, a frown on his lips. "I am tired of arguing with you, Ruth. This is no different than the offering of firstfruits we give to the priests in Israel. Olive harvest is a time of celebration and joy. What are you so worried about?" He scowled for a lengthy moment, then moved closer into the room, his expression changing to a smile. He cupped her cheek and tipped his head in that charming way he had. "Come with me, beloved. Don't make me beg."

She looked down at her hands clasped in her lap. If only she could make him see. But she had explained the festivals, nearly all of them—how the first one led to the next and the next, and they all seemed so much like the festivals Mahlon knew in Israel . . . until the final one at the end of the year where human sacrifice took place.

"Has your god required the yearly sacrifice of one of your

poor men, women, or children?" Ruth spoke softly, her stomach in knots as she met his now hardened gaze. Mahlon did not realize, did not see, that the rich paid the redemption fee, but that same fee was always set higher than the "chosen" poor could afford. That way the priests grew richer and the governor kept his coveted hold over the people.

"I've told you before, when it comes to that feast, we will not go. This one is not like those. Even you said so, did you not?" He backed a few steps from her, arms crossed. She'd seen his temper rise in a flash or come slowly like that of water boiling over the dung heap. She did not wish to experience that anger now. Would it be so bad to attend with them?

"Your mother will be left alone." Did he not care that his mother often spent too many nights by herself as it was? Naomi would worry over all of them attending a pagan feast.

"My mother is used to having the house to herself. She prefers it so." His scowl deepened, but she knew his words were not true. Naomi did not like the solitude and had confided so on more than one occasion. "Stop making excuses, Ruth. Either put on your best robe and come with me now, or I'm leaving without you."

She looked at him, their gazes locked for the space of too many racing heartbeats. Ruth stood, walked to the peg where her best robe hung, and quickly changed. She looped her grandmother's earrings into her ears and wrapped a veil over her head. If she cared, she would have added kohl to her eyes, but she was going in protest.

"I'm ready." She stood in front of him, allowing him one scrutinizing gaze. He lifted a brow as though he expected better from her but said nothing.

He turned on his heel, and she followed with a parting

glance at Naomi, then caught up with Chilion and Orpah, who already stood pacing in the courtyard. Naomi was not smiling.

The town of Dibon was alive with music, and torches lit every street corner. Vendors plied their wares despite the late hour, and a path to the center of town where the temple stood was lined with flowers and ornate vases of olive oil. Men held cups of wine loosely in their hands and stood in groups, laughing and singing.

"Come," Orpah said, pulling Chilion behind her. Mahlon was close on his brother's heels, but he did not take Ruth's hand, seemingly not caring whether she was lost or whisked away in the crowd.

Ruth pulled her robe tighter and quickened her pace, fighting the tears his indifference wrought. If she had known Mahlon carried such an uncertain temper, if she had known he would not listen to reason, she would never have married him. Her heart thudded to the beat of the drum as one horrible, sudden thought took root inside of her. If *their* child was chosen, would Mahlon pay the high price to buy the child back? Surely he would fight for her, for any child she might bear. *If* she bore one. Enough time had passed to cause her to share Orpah's concerns . . . and doubts. She stumbled, nearly falling to the stones, but the crowd pressed in, keeping her upright. She hurried to catch hold of Mahlon's arm, grateful when he glanced at her and did not pull away.

She released a sigh as Orpah led them to a place where her uncle had a shop not far from the main square. His business of selling images of Chemosh and other Canaanite deities had grown lucrative over the years, and his location allowed them to climb onto his roof with a grand view of Dibon's blinking torches and colorful displays. Women in multicolored, revealing tunics twirled in the streets, lining the parade route toward the temple.

"Isn't it beautiful?" Orpah pointed to the priests in white robes following the twirling women.

Trumpets from the horns of a ram blared at the head of the procession, and more priests followed, carrying golden vases of the first pressings of the olive crop. A hush fell over the crowd, and the women danced without the music as the priests moved solemnly to the steps of the temple. They stopped at the first golden landing and poured a circlet of oil before them, moved up to the next landing, and repeated the process for the entire thirteen steps. A collective sigh released from the people when the last drop spilled from the jar in the exact amount needed to enter the temple doors.

The golden doors swung open as moonlight fell upon the oil one step at a time. The priests watched as though the moon's light spelled either blessing or cursing upon the town, but this night the moon lit the oil in exactly the way they always hoped. Moments later, the governor emerged and climbed to a platform near the roof of the temple and spoke to the people.

Ruth felt her breath escape. Sometimes, when the clouds hid the moon's glow and the priests did not receive the omens they sought, an unexpected additional sacrifice was offered. Sometimes it was a virgin taken into the temple to couple with the high priest. Sometimes it was a newborn child offered on Chemosh's brazen arms. But the governor spoke of no such thing, and by the time his speech ended, Ruth felt her body go limp, her energy spent.

"There, see?" Mahlon bent low and spoke softly in her ear. Did he even notice that she had no strength left to stand? "What harm was there in that? No one was hurt or sacrificed. Simply oil poured out to give thanks for the harvest, much like we do in Israel in our drink offerings."

Ruth only nodded and offered him a tentative smile, praying—or at least hoping, for she did not know whom to pray to—that he did not notice her disapproval. When Mahlon took her hand and returned her smile, she wondered if her prayers were heard, but she did not question by whom or why.

14

Naomi stared at the loom Elimelech had built for her, the colorful strands held in place by weighted stones, mocking her. She had barely worked on it since Elimelech's death and the girls had come to live in her home. Her heart was simply not in her work. *Will I ever feel normal again, Adonai?*

Her husband's loss still caught her unawares at times despite the passing years. Sometimes the grief hit like a blow, sometimes woke her sweating and shaking from dreams she could not remember in the dead of night. But always the same thoughts accompanied her waking. If they had never moved from Bethlehem, might Elimelech still live? Would God have allowed the bear to attack him there?

Of course not, for there, Elimelech would have stayed within the city's gated walls. He would not have traipsed from their home to a town he did not know. Why had they ever come?

The questions haunted her.

She shook her head and went outside to clear her mind, something she did even in the still of night, fear of wild animals or not. She cared little what happened to her now. Her sons were wed. They did not need her like they did when they were young or sickly in their youth. Even now when Chilion suffered the strange maladies that came after eating foreign food in Dibon, it was Orpah who tended to his needs, not Naomi.

You could demand your right to help them, an inner voice taunted. *This is your home, and they owe it to you to respect you and what belongs to you.*

But despite the hurt or anger she felt surge within her from time to time, she also felt no right to demand anything. If she had carried any weight with her sons when their father died, she would have insisted they take her back to Bethlehem then. But she couldn't then and she couldn't now, for she was helpless against their pleading, their desires.

She was more wretched than she ever thought possible.

Ruth carried a basket of soiled linens over one arm, and the jug for water rested on her shoulder, held in place with her other hand. Orpah walked beside her, her basket and her step lighter than Ruth's.

"And what makes my sister so happy this day?" Ruth knew the question needed to be asked, but she feared the response she would receive. Two more years had passed—seven years wed to Mahlon and still no child. Yet with each passing year Mahlon's wealth had increased, and his fascination with the festivals and culture of Dibon increased to match it. He hadn't exactly blamed her for her barrenness as he did in the beginning—he seemed to just accept it—but he had courted the idea of offering sacrifices to Chemosh or taking a concubine. Ruth shuddered at the thought.

"I finally do not have as many linens to wash in the river today." Orpah's smile reached her eyes, and her voice held a lilting quality.

"And why would that be?" The sinking feeling inside of Ruth already told her the reason.

"I believe I am with child!" Excitement seemed to fill Orpah's whole being, and she nearly skipped as they neared the Arnon. "It's been two months since my last cycle, and I only have to confirm my suspicions with the town midwife before I tell Chilion." She stopped abruptly, her gaze suddenly scrutinizing. "You won't tell Naomi before I do, will you? I know you are closer to her than I am."

Ruth shook her head. "No. Of course not. It is not my news to tell." She offered the best smile she could summon. "I would hug you, but my arms are rather full." She laughed so that it would seem to Orpah she was happy for her, and she tried to be, truly she did. But deep down she felt only pain.

Why Orpah and not me? "Are you feeling well then?" Ruth had heard the first few months often brought on certain nausea or inability to eat.

Orpah laughed. "Never better. Though I am hungry all the time. I don't understand it unless the child is also hungry." She patted her middle. "I'm going to grow as big as Naomi's house."

They had reached the bank of the Arnon, and Ruth set her soiled linens near the river's edge. Linens that proved her barrenness. She forced back a sigh. Orpah had remained barren for nearly as long, so perhaps there was still hope for Ruth.

"So tell me, did you do anything to help you produce a child? Have you found mandrakes you did not tell me about?"

They both laughed as Ruth recalled the story Naomi had told her of the mandrakes Rachel had purchased from Leah's son, hoping to become pregnant, but it was Leah whose womb bore fruit instead. Would Ruth be like Rachel, or like Rebekah or Sarah before her? Had she offended the Israelite god or the Moabite god somehow that Orpah should beget and she did not?

"I hope my news does not sadden you or make you jealous." Orpah set down her basket and filled the jug with water, glancing back at Ruth.

Ruth was quick to reassure her. "Of course not! I am pleased that at last there will be the voice of a child in the household. Naomi will be pleased."

Orpah stood and set the jug on the ground. "Will she?" She rubbed the small of her back. "I think she would have preferred it be you. Mahlon is her firstborn, after all."

"A child is still a child. It matters little whose womb bears it." Ruth bent to dunk the first of the cloths into the rushing waters and scrubbed the stains with a rough stone.

"I hope you are next, and soon," Orpah said, touching Ruth's arm in a gesture of kindness. She laughed again and placed a hand on her middle. "And I hope it is a boy."

Ruth smiled. A boy. Yes, a boy. For all men wanted sons to follow in their footsteps. Daughters, as Ruth knew too well, were a burden more than a blessing until they were married off.

But was she becoming a burden to Mahlon because her womb would not bear? She turned from Orpah as she dunked the cloth again, hiding her tears with the need to wash it clean.

"Such wonderful news," Naomi said a few days later. Orpah sat with her and Ruth, all of the women spinning or weaving. The town midwife had indeed confirmed Orpah's hopes, and she nearly burst as she gave Naomi the news.

"I'm sure it will be a boy," Orpah said, lifting her chin in confidence. "I have offered grain and fruit to Chemosh at every festival, and Chilion gave gold to the priests to pray for a child."

The news came as a blow to Ruth, and one glance at Naomi told her this stunned her as well. Was that why Orpah had conceived? Should Ruth be doing the same? Perhaps she had offended her city's patron god by her attitude and hesitance to attend the festivals and her refusal to participate in the monthly sacrifices.

Naomi cleared her throat even as her fingers worked the loom, something she had only begun to do again in past months after years of letting it stand useless. Her grief was to blame, she had said, and Ruth had not faulted her. She and Orpah had looms of their own to keep the family's clothing needs met.

Naomi chose a black strand to weft through the warp and at last looked up to meet Orpah's gaze. "I am glad you chose to pray for a child, my daughter. Though I must say that I believe only Yahweh gives life. Chemosh is simply a figure made of wood and stone. I do not think offering fruit and grain to a figure made with human hands has brought about the child in your womb." She held Orpah's

104

gaze until at last it was Naomi who concentrated again on the loom.

Orpah tilted her chin, and the look in her eyes remained defiant. "Do you think I would have gotten pregnant without the offerings?" Her voice held only the slightest hint of doubt. "Because Chilion had prayed to your god and he did not answer." The proud look continued as the distaff turned in her hand. "So we took matters into our own hands."

Ruth stared at her friend, hardly recognizing her. But the truth that she was no longer barren while Ruth still waited could not be disputed. *Why?* She longed to pray but could not force her heart to obey past the ache and the inability to understand. If only one of the gods would explain it to her. If only someone would tell her what she could have possibly done wrong to be barren. She threaded another black strand into the weft and helped Naomi in silence.

15

Lush green foliage lined the banks of the Arnon and spread through the fields, the barley ripening, the colorful flowers bursting upon the hillsides. Ruth walked alone from the river with the water, her third trip that morning, as Orpah had been in labor most of the night.

Exhaustion weighted her steps. For though there was little she could do to help her sister-in-law, having no experience with birthing children, she had been kept awake by the girl's screams.

She approached the gate and closed her eyes for a moment. Orpah's cries and the assurances of her mother and the midwife could still be heard through the walls. Naomi, though Ruth knew she was present in the room, remained silent. Mahlon met Ruth as she approached the entry.

"Chilion left for the fields hours ago, and I can no longer get a moment's peace." He bent to kiss her cheek. "Pray this ordeal is over soon so we can all get some sleep."

She smiled into her husband's shadowed gaze and brushed

a hand near his forehead. "I fear this is just the beginning of sleepless nights, my love."

Mahlon's brows knit in the slightest scowl. "That is not something a man wishes to hear." He touched her arm as he passed her, sickle over his shoulder. They would begin cutting the barley today, and with little sleep the job would not be an easy one.

Ruth watched him go, wishing for a moment that she could join him and glean among the sheaves. But Naomi would need her now more than ever to help feed and tend to the extra women—the midwife and her helpers who remained crowded around Orpah's side.

She set the water on the stones in the court and walked slowly into the house. A loud cry burst from the room where Orpah labored, followed moments later by a baby's wails.

A deep, relieved sigh escaped Ruth's lips. She hurried to the chamber, which seemed overcrowded with women, and stood to the side, watching. Orpah's exclamations went from laughter to tears, and Ruth felt an ache in her heart, both of joy and of pain.

"It's a boy!" the midwife exclaimed.

Ruth looked on, happy for Orpah, but she could not deny her own disappointed pain mingled with the joy. She caught Naomi's eye and smiled, glad that the woman at last had a grandchild. The house needed the sound of children. After nearly eight years, it was time.

Ruth slipped from the room to begin grinding the grain when the sound of male voices came from beyond the courtyard. She glanced up, assuming Chilion had been told the time was near, fully expecting to see him rushing toward the house.

But at the sight of the governor's son, who had taken on

many of the duties from his father these past few years and married a woman whom Ruth found arrogant and difficult, she paused. What was he doing here, followed by an entourage of dignitaries and priests as though he were a king?

She swallowed hard as Naomi emerged from the birthing room, and somewhere in the distance Mahlon called for his brother. Chilion ran toward the house, but not in time to arrive before Te'oma and his followers. A knot the size of a boulder settled in Ruth's middle. Something was terribly wrong.

"Chilion, my friend, I hear congratulations are in order." Te'oma's smooth voice grated like the grinding stone with no wheat kernels to soften the noise.

How had the man possibly heard so quickly?

Chilion's face colored, and Ruth knew in an instant that it was he himself who must have told the governor's son that the birth was imminent. Was that where he'd gone to escape the cries of birth?

"Yes, I assume so. I just now returned from the fields to see for myself." He tried to push past Te'oma, but the man's guards halted his efforts.

"Is it a boy?" Te'oma glanced at Ruth now, his gaze fixed with a gleam she well recognized and did not like.

She nodded, unable to voice the words. Naomi and Orpah's mother appeared at her side.

Naomi touched Ruth's shoulder. "What's going on?"

Mahlon rounded the bend and jumped over the courtyard wall. "Allow my brother to pass to see his son." His commanding voice brought the first hint of peace to Ruth's heart since she'd spotted Te'oma's overstuffed body marching in their direction.

Mahlon looked at Chilion, as if silently ordering him to also jump over the wall. But Te'oma stopped him with a look. "I'm afraid that is not possible."

His telling smirk made Ruth clutch her stomach, the pain nearly doubling her over.

"You see, Chilion made a vow to the gods that if his wife would bear a son, his firstborn would be given in dedication. The priests' men"—he waved a hand at the white-robed men with him—"are here to take the boy, to be sure Chilion keeps his promise."

"Given in dedication?" Naomi's voice was high-pitched, agitated. "What does that mean? Dedication?"

Naomi had told Ruth how the firstborn sons of Israel were given to Adonai with a special offering, how they belonged to him, but Ruth did not believe these men were here to claim Orpah's son in that way.

"A dedication is a sacrifice," Orpah's mother said, her once happy tone now lifeless.

"Our god requires a pure sacrifice once each year, and by Chilion's own words, this year the offering is his son." Te'oma lifted a curled hand to his mouth and blew on his knuckles. "It is a simple thing, really. You give us the child or I take Chilion." He looked Chilion's way, the gleam more evil than Ruth had ever seen.

"No!" Naomi screamed and rushed for her son. "You leave right now. You cannot have my son or my grandson. You do not own us here. We are not Moabite and we do not worship your god!"

Mahlon's arm came around Ruth in the exact moment she thought she might faint.

"Oh, my dear woman, I am afraid that is not true at all.

Your husband sought alliance with us, and this son of yours offered sacrifices to our priests so that his wife could bear a child."

"To keep the child, not give it to the flames!" Naomi was screaming at Te'oma now, and Ruth wondered if the man would strike her. But he seemed amused by her outburst.

"Orpah is young. There will be more children now. But the agreement was made and the child will come with us." His guards took hold of Chilion, restraining him against every effort to break free.

A priest pushed past the gate and into the courtyard, past Mahlon who seemed frozen in place, past a screaming Naomi who was restrained by another guard, and into Orpah's bed-chamber.

Ruth listened, her heart beating fast, waiting for Orpah's cries of disbelief and refusal. But the midwife followed the priest outside, carrying Orpah's child, with no sound from her sister-in-law. Had they killed her?

But hours later when the men and child were gone, Ruth found Orpah on her bed, drugged, and Chilion weeping at her side. Naomi sat in the corner near her loom, numb, unmoving, and Mahlon paced, making and discarding plans to rescue the child.

Ruth said nothing as she moved in silence from room to room, offering water or flatbread, feeling nothing but pain. She knew there was nothing to be done now. Orpah must have also agreed to this foolish plan when she made the of-ferings to the gods and when she begged Chilion to pay the priests to pray for a child.

They'd paid for a child, that was true. And the priests took exactly what they'd purchased.

16

Ruth kissed Naomi's cheek and glanced again at Orpah, who sat in a corner of the room, silent, unmoving. She had been like this for the past three weeks, once the drugs wore off, the screaming subsided, and the sounds of the festival to Chemosh—one none of them would attend—ended.

"I will be back soon," Ruth promised Naomi with a worried frown, looking from one woman to the other. "Unless you would rather I not go?" She felt torn with the thought of leaving her mother-in-law alone with an unresponsive daughter-in-law, but she needed answers that only her mother could give, and she had promised Mahlon she would try to find them.

"We will be fine, my daughter. Go quickly, and hurry with whatever you need to discover." Naomi did not smile, only nodded as she worked the loom, barely looking at the device or the colors of the threads.

Ruth did not tarry, but accepted Naomi's nod as understanding. She had not told her mother-in-law her reasons or her questions, only that she needed to visit her mother. If what she suspected was true, then any children born to her and Mahlon or future children born to Orpah and Chilion could be in danger.

Her heart skipped a beat at the thought, and the sick feeling in her gut that had begun three weeks ago would not leave. She hurried through the gate and across the field toward the town, whose large stone gates stood guarded by towers and men on either side.

When she approached the first guard, he recognized her and waved her through. She breathed a sigh that she still had no trouble entering the town she had known most of her life.

She greeted merchants with a passing nod or wave but did not stop to talk. If she turned to the right or to the left, she would never finish with her mother in time to return to Naomi before the men came in from the fields. Besides, a few moments with her mother was long enough. Sometimes a few moments felt like hours.

She turned a bend in the path and continued through the center of town, past the temple to Chemosh, trying to avoid looking in its direction. A shudder worked through her at the very thought of the bronze image and its heated arms and tongue. When she closed her eyes, she imagined a snake licking the ashes of the dead.

The thought made her nearly sick, and she clutched her arms to herself and picked up her pace. She turned another corner to a row of stone houses all near each other, some sharing a common courtyard. She came upon the home where her mother and sister resided, pushed open the gate—surprised to find it unlocked—and walked to the door of the house.

"Ima?" she called loud enough to be heard through the

open window, then turned the latch. Finding the door open as well, she walked into the house, darkened except for a lone clay lamp and the light spilling from windows set high in the walls. "Ima? It's Ruth."

Her sister, Susannah, emerged from the back room, rubbing sleep from her eyes. "Ruth?" She rushed forward into her sister's arms and hugged her tight. "It is so good to see you!"

Ruth returned the embrace and held her sister at arm's length. "It has been too long. Look how you have grown!"

Susannah smiled and twirled in a circle. "Ima says I am to wed by next year." A blush filled her cheeks at the announcement.

"So you are betrothed already?" Why hadn't she been privy to this news long ago? But she had avoided even her sister these past few years.

Susannah nodded and smiled. "Yes. He is the potter's son." She clasped her hands in her lap. "The younger one," she added.

Ruth tried to picture the boy, now a man, but could not recall of whom Susannah spoke. "And you will have to tell me all about him. But first"—she tweaked Susannah's nose—"I must speak to Mother."

"She is not here."

No wonder Susannah had lain abed so long.

"Where is she?"

"She spends many a night at the governor's mansion and doesn't come home until late morning. Especially when there has been a festival. Ima helps plan them now."

Ruth sank onto one of the cushions, absorbing this information. Susannah came and knelt at her side. "When did this start?" The words felt weighted even as she said them.

Susannah looked away, as though she was ashamed to tell Ruth the truth.

"Tell me," Ruth insisted. "Was Mother part of the last festival? Did she have anything to do with the choosing of the sacrifice?"

Susannah's attention snapped back to Ruth. "No!" She looked away again and drew a deep breath. "She has nothing to do with the chosen ones, but she did say that you never should have married the Israelite. Te'oma has been angry ever since, and the governor has been plotting a way to get back at you. So when Mahlon's brother came to the priests, they finally had their plan."

Ruth leaned against the cushions, stunned.

"Te'oma wanted it to be your child that was chosen, but you haven't had one yet." Susannah glanced around as if afraid the walls would hear them.

Ruth sat up again, her eyes widening in sudden understanding. "So if I bear a child, boy or girl, the governor will make sure the child is chosen as a sacrifice just because I did not want to marry his son?" Anger flared as she spoke, though she hushed her words.

Susannah nodded, fear showing in the whites of her eyes. "Forgive me, my sister, but I have prayed to the gods that you would be spared a child, for I could not bear to know they would take it from you. Promise not to tell anyone?"

Ruth looked long at her younger sister, surprised and touched by her loyalty. Though she doubted any prayers to Chemosh were the reason for her barrenness. Look at what such prayers had gotten Orpah!

The thought of her sister-in-law caused her stomach to

churn again. "So Mother has no power or say over the choices. It is Te'oma making the decisions now, isn't it?"

Susannah nodded slowly. "Though his father still governs, he has given much power to Te'oma. Ima says repeatedly that you could have been powerful and wealthy if you had just wed the man. I think Ima resents your marriage too because if you had wed Te'oma, she might have gotten the governor to wed her."

"She is tired of simply being his mistress? He has a wife. The best she could hope for is the status of a concubine."

"That is better than a mistress. She would have protection." Susannah looked away. "She is afraid, Ruth. And vulnerable. That is why I agreed to Mother's choice of the potter's younger son after the older married someone else. At least once I am wed she will have someone to take her in if the governor finds her in disfavor."

Ruth pressed her hands to her knees, holding her sister's gaze. She had not realized until that moment that her mother's anger had been a mask for her fear. She had acted as though she had the best life, that all was well, that the governor had made great promises to her. But she had not been the same after Ruth's father died, and the governor's promises were never to be trusted.

"I have to go." She stood abruptly, sick with the realization that she could have done more for her mother and sister and would have saved Orpah the pain of such loss. If only she had married Te'oma instead of Mahlon.

"Just take care about getting pregnant," Susannah whispered as she neared the door. "And warn Orpah the same. As long as you are married to those Israelites, your children are not safe."

Ruth kissed her sister and left, thanking her with a nod.

But on her way through the town and back to Naomi's home, she wondered what it would take to convince Mahlon and Chilion to leave Moab. They had established lands here, which were showing signs of success. And Bethlehem was still under the curse of drought.

But the curse of drought sounded like a safer thing than the curse of Chemosh and the governor of Dibon, who chose victims on a whim or in vengeance, leaving Ruth feeling frightened and shaken.

Mahlon paced the small room that was exclusively theirs, his anger evident with every step. The urge to flee from her husband had never crossed her mind until this moment, but his wrath caused her heart to pound and sweat to break out on her brow.

"So you are telling me that my brother's only child was taken because you would not marry another man? Then why did your mother even offer me the chance to pay a higher bride-price for you?" He stopped, staring into her eyes as though their marriage never should have taken place and all that had happened to Orpah's child was her fault.

"She was bargaining, but I do not think she expected you to be able to pay," she said, keeping her voice low, though Mahlon did not seem to mind raising his. "I had told my mother no to her requests that I marry the governor's son for over a year before I met you. In our country, a woman has a right to choose, especially without a father to settle the matter for her."

Mahlon's gaze did not waver, but a moment later he moved away from her and walked to one of the two high-set windows, where his height allowed him to look out on the fields beyond. He released a long, steady sigh. Silence followed, and Ruth did not know whether to draw close to him or stay where she was.

At last he extended a hand toward her without looking in her direction. She came to him slowly. He looked at her, his dark eyes no longer filled with the rage she had witnessed moments before. Relief filled her.

Mahlon took her hand and squeezed. "I am glad you did not marry that man. Everything I have ever seen in my dealings with him has not impressed me." He glanced beyond her toward their closed door. His voice lowered. "I wish my father had never made us beholden to the governor, nor purchased land from him. I wish my brother had not included your priests in his quest for a child."

"They are not my priests," Ruth corrected gently. "I have wanted nothing to do with Chemosh or any other gods of Moab for quite some time, even before you came here."

Mahlon studied her. "I sensed that in you from the beginning. It was why I wanted to marry you." He took both of her hands in his and kissed her cheek. "But I am afraid your little sister is right. Though Adonai has not yet given us a child, we must not chance having one as long as we live in this place. It is too risky." His smile was sad. "I will tell my brother to do the same. Orpah must never bear again until we can move back to Israel or far from this city."

Hope rose in Ruth's heart at the mention of Israel. "Why not move us back to Bethlehem even now? Your mother would be glad of it, and it wouldn't take long to make the journey."

He shook his head and then slowly released his grip on her hands. "It's not possible. Bethlehem is still suffering from the drought and famine. We would have little food to eat and nothing would grow there." He turned back to the window. "Besides, the wheat harvest is nearly upon us here, and we will soon have the grape and olive harvests to bring in. We cannot leave until we have harvested all our crops."

"But then we could take the crops with us and return? Surely there would be enough to eat for a time from what we gather, and by then the rains would certainly have returned to your land."

He glanced at her for a brief moment. "The famine in Bethlehem has gone on many years."

"But are we sure it is still going on? Has someone come from Israel with news?" She knew travelers came and went and the merchants shared their gossip. Her husband must have heard something when he went to the city in the evenings to drink in the gaming houses.

Mahlon blew out an exasperated breath and ran a hand over his hair. "Would I not have told you if I had heard such news?"

Ruth did not flinch despite her desire to take a step back. His anger was so temperamental, but he had never struck her. "I suppose you are right," she said carefully. "I just thought it might be possible that perhaps the townspeople had with-held such information from you and Chilion. Some of the men could have reason to want you to stay." To take her husband's money as quickly as they could—but she did not say so. Without a doubt, Mahlon and Chilion had made a profit off the land their father had obtained, and even since the marriage feasts that had cost them so much, it seemed that blessings had followed them where the crops were concerned.

Until Orpah began giving gifts to the gods for a child.

Truth dawned as Mahlon's earlier words filled her mind. If Mahlon was not willing to move to Bethlehem soon, and he did not want her to bear a child . . . "What are you saying, my lord? Regarding children?"

Mahlon did not look her way. "I mean that we will share separate sleeping quarters. You and Orpah will share a room, and I will go back to how things were with Chilion before we wed. Until the danger is past, we cannot take any chances."

Ruth looked at him for the space of too many breaths. She had been married for nearly eight years and now she would live as a widow? "The danger will never be past. Not while we live here."

He moved closer and met her gaze then. "I promise you that once the harvests are in, I will send word to Bethlehem to see how the famine fares. And if the land is still barren, I will look for another place where we can go back to living as husband and wife." He touched her cheek. "Please tell me you understand."

She nodded to appease him, but she could not bring herself to say the words. Tears threatened, something Mahlon could not abide. He bent to kiss her cheek, then strode from the room, leaving Ruth reeling from his words.

17

1284 BC

Two years passed. Two harvests brought in, with no sign of Mahlon keeping his word. There had been no messengers from Israel, and whenever Ruth attempted to pull information from her husband to see if he had sought a place away from Dibon where they could safely move, he said nothing.

"It is as though Chilion has shut me out of his life," Orpah complained for the hundredth time as the two of them walked to the Arnon for the morning ration of water. "Has anything changed with Mahlon?"

Ruth shook her head. "Nearly ten years of marriage, yet it feels as though we are virgins again, only living in a different home." She swallowed the emotion that often accompanied that thought. It wasn't so much the lack of physical affection with her husband, it was his unwillingness to talk to her, to share his thoughts as he once had. To hold her when she was afraid, and explain why hoarding an abundance of crops or selling them off to buy things they did not need mattered more than living in the safety of a place that might offer them the possibility of a child, a family.

"Have you spoken to Naomi about this?" Orpah's question was one Ruth had pondered but never voiced.

"No." She looked at her friend's shadowed expression. Orpah had never recovered from the loss of her son, and if she did smile, it never reached her eyes. "I honestly do not think there is anything she can do." They were grown men, and she was a small, insignificant woman in their eyes.

"Have you heard anything from the women at the market? Has there been any news of the famine in Israel?" Orpah was more talkative today than at most times in the past two years, and Ruth wondered at the change. Perhaps her friend was finally feeling hope again.

"You are hoping there will be a way to convince our husbands to return to Israel?" Ruth stopped at the river's bank and set down her jar, kneeling beside it and urging Orpah to do the same.

Orpah sank to the grass, but her gaze skittered beyond Ruth's to the rushing waters. "Many times I have thought to throw myself into the river and let it take me away," she admitted, clasping her hands in her lap. "It seems obvious that no one would miss me, and without my son . . ." She choked on a sob and put a hand to her mouth. It was the most Orpah had said since the incident.

Ruth touched her arm. "Of course we would miss you!" She coaxed Orpah to look at her. "I am very sorry for your loss, my sister, and even sorrier that Te'oma seems to have vengeance in mind against all of us because of me."

Orpah's eyes narrowed the slightest bit, but she did not

scowl. The truth had come out to all in the past year, even sooner, once the brothers had separated themselves from their brides.

"Do not blame yourself, Ruth. It was my unfortunate curse to carry a child before you did. If Chilion had not given that offering to the priests . . . if I had not coaxed him to do so—" She stopped abruptly, looking again at the rushing waters. "I wanted a child to love, to love me."

"We all love you," Ruth said, her words forceful, willing Orpah to believe her. "A child would be a blessing for both of us, but even Naomi's god has not seen fit to allow it. Look how long it took for you even with all our prayers."

"And now without our husbands it is impossible." Orpah's bitter tone matched the feelings in Ruth's heart.

"If only we could find a better place that would allow them to be fruitful and gain wealth without having to return to the land of famine." Ruth spoke mostly to herself, but Orpah absently nodded, her gaze still on the river. Would she really throw herself into the rushing waters and allow her life to be swept away? A shiver rushed down Ruth's spine at the very thought.

"I will speak to Mahlon again," Ruth promised, though her stomach twisted at his possible response. Did he not miss spending time at her side? "Perhaps this night." She could seek divorce from a man who deprived his wife of such rights. Though the thought of reminding him of that fact drew another shiver from her.

"That might help." But Orpah's tone had returned to its numb state . . . the one that she had carried since her child's death. As though it didn't really matter what happened to her the rest of her life.

Ruth stood and filled her water jar, and Orpah did the same. But their return home was not nearly as talkative, and all Ruth could think about was how to approach her moody husband with such a difficult topic.

Ruth poured wine from a flask into the clay cup Mahlon held out to her as he sat eating with his brother in the court-yard. The women would dine after the men were fed, something they had taken to doing for lack of conversation when the men were near. The house had grown so quiet in the past two years that Ruth ached for human connection.

She shook herself as she capped the flask. "And how was your day in the fields, my husband?" She looked Mahlon's way, waiting for him to glance up at her.

He wiped his mouth on a linen towel and met her gaze. "The same as it always is." He placed the towel beside the clay bowl and stood.

"May we walk together before the sun fully sets?" It was a bold thing to ask, but he had been more distant these past few weeks than ever before. Was he seeing a prostitute in the city? The thought brought a sick feeling to her gut. It had been so long since they were together.

Mahlon cleared his throat and grunted. "If you want to," he said, though he did not sound happy.

Ruth glanced at Naomi, who bid her go. She quickly followed Mahlon through the gate into the fields beyond the little house, which was as unprotected by the city's walls as her heart felt without her husband's love. They walked in silence for several moments until they came to a large rock where they used to meet during the late morning, when Ruth would bring him fresh goat's milk or a slice of fresh cheese. How long had it been since she had done such things?

"What did you want to talk about?" he asked, his tone clipped. He sat on the rock and looked up at her. No invitation for her to sit beside him.

"I wondered . . ." She paused. How best to frame the words, to help him understand?

"Wondered what?"

She looked at her feet, finding it more and more difficult to meet his gaze. Had their love grown so cold?

"I wondered if you had given any more thought to moving away from here . . . so that we all could live as husbands and wives again and not fear bearing children." She blew out a breath, released of the weighty words.

Silence lingered between them.

At last she spoke again, longing for some closeness. "I miss you, Mahlon. Orpah misses Chilion. We long for families. But we know it is not safe here."

He looked beyond her as though ashamed. He had promised her. Two years ago. And still he had not kept his word.

"Are you not interested in remaining married to us? Has someone else come along to take your affection?" The questions came despite the urge to stop them. Why was her tongue suddenly so loose?

"No." His words were quiet but firm. "There is no one else for either myself or Chilion." He looked into her eyes. "At least there is no one else for me. Chilion would have to speak for himself."

"And the other?" She implored him with a look. "Can we not go back to being husband and wife?"

He looked away, and she saw the pain in his expression. "I

want to," he admitted. "I've been so caught up in the yields. The fields here have been so fruitful—" He stopped.

"And I am not fruitful."

"We had over seven years to try, and so I thought . . ."

"You think I am barren, so you would work the land and leave things be."

He shook his head. "No, beloved. No."

Tears stung and she turned away.

He stood. Cupped her shoulders. "I will do something to make it right. Tonight we will sleep again as husband and wife. If you should come to be with child, we will move before anyone in town can become aware of it." He turned her to face him. "Will that solve the struggle between us?"

She nodded, though she did not know if she truly agreed. She *would* be grateful to have her husband again. But she was not so sure he would move if the land remained so fruitful. Especially when she knew he didn't think she ever would be.

18

Shebat (January) 1283 BC

Naomi looked up from her weaving at the sound of heavy footfalls entering the courtyard. She glanced at Ruth and Orpah, then let the loom rest and hurried to see who it was. Chilion stumbled toward her, and she barely reached him before he fell to his knees on the hard stones.

"Ima. Help me." His words were a mere breath, and Naomi stared at him.

"Orpah, Ruth, come quickly!" She tried to help him stand, to get him into the house, but until the girls aided her she was not able to lift his large frame.

"Chilion!" Orpah's cries sounded like a wounded she-cub, causing the pulse in Naomi's throat to throb. No. It couldn't be.

They managed to carry him to his pallet, and Ruth ran to get water while Orpah dipped cloths into the tepid water already there. She wrung them out and placed them on his forehead.

"What's wrong, my son?" Naomi felt Chilion's neck to count the thready beat of his heart, her mind whirling with memories.

"Your sons are very sick, Naomi," the town's physician had said. "How long have their throats burned and this rash covered their chests?" He'd held his ear to their chests and pressed on their bellies, then stood and shook his head. "Very sick," he repeated as though she had not heard him the first time.

"Will they live?" She heard Elimelech ask the question, his tone too pragmatic. Of course they would live! They had to live!

The old man, who understood the way of herbs and healing remedies, just shook his head again and walked from the room. Elimelech had followed him, but Naomi would not leave her sons' sides. *Please, Adonai*, she had pleaded.

This could not be the same thing, but she felt for fever, asked Chilion if anything hurt, and checked his chest just the same. No rash, no burning throat. But when Naomi felt for his heartbeat, it seemed slower than it should be, and Chilion's color had paled even in the short time he had been home.

"Where is your brother?" Could the same malady have afflicted Mahlon and he be lying in a field somewhere?

Chilion's closed eyes fluttered. Naomi bent close to his ear. "He is well, Ima. I . . . I just felt very weak today."

Naomi wiped her brow. Why today? It was not abnormally hot, nor was the work of harvest yet upon them. Why then would Chilion grow so suddenly weak . . . as he had as a child?

Fear gripped her as she stared down at her son. She glanced at Orpah, who knelt at his side, her eyes wide, disbelieving.

Orpah continually draped cool cloths over Chilion's brow, and Naomi slipped from the room.

She found Ruth in the sitting room, a fresh cup of water in her hand. "Take it to Orpah to give to him," she said softly. "Then I want you to go to the fields and find your husband."

Ruth rushed from the house, heart pounding. Dear gods . . . which god? What was wrong with Chilion? She had never seen a man so weak, so listless on his bed, in the middle of the day. Had he found some poisonous root or drank from a stale pond rather than the life-giving rushing waters of the Arnon?

Many a Moabite had learned the hard way to avoid waters near the places of sewage, and children were taught from childhood to avoid certain plants. But did such plants grow in Bethlehem? Were her husband and his brother aware of the dangers?

Her mind raced, and she tripped and righted herself again as she ran across the fields toward the standing barley where Mahlon and Chilion were supposed to have worked that day.

"Mahlon!" She called out his name as she drew nearer the place he was supposed to be. But she did not see him. "Mahlon!" She stopped and bent forward, her breath coming fast, hands on her knees.

She glanced about, then began a slow walk, looking down each row for some sign of him. *Please, god of Naomi, where is he?*

"Mahlon!" She reached the edge of the barley field and headed toward the wheat field, where the stalks were not as high. Much easier to see across the expanse of the land. She stopped, looked from side to side. No sign of him.

Her heart skipped a beat, then began to race again with a fear she dare not name. They could have both eaten something poisonous, and Mahlon might not have had the strength to even make it home.

Please, god.

"Ruth?"

She whirled at the sound of his voice and fairly flew into his arms, weeping.

"What is it, beloved?" He stroked her veil at the back of her head and pulled her close.

"I thought . . ." She glanced up at him and released a shaky breath. "Your brother came home so weak and sick and your mother said to find you, and when I couldn't, I feared . . ."

He pulled her to his chest and rubbed her back. "Hush now. Stop and breathe a moment."

She obeyed, but too soon he held her at arm's length. "My brother has come home sick?" His brows knit, and she could see he was trying to assess whether or not her alarm was justified.

She nodded. "Very sick, my lord. So weak we had to help him to his bed. Your mother seems as though she is trying to remain calm but . . . is quite frightened." Ruth met his gaze, and his own calm suddenly shattered.

"This is not the first time," he said, his tone carrying much more worry than he had exhibited moments before. "When we were small, both of us contracted something . . . No one knows what it was, but we nearly died. My mother would naturally fear it happening again." He looked at her. "Come. We must comfort her and see what is to be done for him."

He grasped her hand and ran with her back toward the house.

19

They arrived at the house, but Mahlon remained only long enough to check on Chilion and run into Dibon to seek a physician. Ruth ran to the garden to find herbs to make into a poultice, though she had no idea where to put such a thing, for Chilion had no boils or rashes or anything to show them where a poultice might help. And Ruth had no knowledge of what types of herbs might heal the slowing weakness of a person's beating heart.

"Is he going to die?" Orpah whispered to Naomi in the hall outside of the room, where the three women stood waiting for Mahlon to return. "I have never seen such a thing. I have tried to ask him if he ate or drank something, for then perhaps we could give him something to coax it out of him." Tears filled her eyes, and she did not swipe them away. "But he can barely speak. All he could do was shake his head no."

"Mahlon did not think Chilion would have drunk water from a stale source, and he knows which plants to avoid,"

Ruth said, placing a hand on Orpah's shoulder. She looked to Naomi. "Mahlon said they were both sickly when they were very young. Could this be the same malady? Has such a thing happened to others in your family?"

Naomi did not speak for many breaths. She looked from one daughter-in-law to the other. "They were very sick in childhood. There was nothing to be done for them but pray."

Ruth saw fear fill Naomi's dark eyes, the lines along her brow grow deeper. "He does not have the symptoms he had then," Naomi said softly, glancing at the room where Chilion lay. "I do not understand it."

The three women stood in silence until Orpah returned to Chilion's side, and Naomi followed her. Ruth went to the courtyard to look for Mahlon's coming. She spotted him in the distance, hurrying toward her with a man and woman in tow.

He arrived at the gate out of breath, sweating profusely. Ruth hurried to retrieve a cup of water for him as the couple pushed past him and into the house toward the sickroom.

"The physician and his wife," Mahlon said between gulps of water. "They work together preparing and growing the herbs."

Ruth nodded, took the empty mug from Mahlon, and refilled it. "You ran so hard, my lord. Won't you sit?" She had never seen him so flushed.

He looked at her, seeming to want to argue, but sank onto the stone bench of the court instead. He accepted the second cup of water and drank slowly.

A loud cry from down the hall carried to them. Mahlon's hand trembled, the cup slipping from it and breaking on the stone floor.

"Chilion!" Orpah's loud cries split the air, and Ruth knew in an instant that her brother-in-law was beyond the help of the two who had just arrived.

She turned, thinking to go to them, but a moment later whirled back just in time to see Mahlon slump to the ground at her feet. A scream escaped—was that her voice? She knelt down and quickly rolled him to his side, feeling his forehead, his neck, his arms.

"Mahlon," she whispered, for her voice seemed stuck within her. "Mahlon." She bent close, feeling his chest, searching his neck for the thumping of his pulse.

Naomi appeared and knelt on the stones beside her. She took Mahlon's head in her hands, probing. But one look into the man's face told both of them what they could not, dare not, believe. Mahlon's eyes were blank and rolled back, his chest did not lift, and no air came from his nostrils. His sweating skin now felt clammy to the touch, and his once flushed face had drained of color.

"He's gone," Naomi said, her voice flat, lifeless. "They are both gone." She looked at Ruth and met her gaze. "In one swift moment God has taken both of my sons."

Ruth glanced at the prone form of her husband. She did not need to see Chilion to know that Orpah's keening was for the same purpose. How was this even possible? Men did not just drop dead in the finest years of their lives. They died in battle or during blight or years apart from each other. Brothers did not go to work in the morning and die together in the middle of the day.

But they had.

And no explanation on earth or among the gods made any sense for it.

This isn't real. The phrase turned over in Ruth's mind as she stared at the bier holding her husband's body. The words followed her like a relentless shadow from Naomi's home, past the barley and wheat fields, past the wailing women and forlorn shopkeepers who had come to line the path to the outskirts of town, where burial caves lined the incline that led westward toward the Dead Sea.

Ruth trudged behind a weeping Naomi, the woman who had become like a mother to her in the past ten years. How often had the woman tried to convince her sons to return to Israel? If only they had listened.

Did Naomi resent her, resent Orpah, who represented everything Naomi despised? Everything Moabite as her sons' reason for staying?

Ruth glanced at Orpah, who clung to her arm, dead weight that it was, weeping like a caring wife should, like Ruth should . . .

Orpah stumbled once, twice, and nearly dragged Ruth to the ground. "Chilion! How could you leave me?" Her high-pitched voice carried fierce emotion.

Ruth squeezed her hand. She could find no words to comfort her sister-in-law. Orpah's losses were greater than Ruth's, and yet if Orpah had not encouraged Chilion in the festivals of Chemosh . . . the worship that had taken their child . . . Had Naomi's god struck both men because her sons had disobeyed some commandment of their god?

This isn't real.

The thought held the acrid taste of bile. She stopped, put a hand to her middle. She could not be sick. Not here. Tears stung and filled her eyes as she swallowed the bitterness, hating every step. To lash out at Orpah—it would do no good. She could not blame Orpah for believing in the gods of their people. She had thought her actions would do them good, give them children.

Had Ruth and Orpah been cursed the moment they joined the Israelite family? Or had the family been cursed by their presence?

The sun's heat created beads along her brow and dampened the ashes she had poured over her head. Stones crept into her sandals. She stopped. Brushed them away. Orpah released her hold and stumbled after Naomi as the caves drew nearer. Ruth stared at the wide mouth of the cave, aware of every sound, of the grunts and whispers of the men and women on the fringes of the circle they made—she, Naomi, and Orpah.

This is not happening. I will awaken soon, and Mahlon will laugh at my foolish nightmares. Hadn't she feared and sometimes dreamed such things on more than one occasion? Though she had rarely spoken of it to anyone, she feared loss—had feared it since her father's death those many years ago in battle. Had feared it with every yearly sacrifice to Chemosh. And feared doubly so when Chilion convinced Mahlon to attend those festivals.

She jolted at Naomi's bitter cry. The squeal of the heavy boulder being moved from the burial cave grated harshly on her ears. Tears blurred her vision as she placed one arm around Naomi's shrunken shoulders. The poor woman had lost everything. First her husband, now her two sons.

I can't bear it. Her heart cried with a pain so fierce she longed to run to the hills and scream until her lungs burst. This could not be happening to her, to them. ·

The men carried first Mahlon's then Chilion's body into the dark tomb. Naomi sobbed aloud, Orpah quickly joining in. Ruth wept quietly beside them both.

As the sun banked lower in the west and the men rolled the protesting boulder back over the cave's opening, the truth hit Ruth with the force of a mighty wind.

This *was* real. Naomi's god or the gods of Moab had exacted a heavy price upon the three of them, especially Naomi.

And left them all completely bereft.

20

As night began its descent, Boaz paced the hills, searching for the lamb. Adi had favored the ewe since its birth, treated it like a daughter at times. They had laughed that God had given them sheep instead of children, but he had not minded. At least the animals brought the smile once more to her lips.

How could the animal have strayed without his notice? He had told Adi to stay abed that morning when she felt ill, and he promised to care for her small flock. She trusted no one else with the animals. During the famine they had become her children, and she had spent days and nights in the fields, traveling far in search of green grasses, sometimes with only a sling for protection. But how could he deny her? She had found no joy in her normal tasks, and when Reuven had promised to teach her all he knew, having been a shepherd in his early life, Boaz relented.

She would not be happy with him now if he could not

find her favorite. Where was the animal? Dusk threatened with each step away from home, where he had sent the other sheep with a servant. If the boy could be trusted, more men would soon join him in the search. The whole town would celebrate as they always did over even one lost lamb. But not if he couldn't find the foolish animal.

He shaded his eyes against the blaze of the sun's last glorious rays, walking carefully toward a nearby ravine. The rains had only recently begun again, but wadis could quickly flood with rushing waters, especially after such a drought. The ewe could be swept away and lost forever.

Boaz felt the sweat beneath his tunic as he quickened his pace. He called out, but the sheep did not know his voice as they did Adi's. She should be here to help him. But he could not let her weaken herself when she had already spent the night coughing in the room next to his.

He rubbed his face and called, "Sheep!" again. Adi had names for them all, but for the life of him he could not keep them straight. He picked his way over the dry ground and hurried toward the wadi before he lost all light. One glance toward the town told him the men with torches were still some time in coming. He looked back toward the wadi and made his way to the bottom. Looking right and left, he strained to see, calling as he walked slowly in one direction, away from the sun's final glare. And there, when the sun held barely a thread of light in the sky, he saw her sprawled on her side, unable to get up.

Boaz knelt and examined the ewe, running his hands gently over each leg. Nothing broken. He peered at the bottoms of her hooves, feeling for stones. Nothing. At last assured that she had simply fallen onto her back and couldn't roll over in this narrow part of the wadi, he lifted her heavy body and set her upright. She stood a moment, shook herself, then looked up at him.

"Come," he said, leading her up the embankment. How did Adi manage with these animals—and at her size? Adi was such a slight woman, much too thin since the last pregnancy and two miscarriages to follow. He had feared for her life each time and was almost relieved when she seemed to take to shepherding instead of making baby clothes.

"How did you manage to get down there?" He spoke to the sheep to comfort her, to make sure she continued to follow as he walked toward home. Adi would be glad he had been the one to find her. They would celebrate, perhaps, if the cough had left her and she was feeling better. Naomi would have made sure of it had she been here. But Naomi had been gone over eleven years. By now Boaz was certain they would not see her or her sons again.

The town drew closer, and he met the servant boy near the city gates with instructions to take the ewe to the pens near his home. He passed through the door, assured the men at the gate he no longer needed assistance, and heard the gate barred behind him.

The desire to whistle filled him, and he almost gave in to it as he walked Bethlehem's streets toward home, but he held back his exuberance. He never could carry a tune he would want the city to hear. But his step was light as he neared his courtyard, saw the torches lit in welcome.

He entered the house and waited while a servant washed his feet.

"There you are, my lord." Reuven had aged much in the years since the famine first began. He walked with a limp now, and his hair was purest white. How much longer would Boaz have him to lean upon?

"Yes, I'm home at last. One of the sheep wandered off and fell into a ravine. She is fine though. And here we are." He smiled wide until he met Reuven's troubled gaze. "What is it?" He was used to the occasional squabble Reuven was forced to bring to him in the evenings, though tonight he wanted only to find Adi and enjoy a fine meal.

"I fear . . . that is . . ." Reuven paused and cleared his throat. "She did not wish it, but I sent for the town physician and the midwife to attend to Adi, my lord. She has not stopped coughing since you left, and I feared . . . well, perhaps it is also a womanly thing."

Boaz jumped up before the servant could dry his foot. He raced down the hall, Reuven slowly following, and stopped at the room where Adi lay sleeping.

He breathed a sigh. Reuven was simply overreacting. She was fine, as she had been every time she had lost a babe. "She seems to be resting well now, which means she will soon recover," he said, glancing at his servant. "Did you say the physician came earlier?"

Reuven nodded. "The man gave her something to stop the cough and help her sleep. The midwife did not tell me anything. She will stop again tomorrow."

Boaz stared at him for a lengthy breath. Adi had said nothing about another pregnancy. In fact, it would be much too soon because she had just recovered from a miscarriage barely two moons ago. "She wouldn't be coughing unless she was sick." He spoke to make sense of Reuven's obvious concern. "Did the doctor give a cause? Is she feverish?"

Reuven shook his head. "The doctor did not know the

cause. But he did suggest that Adi is worn out from too many pregnancies and too much exertion with the sheep. She is not strong, my lord."

In his mind's eye, Boaz felt again the weight of the sheep he had lifted. Adi cared for thirty of them, all of similar size. Why had he not sent a servant with her to help each day? A strong man or woman, someone to lift the fallen or care for the larger animals? What kind of a husband was he to let her care for them alone?

"When she is well, she will not handle the sheep alone again," he said, already thinking of which servants would be best suited to helping his wife without making her feel weak. She would not want him to think her incapable.

"Very good, my lord. I shall make a list of possible candidates for the position of hireling shepherd to Adi." Reuven's gaze drifted beyond Boaz to Adi's sleeping form. How peaceful she looked.

Please, Adonai, give her rest. He walked into the room and knelt at his wife's side. How he longed to stroke her hair, her cheek. But he resisted the urge lest he wake her. In a few days she would return to normal, and he would speak to her about rearranging her duties so they didn't tax her so. He would have to think carefully about how to word his requests. Adi could be stubborn when she wanted something badly enough.

A smile formed as he gazed on her beautiful face. *Thank You, Adonai.* He might not have sons, but at least he had Adi. And despite what anyone else thought, that was enough.

The following morning, a knock on the door interrupted Boaz's quiet meal. Adi had slept without waking and still lay abed, so he had chosen not to disturb her. Reuven returned from answering the door with the midwife in tow. Boaz stood as the woman entered the room. He ushered her to the sitting room and invited her to rest among the cushions.

The woman glanced at Reuven, who quickly excused himself, but she refused to sit as Boaz had instructed. Instead, she lifted her wizened head and stepped closer to him, her voice low.

"I did not wish to convey this news to your servant, my lord," she said.

He looked into her dark eyes. His stomach clenched at the knit of her brow and the slight scowl on her wrinkled face. "Tell me."

"I spoke with the physician after I examined her. She is bleeding, my lord, and not in the normal way of women. That is why she is so weak." She stepped back, her gaze assessing.

Boaz stood, unmoving. Every fiber of his being rejected the words and their implied meaning. Adi was ill, yes, but she had been ill in the past and always recovered. She was slight of build but strong in spirit. She would be fine. Of course she would.

"I would like to examine her again to see if the poultice I used yesterday did any good. If you are willing, my lord." The midwife still spoke softly and glanced quickly about the room as if she feared being overheard.

"You gave her a poultice?" Why did his words sound so wooden, as though they came from another? "And the physician approved of this?"

"He was in full agreement, my lord." She met his gaze. "I do not want to alarm you." She stepped closer and placed a hand on his forearm. "I know how much your wife longs for a child, how hard it has been to lose them all."

The woman did not know the half of it. She was not the one holding Adi's weeping form in the dark of night when no one else could hear. She did not know that the sheep only brought small comfort, for her empty arms longed for so much more.

"I fear," the woman went on, though Boaz wished her words would stop, "that she attempted another pregnancy too soon and something has caused the bleeding. Either she has lost the child already or is in the process."

Boaz stared at the woman, pulled his arm from her attempt to comfort, and crossed both arms to ward off a chill that he knew came from deep within him. He had not been with Adi often, had purposely avoided the times . . . hadn't they? "But she has shown no sign of pain as she has in times past."

The woman nodded. "It is why I am uncertain of the cause. May I check on her?"

"She is sleeping." But he nodded regardless and led the woman to Adi's chamber.

She slipped past him and he waited, pacing the hall. Adi's quiet voice drifted to him in answer to questions the midwife asked her. But they spoke too softly for Boaz to hear their words.

Adonai, please heal my Adi. Please make her whole again. I care not whether I have a son as long as I have her. His stomach knotted with the prayer, and he stopped at the threshold of the room just as the midwife bid Adi farewell. She came out carrying a basket of soiled linens. He averted his gaze and glanced beyond her to his wife's pale form drifting once more into sleep.

He followed the midwife like one of Adi's lambs and stopped with her near the entry to his home. "Tell me what you know." He would not be kept in the dark about this, womanly business or not.

"The bleeding has eased. Her cough also seems to have abated, and she said she is feeling better. She is simply tired. I think another day or two of rest and she should be back to her normal self." The woman offered him a tempered smile. "But I would warn you, do not go to her for at least three months. Her body cannot take another loss."

He nodded, heat creeping up his neck at the intimate comment. He would stay away six months if that was what Adi needed. "But she will recover. You are sure of this?" How desperately he wanted that relief, to know for certain.

"I believe she will recover," the woman said, stepping into the courtyard. "But I am not a physician. I think you will want his opinion as well in a day or so."

Boaz watched her leave, then gave orders to have the physician summoned today. He needed assurances now, not days from now. But somehow he wondered if even that man with his knowledge of herbs and ailments would be able to give him the guarantee he needed.

Weeks passed, and Adi improved as the midwife and physician had assured Boaz she would. Color filled her cheeks once more, but the bleeding had not stopped. She was unclean to him and to anything she touched and to anything sacred, which meant she could not attend the Festival of Firstfruits coming in a few months unless the bleeding stopped soon. The thought both worried and saddened him, all the more because he saw the way it weighed on her as she left for the fields with the sheep each day.

He watched now as she called each lamb by name and walked away from him. Usually she turned and waved, but today she kept walking as if there was nothing else to say between them. This ailment was driving them apart, and he didn't know how to get her back.

He turned away and rubbed the back of his neck. Reuven hobbled across the courtyard stones and met him as he took the reins of a saddled donkey from a servant and led the beast forward.

"My lord." Reuven crossed his arms, then let them fall to his sides again, a sign of his frustration, his uncertainty.

"What is it, Reuven?" He needed to meet Ezra in the fields, and he was already late for having watched Adi for so long.

Reuven shook his head. "It is nothing, really. It is just . . . I am concerned for Adi, my lord. She seems too resigned."

He looked at his steward, processing his words. "Resigned? Well, of course, she has no choice but to accept what is happening to her. She cannot heal herself. She cannot give herself a child." He turned away, heat filling his face. *And God is not listening.* He couldn't say the words aloud, but oh how he felt them! Why did the Almighty not hear his prayers for his wife? Why did she languish day after day? She had never done or said anything unkind in her life, and yet she suffered. Why?

Anger filled him as he hopped onto the donkey's back. "I'm sorry, Reuven, but I have to go. I do not understand why God allows the innocent to suffer. I do not understand why those who fear Him still undergo so many trials. Adi has faced trials all of her life, and God has done nothing to stop them." There, he'd said it. He kicked the donkey's sides and trotted away from his house, not waiting for his steward to respond.

The stars were already out that night as Boaz finally returned to his courtyard and handed the reins to a servant.

"There you are at last!" Reuven looked haggard and a little out of breath.

"Yes, I'm sorry. I was roaming the hills. I thought perhaps I would run into Adi with the sheep, but she must have come home because she was not in any of her usual haunts."

Reuven wrung his hands, an action Boaz had never seen him do. "I'm afraid that is not the case, my lord. Adi has not returned."

"What do you mean, she has not returned?" His heartbeat increased its pace. Where else would she have gone? Adi no longer spent the night in the field with the sheep as some shepherds did. She wasn't strong enough, and Boaz could not bear to let her stay away.

"I sent men in search of her—hours ago, in fact—but none have returned." The old servant sank onto a stone bench as though all strength had left him.

"Which way did they go? I will join them." He called to the servant who had taken his donkey to retrieve a fresh one.

"I have sent men in all directions, my lord. I told them to check the Jordan and its tributaries." Reuven's words cut deep, and Boaz felt that his heart might pound right through his chest.

"She wouldn't go too close to the river. Not at its height. She wouldn't risk losing one of the sheep into the rushing waters." He ran a hand through his hair and glanced toward the stables. Where was that servant?

"You are right, my lord. The sheep would fear the sound of rushing waters. She would seek quiet waters for them. But it seemed prudent to check those areas just the same."

"And with the recent rains . . ." He didn't finish his thought. Even the tributaries had fewer quiet places now that the long drought and famine had passed.

"I could go with you," Reuven said, his aged face lined with worry. "I know the places shepherds go."

Boaz looked at his friend and shook his head. "Just tell me where you think she might be."

Had Adi been in her right mind this morning? She had been sad for years, even more so since she'd been ill, but she wouldn't do anything foolish. Would she?

"I would ride along the banks of every river you can find, despite the rains. I would check every ravine, every dip in the ground. Even every cave."

The servant appeared with another donkey saddled and ready. Reuven pulled a torch from the wall, handing it to Boaz. "You will need this."

Boaz looked into Reuven's worried gaze. His stomach did a flip. Reuven did not fret without good cause.

"I'm sure she is fine," Boaz said to convince himself. "Probably chasing after a lost ewe. You know how she is." He turned to the servant, who handed him the donkey's reins. "Go, saddle another donkey and come with me." If something had happened to Adi, he would need help, for he wasn't sure he could survive what he knew deep down Reuven feared.

Despite her sadness of late and her illness, Adi would not

throw herself into the rushing waters. She would take care of the sheep like the good shepherdess she was.

But as he rode with his servant in the dark toward the Jordan's banks, his fear grew.

The search lasted throughout the night, to no avail. At dawn the following day, Boaz stood near the edge of a ravine. He stepped carefully, noting loose rock and what looked like the broken edge of a cliff. The fear that had never really left him rose higher as he looked down. A body lay sprawled at the bottom, and a bleating fallen ewe unable to get up on its own lay nearby.

Boaz left the servant and the other men who had joined him in the night and picked his way down the ravine, his heart pounding. *Please, Adonai, no!*

But the closer he got to the floor of the ravine, the clearer his vision. He would recognize Adi's robe anywhere, and her ashen, bloodied face sent him to his knees. Her body lay at a crooked angle as though she had fallen. Adi would not fall off a ledge. She was too smart and agile for such a thing. And yet . . . she had been so ill only weeks before. Guilt and despair filled him as bile rose in his throat. One glance back at the cliff told him that the ground, perhaps from the recent rains, had given way at least a little. Perhaps the ewe had fallen first and Adi misjudged the distance to the edge? Or the soft ground?

He looked back at her face. There were no marks of mauling by a wild animal, praise Adonai, except for the caked blood in her hair. Hands shaking, he gently gripped her shoulder and turned her toward him. Looked at the back of her head. Saw the rock where she had obviously landed and hit her head.

Tears fell, and he made no attempt to stop them. "Adi." Her name was a whisper on his tongue.

"Boaz?" Ezra's voice called to him from a distance. "Boaz, where are you?"

He swallowed hard. The words were nearly impossible to utter. At last he turned and called, "Down here."

Ezra's form appeared above him. His steward looked around him and began the slow descent to the bottom, his expression grim. "She fell?"

Boaz could not speak. He nodded slowly.

Ezra glanced up again. "The clay is weak just above us. Perhaps it was too dark for her to see." He looked at the struggling ewe not far from Adi's body. "She was trying to rescue the one that was lost."

His observations, true though they may have been, did not comfort. "She was more careful than this."

"It was dark." Ezra bent and touched Boaz's shoulder. "She was small and weak. Perhaps she just did not see the edge." He squatted, meeting Boaz's gaze. "Let the men take her body and prepare it for burial. There is nothing more you can do here."

Boaz stared at him, numb. Ezra stood and called up to the other men, who descended the ravine to carry Adi's body from the ground and up the hill.

Ezra placed a hand on Boaz's shoulder where he still knelt in the dirt. "Boaz, come home." His strong arms lifted Boaz to stand.

Tears fell silently into his beard and he tasted the saltiness, not caring what Ezra thought of him. Two other men put the ewe on its feet, and Boaz numbly watched it climb the hill. Something Adi would never do again.

All he'd ever wanted was this woman to be in his life for as long as he lived. He was supposed to go into Sheol before her, not have her leave him empty and alone. Had he done something to deserve this? Held too much anger over the lost children?

Did You take her because of me?

Fear crawled up his spine. Surely not. The Almighty did not reward a man's honest hurt with more pain. Surely the Almighty desired his good.

"But this isn't good."

"No, it's not," Ezra said as they climbed the steep hill on hands and knees, not realizing that Boaz was speaking aloud to God. But death was never good—whether physical death or death of a relationship in life. And death of one beloved was the worst thing of all.

Why, Adonai? Why did You allow this now?

His question met only silence.

PART 2

Then she [Naomi] arose with her daughters-in-law to return from the country of Moab, for she had heard in the fields of Moab that the LORD had visited his people and given them food. So she set out from the place where she was with her two daughters-in-law, and they went on the way to return to the land of Judah.

Ruth 1:6–7

21

NISAN (APRIL) 1283 BC

Naomi moved from room to room in the house now so empty, so lifeless, barely noticing the presence of Ruth and Orpah moving about like silent statues, attempting to keep up with the daily tasks. Her loom stood in the corner with the same threads clinging to it as they had the day Chilion had stumbled into the courtyard, sick. She would never weave again.

A sigh escaped, and with it the wish that she had never loved weaving garments for her family. But she had, which made the loss seem even greater. She had no family any longer, no one who needed her, no one to love. Her throat grew thick with the same grief and pain she'd felt the day Elimelech died, but this time . . . there were none to comfort.

"Mother Naomi." She felt Ruth's touch on her shoulder and flinched. "I'm sorry, my mother. I didn't mean to startle you."

Naomi shook herself and turned to face this girl who had remained in her home since the loss of her sons. Two months now, and still they stayed in a house with no life. As though the place had become its own tomb.

"It's all right, my daughter. What do you need?" Did the girls need her? What was left of her life to give them? A house with the air of death, in a land that meant nothing to her? And her womb as dead as her sons. She could have no more children to wed to these women. Why did they stay?

They feel sorry for you. Of course, that was it. The poor widow Naomi. They couldn't just walk away and leave her. They couldn't return to their homes to have their mothers or fathers find new husbands for them as long as they felt an obligation to her.

She glanced at Orpah, who sat in a corner, her dark eyes clouded as though she too had lost all vision of hope. The woman had wept inconsolably at Chilion's side, while Ruth's tears had been quieter, as though she held her grief close to her heart.

She looked again at Ruth, who still stood patiently waiting for her attention. "What is it?" she asked again, impatience rising. *Just speak!* She wanted to scream at the girl, to scream at the walls, at the air, at God, but she dared not. What good would it do to argue with the Almighty, who had dealt her a blow worse than death?

"Some women have come from the market," Ruth said, pointing toward the outer court, where a small group of merchants' wives stood huddled like gossips at a well. "There has been a caravan from Syria that took on a traveler from Bethlehem."

Naomi's brows rose at the name of her hometown. How long had it been since she had heard it?

"They come with news, Mother." Why the girl insisted on

calling her "Mother" when she was only her mother-in-law she did not know, but she allowed it. She had no strength to argue with these women or to send them home.

"Then we must not keep them waiting." Naomi pushed slowly past Ruth and paused at the threshold to the court-yard. She drew a breath and lifted her head. "Welcome to my home," she said with false cheerfulness, hoping her tone did not sound as flat as she felt. "Please sit." She motioned to the benches of the court and looked at Ruth, who quickly retrieved cups of water for the women. "Tell me how I can help you today." How easy it was to say the normal niceties without feeling in any way a desire to fulfill them. She felt as though lies were dripping from her lips and kindness was a thing long past.

"We thought you would want to know," the potter's wife said, glancing at her friends for apparent moral support. "That is, we know that you have never been happy living in Moab." She paused as if waiting for Naomi to agree.

Naomi nodded but said nothing.

"We know you miss your own land," another said, trying to soften the sound of the other's words. "But your sons stayed because of the famine in Israel."

Naomi let her eyes roam heavenward in an attempt to stave off tears at the mention of her sons. A moment later she blinked them back and looked at the speaker. "The famine in Bethlehem is what led us here, yes." *And kept us here far too long.*

Suddenly, she had an urge to see her old home and the family that had remained, if any still lived—Boaz's sisters and Neta. Did Ziva still care for the home she and Elimelech had left behind?

The thoughts churned as she met the speaker's gaze once more. "What does this matter to me now?"

The potter's wife cleared her throat. "We have heard . . . that is . . . a passing traveler from Bethlehem said that the famine has lifted at last. The winter rains have come again and the barley has taken root. Even now it is nearly ripe unto harvest."

Naomi stared at her. None of these women from Moab had given her the offer of friendship in all of her years near Dibon. But now that she had lost everything, perhaps they felt as sorry for her as her daughters-in-law did. Or perhaps they hoped to now be rid of her as well.

How bitter your thoughts, Naomi. But she did not care, for her heart felt nothing but pain. The Almighty had dealt her a blow that pierced sharp as an arrow. Why had He not taken her out with that arrow as well? Why punish her by letting her live? She had nothing to live for.

But Bethlehem. How strange that the sound of that word should carry a glimmer of hope.

"How long ago did the man leave?" Unfortunate that she could not have spoken directly to him. Maybe she would have recognized him as a relative or a friend's son.

"The Syrian caravan came yesterday, and we only heard this morning. Apparently the man left the caravan before it entered Dibon. It was one of the camel drivers who gave us the news." The potter's wife pointed to the weaver's wife as the one who had spoken with the driver.

"So the man never came to Moab?" Disappointment shot through her. Every man and woman in Bethlehem had probably been told of the folly of her husband and what happened to those who associated with Moabites.

"I don't know for certain," the weaver's wife said. "Only that someone in the caravan spoke with a traveler from Bethlehem. No one seems to know where the traveler was headed. I never saw him."

Naomi simply nodded. Perhaps someone had been sent to deliver a message to another kingdom. Or perhaps someone had been traveling south to Edom, though Naomi could not imagine the purpose.

"So the famine has lifted in Israel," Ruth said, coming up beside her.

"Yes," Naomi said, thoughts of home whirling through her head again. She glanced about, barely seeing the women who seemed almost uncomfortable sitting in her court. She had the presence of mind to thank them as they stood and hurried back toward town.

"Then we should go home," Ruth said, taking Naomi's hand. "If your god has seen fit to bless Bethlehem, then perhaps he is telling us to return and be blessed as well." She offered Naomi a hesitant smile, but Naomi could not return it.

"There is no blessing left in my life." She winced at her tone, wishing she could offer some kindness to this girl who had shown nothing but kindness to her. She forced a half smile, regretting her harsh words. "Except you," she added, squeezing Ruth's hand. She turned to hurry away from Ruth's scrutiny and caught sight of Orpah standing there watching, hearing every word.

22

Ruth chewed the parched grain in silence, listening as Naomi recounted the things she still needed to do. "I can think of very little that needs to go with us." Naomi glanced about the sitting room where the three women sat sharing a simple meal from the early garden produce and some of the dried fruit and nuts and grains they had stored from last year's bounty. "We will need food, of course, and one donkey should be able to carry the load. And we can take one of the goats." She paused, her thoughts obviously far off. "Do you think anyone in town will purchase the land quickly from me, or some of the furnishings?"

Ruth nodded, glancing from Naomi to Orpah. "I am sure any number of the women will take what we cannot carry. But you will keep the loom and bedrolls and cooking utensils, will you not? We cannot travel without some provisions."

Naomi studied her hands a moment as though the question needed much pondering. What thoughts went through her mother-in-law's mind? Had she said something to trouble or offend her?

"I do not think I can ever look upon that loom again," Naomi said at last, her gaze shifting to the loom that still stood in a corner and then to the window beyond it. "Elimelech built it for me."

Silence followed the remark.

"Then you should keep it," Orpah said, her tone confident. "Perhaps you will pass it down to grandchildren one day."

Her words caused a gasp from Orpah herself, and she held a hand to her mouth. "Forgive me. I spoke rashly." Emotion made her voice waver, and she jumped up and ran from the room.

Ruth looked at Naomi, who watched Orpah flee. What could she possibly say to mend such words? For the glaring truth was that Naomi would never have a grandchild and had no more children to become her heirs. Two Moabite daughters-in-law meant little to her. Didn't they?

"I will keep the loom," Naomi said without emotion. "But we will take only what one donkey can carry, and the goat will give us milk and cheese."

"Only one goat?" They had a small flock, as did all families who lived outside the main city, and even some within the town walls kept more than one.

"We will sell the rest." Naomi did not even meet Ruth's gaze. "We cannot afford to keep them," she said after a lengthy silence.

Ruth did not quite understand Naomi's reasoning, but she did not argue. "I can go into town in the morning and talk to my mother. She can speak to the governor about a possible person to purchase the land."

Naomi nodded. "Yes, that would be helpful."

When more moments passed without comment and Orpah's weeping could be heard from her bedchamber, Ruth slowly stood and cleared the food away. Her mother had finally wed the governor in a civil ceremony that made her a lesser wife rather than a mistress to the man, so the governor now considered himself Ruth's father. But she would never consider him so, and she would not go to him directly. She had not trusted him in the past and she did not trust him now.

But it would be helpful if he would buy back the land he had once sold to Elimelech. Surely he would not lay claim to it and leave Naomi destitute. Ruth would search the entire town for a man to buy the land before she would allow that to happen.

As dawn crested the horizon, Ruth wrapped her robe tightly about her, took Mahlon's walking stick, and kissed Naomi's cheek. "I will return before nightfall." She said the words to bring some light of reassurance and hope into the woman's lifeless eyes.

"We will be waiting." Naomi glanced over her shoulder. Orpah's fingers had found use in the spindle and distaff, but she had not spoken a word since the night before.

Ruth offered Naomi a smile but did not linger. She could not help her sister-in-law, whose grief lay so deep Ruth wondered if even Naomi's god could reach it.

She moved with hurried steps once she passed the courtyard walls, aware of every sound and the things that moved in the grasses beneath her feet. The hint of dew still clung to the blades, tickling the sides of her feet. In her early years, she would have run and laughed among the fields, and there had been times Mahlon would have run with her, caught her, and twirled her around, laughing the whole time.

She swallowed the lump that accompanied the memory. Mahlon was gone. And she had a mission to move on, to make his mother smile again.

She hurried faster until she slipped through the city gates, stopping first at the potter's house, where her sister Susannah now resided. She rapped softly on the door, but Susannah was not abed or sleepy-eyed as she had once been in her youth. In the home of her husband there was too much work to be done.

"Ruth!" Susannah flung open the door and welcomed her sister with open arms. They held each other in a fierce embrace until at last Ruth pulled away.

"I must speak with you. I need your help," she said.

Susannah pulled Ruth into the inner courtyard, where she could grind the morning's grain and listen. "Tell me," she said as she tossed kernels of wheat onto a weathered stone.

"I must find someone to purchase the land Elimelech bought from Governor Aali. Naomi is returning to Bethlehem, and Orpah and I are going with her." The words came out softly but rushed.

Susannah abruptly stopped the grindstone. "You're leaving?" Her wide eyes told Ruth the news was quite unexpected.

Ruth nodded. "I will go with her. I cannot let Naomi go back alone."

Susannah studied her for a lengthy moment, then took up the grinding again. "It is not a wise choice, but you are old enough to make that decision, I suppose." After all, a widow did not have to return to her mother's house. "I would not leave if it were me," she added. "Whatever will you do in such a foreign land?"

"The same thing Naomi has done in ours all these years. Learn their ways. Take care of Naomi as she cared for those she has lost." Ruth looked at her work-worn hands. How would she find work to provide for their needs? Surely the money from the land would help for a time.

"As for the land," Susannah said as if reading her thoughts, "I think you will find trouble there."

Ruth looked up and met Susannah's gaze. "In what way?"

Her sister looked beyond her. "Mother has confided," she said, lowering her voice. Ruth scooted closer to hear above the noise of the grindstone. "Governor Aali has been biding his time. He has seen the prosperity of the land he allowed Elimelech to purchase and his sons to keep after his death. But he will not give a fair price to get it back. In fact, I doubt he will pay anything at all."

Ruth stared at her sister as the younger woman put more weight into turning the stone. Sounds of Susannah's young children could be heard in the house, accompanied by instructions from their grandmother, Susannah's mother-in-law. An ache accompanied the sound, one Ruth did not expect. How long would she be troubled by feelings of inadequacy for never having born Mahlon a child? For having no son to rest on Naomi's knee?

She shook herself, ashamed of her selfish thoughts. She wanted a child for herself, if the truth were known. And now she would never have one.

"Then I will not go to Mother or Governor Aali," she said, lifting her chin. "Surely someone in this town would be willing to pay a price for such fine land." But a sinking feeling accompanied that thought, further affirmed by Susannah shaking her head.

"You know better than that, dear sister." She stopped to sift the grain through the sieve to remove as many pebbles or scraps of stone as possible. "If anyone dared buy that land out from under Governor Aali, you can bet they or one of their family would be chosen for the next sacrifice." She shook her head again. "It is a risk no man in this city would take."

Ruth sank lower into the bench, the air escaping from her lungs, her heart defeated before the sun had fully crested the rise.

"Then what will we do?"

They couldn't stay. Naomi would not hear of it. In a flash she wondered if those women who came to tell of a traveler from Bethlehem had reported a true tale. *Had* Naomi's god revisited his people and brought water to the land once more? Was the famine truly past? Or was it a ploy to get Naomi to leave so Governor Aali could have what he'd wanted all along? Land he'd never intended to let go of indefinitely. What Mahlon and Chilion had made prosperous, Governor Aali and Te'oma would take for themselves.

"I wish I could advise you, Ruth," Susannah said, adding more grains of wheat to the stone. "But if Naomi plans to leave, the best she can do is to take what she can carry and go. No one in Dibon would purchase anything that belonged to an Israelite. And no one but the governor will lay claim to the land."

"Then she is truly destitute." Ruth felt as though the millstone Susannah turned had sunk to the pit of her stomach.

"*You* don't have to be," Susannah said, meeting her gaze. "Go back to live with Mother and the governor. They will find you a new husband and you will live in peace. Let the Israelite find her own way home."

Ruth stared at her sister for a long moment. "It is a dangerous journey for a woman alone."

"It is just as dangerous for two or three. You have no men to protect you, my sister." Susannah's tone had grown pleading now, and the look in her eyes held deep concern. "You don't have to go with her. You are no longer bound to her family."

She is right, you know. The thought flitted through Ruth's head, but her heart rejected it. She abruptly stood, knowing she had failed Naomi already but could not fail her again.

"I am bound by duty and by love," she said, gazing down on Susannah one last time. She would likely never see her sister again.

Susannah stopped her work and stood as well. "Will you even tell Mother goodbye?" Tears filled her eyes, and Ruth could not stop her own.

"I will stop at her house on my way out of town." She reached for her sister and held her close once more. "I will miss you," she whispered in her ear.

Susannah repeated the same. Soon her three children surrounded them. Ruth bent to kiss each one, tears falling freely now. The sun's yellow rays splayed over the courtyard when she at last pulled the youngest child from hanging on her leg and bid them farewell. Sorrow welled near to the breaking point as the potter's house slipped from view, but Ruth knew the harder confrontation was around the next bend.

Ruth entered the courtyard of the governor's grand estate, passing beneath two guards who recognized her and allowed her to pass without question. How different life would have been for her had she wed Te'oma and lived here. How strange it would be to have mother and mother-in-law under the same roof.

She shook the ridiculous idea aside. There was no point in dwelling on the impossible, and she was very glad, despite her losses, that she had never given in to the selfish ways of the men in this house.

She waited in the entryway to be announced, and a servant came to wash her feet while she sat on an ornate wooden bench. "There is no need. I won't be staying," she almost said, but to stop the servant from doing his work seemed rude. The last thing she wanted was to get some poor person in trouble.

Time elapsed more slowly than if she had watched the sun move, but at last her mother breezed into the entryway and pulled her to her feet.

"Ruth, my darling! How good of you to come." She coaxed Ruth into the large sitting area where more servants roamed. Trays of dried fruit and cheeses and nuts sat on several low tables, while sweating golden cups of cold water sat beside the couch where her mother took her seat. Ruth sat opposite her on the edge of the couch, wishing for the wings of a bird to let her fly away.

"Sit back, my love. Stay. There is no rush." Her mother plopped a date into her mouth and pulled the pit from the center, setting it on the silver tray beside a pile of others. "There is plenty of food. Eat."

Ruth glanced at the food, but her stomach rebelled. "I'm not hungry, Mother. I had my fill before I came." Not nearly as much as was staring at her now, but the parched grain and dried raisin cakes with Orpah and Naomi had been enough.

Her mother pulled the goblet to her lips and drank. "Then tell me why you have come," she said, her voice no longer quite as inviting. "Come home to beg for a place to live until Aali can find another husband for you?" She ran her finger along the rim of the cup. "Too bad for you that Te'oma has already wed two wives. You would not enjoy third place, my dear."

I would not have enjoyed first place. But she bit her tongue lest the words slip past.

"I came to tell you that I am leaving. I am going with Naomi to Bethlehem." She clasped her hands together to stop a sudden chill. "I came to say goodbye."

The sudden silence was not the surprised yet pleasant kind that she had had with Susannah only moments before. The air held the foul scent of anger.

"What did you say?" Though her mother had clearly heard her.

"I am going with Naomi. We had intended to sell the land and go, but I am told by my sister that your husband will not allow the land to go to anyone but himself." She met her mother's gaze with sudden challenge. Could it hurt to try one last time, even though she knew without a doubt Susannah spoke the truth?

Her mother's eyes narrowed, her gaze holding a hint of threat. "Your *father* owned that land, which he allowed Elimelech to rent for a time, my dear child. It never belonged to him or his sons. There is nothing for Naomi to sell."

Ruth swallowed back the urge to tell her mother that she was wrong, but suddenly she did not know. Had Elimelech merely paid for the use of the land for a time? Would Naomi even have known that? Mahlon had never spoken of anything

166

related to money except to assure her that all was well and growing more prosperous with each passing year.

She stood then, knowing she would get no more help from this woman who had given her birth. Certainty swept over her that Naomi had been more mother to her in the past ten years than Shiphrah had been since her father's death.

"Goodbye, Mother," she said, turning to go. She half expected the woman to jump up and follow her to the door, to request one last hug as Susannah had done. But no footfalls sounded upon the tiled floors, making her decision and her defeat all the more real.

23

THREE DAYS LATER

Naomi stood in the courtyard of the house for one last look at this place she had called home for far too long. Memories whispered from the walls—of conversations, love, laughter . . . and pain. So much pain.

She turned and grabbed the donkey's reins, glancing to make sure the goat was secured to the donkey's tether. Cooking utensils jangled from the animal's sides, and their sleeping mats lay folded to make a seat should one of them need to ride. Sacks of grain and jugs of oil would last them until they arrived at Bethlehem, perhaps beyond if they were careful with the amount they ate.

Naomi wondered if she could eat a thing, given the way her stomach continually twisted in knots. Why had they ever set foot in this godforsaken land? Emotion clogged her throat as she urged the donkey forward.

"Are you all right, Mother?" Ruth's kind voice jolted her

from the spiraling feelings of melancholy. The girl had been such a blessing to her these past few months since . . .

The sudden image of her laughing sons brought the thoughts to a halt. They had been happy here, with these women. *Why, Adonai?*

"I will be fine once we reach Bethlehem," she said, avoiding the truth that she was not fine at all. There was no sense in upsetting Ruth and Orpah now when they had a seven- to ten-day walk ahead of them.

Naomi headed them south through Moab to avoid going north and crossing into Ammon, taking the path by way of the Dead Sea. The same path Elimelech had followed, one where they might join a caravan that traveled these roads.

But as they set up camp for the night along the shores of the Dead Sea, Naomi's heart ached with the realization that she could not ask these women to continue on with her. In another day they would leave Moab's lands, and who knew what might happen to three women alone along the road home?

If she were harmed, she cared little. She had nothing left to bring joy in this life. She might as well rest with her men in Sheol. But Ruth and Orpah were young, vital women who deserved to have what Naomi had once loved above all else. A husband and sons. Her daughters-in-law did not need to spend their days keeping company with an old woman who had nothing to offer them but pain.

The stars illumined the night as she stood outside her tent looking out at the blackness of the Dead Sea. She would confront the girls on the morrow. The water softly lapped the shore, and she moved closer, careful to avoid its oily feel from creeping onto her sandals.

It would be hard to leave them in this land, but it was the right thing to do. They didn't belong in Israel. She glanced heavenward, but even the stars seemed frozen in their places, without a wink or nod to indicate that their light would guide her home.

No, she would be going home alone. And in that moment she wondered if even God would be going with her.

Morning dawned too soon, but Naomi rose, body aching from the hard ground, her feet still sore from the walk the day before. She dressed in the dim light and left the tent to find Ruth already bending over the fire, cooking quick flatbread for the journey.

Orpah poured water from one of the flasks, carefully measuring just enough to wash down the bread. She handed one to Naomi. "I hope you slept well, Mother Naomi," she said, her expression distant, unreadable.

Naomi nodded, taking the cup from Orpah's hand. "As well as anyone does on hard soil. Though I will say at least some of the land near the water is smoother. It was just too much to risk pitching a tent right on the shore."

"At least we would have floated if the sea had decided to crest its banks." Ruth laughed lightly, a pleasant sound, but Naomi was in no mood to be pleasant.

She sat on the ground and accepted the flatbread Ruth had made without another comment. The three ate in silence, though Naomi's mind was anything but quiet. She pondered a number of different thoughts, trying to figure out which way to speak to these women who had been with her for so many years. Her heart felt as though the words themselves would rip her in two once she spoke them. But speak them she must.

"I have something to say to you both," she said at last, once the meal was done and everything packed up again. They stood near the donkey, ready to head out for another day, but Naomi made no effort to start walking.

"What is it, Mother?" Ruth's brows drew down, causing lines to appear across her brow. "I know something troubles you."

"Yes, please tell us," Orpah said, her perpetually sad expression unchanged.

"I want you to go, return, each of you to your mother's house." She paused only a moment at the shocked look on each beautiful girl's face. "May the Lord deal kindly with you," she said, hurrying on, "as you have dealt with the dead and with me. The Lord grant that you may find rest, each of you in the house of another husband."

She looked from one to the other, leaned close and kissed Orpah's cheek, then did the same to Ruth. She choked on a sob at the sound of Orpah's weeping. But when Ruth could not keep the tears from streaming down her face, Naomi could not stop herself from crying with them.

For the space of many breaths they all wept aloud, their posture telling Naomi that they would not be so easily convinced.

"No," Orpah said, "we will return with you to your people."

Ruth nodded. "Orpah is right. We will go with you. It is not right to leave you . . . and we don't want to."

Naomi swiped at her wet cheeks and shook her head. "Listen to me, my daughters. Turn back. Why will you go with me? Have I sons in my womb that they may become your husbands?" She placed a hand over her middle where her dead womb lay, for she knew, as her daughters-in-law also surely knew, that she was long past the days of childbearing.

"Return home, my daughters," she said. "Why would you come with me? Am I going to have any more sons, who could become your husbands? I am too old to have another husband. Even if I thought there was still hope for me—even if I had a husband tonight and then gave birth to sons—would you wait until they grew up? Would you remain unmarried for them? No, my daughters. It is more bitter for me than for you, because the Lord's hand has turned against me!"

Naomi leaned into the donkey, her words taking the last of her strength. Why had God been so against her? Hadn't it been Elimelech's decision to move them here? Hadn't she tried to get her sons to return home, to no avail? Why then was she punished by so great a loss?

Tears came again, silent and unyielding, but Orpah's and Ruth's cries carried far beyond their little camp. She looked from one to the other. They knew without a doubt she spoke sense and truth. Orpah's tears were real, but for the first time in many years, Naomi saw a spark of hope in her eyes. She was doing right by the girl in letting her go.

Orpah turned first to Ruth and clung to this sister-in-law who had also been her best friend since childhood. But at last, when their tears seemed spent, Orpah turned to Naomi.

Naomi opened her arms as Orpah came toward her, hugged her tight, and accepted her kiss of departure.

"I will miss you, Mother Naomi," she whispered, her tone still carrying a wobble of grief.

"And I you," Naomi said, knowing that despite the girl's foreign ways, it was true. "Chilion loved you from the moment he first saw you." She touched Orpah's cheek. "May God grant you another husband who loves you just as much."

Orpah smiled but could not speak as tears slipped down her comely face, dampening her hair, her headscarf. At last she turned, gave both women one last look, and walked back the way they had come.

Ruth watched Orpah leave, her gait slow at first, but before she rounded a bend that would take her out of sight, Orpah picked up her skirts and ran like they used to when they were girls. She would be home in half the time it had taken for them to walk with Naomi the day before. The sight felt like the twist of a knife in her middle.

Why would you leave us? But she knew the answer, had always known. Orpah had never embraced even the slightest teaching Naomi had offered, nor asked any questions about the God of Naomi's people. She had hated Chemosh after the loss of her child, but it wasn't enough to allow her to let go of the belief she had known for so long.

When Orpah was nearly out of sight and hearing, Ruth turned to her mother-in-law. Naomi still leaned against the donkey and suddenly seemed small and frail in Ruth's eyes. She stepped closer, arms open. The two met in the middle and Ruth clung to Naomi, as though to part them would rip more than the fabric of their tunics.

After more tears mingled between them, Naomi pulled back. Affection showed in her eyes, accompanied by deep sorrow. "See," she said, pointing in the direction Orpah had gone, "your sister-in-law has gone back to her people and to her gods. Return after her."

"Please." She took Naomi's hand in hers. "Do not urge me to leave you or to return from following you. For where you go I will go, and where you lodge I will lodge. Your people shall be my people, and your God my God." She glanced toward the road that led to the caves where their men were buried. "Where you die I will die, and there will I be buried. May the Lord do so to me, and more, if anything but death parts you and me."

Naomi met Ruth's gaze for a lengthy moment. At last she nodded and took the donkey's reins, and the two began the long walk toward home.

24

Boaz rode his donkey from the house in Bethlehem to check on his barley fields. Passover and the Feast of Firstfruits, Reishit, would soon be upon them. How could he bear to attend either without Adi?

His stomach tightened at the memory of Adi's joy over each harvest in the days before the famine had hit them, of her insistence they leave the edges of the fields for the poor to glean. How long would every thought of her bring pain, when she had rested in Sheol now more than thirty days?

He ran a hand over the back of his neck to keep the sweat from trickling down his back. Already the sun was nearly directly overhead. His workers would stop soon to rest in the shade and eat the midday meal. He should have come later, when he could have watched from the sidelines and escaped interacting with them. He had turned inward and avoided the townspeople since her loss, hating the weakness, the anger, that still rose within him at every turn.

Why had she gone so near the edge? Couldn't she tell the

ground was loose from the rains? If he had been there, he would have stopped her from getting so close . . .

He gripped the reins tighter, feeling the tension rise. His shoulders ached from the constant clenching, and he found it nearly impossible to relax even on his bed at night. Perhaps he would never sleep again. He rubbed a hand over his face. How dark the circles must look under his eyes. Adi would have noticed, would have told him to trust Adonai, to rest and not worry—as she had done so often during the famine.

He shook his head, willing—begging—the thoughts to stop plaguing him. He passed the young girls who gleaned in the fields behind his men. At least here these women were safe, unlike other fields where women were sometimes caught unawares. He clenched his hands at the very thought. Men could be despicable, especially in this era when too many ignored the law.

He drew close to an overhanging oak, where he spotted Ezra. He should turn around, come back when he was in a better frame of mind, but his overseer saw him and waved him over. Boaz released a pent-up breath and came up beside him, dismounted, then tied the reins to a tree limb. A low table sat beneath an awning in a clearing near the field.

"Peace be with you," he said to Ezra. The workers approached, and he gave his traditional welcoming wave and repeated the greeting.

"And also with you, my lord." The return blessing came unanimously from several lips.

Ezra met his gaze as the men took their seats. "You're early today. I expected you to stay away until the meal had passed."

"I should have," Boaz said, knowing his tone matched the anger still brewing in his heart. "I am afraid I am not good company."

Ezra stepped closer and placed a hand on Boaz's tense shoulder. "Never mind what type of company you are. The men are glad to see you. I'm glad to see you. And it will do you good to be in the fields instead of moping about that big house, scaring your servants half to death."

Boaz lifted a brow. "I don't scare my servants."

Ezra gave him a look that said he did not agree. "Have you spoken to them lately in a tone that didn't sound like a barking hound?"

Boaz frowned. He put up with far too much from this man. "So now my servants are complaining to you behind my back?" He should replace them all! But Adi would have objected and told him he was being completely unreasonable.

"One or two have mentioned it." Ezra held his gaze, un-flinching. Boaz had always appreciated the man's straight-forwardness, but sometimes he was exasperating.

"Give me their names and I will speak to them."

"Not while I live and breathe."

Boaz crossed his arms, glaring at his overseer. But a moment later he lowered them again. "Am I really that bad?"

Ezra patted his shoulder. "Sometimes. But people under-stand you are grieving. I just think it is time you come back from the land of mourning and help with the harvest. It will give you something to do and less time to think about your troubles."

Boaz nodded. He followed Ezra under the awning and took his seat at the head of the long table. His cooking servants had prepared a stew that morning and brought it to the men and women to enjoy, now that the majority of the morning's work was past.

"Good day to you, my lord." He turned at the sound of female voices and caught the looks of interest in the eyes of several. A few giggled behind their hands.

Did they really think he was interested in flirting with them? He scowled but managed, "And to you." He avoided meeting Ezra's disapproving gaze and ate his meal in silence.

The following morning, before Boaz had even donned his sandals, a knock on his door brought Reuven with a message.

"Your cousin Hamul has invited you to dine with Melek tonight, my lord. Shall I tell Hamul that you will accept?"

Boaz rubbed his chin and wiped his hands on a linen cloth, removing any remnants of the morning's goat cheese and date sauce. "Why would my cousin want me to dine with him in the middle of the week?" Melek was never one to send Hamul, his only son, on a servant's errand. Hamul had probably begged for a chance to leave the overprotective confines of his father's house. Melek set great store by the boy, finally conceived after several daughters. The child would never grow up properly if Melek didn't stop hiding him indoors. He glanced around at his own house, so empty without Adi's presence, and wondered briefly if Ezra was right. Was he a raging bear of a man in this place, hiding from life as Hamul was sometimes forced to do? How long would it take for the ache of grief to subside even a little? No meal with a cousin or sister or anyone else could bring her back, and he was in no mood for any type of socializing.

He looked at Reuven. "Send the lad to me."

"Yes, my lord."

Boaz shook himself as Reuven left him to his disparaging thoughts and led Hamul into the sitting room, where Boaz joined him.

Boaz looked at the boy, taken slightly aback at how much he had grown since he last saw him. He had the new growth of hair on his chin, and he now towered over Reuven. "You have grown from a child to a man without my notice, Hamul." He motioned for the young man to sit on one of the couches, but he shook his head and remained standing. Boaz did the same. "Tell me, Hamul, why has your father asked you to come here today?"

"My father did not send me, cousin Boaz. My mother did." He glanced around at Boaz's sitting room. Since Adi's death, Boaz had changed nothing lest somehow he forget her. He barely allowed the servants to dust the urns and other pieces of pottery she had made. Was he losing his mind in his grief?

"Why would your mother wish me to come to your house and choose to send you rather than a servant with the invitation?" He had a rather tenuous relationship with Melek and could see no reason to spend any more time with the man than necessary. The boy, on the other hand, reminded him that had his first son lived, they would be the same age. He covered a wince with a hand over his jaw.

"My father's wives made me promise not to tell." Hamul smiled, tentative, as though he, like Boaz's servants, were afraid to speak much in his presence.

Boaz walked to the threshold between the sitting room and outer court. "If I cannot know the reason, then please tell them I cannot come." He did not look at Hamul as he spoke and waited to hear the boy walk out of the room.

But Hamul stepped closer, bolder than Boaz expected.

"Is something wrong with my answer, Hamul?"

"It is just that they told me not to accept no from you, and that if you did not say yes they would make me pluck the pits from every date in the jar."

Boaz nearly bit his tongue to stave off a sharp laugh. Foolish women.

"How old are you now, Hamul?" The boy should not be doing such work at his age. He should be in the fields helping with the crops.

"Thirteen years," he said, lifting his chin. "My father has promised to declare me a man after the harvest."

"I see that you are already carrying the look of one." Boaz stroked his chin. "It takes much more than height and a beard to make a man."

"I know that a man would not be taking orders from his mother or doing the work of women." Hamul's tone had turned hard, and Boaz saw the hint of rebellion in his gaze. What had this son of Melek lived with all these years that should harden him so?

"Don't think that just because you are a man, you will never have to listen to your mother or your wife. Women are treated with respect under the law, and you never outgrow the need to honor your mother and your father." Boaz looked at the boy, but Hamul merely shrugged. Perhaps Boaz should accept the invitation just to see what really went on in Melek's household. Perhaps he could do the boy some good.

"Tell your mother I will come." He crossed his arms. "But only if they let you come with me to the fields tomorrow."

Hamul lifted a curious brow. "Why?"

"Because it is time you learned the ways of a man."

If his cousin would not step up to the task, he would. At

least it would give him something else to fill his mind. And perhaps save him from going mad in this house where Adi's face never faded and their unborn children's voices called to him in his dreams.

Hamul nodded, but Boaz could not tell if the thought pleased the young man or not. Was it too late to remove that seed of rebellion from his young heart?

The room was already abuzz with the voices of women the moment Boaz arrived at his cousin Melek's large estate. An uncomfortable prickle crept up his spine, and he felt sweat trickle down his back. He should not have come. He had been at odds with Melek since the day Elimelech moved to Moab. They had disagreed over so many issues regarding the famine, and when Melek discovered that Elimelech had sold his land to a neighbor outside of the family, the man nearly burst a vein in his neck.

Boaz had never enjoyed visiting this house, but Adi had made it bearable, always the peacemaker. How acutely he felt her loss now. But for Hamul's sake, for his dignity's sake, it was too late to turn back. He lifted his chin and gathered his courage as he strode into the sitting room.

"Boaz." Melek greeted him with a kiss to each cheek. "Welcome! Welcome! It has been far too long since you have come to visit." He motioned for Boaz to sit among the plush cushions.

Boaz eyed him, gauging the man.

Melek sat across from him, and both men accepted wine from a servant girl.

"Tell me," Melek said once the girl left them, "how goes the harvest in your fields?"

Boaz sipped from his cup. "Things are going as one would expect. The crop is the best I've seen in years." Of course, after such a famine anything seemed better than nothing. "We can be grateful Adonai has seen fit to finally send the rains." People expected him to give Adonai the credit and glory, though in his heart he struggled to be grateful for even one thing when the most important thing to him was lost.

"It is too bad Elimelech did not stay to witness this," Melek said, looking first into his cup, then meeting Boaz's gaze. "One wonders . . ." He left the sentence unfinished.

"One wonders what? That Elimelech was responsible for his own death? Perhaps you would say the same for Adi?" He gripped the cup too hard and felt immediate remorse for speaking so forthrightly when he was here as a guest.

"No, no, of course not." Melek's appeasing tone grated, but Boaz bit back the retort dangling on his tongue. "I only wonder . . . was it not unfaithfulness on his part to leave Israel? And to sell his land to someone other than family?"

The land again. Of course. Melek's concerns were always surrounding wealth. He would have been only too happy to purchase Elimelech's land and then find excuses not to sell it back seven years later.

"The land would have reverted to Naomi several years ago regardless," he said, forcing a civil tone. "If she were ever to return to claim it, I'm sure the man would give it to her. In any case, we have the right of the law to persuade him."

Melek waved a hand. "It is of no consequence to me. I doubt we will ever see any of Elimelech's family again, considering how long they have been in Moab."

"So there has been no news since Elimelech's death? Surely your wives hear gossip from the merchants." Adi had rarely participated in the gossip, though she did share news with him if it was something he needed to know.

"None that I've heard," Melek said, downing the liquid in his cup and accepting more from the servant. "It is simply too bad my brother thought he had no choice but to move." He shook his head as though he truly missed the man.

"I wonder how Naomi and her sons are faring with him gone." Though it had been more than ten years, Boaz could still see the sad parting at the city gate in his mind's eye. Adi had walked around in a melancholy state for weeks after Naomi left.

Melek shrugged. "The last caravan that passed this way heading north said nothing, and that was weeks ago. Before that, I did hear that Mahlon and Chilion had taken Moabite wives." His lip curled in disgust. "Hamul will marry an Israelite in our clan, a woman of the highest breeding. I cannot believe Naomi allowed her sons to do otherwise." He glanced toward the courtyard where Hamul was sitting outside rather than joining the men in the sitting room.

Boaz sat in silence a moment, glancing toward Hamul. He had no doubt Melek would get his way in choosing Hamul's wife. But Naomi could have been hard-pressed to fight against the will of two strong sons. "Perhaps she had no choice," he said at last. "It is not like Mahlon and Chilion are children. And with their father dead, they might have found Naomi easier to convince. You cannot put all of the blame for their choices on her."

Melek's face darkened in a slight blush as though he was ashamed. "I was not suggesting she was to blame." He glanced beyond Boaz toward the cooking rooms. "Still . . . my brother should not have left Bethlehem. That much I think we can agree upon, can we not, cousin?"

"At least on that much we can agree, yes." He looked up at the sound of the servant calling them to the evening meal.

"Shall we?" Melek pushed up from the low chair, no easy task given his girth.

"While we are in an agreeable mood," Boaz said as he moved ahead of Melek into the area where they would recline at a table, "I want to ask your permission to show Hamul some of my barley fields."

Melek gave him a sharp look. "Hamul has work enough in our own fields."

"If that were true, then he would not still be taking orders from his mother to do the work of women." Boaz waited for Melek's response before he sat. If he had roused the man's anger, this would be a very short meal.

Melek's brows drew down, his scowl evident. But a moment later, he laughed as though Boaz had made a humorous statement, and sank onto the cushion. "Women's work! My son? You do not know of what you speak, cousin. But I will humor you. Go ahead. Take Hamul to your fields and show him a thing or two. It will make him a better overseer of my own fields someday." He reached for a platter dripping with the fat of a lamb's leg and offered it to Boaz, who still stood, feeling outwitted—by either Hamul or Melek, he could not tell. Had the boy lied to him? Or was Melek simply covering his embarrassment by denying what Boaz had sensed was truth? Had Boaz become too trusting of the lad simply because he reminded him of all he had lost?

He sat, accepting the platter from Melek's hand, but his guard went up, and he determined to keep a sharper eye on both this wily cousin and his son.

25

Boaz walked with Ezra and every able-bodied man, woman, and child through Bethlehem's gates. The road to Shiloh wound north past Jerusalem, where Jericho had once stood, and the remains of Ai. Shiloh had been set up during the days of Joshua as a place where God put His Name, and the priests ministered to the Lord there at the tabernacle.

The journey toward Passover was a few days' walk, a joyous time when no regular work was done but the people gathered to sacrifice to the Lord and eat the Passover meal of remembrance. Boaz glanced at the donkey at his side, where a large sheaf from the first cuttings of barley was strapped to its back. Boaz would offer a thank offering, an early firstfruits of gratitude, though the act felt like mere formality instead of the true gratitude he should feel after so many years of famine.

How did one rejoice during grief?

He felt a knot in the pit of his stomach as he trudged

with the throng, listening to the songs of praise. Maybe he should have taken Adi away from Bethlehem as Elimelech had done with his family. Maybe it was the famine that had weakened her and caused her to lose so many babes. But his mind discarded the thought as quickly as it came. Elimelech had moved, and he was dead.

He glanced again at the sheaf on the donkey's back and felt the weight of the sacrificial lamb draped over his shoulders. Despite his grief, he had picked the best from the small flock—just not one of Adi's favorites.

"Want me to take the lamb for a time, my lord?" Ezra pointed to the animal, his gaze sober. "You shouldn't have to carry the burden the entire way. Not when we are sharing the Passover meal." He stopped, arms outstretched.

Boaz patted the lamb, so content on his shoulders. He should feel the weight of his sin with the weight of the lamb, knowing that in a few days its life would end on his account. And Ezra's. And Ezra's family.

But as he lifted the small animal and handed him over to Ezra, he felt nothing. No sorrow over its coming loss, as Adi would have felt. As he should have felt. All he could pull from his emotions was anger. He clenched his hands as he continued to walk, his mind whirling. How could a good God do this to him? He'd done nothing against the law, nothing to deserve to lose every child Adi ever conceived, nothing to deserve to lose Adi too. He swiped an unexpected tear as a sense of injustice, even rage, burned within his chest.

Ezra settled the lamb on his broad shoulders and continued walking, saying nothing for many breaths. "'Tis a hard thing," he said finally, glancing Boaz's way. "Celebrating a feast when you are barely past the grieving period."

People walked with them before and behind, and conversations rose and fell around them. Children darted between carts and people, laughing and joyous. Boaz looked about at the throng, felt the heaviness grow within him.

"There can be no set grieving time for such loss," he said, meeting his friend's gaze. "I would not have come at all if you had not been so stubborn." Ezra had not stopped nagging him like an old crone the entire week before the festival.

"You cannot stay cooped up inside your house for months and do nothing, my friend." Ezra gave him a concerned look. "The fields are nearly ready for the full harvest, as you can see by the firstfruits. I cannot manage it all without you." He touched Boaz's arm, but Boaz did not respond, though neither did he shove his friend aside.

"You could manage just fine and you know it." How bitter he sounded. He clamped his mouth shut when he saw several women look in his direction. Of course they had heard him, for he had fairly shouted the words.

"Well, I am glad you came. Even if your heart is not in it"— Ezra patted his own chest—"God knows. He understands why sacrifice is so hard for you—for all of us, really, for isn't that why it is called a sacrifice? If it was an easy thing to give our best—the best of our flock, the first of our harvest, not knowing if there will be more—and to give our thanks when we are not thankful, then where would the sacrifice be?"

Boaz said nothing, unwilling to agree or disagree. He simply could not bring himself to care. He glanced at the animal Ezra carried. The young male had been his favorite, for he could not bear to part with anything that Adi had ever preferred or loved. But what did it matter if he gave away everything he owned that wasn't hers? He had nothing left worth caring for. Nothing left worth living for.

Sometimes he wished, like the ancient patriarch Job had wished, that he'd never been born. Living cost too much. It hurt too much. And loving was the hardest thing of all.

His throat ached at the thought. He kicked a stone in the path off to the side, his heart heavier, if that were possible. He hated his life, the life that his had become. Where were the days of joy now, when those days had once held so much promise?

And Passover—it was a time to celebrate their delivery from Egypt when their slavery had ended. It was a time to rejoice in God's provision. And yet all he felt was bondage to his loss. Bondage to anger and disillusionment.

"Tell me about Bethlehem," Ruth asked each morning as they broke camp and began the journey around the Dead Sea. "I want to understand the God of your people, His laws, His ways. I want to understand the differences between Moab and Israel."

Naomi looked up from saddling the donkey, her mood pensive. The girl would not be thwarted, and her questions only added to Naomi's bitter memories. "I am afraid I am not much help to you, my daughter, when it comes to telling you about our God. I used to think I understood Him, but I realize now I do not understand Him at all." *And I am not sure I want to.* But she kept her thoughts hidden, given the hopeful look Ruth was giving her now.

"But your God is not at all like Chemosh," Ruth said, her tone kind. She placed a comforting hand on Naomi's shoulder.

"No," she said, shaking her head. "Our God is not like Chemosh. He may give and take life at His appointed times, but He does not require the blood of the innocents on brazen altars. In fact, He abhors it, as He proved to our father Abraham. Our God does not abide immorality and the worship of animals or stars or sun or moon. He will have no other God before Him. Even Chemosh must bow to Adonai Elohim."

Ruth nodded as though pondering Naomi's words. "And yet you are angry with Him for taking your men because He could have prevented their deaths." The observation was said in a tone of acceptance, the bitterness of Naomi's heart missing from Ruth's quiet voice.

"I would think you would be angry as well," she said, hating her curtness, which surely hurt the faithful girl.

When they reached a ridge that the donkey would take time to climb, Ruth took the reins from Naomi to allow her a break to walk freely. "I am not angry," she said at last. "I am sad. I miss Mahlon and Chilion. I miss what might have been." Her voice trailed off. "But I cannot change what has happened. I can only change how I view things."

Naomi stopped a moment, pretending to readjust her headscarf, while Ruth continued to guide the donkey and goat up the hill. At last she gathered her courage and caught up with the woman.

"Why did you not return to your mother's house?" She knew there was no turning back, as Bethlehem was not far now, and Ruth had made it clear that she would not leave Naomi's side. But why should she care for an old, broken woman?

Ruth stopped the donkey at the top of the rise where Bethlehem spread out below them. Naomi took in a breath, thrilled by the sight. "Home," she whispered, her heart feeling suddenly lighter than it had in years. Yet home was where her family resided, and her family was no more.

"I did not want to return to my mother," Ruth interrupted Naomi's melancholy musings, "because my mother had married Governor Aali, who would have considered himself my father and claimed a right to choose a husband for me. He might have given me to his son Te'oma, as was once his desire, as a third wife. I could not abide such a thing. My children, should I have any, would always live in the shadow of Chemosh, and I would live in fear of them being chosen as a sacrifice if I somehow upset Te'oma or the governor." She paused, placed a hand on her heart. "Besides"—she glanced at Naomi—"I want to be where you are."

Tears stung Naomi's eyes at the admission of such love, but she blinked them quickly away. She didn't deserve the affection of this woman, and yet here they were. "Come," she said, shoving the conflicting feelings aside. "Let us hurry before the sun gets too high in the sky. Not only do we have to enter Bethlehem's gates, but somehow I have to see if my old home is still intact and able to house us tonight."

She picked her way down the hill with Ruth following in silence. Her heart pounded with every step, and as the gates loomed before her, she fought the sense of panic that she couldn't do this alone. She had left these gates with her family, and now they were buried in caves in Moab.

Oh God!

The pain of it hit her like a mighty wind, and she nearly doubled over. She paused near the stone gates and waited for Ruth to come alongside her.

I can't do this.

"You can do this, Mother Naomi," Ruth said, clasping her hand. "We will go together."

Naomi merely nodded, too overcome to speak.

They passed the guards, who gave Naomi a curious look but gazed overlong at Ruth, who had covered her head and tucked the scarf in such a way as to try to appear invisible. But her beauty peeked through from her lovely face, and Naomi did not miss the way the men looked at her.

They moved through the wide stone structure and entered the market stalls that lined the main thoroughfare. Naomi looked to the right and left, searching for a familiar face. Women paused in their haggling over wares and turned to stare at the two of them with the donkey and the lonely goat.

"Is this Naomi?" one of the women asked, drawing closer.

"Neta?" She almost didn't recognize Melek's second wife, now much older than she had been eleven years before.

"It is you!" Neta raced closer and pulled Naomi into her arms. "You've returned!"

The women crowded around her then, all asking questions at once.

"How was your trip?"

"How long you have been gone!"

"Why did you leave?"

"Who is this with you?"

"Naomi," Neta said, interrupting the barrage of questions, "you must dine with us tonight." As she spoke, she glanced Ruth's way.

"Do not call me Naomi," she said, a catch in her voice. She saw the way the women glanced beyond her as though looking for Elimelech, Mahlon, and Chilion. "Call me Mara, for the Almighty has dealt very bitterly with me. I went away full, and the Lord has brought me back empty. Why call me pleasant Naomi, when the Lord has testified against me and the Almighty has brought calamity upon me?"

Neta rested a hand on Naomi's arm and offered her a comforting smile. "We had heard the rumors of Elimelech." She looked at Ruth. "We expected that Mahlon and Chilion were still with you."

"They passed on only a couple of months ago," Ruth said softly, drawing the women's attention to her.

Naomi nodded, relieved that Ruth had spoken for her, for she was not sure she was capable of saying the words.

"And who is this with you?" Neta asked, her tone kind, though some of the other women's faces held skeptical gazes.

"This is my daughter-in-law Ruth, a Moabitess. She was Mahlon's wife and has come with me to comfort me, to live with me, and to become one of us."

Silence followed her announcement. Naomi looked from one woman to the next, daring them to disagree with her or try to push Ruth out.

"I think that is wonderful." Neta spoke first, then walked to Ruth and offered her the kiss of greeting. "Welcome to Bethlehem."

"Thank you." Ruth smiled at each woman in turn and put an arm around Naomi's shoulder. "It has been a long journey," she said, suddenly taking charge as if she sensed Naomi had lost her strength. "I know Naomi would like to return to the home she left here. Would one of you be willing to show us if it still exists and lead us there?"

"And does Ziva still live?" Naomi asked, suddenly needing to know that her old servant had been cared for in her absence.

"Ziva passed into Sheol some years back," Neta told her as she led the two of them toward the old house. "But her daughter has tried to keep the place up for your hoped-for return." She paused. "There is something else you should know."

Naomi met Neta's gaze, a sense of dread filling her already grieving heart. "Tell me."

Neta looked at her feet. "Not long before Passover, Boaz's wife Adi also passed into Sheol."

Naomi stared at her sister-in-law. "Adi?"

Neta nodded. "She lost several babes in the years you were gone, but she died caring for the sheep. She fell into a ravine when the earth gave way at the edge of a cliff. Boaz has been bitter with grief ever since."

How well she understood. But Adi! *Oh Adonai, why?* She glanced up at the darkening sky, feeling Ruth's gaze resting on her. Of course, the poor girl did not know Boaz or Adi or anyone here. And Naomi realized yet again how grateful she was to have at least one person to care for in her grief. But Boaz had no one.

"Take me home," she said, not wanting to hear more. Her heart could bear no more bitterness.

26

Ruth held on to Naomi's arm as they followed Neta in silence through Bethlehem's city streets around several bends, until at last they came to a broken-down courtyard and a house that had seen better days. Naomi had sagged against Ruth from the moment Neta mentioned the woman Adi, God rest her soul. But this house—the sight was clearly troubling.

"Is this the place?" Ruth asked softly, for lack of something else to say.

Naomi nodded.

Neta carefully picked her way through the broken stones of the courtyard and led them to the door, which hung crooked on frayed leather hinges. Ruth tied the donkey's reins to a post she hoped would not crumble if the animal chose to tug against it, and helped Naomi, guiding her steps.

"It has fallen into much disrepair since Ziva passed into Sheol. The old woman did her best to keep it up, and Adi came to help now and then, until Boaz told her she was too weak—the poor girl lost too many babies—and Ziva grew too frail herself to attend to it after a few years. Her daughter comes by now and then, but she has a large family of her own, and, well . . ." Neta paused, glancing at Ruth, then settled her gaze on Naomi's. "I'm sorry no one else has had time to keep things in order, but we did not know if you would ever return."

Neta looked away and walked into the house. The floor was bare earth with only a few boards still visible. Someone must have taken things from the place.

Naomi sucked in a breath, and Ruth's grip tightened on her arm. "They have destroyed everything. God has left me nothing."

"I am still with you, Mother Naomi." Ruth spoke in a whisper, for she wondered if perhaps she really was nothing in her mother-in-law's eyes. She looked around the place, a sinking feeling of loss and weariness threatening to engulf her. Was she wrong to have come? To this?

A broken basket, old and weathered, looked as though someone had tossed it to the side. Some clay jars, cracked or chipped, rested against what once must have been bright, whitewashed limestone walls.

"I'm afraid the food you left ran out long ago, and once Ziva grew ill, thieves broke in and took anything of value that you left behind." Neta's explanation was accompanied by a look of genuine sorrow. "I'm sorry, Naomi."

Naomi looked over the immediate area, then slowly walked into the adjoining spaces. Ruth followed but said nothing. The sleeping rooms and cooking area were no better than the sitting room they had first entered. At last Naomi returned to Neta.

"It is not your fault, Neta. God is the one who has turned against me. My husband chose to leave this place. What was I to expect? To return to prosperity? No. I am destitute with no men to care for me. My life is worth nothing."

"That's not true," Neta said, her voice growing stronger, more confident now. "You are here. God preserved your life to bring you back." She reached for Naomi's hand and squeezed it. "Things will improve. I promise."

"You cannot promise something you do not know and cannot control." The bitter tone in Naomi's voice matched the pain in Ruth's heart. Perhaps they should not have come. If she had found a kind man in Moab, perhaps he would have cared for Naomi too. But she knew without a doubt that no such man existed. Naomi would have returned here in any case, with or without her. They must simply learn to live with little and work to improve what they had.

"She cannot promise," Ruth said, placing an arm around Naomi's shoulders, "but if all of the things you have told me about your God are true, then He will care for us, won't He?"

"If He cared for us, He would have allowed our men to live."

Neta touched Ruth's arm and smiled. "Bring Naomi to Melek's house to dine with us tonight. I will send a servant to show you the way."

She left them in the broken-down house with nothing except what they had brought with them. But Ruth determined that what they had camped with along the way they could camp with inside the house.

She kissed Naomi's cheek and went to retrieve their belongings from the animal's back. Then she would make a plan for what to do next.

Naomi stood in the empty sitting room and stared at the dark interior. Memories of happier days flooded over her in waves. Mahlon chasing Chilion from room to room until Naomi shooed them into the courtyard or out to the fields to find their father. Mahlon and Chilion arguing or pretending to fight enemy invaders, or begging their father to accompany him to the fields once they were barely old enough to carry a sack of seed.

Mahlon and Chilion sick in bed, too achy and feverish to move.

No. She blinked, forced back the emotions that joined the memories. She glanced down at what was once a floor made of shaved boards that Elimelech had painstakingly crafted from an oak tree. Why would someone tear up the floor?

Looking for a jar of gold or grain, no doubt. But Elimelech had left nothing hidden when they moved.

She shook herself, taking in the broken remains of what once was. Oh, to have life the way it used to be! This time the tears did fill her eyes. She had been so blessed and had taken it for granted. She never dreamed she could lose so much.

The sound of Ruth's footsteps caused her to look up. The girl held a flaxen broom in one hand. "I borrowed it from a neighbor," she said, her cheeks showing a hint of a blush as though the admission embarrassed her. But of course she would have to borrow such a thing. They did not think to bring every household item from Moab.

"I will sweep up the floor in this room and then move on to the others." She met Naomi's gaze with a smile and began to sweep in the far right corner and worked her way toward the door to the courtyard.

Naomi stared. Why had this young woman, who could have married into a wealthy noble family in Moab long ago, chosen her son and now her? Chosen poverty over riches and an old woman over love? It made no sense.

Perhaps God has not left you as completely as you think. The thought felt like an arrow to her heart, filled with accompanying guilt. Naomi turned away from the sight of Ruth's sweeping and moved into the courtyard. She could take an accounting of what they had left from the small store of food they'd brought with them. Perhaps Melek could be persuaded to buy her as a slave until she could earn enough food for Ruth to live.

But at the thought of her brother-in-law and his greedy ways and his many wives, she felt a sudden protectiveness of Ruth. If she asked Melek to purchase her, Ruth could end up in the bargain. Naomi would not allow Ruth to come all this way to become a slave in her new land.

By the time evening shadows lengthened, Neta proved true to her word and sent a young servant girl who appeared outside the courtyard and called out to Naomi. Ruth, who had finished sweeping the rooms, laid out their sleeping mats, and managed to make a saddlebag into a cushion for Naomi, stood from the quick respite she had taken on the floor and joined Naomi at the door.

"Mistress Neta said to tell you to follow me." The young girl, possibly an Ammonite or from another Canaanite tribe, waited a moment for Naomi to close the door to the house, where the goat was secured in the back room. Then Naomi rode the donkey with Ruth walking beside her.

The child led them through winding streets and through the gates to an area outside of Bethlehem's walls but surrounded by a high wall of its own. Barley fields high with uncut grain waved in the distance beyond the house. To the right of the village gate not far from the fields stood a large stone structure Ruth guessed to be the place the men would thresh the grain once the harvest was completed.

"I did not realize your relative had so much wealth." Ruth leaned closer to Naomi as they approached the gate to the outer courtyard, where women lit torches and servants stood waiting to wash their feet.

"Melek thinks himself a king," Naomi said softly, her tone derisive. "He has long considered himself an important man in Bethlehem."

"Then why does he not live within the protection of its walls?" Ruth gazed over the vast estate. "Though I see he has built his own protection."

Naomi dismounted the donkey, handed the reins to a servant, and waited to respond until the man was out of hearing distance. "Melek is Elimelech's older brother. Both men's lives started differently than where they ended up. That is, Elimelech did not think the protection of Dibon necessary for us, and Melek appears to have made a similar decision. But Melek has wealth enough to hire plenty of guards and servants, so I daresay he could defend against most foes. If an army came against us, he could flee into Bethlehem, for he still keeps a home there."

"He is a powerful man then." Ruth sat on the bench a servant indicated, Naomi beside her, and waited while the servant proceeded to wash their feet.

"He thinks he is." Naomi said no more, and Ruth did not press her.

At last they were ushered into the women's dining area and seated with Neta and Melek's two other wives—Chanah, who had borne Melek's only son, Hamul, and Elke, his first wife who had given him only daughters.

"Naomi," Neta said, coming quickly toward her. She kissed each cheek in greeting. "I am so glad you were able to come."

Ruth watched Naomi's face, saw the tightness of her jaw, and wondered what bitter words would spew from her tongue. She'd seemed to hold only hurt and anger in her tone from the moment they entered the town.

"I am also glad to be here." Naomi returned Neta's kiss. "Thank you for having us." She looked about her. "Are Boaz or his sisters coming?"

Ruth lifted a brow but quickly masked her surprise at Naomi's gentle, grateful tone. Of course Naomi would be polite to those who would feed them. They were little more than beggars now, and unless Naomi's God somehow provided for them to find work for food, they would soon starve.

"Boaz came for a visit before Passover and the Feast of Firstfruits, but he and Melek are not on the best of terms," Neta said softly. "Between their constant disagreements and Boaz's grief . . . let's just say that no one sees much of Boaz these days except his men in the fields."

Naomi's look held empathy, something Ruth had not seen in her gaze for some time, and Ruth felt a sudden sadness for the man who had lost an apparently beloved wife.

Neta smiled. "But you are here, so let us put off talk of distressing subjects, shall we?" A servant came and set before them platters of meat and fish and more vegetables than

Ruth had seen in months. The bounty was like that of Moab, and more.

Hope lightened her mood as laughter and conversation drifted around her. Melek was Naomi's brother-in-law. Surely he would help his destitute family.

"So, Naomi," Chanah said after the second glass of wine had been poured into their cups, "tell us what Moab was like. Even more, tell us what happened to your sons. I mean, we know our God has taken them, but how? Were they hurt by wild animals, did they fall ill?" Chanah tsked. "Such dreadful sorrow you have faced, my sister."

The others nodded, and Ruth tensed. To ask such questions seemed rude when one still grieved, but Naomi did not brush aside their comments or scowl at her relatives.

"You have heard, of course, that my Elimelech was mauled by a bear."

Exclamations of horror and shaking heads and comments of "such a terrible thing" went around the table before Naomi continued.

"But my boys . . . it is a strange thing indeed." She paused to look at each woman. Ruth glanced up at that moment to see a man she did not know standing near the arch of the door, intently listening. Probably Melek.

"You know how they were so sickly at one point as children," Naomi said.

Everyone nodded again with more comments of "such a terrible thing" and "you almost lost them then" before at last the women quieted once more and Naomi continued. These women did not tell a tale the way the women of Moab did, and after a time Ruth wondered if Naomi would ever finish the story. But after the fifth interruption of exclamations, she at last drew in a long, slow breath.

"The illness came on Chilion so suddenly, and then Mahlon was stricken the moment he returned from fetching the physician. Both boys on the same day and for no reason!" Naomi's voice rose in pitch, and Ruth noticed her hands clenched in her lap. "Our God, blessed be He, took my sons faster than He gave them and left me with two Moabite daughters-in-law. No grandchildren. And in the end, only Ruth"—Naomi pointed to her—"was willing to leave her homeland and return with me to Bethlehem."

"What a blessing that she did not leave you alone," Neta said after a weighty silence. She smiled at Ruth, who suddenly wondered if everyone in the room hated Moabites as much as Moabites hated Israelites.

"Yes, a blessing," Chanah and Elke agreed.

An awkward moment passed when it seemed as though the conversation was at an end and yet no one knew what to say next.

"How will you manage?" Neta finally asked as the serving girls began to clear the food away.

Ruth darted a glance toward the door where the man had been, but he had departed at some point without notice.

"I do not know," Naomi admitted, looking to each woman. "The grain and oil and wine and raisin cakes we brought with us are very low. It was not quite the start of harvest when we left Moab, and with Mahlon and Chilion gone, there was little we could do."

"But surely you could have brought in the harvest with help from the people of the land." Chanah shook her head. "Such uncivilized people to not offer to help you."

Ruth cleared her throat. "The governor of the city planned to take the land from Naomi. With no husband or sons to

protect her, there was nothing she could do. We took everything we could carry."

Compassion filled Chanah's eyes. "You are a kind young
woman to help your mother-in-law then."

"She is a blessing of the Lord," Naomi boasted. Ruth
glanced at her mother-in-law. Did she truly think of her as
God's blessing?

Chanah and Neta stood and went to another area of the
room and returned with two sacks. Neta leaned close to
Naomi's ear as she pressed the bags into Ruth's hands. "This
isn't much, but it is all we can give you. Melek is charitable
. . . to a point."

Ruth felt the weight of the sacks. *A very small point.* But
she only said, "He is very generous to look after his widowed
sister-in-law."

Melek's wives looked toward the door but said nothing.
Ruth glanced in the same direction. There was no sign of
Melek, but his wives obviously did not think it wise to speak
another word about him lest he hear. What kind of man was
this relative of Naomi's? The image of Governor Aali flashed
in Ruth's thoughts and she cringed.

Naomi stood quickly, and Ruth was just as happy to follow her from the house to the waiting donkey.

"Thank you for your hospitality," Naomi said loud enough
for the household to hear. "God bless you for your kindness
to us."

The women parted with farewell kisses, and Ruth hurried
after Naomi, holding a torch to guide the way back through
Bethlehem's gates to their humble house. But in that moment she was glad of the lowly estate Naomi still owned. She
would rather live with modest means with a person she loved
than in a house of fine furnishings with a man like Melek.

27

Ruth felt the two sacks Neta had pressed into her hands a week ago and met Naomi's gaze. "The grain runs very low, my mother." She held up one of the limp sacks. "There may be enough for one more meal or two if we are careful, but then we will have nothing. All of the food we brought from Moab is gone, except for the oil." But oil needed to be mixed with the flour from the grain. They could not eat oil alone.

Naomi glanced over the room where they took their meals, a wistful look in her eyes. "Years ago, it was I who took food to the widows and orphans. I never expected to be needing help in the same way."

Ruth set the sack inside a clay jar to protect it from rodents and walked to Naomi's side. She cupped the older woman's frail shoulder, feeling the bone sharp against her hand. They needed food. Much food, or she could lose her.

Oh God of Naomi, please do not take her too.

"Let me go to the fields and pick up the leftover grain

behind anyone in whose eyes I find favor. Surely I can find a farmer who will allow such a thing. Have you not told me that your God provides for the poor through gleaning? Are not the men to keep from harvesting the corners of their fields so that the alien and the widow and the orphan can have food to eat?" Did the people of Israel keep their God's laws in this way as Naomi had said?

"Yes. I have told you that." Naomi's eyes brightened for the first time in weeks. Clearly she had hoped for more help from Melek, but no more food had come to them from Neta or Chanah or anyone else in Melek's household. She sighed. "I hate to ask it of you, my daughter. Gleaning is hard work, and you are such a help to me here."

"But we need food to eat, Mother, and I will be home by nightfall. Let me do this. Let me see if your people obey the laws of your God so that we can both find comfort." Ruth straightened, her chin jutting forward. "And you need not worry. I am a strong worker. I can glean as easily as I can sweep or grind grain."

Naomi smiled and patted Ruth's arm. "Go, my daughter. But the fields are outside of the city walls, and you must take great care to be watchful. A woman alone . . ." She did not finish the sentence, but by her look, Ruth did not need her to do so.

"I will be careful." She kissed Naomi's cheek, then picked up the broken basket they had found when they first arrived, which Ruth had spent her evenings mending. She strapped it to her back and waist with strips of the goat's hair blanket she had carefully torn.

Naomi followed her into the courtyard, and Ruth glanced back and waved, then made her way through the now familiar streets and out to find a friendly field.

Boaz stopped at the city gate on his way to his barley fields. The Feast of Firstfruits behind him now, he was anxious to get started with the rest of the harvest but knew Ezra could manage a little longer without him.

He climbed the steps to the room within the gate and sat opposite Melek and several other merchants and landowners, most of whom had also gone to Shiloh—except for Melek, who managed an excuse to send someone in his place, something Boaz had longed to do if not for the guilt he would feel. He tamped down his frustration. He had gone. He had obeyed the law. God forgive him if he could not obey it from his heart—a heart too raw with pain to feel anything but obligation.

"The Lord be with you," he said, again using the obligatory greeting.

"And with you, Boaz," each man said in turn.

"It is good of you to join us again," Melek added, his smile too pitying.

Boaz nodded but only half listened to the daily updates on town business. Why had he bothered to come today? He had no interest in the town's trivial matters. Not like he once did when he'd had Adi to go home to and share them with. But even two months seemed not nearly long enough to get past his grief, though his sisters had already made a few suggestions that there were widows in the town who could use the protection of a husband. Of course they would think thus. People married for convenience all the time. He could do so to help some poor, lonely woman. But his heart recoiled at the thought.

"I'm sure we are all aware that my brother's wife has re-turned from Moab and brought a Moabitess with her," Melek said, jarring Boaz from his thoughts. "Unfortunately for her, Naomi has lost everything—my brother and both of her sons. Except for the foreigner and a run-down house, she is destitute. I don't know about the rest of you, but I cannot afford to support two more women."

Boaz stared at this cousin who had been a continual thorn in his foot and could most certainly afford to help Naomi. "Surely with such a promising harvest we can both find a way to help her. We cannot let her starve."

Melek scoffed. "She won't starve. Behind my back my wives have already given her food from my storage, and I'm sure they will find ways to continue. Or perhaps your sisters will help her." He leveled his gaze at Boaz, his meaning too clear. "At least the Moabitess is comely to look upon. Now, if she were an Israelite . . ." He left the sentence unfinished, but Boaz caught his meaning. If the Moabitess were of Is-rael, Melek would happily snatch up another wife. Or so he wanted Boaz to think.

"The Moabitess left her homeland and all she had to come with Naomi," one of the elders said, giving a detailed account of this woman who had pledged herself to her mother-in-law. "The least we can do is be accepting of her."

Boaz looked about the group and abruptly stood. "If Naomi is in need, it is our duty to help her." He paused, recalling Naomi's pride, her willingness to help others even against Elimelech's wishes. Would she accept help in return? It was far easier to give than to receive.

He strode to the steps. "Without offending her pride, I trust you gentlemen can come up with ways to see that after all her generosity toward our poor, Naomi does not end up worse off than the people she helped before they left Bethlehem."

He turned and took the steps two at a time, heat filling his face. He shouldn't let Melek frustrate him so, but the man was impossible. He blew out a breath and untied the donkey from the post where it waited, climbed on its back, and urged it through the gates.

Why had no one told him of Naomi's plight until now? She had been back a week or so, the men had said, and apparently Melek had already laid eyes on the Moabitess. He would have to stop at the house Naomi and Elimelech had owned and see how she fared. Melek might not want to help the women, and Boaz could well imagine how much he would ration any "help" he allowed his wives to give, but Adi would haunt him from her grave if Boaz ignored such a need from family.

Adi. She would have already told him of Naomi's return. In fact, she would have welcomed Naomi and the Moabitess to their home until Naomi's home could be repaired. He shook himself. He couldn't very well do such a thing—a man alone—servants about him or not.

He rubbed the back of his neck as he rode alongside the fields until he came to the area where the reapers were working. He jumped down and tied the reins to a shade tree and walked to where Ezra stood near the crew of men.

"The Lord be with you!" he called out to them. The greeting slipped out before he could think. He glanced heavenward. Did God grow angry with men who spoke blessings with their lips but whose hearts were far from Him? Boaz used to feel close to the Almighty, especially out here in the fields or with Adi and her sheep. But sometimes breathing was the only prayer he could muster, and it was wordless agony to think anything more.

"The Lord bless you, my lord," his men responded in kind.

Boaz walked the length of the field from where the reapers worked to where the young women gleaned behind them. He caught up with Ezra not far from the women.

"My lord, you have come at just the right time." Ezra smiled and touched a hand to his head in greeting.

"Have I now? And why is that?" He glanced Ezra's way and turned his gaze to the workers to determine for himself how things fared.

"Things are going quite well. We are actually ahead of schedule, as the men seem quite energetic today and eager to get the crop in," Ezra said.

Boaz only nodded, still looking over the workers. Was that the Moabitess Melek had mentioned?

"Did you hear what I said, my lord?"

"Yes, yes." Boaz looked at Ezra and pointed toward the foreign woman. "Whose young woman is this?"

Ezra's toothy grin made Boaz frown. "She is the young Moabite woman who came back with Naomi."

So she had found a way to help Naomi even if Melek's "help" had been of little use. Good.

"She said, 'Please let me glean and gather among the sheaves after the reapers.' Of course, knowing how you would feel about it all, I couldn't refuse her. So she came, and she has continued from early morning until now, except for a short rest."

Boaz nodded again. Adi would have been pleased. "Good. Good. You did well." He strode away from Ezra as though some unseen hand propelled him forward. He would see for

himself this woman who seemed to command the attention
of the town elders. He walked across the field until he came
to the Moabitess.

"You are the young woman who came back with Naomi,"
he said.

She straightened from picking up some of the gleanings
and placed them over her shoulder into a basket that had seen
better days. "Yes, my lord," she said, her voice soft, respect-
ful. "I am Ruth the Moabitess. Naomi is my mother-in-law."

Boaz looked down at her, silently agreeing with Melek that
she was comely to look upon. But a guilty feeling quickly
followed. Widow or not, he could not do as his sisters had
suggested. And surely not with a foreigner. Besides, one more
glance told him that she was much too young for him.

"Now, listen, my daughter," he said, emphasizing their
age difference for his sake as well as hers. If she still grieved
her husband, she would not be entertaining such thoughts
regardless.

She tilted her head. "Yes, my lord?"

He shook his head. "Do not go to glean in another field
or leave this one, but keep close to my young women. Watch
the field where they are reaping, and follow after them. I will
charge the young men not to touch you." Which he would
do the moment he left her side. The least he could do for
Naomi was to protect her daughter-in-law.

He cleared his throat, searching for more to say, feeling
uncharacteristically tongue-tied. He watched the way she
pressed her hands together and kept her head slightly bent
rather than hold his gaze. Compassion filled him. Of course
she would not feel his equal, and as a foreigner she probably
wondered what she should and should not say and do.

"And when you are thirsty," he continued, "go to the vessels and drink what the young men have drawn." He would invite her to eat of their food as well, but that could wait until the sun hit the midpoint in the sky.

Ruth knelt among the gleanings and put her face to the ground. "Why have I found favor in your eyes, that you should take notice of me, since I am a foreigner?"

Boaz bid her rise with a gentle touch on her shoulder. "All that you have done for your mother-in-law since the death of your husband has been fully told to me, and how you left your father and mother and your native land and came to a people that you did not know before. The Lord repay you for what you have done, and a full reward be given you by the Lord, the God of Israel, under whose wings you have come to take refuge."

"Thank you," she said, her voice low, almost musical. "I have found favor in your eyes, my lord, for you have comforted me and spoken kindly to your servant, though I am not one of your servants."

Would that you were.

28

Ruth picked up another sheaf of grain the reapers had missed and tossed it into her basket. Boaz's words turned in her mind as she followed his girls back and forth through the barley fields. The sun beat down on her as it rose higher in the sky, causing trickles of sweat to glide down her back and dampen her face along her brow.

She straightened and noticed the other women had carried their baskets to the shade of a large oak. They took turns drinking from the dipper used to scoop water from a number of large jars set in the ground near the area where the workers took their meal.

She stood at the end of the line, feeling the eyes of several of the male workers on her. She kept her head down, refusing eye contact, and wondered not for the first time if life would have been better if she had stayed in Moab. Was it hostility she sensed in the air between her and the workers—or interest?

She took her turn and drank from the dipper, wiping a remaining drop of water from her mouth. Straightening, she glanced toward the women. She had no food with her, for there was barely enough left for Naomi to eat today. Somehow she'd believed she could endure the hard work without food. But the rumble in her stomach and the weakness in her knees told her she was wrong.

"Come here and eat some bread and dip your morsel in the wine." The voice was one she could not easily forget. She glanced up to see Boaz standing near the table where the reapers were already seated on the ground around it. His welcoming smile warmed her. This was a kind man.

She breathed a sigh and walked slowly toward them and sat where he pointed. She startled when he sat opposite her, so close that their hands could touch if he reached out to her. And that seemed to be his exact intention as he passed her roasted grain and bread and wine for dipping.

"Thank you, my lord," she said when the meal was nearly finished and she had food left over. Enough to take to Naomi for the evening meal. A small smile touched her lips. Perhaps Naomi's God really did care for the widow and orphan and alien among His people.

She rose with the rest of the young women and again nodded her thanks to Boaz, then hurried to gather her basket and return to the fields. She tucked the roasted grain into a pocket of her robe, her heart almost light enough to sing.

Boaz watched Ruth follow his girls, a lightness to her step that had not been there when he saw her earlier that day. Had she eaten nothing until now? The thought troubled him. He should have known that Melek's "provisions" to Naomi would not be enough to sustain them for more than a few days. But as he glanced at the reapers still finishing the last dregs of water and wine, another troublesome thought pushed all others aside.

"None of you are to do anything to cause Ruth to feel fearful or ashamed," he said, drawing each man's attention. He paused, making sure they understood his full intent.

"Yes, my lord," one said, followed by the others.

"Good." He cleared his throat. "Furthermore, let her glean even among the sheaves. And also pull out some barley from the bundles for her and leave it for her to glean, and do not rebuke her."

A quizzical brow rose among one or two of the men, but most simply nodded. They stood to return to work, and Boaz walked with Ezra to watch them all before he would head back to check on his other fields.

"She is a comely young woman," Ezra said, giving Boaz a sidelong glance. "And a widow."

"Yes, I am aware. Is there a point to your comment?" He returned Ezra's glance, taken aback by the sudden wistful feeling that came over him.

"No point . . . just an observation." Ezra offered Boaz a wide grin.

"Let's just watch over her and protect her while she is here, shall we?"

Boaz waited for Ezra's nod of acceptance, then turned and headed back toward his donkey. He had no time to worry about the plight of one young foreign woman. But he was concerned about Naomi's well-being. And he could not concern himself with one and not the other.

The sun had nearly set by the time Ruth finished gleaning and beat out the barley, which filled the basket—nearly an ephah of grain. Such great bounty for only one day!

She hefted the basket onto her back and walked toward the city, grateful to see a few other women walking in the same direction. There was safety in numbers, and after the warnings she had received, she realized that even in the land where Naomi's God ruled, men could still be cruel and she could be in danger from them. If not for Boaz's kindness . . . She did not let that thought linger.

She strode through the gate and hurried down the darkening streets, breathing a sigh of relief when she saw the familiar house of her mother-in-law come into view.

"Mother Naomi!" she called from the courtyard. She rushed into the house and set the basket on the ground. "Come and see!"

Naomi entered the room from the cooking area, though Ruth could smell no aroma of cooking food. Perhaps her mother-in-law had prepared the place in order to roast what she hoped Ruth would bring.

"All this?" Naomi bent and looked at the basket, holding a small lamp close enough to see, as the sun had fully set now.

"Yes," Ruth said as she pulled out the roasted grain she had left over from the noon meal. "And this!" She handed the parched grain to Naomi. "Eat, Mother. Taste and see how good your God has been to us."

Naomi's hand shook as she brought the grain to her mouth. "Where did you glean today? And where have you worked? Blessed be the man who took notice of you." She took another bite and met Ruth's gaze. "Tell me."

"The man with whom I worked today is Boaz. Is he the

same man you spoke about with Neta, the one whose wife recently passed on?" Ruth flushed at the question, for to mention him reminded her of the strength of his presence.

"Yes, yes. There is only one Boaz in Bethlehem. It is the same man. And may he be blessed by the Lord, whose kindness has not forsaken the living or the dead!" Naomi said, taking Ruth's hand. "The man is a close relative of ours, one of our redeemers."

Ruth tilted her head, not fully understanding. "Redeemer? You mean like the kind of buying back of the chosen ones in Moab so they would not suffer the fate of sacrifice?"

Naomi looked at her with a lifted brow, but a moment later she shook her head as though a light had dawned. "No, no. Our kinsman redeemer is nothing at all like Moab's 'redeemer' of the chosen sacrifices. Your redeemers pay corrupt priests in order to save their own lives or the lives of their children. Our kinsman redeemer marries the widow of a childless man in order to raise up offspring for the man, so that his heritage is not lost in Israel."

Ruth stared at Naomi, her cheeks heating again. "Boaz is a man who could raise up a son for Mahlon? I still don't quite understand." How would the child not be Boaz's son? And wouldn't that mean Boaz would have to marry her to accomplish such a thing? She shivered at the thought.

"Our law allows protection for our people in many ways, my daughter. But it is too soon to think about such things. The fact that Boaz took notice of you and offered you his protection is enough."

"He did say to me, 'You shall keep close by my young men until they have finished all my harvest.'" Ruth felt again the awe and embarrassment of that moment when he had spoken to her. "Of course, he did tell me to follow after his young women as we follow his reapers," she added. The men would not harm the women, and it was fitting that she would stay with women rather than men.

"It is good, my daughter," Naomi said, intruding on her thoughts, "that you go out with his young women, lest in another field you be assaulted." Her look matched the concern Ruth had seen in Boaz's eyes.

"I will do as you say," she said. But suddenly her heart wondered if her desire to obey was strictly for her safety.

29

"Had we come home sooner," Naomi said one evening as she and Ruth ate parched grain, their daily staple, and drank a little wine from one of the flasks Boaz had brought to Naomi, "we would have been here to celebrate the Passover."

Ruth looked up from sipping from her cup and set it beside her as they sat inside the still broken-down house—another thing Boaz had promised to repair for Naomi when he could spare servants now working in his fields. "Passover is your feast of remembering." Ruth sought to recall what Naomi had taught her during their years together. "It is to commemorate the time your God brought the Israelites out of Egypt."

Naomi nodded. "Yes. And the reason it is called Passover?" Naomi loved the role of teacher, Ruth had long realized, and she enjoyed playing along for the joy it brought to her mother-in-law.

"Because the Lord passed over the firstborn of Israel to spare them, but not the firstborn of Egypt." Ruth returned

Naomi's ready smile, then took another bite of the parched grain. She pondered the answer she had given a moment earlier, troubled by the questions it raised in her heart. She had never voiced them in their home in Moab, but now she needed answers. Needed to understand.

"Why was Egypt punished in that way, Mother? Does your God love only Israel? Did He not care for the Egyptians too?" She folded her hands in her lap, realizing that she asked for her own sake. Did the God of Israel accept a Moabite who wanted Him?

Naomi set her food aside as though she was no longer hungry and moved closer to Ruth, taking her hand. "My dear girl, I know how hard this must be for you to understand. It is not that our God loves only Israel, it is that everyone turned away from Him the moment sin entered the world through Adam. God saw the hearts of men, that they were only evil continually, so he destroyed the earth, saving Noah and his family. But even then, sin would not be eradicated. Noah's son Ham, by his actions, caused Noah to call down curses on him and his children. One of those children was Egypt."

"Why would a man curse his own son?" Ruth couldn't imagine doing such a thing. Orpah's infant, stolen so quickly from their home, flashed in her mind's eye. Offered on Chemosh's altar because of the vengeance of greedy men and the "wish" of their god.

"Noah cursed his son because he witnessed his father's nakedness and did nothing to protect him, to shield others from seeing him in such a state. He did not honor his father, but by his actions disdained him." Naomi stood, drawing Ruth up to walk outside into the courtyard. "Noah's son left the family and took his wife and children to the land of the Nile. If Ham had repented and worshiped Yahweh, Egypt would have been much different than it became, but Ham and his sons created their own gods, or perhaps resurrected gods destroyed in the flood, and soon Egypt was flourishing with gods named for nearly every creature. From the sun to the Pharaoh to the river Adonai had made, the descendants of Ham worshiped the creature rather than the Creator, blessed be He." Naomi pointed to the stars, and Ruth looked up, watching as the darkness began to fill with thousands of blinking lights.

"How clear it is tonight." Ruth loved the night sky when the clouds did not hide its brilliance.

"As I hope my explanations are clear to you, my daughter."

"I am trying to understand." Ruth looked at Naomi and slipped a hand around her thin shoulders. "Israel went to Egypt to escape a famine, but they stayed too long and became slaves to its people. So your God brought them out and gave them this land." She moved her free hand in an arc.

"But he punished the Egyptians," Naomi said, "including the death of the firstborn, not only because they treated His people with cruelty but because they would not acknowledge Elohim as God alone. He showed through many miracles that His power is greater than the might of Egypt, and yet the people still did not repent." Naomi touched Ruth's cheek in a gentle gesture. "My daughter, the Passover does not tell us we are better than the Egyptians. It reminds us that God's discipline, even punishment, is also a warning and a measure of grace. He wanted the plagues to bring the Egyptians to Him, but they refused. Our God does not force people, even His own people, to trust or obey Him."

"Yet your God commands obedience, not unlike Chemosh."

"Chemosh is not a god, dear girl. He is an object of men's creation, something they can see and touch. Our God is a Spirit. He cannot be held by human hands." Naomi waved a hand overhead toward the stars once more. "Could Chemosh make those?"

"My people worship the moon as well. But no, we do not acknowledge one great creator." Ruth thought back to the festivals to the gods of her people, the wild dancing, the orgies, the sacrifices that always left someone in mourning.

"Our God will have no other gods before Him," Naomi said softly, her tone one of awe. "Passover reminds us of that. For if our people had not obeyed Moses, if they had not covered the doors and lintels with blood, their rebellion would have been the same as those who worshiped other gods. Whenever we follow our own way instead of His, we are acting as though He doesn't exist. He won't force our obedience, my daughter. But He won't let us go our own way without wooing us back."

"Did He woo you back when you left this place?" Ruth suddenly wondered if her mother-in-law spoke more from experience than simply of tales of her heritage long past.

Naomi released Ruth's hand and walked to the edge of the court. Ruth strode with her, and the two looked down the street.

"I believe Elimelech's death was a warning to me, to my sons, that we should have heeded. I never wanted to leave Bethlehem, but I could not allow my family to go on without me." She turned, faced Ruth. "If I could go back and see then what I know now, I would have tried harder to change things, to convince my sons to leave the moment their father died. But what is done is done."

Naomi turned and walked back into the house. Ruth's stomach twisted. She should be more understanding. After all, the woman had lost everyone she loved. Never mind that Ruth had given up all to accompany Naomi to this place, to embrace her God, to show her love.

But in that moment, with Naomi's admission, she wondered whether Naomi was even glad of her presence. She undoubtedly would have been much happier living here with her two sons married to Israelite women than stuck with a foreigner who struggled to understand Israel's ways.

Boaz sat at his table alone, eating the food his cook had prepared for him. The food was tasty, though it could never compare to what Adi had made. Her food carried the sweetness of honey, as though it dripped from her fingers to his tongue.

Adi. His appetite left at the thought of her. Again. He closed his eyes but opened them at the sound of footsteps. Reuven entered the room.

"My lord, there is trouble." The old man's face was flushed as though he had run from the courtyard to the house.

Boaz stood. "Take a moment to catch your breath and then tell me."

Reuven accepted a cup of water from Boaz's hand and drank, then set it down and started walking with Boaz to the court. "It appears one of the young maidens was waylaid in the fields."

The news cut to his heart. Boaz's stomach churned, and he clenched both fists as he walked. *Not Ruth. Please, Adonai, not her.* He stopped abruptly. How could he possibly think of Ruth when Adi had just brushed his thoughts? How fickle he was!

Still, Ruth had worked his fields for the past month with no incident. And he could not bear the thought of her—of any of his young women—being harmed.

He hurried into the outer court where several of the elders stood with a weeping young girl, barely a woman, who knelt among the stones. He looked from one man to the other, then knelt beside the girl and briefly lifted her chin in his hand.

"Who did this to you, and how did it happen?" Her clothes were clearly torn, and Boaz recognized her father standing behind her.

The girl choked on a sob, and in the dim light of the torches Boaz could see that she had tossed ashes on her head. "I was in the field gleaning," she said so softly Boaz had to lean closer to hear her.

"My fields?" The thought sickened him.

"No, my lord," her father said from behind. "A field neighboring yours. Melek's field."

Boaz felt his face heat. His cousin had always been more lax with his workers, less concerned with their welfare. He turned to the girl again. "Go on," he gently coaxed.

She swallowed a sob and spoke again. "The other girls had headed to the area where we beat out the grain, but I was behind them a little ways, for I had not gathered as much as I needed." She could not meet Boaz's gaze.

Boaz released a breath, held his impatience in check. "Then what happened?"

She swallowed, then glanced at her father's stricken face. "I had picked up a few more gleanings and walked over to join the others when a man came from the grain that was still standing and grabbed me." She stopped, choking on the words once more. "He pulled me behind the standing grain and dragged me far from where the other girls were beating their sheaves. His hand was over my mouth so that I couldn't cry out."

Boaz felt the pulse in his neck pound and heat pour into his veins. He forced out one more question. "Did you know this man?"

She nodded but did not speak.

Boaz looked at her father, whose eyes held a glint of fear, as though he too dare not say the name.

"Is your daughter betrothed?" The law differed concerning a virgin versus one who was betrothed, and Boaz needed all of the facts before he could make a judgment.

The man shook his head. "No, my lord."

"You know who did this, don't you?" Boaz addressed the father now, for the girl had begun weeping again.

The man glanced at his friends, who by their nods urged him to speak. The man cleared his throat, looked quickly around him, and lowered his voice. "Your cousin's son, Hamul, did this, my lord. Melek's only son."

Boaz felt like someone had dealt a deep blow to his gut. Melek's son. This was not good. He would not take kindly to what the law required for his only son.

But obedience to the law, to Adonai Elohim, mattered more than pleasing a stubborn man.

Boaz rose, glanced at Reuven. "I don't know when I will return."

Reuven nodded as though he'd expected as much.

"Come," Boaz said to the men and the girl. "I will summon Melek and Hamul to the city gate. Gather the rest of the elders on your way and meet me there."

The men seemed to breathe easier as Boaz walked with them, the father half dragging his broken daughter. But Boaz knew this was by no means going to be an easy night.

Boaz grabbed his walking stick and marched through Bethlehem's gates, past curious guards and elders who had begun to gather, and called two guards to follow him across the narrow valley to Melek's house.

"Summon your master Melek and his son, Hamul, at once," Boaz said to the servant standing guard, his voice smooth yet unyielding.

"He will surely be in the middle of his meal, my lord." The protest was weak.

Boaz brushed it off with a wave of his hand. "He can finish it later. Get him now."

He paced in front of the gate as the servant hurried off. How could this boy, the cousin who was barely a man, do such a thing? He'd clearly shown little respect for women the last time Boaz had met with him in his home, but later when he had given the young man a tour of his fields and explained the work involved, even teaching him how to wield the sickle in just the right place among the sheaves, Hamul had seemed interested, as though he wanted to learn. He had not even seemed to notice the women working the fields.

How naive Boaz had been. He should have seen something, been able to stop this atrocity, warned Melek . . . *something*.

Footsteps drew his attention to the court beyond the gate, and it occurred to Boaz that the servant had not even invited him to enter Melek's residence. Had Melek known Boaz would come?

"Boaz." His cousin walked toward him. No sign of his son. "What brings you out at such an hour? Are you hungry? We have plenty." He motioned with his hand. "Come. Dine with me."

Boaz stood his ground and glanced at the two guards with Melek. Would Melek fight justice and refuse him? Perhaps the truth should wait until they were assembled with the elders at the city gates.

"I'm afraid a matter has come to my attention that needs your counsel and that of your son." Boaz spoke as though having Hamul at a council meeting was a common occurrence, but Melek's narrowed gaze told him his cousin found the request suspicious.

"What matter is so important it cannot wait until morning?" Melek kept his distance several paces from Boaz and crossed his arms.

"It would be best if we let the elders explain it to all of us." Melek need not know that Boaz would be leading the elders in this. "Please, Melek, just get Hamul and join me. We cannot start without you." He knew he was appealing to the man's ego, but so be it. Melek was not an easy man to convince of anything.

"You have no idea what is so important?" Melek still had not moved, but he raised a brow as though in scrutiny of whatever Boaz might say next.

"Something has happened that needs our immediate attention," Boaz said, weighing his words. "It is a serious matter and cannot wait." He raised a hand in supplication. "Will you come?"

His cousin stared at him for a lengthy breath but at last gave a curt nod.

"And you will bring Hamul." He did not ask lest Melek think he had a choice.

Melek turned toward the house to gather whatever he needed. "I will bring Hamul."

Boaz waited for the two to join him, praying Melek would not make this more difficult than it already was.

30

Boaz followed Melek and a quiet Hamul up the steps into the inner room of Bethlehem's city gate. Elders already took up most of the benches. The young girl, Hava, stood against the wall, arms wrapped about her, silent tears falling.

Melek sat in his normal place, but Hamul stood behind his father, unwilling to sit even when his father pointed to a seat next to him. Boaz stood as well in the center of the gathering.

"It has come to my attention," Boaz said, turning his gaze from one man to another, "that this young woman in our midst was taken advantage of in the fields belonging to my cousin Melek." He faced Melek, whose eyes narrowed, but he did not speak.

Boaz paused. "The girl, Hava, knows her attacker." He tried to make eye contact with Hamul, but the young man would not meet his gaze. He again looked to Melek, whose hands were clenched tight around the edge of the bench. Did he know? Or simply suspect?

"Hava and her father and uncles and friends came to me tonight to explain what happened." Boaz related the details as he had been given them, not wanting to put the girl to any more shame. He called Hava's father forward. "Does your daughter have any reason not to tell the truth?"

"No, my lord," the man said, his voice nearly choking with the emotion he clearly tried to restrain. "My Hava has always been good and honest and kind." He glanced at his daughter. "She has never given us a reason to doubt her word."

Boaz swallowed, hating the very question he needed to ask. "And has your daughter been examined by a woman who is above reproach? Has the woman confirmed Hava's words?"

The man nodded. "Yes, my lord. My daughter is no longer a virgin. The man who took her violated her."

A deep sigh lifted Boaz's chest. If only the men of the land would follow the Law of Moses. Where was the respect for another's life?

He asked the man again if the girl was betrothed, receiving the same answer of no. He looked slowly at each elder, then faced the girl's father once more. "Tell me who did this to your daughter."

The man seemed to hesitate for the slightest moment as his gaze turned toward Melek. Boaz's cousin, being older, held more power than Boaz cared to admit, and he had a way of intimidating merchants and fellow farmers.

"Who violated your daughter?" Boaz asked again, drawing the man's attention back to him.

"Hamul, son of Melek," the man said at last. He sank onto a bench as though a heavy weight had pressed him there.

Boaz faced his cousin. "You have heard the charges against your son. Do you have anything to say?" A part of him wanted Melek to admit everything, while a warring part wanted to hear that Hamul had been far from that field the whole day. *Some* other explanation. Another man had done this. Not his naive young cousin.

Melek slowly released his grip on the bench and swiveled around to meet his son's gaze. "Did you do this?" His shoulders sagged, brought low by the same heavy, invisible weight that seemed to fall over the entire group, especially the two fathers.

Boaz watched Hamul, saw the glint of rebellion in his gaze, but a moment later, under his father's hard gaze, he bowed his head and nodded.

"Let me hear you say it," Melek demanded.

"Yes," Hamul said just loud enough for the men to hear.

Boaz saw the pride slip from Melek's eyes, pride for this son he had waited for so long.

"The law requires that you pay Hava's father fifty shekels of silver," Boaz told Melek when the man finally turned and met his gaze again. "And Hamul must wed Hava. She will be his wife, and he can never divorce her as long as he lives. He must treat her fairly and with kindness as well." Though Boaz knew what a man did in his own home was hard to know or to control.

Melek did not respond for the longest moment, nor did Hava's father move from where he sat. The elders murmured one by one that this was the law and it was right and good. All of them must obey it if they were to receive Adonai's blessing. They would not allow disobedience and risk another famine.

Boaz listened to the comments, watching his cousin, waiting for acknowledgment. Melek would be the one to enforce this with his son. He would be taking Hava into his home and providing for her. It was protection for the girl, for no one else would marry a violated virgin, but Boaz wondered what kind of life she could possibly have when the marriage had started out so violently.

I don't understand Your laws, Adonai. Not when the hearts of men clearly go against them. They are so easily twisted by the arrogant and rebellious.

Boaz's heart thumped, and he wished to be alone, to walk in the night air and the fields and cry out at the injustice of it all. Part of him could not believe this had happened. And what if it had been Ruth? Hadn't he warned his men not to touch her? He knew the hearts of men, where their thoughts led.

He glanced at Hava and held out a hand. She still cowered in the corner, but then she came slowly forward to stand in the center of the group of men. Boaz extended his other hand to Hamul. He waited too long for the young man to step out from behind his father, but at last he did. With halting steps he came to stand before Boaz.

Boaz looked hard at his cousin. "This is not the way I would have imagined your marriage, Hamul. And I am deeply disappointed in your actions toward this innocent girl." He looked at Hava, whose shaking hand clung to his like a child's. Though the words were not part of the law, he spoke a command he hadn't intended to. "So I am warning you now, I had better never hear that you have mistreated her again. You will love her and cherish her as a wife should be cherished." He paused at the swift memory of Adi that flashed in his mind. He drew a breath and grasped Hamul's wrist, then placed Hava's hand in his. "Here is your wife. You will remain faithful to her all of your days. Do you understand?"

Hamul nodded, eyes wide as a doe's. Perhaps he'd thought he would be stoned, but this act did not require that. Pray God this law would provide security and peace to them both.

He looked to Melek. "Do you have the silver with you?" Melek often carried silver or gold on his person as though he alone could protect his assets.

Melek shook his head.

"Send a guard to get it for you then. We will not leave until Hava's father has been rightly compensated. Then you may take your son and daughter-in-law home."

Melek simply nodded. He stood and walked to the stairs, spoke to a guard, and waited at the parapet.

Naomi woke with the first pinks of dawn and a hint of determination. It was time she paid a visit to some of the women of the town. She had remained in her broken-down home for too long while Ruth worked the fields all day. And with the harvest nearly finished and the Feast of Weeks coming soon, she needed to find a way to show Ruth how Israel honored Yahweh, how they celebrated His goodness.

His goodness. Naomi rose from her bed and bit her trembling lip. She had not thought of God as good in a very long time. Not since Elimelech had taken them to Moab because God had shut up the heavens. If God was good, why did He withhold the rain? If God was good, why did He take her family and leave her with a foreign daughter-in-law, nice as the girl might be?

She splashed tepid water, leftover in a small clay bowl she had used the night before, over her face. Was that an errant tear? Her eyes welled, and she blinked hard, angry with herself. There had been too many tears. Enough!

She dressed quickly and slipped past the chamber where Ruth slept, but one glance told her the girl had already risen. To draw water, no doubt. *Adonai, that girl works too hard. She leaves me nothing to do, and I feel useless.* There, she had admitted it. She ought to be joining Ruth in the gleaning each day. Was she so old that she couldn't put in at least part of a day's work?

Determined to do just that, she went to the courtyard to grind the morning's grain as she waited for Ruth to return with the water. Moments later she saw her walking toward the house, the sun's rays illuminating her like an angel of the Lord. Not that Naomi had ever seen one, but there were tales.

"Good morning, Mother Naomi." Ruth's smile added to the glow about her. She set the water jug in its niche in the stones and took the sieve to help Naomi with the flour. "Did you sleep well?"

"Well enough." Naomi winced at the edge in her tone. She had slept fine and awakened with purpose for the first time in months, and now she was suddenly crabby with the one person who had been most kind to her? *A foolish woman you are, Naomi.*

"I actually had something I wanted to tell you," Naomi said, changing her tone.

"Oh?" Ruth shook the sieve, looking for stones, but glanced into Naomi's eyes before continuing the process.

"I am going with you to glean today." She straightened her back to show determination, strength.

Ruth looked at her for a long moment. "That would be wonderful, Mother, but . . ."

"But what? I am still young enough and strong enough to do the work." Though the very thought of it made her weary.

"Of course you are!" Ruth smiled. "It is just that we only have one basket, so how would you carry the sheaves?"

She hadn't thought of that. She had been meaning to make another basket for Ruth, a better one to hold the grain, for the patched one was growing thinner by the day.

"That would be a problem, wouldn't it?" Naomi looked beyond Ruth, unwilling to admit that the problem gave her a sense of relief. Perhaps she truly was too old for that kind of work.

"I heard news at the well," Ruth offered, pulling Naomi's thoughts from herself.

"What news? Tell me quickly." Naomi realized again how starved she was for the company of the village women, to hear how they were doing, to know who was getting married, who was expecting a child.

"There was an incident at the city gate last night. Apparently your relative's son, the one who had us over to share the evening meal when we first arrived, compromised a virgin in the fields. They say Boaz gathered the elders together and they forced the boy to marry the girl."

Naomi leaned against the wall of the court, the news taking her by complete surprise. "Melek's son? Hamul?"

Ruth nodded. "That's what they say."

Naomi drew in a sharp breath. "Where? When?"

"I didn't hear all the details," Ruth admitted. "They say Melek was so humiliated he could not speak. But I have learned that the gossips often add details to any story, true or not." She poured flour into a bowl and added oil. A fire burned low in the middle of the court, and Ruth quickly made flatbread on a pronged griddle.

"I must visit Boaz's sisters this very day. Gilah and Liora will know more than anyone. Even if Boaz told them nothing, they will have heard."

"And I will go to the fields to glean." Ruth smiled. "One basketful will be enough," she added, patting Naomi's arm. "I would rather have you here, Mother, taking care of our needs as only you can."

Naomi met Ruth's gaze, her heart filling with a feeling she had not had in a long time. Love. For a foreign girl.

Perhaps God was good after all.

31

Naomi watched Ruth walk with sure strides over Bethlehem's dusty streets, the patched flaxen basket strapped to her back. Such a faithful girl she had been these past months, even years.

A sigh lifted Naomi's chest. Barley harvest was nearing its end, with the wheat harvest to follow. Ruth should not be forced to glean and live in poverty the rest of her days. Naomi should do something, do right by the girl, find a home, a husband. She banished the thought. She would lose her as surely as she had lost everything and everyone else in her life. She could not bear it.

Please don't ask it of me, Lord.

When had prayer returned like breath? She had always prayed thus, but of late she had purposely tried to avoid speaking from her heart to the Almighty. She had no guarantee He even heard her prayers, and even if He did, He did not answer them, so why should she pray?

She huffed, disgusted with herself. Her heart betrayed her even when she told it not to. Prayer felt like a war within her.

But hadn't she felt at war with the Almighty since Elimelech's death? Even more since God had taken her sons. Prayer had not saved them.

She shook herself, pushing the thoughts aside once more, gathered her spindle and distaff, and closed the crooked door. She really should try to right the thing so that it closed properly, securely. Surely with Ruth's help they could fix the house without waiting for Boaz or Melek to come to their aid.

Ruth. She would willingly do anything Naomi asked of her, but she was always so weary when she returned from the fields. Naomi did not have the heart to ask her to do more. She glanced at the door, pulling the leather latch closed. Perhaps Gilah's husband would come.

She lifted her chin despite the ache in her heart and walked with purposeful strides toward the home of Gilah, Boaz's older sister. She hated this begging for favors. Hated being on the other side of need. She who always took great pleasure in helping those less fortunate. How had it come to this?

The streets curved several times before Naomi reached Gilah's larger home. Gilah lived with her husband's family, as Liora lived with hers. But the two often met together, and since their homes were in proximity, they were able to remain close, as both sisters and friends.

Naomi stopped in the street, looking up at the impressive gate to the outer court of Gilah's husband's home. Should she have come? But she couldn't very well invite the sisters to the dilapidated house she shared with Ruth. She had no food to offer them beyond the simple parched grains and flatbread Ruth baked over the fire. Soon, when the other harvests came in, there would be almonds and wine and grapes and more oil and dates and even pomegranates. And once the garden took hold, next season or two, they would have herbs and vegetables to offer guests.

But not now.

She sighed again, knowing the feelings were mostly self-pity. She had much to be thankful for if she chose to. But it seemed more comforting to live in the bitterness that had carved a place in her heart, in the spot where compassion once ruled.

Well, there was nothing to be done about it now. She straightened and entered the courtyard. A servant met her at the door.

"I am here to see Gilah," Naomi said before the servant could speak.

"Yes, mistress," the young woman said, smiling. "I will get her for you." The girl hurried into the house, leaving Naomi to look about the court with its whitewashed stones and smooth benches. Fresh water stood in a large clay jar near the bench where servants would wash the feet of visitors. Not so different from the way her home had looked one long-ago day.

"Naomi!" Gilah rushed toward her, arms wide, startling her. So quick she was. So inviting. "I'm glad you came!" She embraced Naomi, and Naomi accepted her kiss of greeting on each cheek. "Please, come inside and take the morning meal with us."

They were still sitting about the table at this hour? But Naomi said nothing. Nor did she tell Gilah that she had already eaten, for in truth she had eaten little. Her hunger had waned since Mahlon and Chilion died, and she saw no sign of it returning. But she followed Gilah into the sitting room and sat with the woman and Gilah's mother-in-law and children.

"The men have already gone to the fields, so we were just finishing a few more bites of bread and dates. Here," she said, passing Naomi a plate of those and more. "Eat."

Naomi thanked her and took some of the food to be polite. She glanced around at the women and forced herself to smile. "I hope all is well with you this day," she said, nibbling the end of the bread.

Gilah nodded. "Yes, yes. But we were up very late last night. You have heard the news, of course."

Naomi nodded, not wanting to sound as though she was ignorant of what went on in Bethlehem. She lifted a brow. "I have heard there was a hasty marriage and that Melek's son violated one of the young virgins in Melek's fields. Surely you know more?"

She watched the spark of interest light Gilah's face. Both sisters loved to tell what they knew. A sense of satisfaction crept over Naomi. She had come to the right place.

Gilah proceeded to tell her the entire tale much as Ruth had already told her, but with embellished detail. Naomi soaked it in, not because she enjoyed the horror of what had happened but for the camaraderie of female friendship. Whether the story was true or not—and she could never be sure that Gilah had all of her facts straight—Naomi enjoyed just being with these women. It gave her a sense of coming home. Something she had not felt in a very long time.

Ruth bent to pick up a sheaf of barley, then another and another, before straightening to put them in the basket on her back. The work was hard, and often she stopped to rub the small of her back to relieve the tension.

"You know, if you set the basket on the ground, you can work an entire row before having to straighten so much." The woman who spoke, Nitza, had taken an interest in Ruth since the end of her first week in Boaz's fields.

Ruth smiled at the younger woman. Might an Israelite consider a Moabite a friend? "Thank you. I had thought of that but feared the basket might not hold from my constant picking it up and moving it to the next row." She patted the basket at her back. "I have mended it several times, but I am going to have to find time to make a new one soon. I only hope this one lasts until the end of the harvest."

Nitza drew closer and examined the flaxen basket at Ruth's back, then nodded. "I can see what you mean. I'm surprised it hasn't torn already." She moved back to her place in the line and continued to pick up the loose sheaves.

"Oh, it has," Ruth said as she followed suit. "Naomi mends it often at night so it is secure enough for another day."

Nitza glanced at Ruth, her gaze curious. "What was it like living in Moab?" She moved through the row as she spoke.

Ruth bent again for more of the wayward stalks of barley, pondering how to answer. "Much like it is here, I expect. We lived in a walled city during my childhood years, but when I married Mahlon, we lived in a home outside city walls, much like Melek lives just outside of Bethlehem's borders."

The mention of Melek caused the conversation to turn away from Ruth. "Did you hear what happened to that poor Hava and Melek's son, Hamul? I heard it said that Boaz was in a temper about it and made them obey the law, like it or not." Nitza glanced about and put a hand to her mouth. "There he is," she whispered.

Ruth looked up to see Boaz walking the length of the field,

stopping here and there to speak to his men, then conversing longer with his foreman, Ezra.

"I have never seen him in a temper," Ruth said softly. "He doesn't seem like the kind of man who would grow angry." Not like Mahlon had done. Not the kind of anger that sulked and yelled or wouldn't speak to her for days when she refused to do something he wanted, like go to a Chemosh festival.

"You don't know him well then," Nitza said, darting her gaze between Boaz and Ruth. "He has not been the same since he found his wife fallen from a cliff, dead in a ravine while watching the sheep. I know it has only been three months, but they say sometimes even now he roams the hills and his cries can be heard all the way to Bethlehem."

Ruth stopped and straightened. "I had heard he was recently widowed." The very thought brought great empathy to her heart, and she wished she had the right to offer sympathy or comforting words.

"He lost a son too, many years ago, and his wife Adi—she was the nicest person—they say she could never carry another baby to term." Nitza sighed. "Any man who loses so much is entitled to rage at the hills if he wants to."

Ruth looked again in Boaz's direction, then quickly bent to continue her gleaning. Heat filled her cheeks at the thoughts and feelings suddenly evoked by Nitza's words. She had noticed Boaz's strength and kindness, his lean, muscular build and dark, probing eyes. And that dark brown hair with the wayward streak of gray she had imagined sifting her fingers through on more than one occasion.

"His sisters have suggested he marry one of the town widows. It would be a kindness to one of them and to him, eventually." Nitza interrupted her embarrassing musings.

"But our master's heart was so bound to Adi . . . I wonder if he will ever marry again."

Ruth nodded. She could not blame him. His loss was too recent and far greater than her own, for though she had loved Mahlon, he was not as kind as Boaz seemed to be. And they had never lost a child to bond them in that way.

"You said the master is devoted to the law of your God," Ruth said, changing the subject. "There is a law that forced Hamul to marry Hava?"

Nitza shrugged. "I guess so. Women are allowed to hear the law read when we go up to Shiloh to the festivals with the men, but most of us never learn to read it, and only the Levites have copies of the law itself. Boaz is an elder, and a respected one here. With his wealth, they say he hired a scribe to make a copy of the law for him, and he reads it or has it read to him daily. That's how he knows to judge the cases that come to the elders."

Ruth stood again and rubbed her back. The ache had grown with the weight of the basket. She glanced at the sky. It was nearly time for the noon meal. Relief flooded her. She could rest soon.

"Don't all of the elders know the law?" In a town the size of Bethlehem, more than one man ought to know how to judge according to what Israel's God had prescribed.

Nitza stood. "Sure they do. But not many take time to read it every day. At least I don't think so, because Boaz knows more than most and the men respect him for it." She looked up. "Come on. It's time to rest and eat. We can talk more later."

Ruth followed Nitza to the area where the food was spread and gladly set her basket on the ground. She straightened, and a deep sigh escaped.

"It looks to me as though that thing has seen better uses long ago."

Ruth whirled about at the sound of Boaz's voice, startled by his nearness. She took a breath to steady herself. "Yes, my lord. It was left in the house and filled with holes. Naomi and I patch it almost nightly." She studied her feet. Why was she admitting such a thing to him? She didn't want his pity.

He cleared his throat, causing her to meet his gaze. "See Ezra before you begin work tomorrow. He will replace the basket with a new one."

She bowed low, but he stopped her with a touch to her shoulder. "Do not bow to me, my daughter." He extended a hand toward the food. "Come, eat and be filled." His smile nearly melted her heart.

32

How generous of Boaz's sister to give you the lentils and cheese," Ruth said as they finished their meal of flatbread and stew made from the lentils Gilah had given to Naomi. "How was your visit there today?"

"Pleasant. I did not realize how much I miss the company of my old friends." Naomi smiled. "Though I wish you could have joined us, my daughter."

Ruth nodded. "Yes, but it is good that you could enjoy the day. And look how your God has provided for us." She pointed to the sack of barley that she had beaten from the sheaves that afternoon. Boaz's men had continued to drop more sheaves than they ought to, though she knew if she asked, they would not admit they were doing so on purpose. But Ruth knew from past conversations with Naomi that Boaz must have given orders to grant her greater provisions than the law provided in gleaning, for she always came away with more than some of the young women who worked farther down the row from her.

"Your relative Boaz is a kind man," Ruth said when Naomi seemed lost in thought, her gaze on the sack Ruth had pointed to. "Please tell me about his wife."

Naomi's attention snapped back to Ruth. "Adi?" She shook her head as though the mention of the woman's name brought Naomi her own sense of sorrow. She sighed. "Boaz married young, and he and Adi were so in love." She paused.

Love was not common between couples who married. Marriages were made for convenience, for sustenance to survive, for companionship, to procreate. Rarely for love, though it sometimes came later.

"It sounds as though they had a rare gift then." Ruth met Naomi's gaze.

"Yes, they did. And everyone loved Adi." Naomi placed a cover over what was left of the stew and hung the pot high above the ground. "They were married for two years when our judge Ehud killed your king Eglon." Naomi glanced at Ruth, who sensed her hesitance to continue.

"I was a child when that happened," Ruth said softly. "Governor Aali was our neighbor then, and when my father was feared lost, he rescued my mother—all of us—and fled with us to Dibon." A small shudder worked through her at the memory. While she had always been grateful the man had saved her family, she had hated what he became. And yet . . . did the God of Israel want His people to hate others, even their enemies?

Naomi sat again, the food stored now, and poured Ruth more water from a jug. "Boaz fought in that war, Ruth. The one that took your father's life."

Ruth did not flinch as she held Naomi's scrutinizing gaze. Was Naomi waiting to see her reaction? What if it was Boaz's arrow or a stone from his sling that had killed her father? But they would never know.

"Obviously, the war was fought because of Moab's oppression of your people," Ruth said slowly. "Your people are my people now, Mother. You do not offend me by telling me the truth."

Naomi watched her another moment, then nodded. "Boaz fought in the war and returned to Adi, and all seemed well for many years except that Adi could not bear a child. Some told Boaz to take another wife, as Melek has done in his desire for a son, but Boaz is a faithful man and refused. He said that if God wanted to preserve his heritage, God would give him and Adi sons. He wanted no one else."

"That kind of man is hard to find in these times." How well she knew it, for in Moab it was common for a man to have a wife, a concubine, and a mistress, and to visit the prostitutes during the festivals. To find a faithful man . . . Sometimes Ruth had wondered if even Mahlon was always truly faithful. Whether he stayed away from the prostitutes during festivals he attended without her. She shook the thought aside.

"Yes." Naomi sipped from her cup. "And one day Boaz's prayers seemed to be answered, because Adi was at last with child." She looked beyond Ruth, and suddenly Ruth did not want to hear the rest of the tale. But she said nothing, for it seemed Naomi needed to tell her.

"Adi was the happiest woman in Bethlehem during those months. But when it came time to give birth, the Lord's hand was as against her as it has been against me. The Almighty took her son before he could draw breath. Boaz was devastated—Adi too. But his sisters tell me that they tried again and again, and at times there was hope. But Adi miscarried one child after another until she grew too weak to conceive again. That's when she took to caring for the sheep instead of the household. Boaz indulged her, for he found no other way to make her happy."

Ruth's heart twisted. Such pain for such a kind man to endure. His handsome face with that strong jaw he stroked when he appeared to be thinking flashed in her thoughts. Too much suffering. *Oh God of Naomi, why?* But she silently chastised herself for asking. She had no right to demand answers of Adonai Elohim—she, a foreigner, an unworthy one. But her heart ached for Boaz just the same.

"I am very sorry for him," she said at last. "Thank you for telling me."

"It was time you knew." Naomi looked at her, her gaze curious. "I don't wonder if God still has plans for Boaz."

Ruth's cheeks flushed at the twinkle in Naomi's eyes. She did not need to ask what Naomi had in mind with that statement. And she could not deny that she might find the idea pleasing.

The following morning Ruth stood in the courtyard debating whether to trust Boaz's word or take her old basket in case Ezra had nothing for her. She glanced at the road, gauging the distance from the house to the field and back again if she had to return for the basket. Precious time would be lost. But how silly of her to worry over something so small. Surely the man could be trusted.

"Is something wrong, my daughter?" Naomi came from inside the house, spindle and distaff in her hands. She would be off to visit another friend or relative while Ruth worked the fields, but she never went without some work to complete, even if it was someone else's wool she helped to spin. They had no sheep of their own to shear or spin the wool into garments.

Ruth shook herself, wishing she could give Naomi more than her gleaning efforts. If only they could afford a few sheep, Ruth could shepherd them and breed them, and they would find greater sustenance.

"My daughter?" Naomi looked at her strangely, and Ruth realized she had not answered the woman's question.

"He said not to bring the basket, that they would provide me a new one." Ruth bit her lower lip. "But what if they forget? Should I take it?" She pointed to the old basket she had mended again the night before.

"Who said not to bring it?" Naomi's eyes carried that same twinkle they had the night before, as if she knew a secret she was not yet ready to share.

"Boaz." His name on her tongue brought joy to Ruth's spirit. "He saw how worn this one is and said they would have a new one today."

"Then the man will do as he said. Believe him, my daughter." Naomi smiled and patted Ruth's arm. "Go. Leave this here."

"But I don't want to appear presumptuous."

"Did he not tell you he would provide this for you?"

Ruth nodded.

"Then why do you doubt?" Naomi slipped her arm through Ruth's and began walking them both toward the outer court.

Ruth glanced back at the basket lying on its side against the courtyard wall. She hesitated but a moment, then allowed Naomi to lead her. "I don't know. Perhaps because most men in my life did not keep their word."

Naomi seemed to ponder this a moment.

"I did not mean to offend regarding Mahlon."

Naomi shook her head. "No need to fear offense, my daughter. I know my son was not always as he should have been to you. But I can tell you that despite Boaz's grief right now, he is not like most men. If he said he will do something, he will do it."

Ruth blew out a breath and nodded. "All right." She only hoped Naomi knew the man as well as she thought she did.

The following day, Ruth's work ended early in preparation for the coming Sabbath. Boaz's sister Liora had invited them to eat the Sabbath meal with her family, and Naomi was quick to accept.

Ruth pulled on a fresh tunic, separate from the one she wore for gleaning, and her best robe, the one she saved for special occasions. She followed Naomi through the winding streets to the house of Liora's husband and family.

They arrived early, before the sound of the shofar called them to the Sabbath. Ruth had grown accustomed to the sound, and the day of rest to come was a welcome respite from the hard labor of her life. But a part of her still felt a need to do something to show her devotion to Adonai. Surely He would be pleased with some kind of service on this day.

"Naomi, Ruth, you are here! I am so glad to see you." Liora embraced Naomi in the customary way with a kiss to each cheek, though with Ruth she simply nodded and smiled. Would the people of the town never see her as anything but a foreigner, an alien in their midst? Though Naomi accepted her, and it seemed others did as well, Ruth did not miss the subtle glances, the curious looks, even the skepticism in the gazes of some.

She sighed, tucking the concerns aside as Liora led them

into the house. No servant washed their feet. Instead, they were led to a large room, where it seemed all of Liora's family and more had already gathered. Small tables were set with bread and platters of cheese and figs and dates and vegetables, all prepared the day before, according to what Naomi had taught her.

"Naomi, welcome, my sister."

Ruth startled at the voice, for she would recognize it anywhere. But Boaz was not Naomi's brother. "Sister" must be a term of endearment, as when Boaz had called Ruth "my daughter."

"Boaz. I was hoping your sister would coax you to join us and meet together for a Sabbath meal. How good it is to see you again." Naomi took the seat offered her, and Ruth sat near her, saying nothing. Though Boaz had seen Ruth in the fields and sent servants to Naomi's house with food and some provisions, he had not been to see Naomi—at least not when Ruth was near.

Ruth's pulse quickened at his closeness, but she fought the urge to blush. He was her benefactor, that was all. And Naomi's relative. Ruth was simply a foreign woman—

"And Ruth, we are glad you could join us." Boaz's comment cut her thoughts short. She glanced up at him.

"Thank you, my lord." She looked down at her hands, suddenly embarrassed to be here.

Boaz moved across the room and joined the men, and Liora and her mother-in-law and daughters sat with Naomi and Gilah and the women of Gilah's family.

Ruth listened and ate in silence, taking in the scene of joy, of a family gathered together in reverence.

"And let us not forget the law," Boaz said when the meal

was finished, "that tells us to remember when we were slaves in Egypt and how our God brought us out with a mighty hand and outstretched arm."

Ruth watched him, leaning close, listening as he told the story of the Israelites' captivity in Egypt, which seemed to take on new life coming from his lips.

"And the plagues our God sent to punish the Egyptians," one of the children said.

"What were those plagues?" Boaz asked as the children gathered around him.

"A river of blood."

"Frogs!" This from a young boy, who laughed at the thought.

"Locusts," a girl said in disgust.

"Darkness," another girl said.

"Why darkness?" Boaz asked, coaxing the girl to look at him.

"Because they thought the sun was God and worshiped it."

"Very good." Boaz smiled and glanced up, catching Ruth's gaze as the children continued to name the ten plagues.

"Did you have a question about the plagues, Ruth?" Boaz asked her later, after the children had been put to bed and the adults who remained were heading home. "It seemed as though you wanted to ask but didn't."

Ruth looked down and moved one foot over the stones of the court. "If I understand correctly, Adonai Elohim sent the plagues to show His power over some of the gods of Egypt—or the things they worshiped."

"Yes, you understand correctly," he said softly. "Our God will have no other gods before Him. That is why He drove out the nations that lived here before us. It is why we have suffered the oppression of our neighbors when we are enticed to worship their gods. The God of Abraham, Isaac, and

Jacob loves His people, but when we put other gods ahead of Him, we suffer the consequences for our actions, as Egypt did. That is why we are to remember Egypt on the Sabbath, and especially at Passover. Not only to remind us that we were once slaves, but to remind us that our God performed a mighty rescue to save us, to buy us back from slavery by His great power. He does not want us to forget, lest we forget Him and then end up despising His goodness to us."

Ruth glanced into his handsome face for the briefest moment, then looked beyond him. "Do you always consider Him good? Even when bad things happen?" She glanced at him, almost wishing the words back, and yet . . . she had seen the shadow cross his face as he talked with the children. His mouth spoke the words, even with the right amount of enthusiasm, but his eyes told a different tale.

He looked at her, his brows drawn low as if assessing how to answer her. "You ask a difficult question." His honesty and the vulnerable glint in his gaze unnerved her. "And I will tell you that no, I have not always considered Him good. When I found Adi in the ravine, I thought Him the very opposite of good. When we lost child after child, I struggled to make sense of Him, of His ways."

"You have suffered much," she said, quickly glancing around, hoping no one had heard her questioning him. "I am sorry for your loss."

He stared at her for a lengthy breath as though he found it impossible to speak. At last he nodded and said, "Thank you."

She gave him a sympathetic look, then quickly moved to Naomi's side, suddenly too overcome with shyness to say more.

33

The morning after the Sabbath, Ruth returned to the field, Boaz's new basket strapped to her back and a few figs in a pocket at her waist. Liora had sent Naomi home with more food than seemed reasonable, but Naomi accepted everything with gratitude, and Ruth did not mind having something to ease her hunger during midmorning.

The sun rose slowly, drinking the dew of the earth while it climbed, as she approached Boaz's barley field. The fields were on a plain above several surrounding valleys that sometimes flooded during the heavy rains. Even now water still rested in them, and Ruth took the path around them to avoid having to wade through water and mud—though water and mud must be a welcome sight to the people here.

Ruth shuddered at the thought of the severe famine they had suffered. How did the town survive so long, and why was it only Elimelech who thought it necessary to seek refuge elsewhere?

She glanced around as she walked, realizing that there were no easy answers to the question, for Naomi had not been here to know how things fared. Perhaps one day she might ask one of the women, but for now such questions seemed inconsiderate.

She came upon Boaz's field, the first of the girls to arrive. How had the others managed to be delayed? She normally tried to time her arrival with theirs, but today she could not help but feel the need to hurry with the rising sun.

She met Boaz's foreman coming from the area where the workers had begun to harvest the rows left standing two nights before.

"The Lord bless you today, Ruth," Ezra said, walking toward her. His skin was darker than Boaz's, his beard black as night. When he smiled, his round face widened.

"And you as well, Ezra." Ruth returned his smile, then glanced toward the area she was to work that day. "May I begin the gleaning?" She saw the men already moving through the rows with their sickles. A few more girls drew up over the rise and came into view.

"Yes, yes, of course," Ezra said, still smiling. He looked at her, and she sensed he wanted to say more.

"Is there something else?" She met his curious gaze.

He tilted his head, studying her. "I have wondered something," he said at last.

A tickle of disquiet filled her, but she simply nodded.

"Are you free?"

Ruth lifted a brow. "Am I free? I don't understand your meaning." She was not a slave. She was here of her own choice.

"Free to marry." His voice suddenly dropped in pitch.

The heat of embarrassment crept through her. Why would he ask her such a question unless . . . Was he interested in her?

She sought an answer but could not seem to pull one onto her tongue.

"Forgive me. I did not mean to make you uneasy. Go ahead and be about your work," he said.

She hurried after the other women but sensed that he watched her just the same.

Boaz walked with Ezra later that day, counting the bundles of barley waiting to be threshed. Several men with donkeys and carts loaded the bundled stalks onto the carts to take to the threshing floor. Once the barley was fully in, they would harvest the wheat. Then the celebration of the Feast of Weeks could begin. Would he feel more connected to this festival than he had the last? Three months had brought only the faintest hint of healing. Adi's scent had faded in the house, but evidence of her presence still lingered in every room. And the nightmares of finding her broken body still brought on a cold sweat, though when he thought on it he realized it had been days since he'd last faced those demons. Perhaps in time . . .

"We have had a great yield so far, my lord," Ezra said, jolting him to the present as the man jotted the numbers on a clay tablet.

"That is good." Boaz glanced heavenward. He should be grateful, and surely he felt some measure of gratitude that the famine had ended. If only he could have shared this good fortune with his beloved.

"Yes, our God is good to grant such bounty," Ezra said,

glancing at him as he tucked the clay and stylus into a leather bag tied at his waist.

"Yes." He could not bring himself to say more, but he was in no mood to argue with Ezra over the issue of thanksgiving.

They walked in silence behind the first cart headed to the threshing floor. He threshed the day's yield each evening, sleeping near the grain to protect it until his men could store the grain in large clay jars and cart them back to his storage rooms the following day. There he could distribute to the needy and save the seed for next year's planting.

"I was wondering . . ." Ezra said as the donkey brayed.

Boaz glanced at his friend and lifted a brow. "What were you wondering this time?" He felt a slow smile cross his lips.

Ezra laughed outright. "I find your people so fascinating, and your ways bring to mind so many questions."

Boaz chuckled, surprising himself at the ability to do so. But they both knew Ezra loved to speak in jest.

"So tell me, my friend, what is it that you wonder?" Boaz asked as they descended the hill toward the circular threshing floor.

"I asked the Moabitess Ruth a question today. It seems that I startled her, and she never did give me an answer. Perhaps you can answer it for me." Ezra looked at Boaz, his dark eyes intent.

Boaz's stomach did a strange flip at the mention of Ruth's name, but he told himself he was hungry, nothing more. "Go on," he said, curious.

"I asked her if she was free to marry. Well, at first I asked her if she was free, and I think she thought I considered her a slave, so I retried my words and asked again. But her face flushed pink and she seemed to have no response." He shrugged. "It was a simple question. If she is bound in some way to Naomi, then she is not free unless Naomi releases her to marry again—is that not correct according to your laws?" He kicked a rock in the path as they walked.

"Naomi is the one who would arrange a marriage for Ruth, yes. Since Ruth is her daughter-in-law, it is up to Naomi to seek a husband for her or to set her free, as she did Chilion's wife." His sisters had told him the tale as they had heard it from Naomi of how Ruth refused to be released. So technically, she *was* free because Naomi had tried to release her along with her sister-in-law, but Ruth would not have it. Would Naomi seek a husband for her here? What man would want to marry a Moabite?

He looked at Ezra. "Why did you ask her such a question, my friend? Is your wife not enough for you that you are seeking another?"

Ezra huffed. "Ach! Why would you say such a thing? I was thinking of you!" He winked at Boaz.

Boaz grew silent, focusing his attention on descending the hill as the decline grew steeper. Marry again, as his sisters had suggested? What would Adi think of him? He had planned to remain as he was until God took him to Sheol to join her.

Ezra's touch on his arm made him look up. "I know you still grieve, my lord. But you know it is common for men to take another wife after the mourning period has passed. And I believe it has passed, has it not?"

Boaz glanced beyond him, then away toward the threshing floor. "Technically, the three months have passed, yes. Practically, I can decide to do whatever I want to. Why do you push me?" His heart had already betrayed him too many times where Ruth was concerned. And he didn't need the reminder that he *could* approach Naomi about her.

"Because I see the way you watch her. And because it is not good for a man to be alone. Is that not part of your own Scriptures?" Ezra met his gaze with a knowing look.

It is not good for a man to be alone. He hadn't been alone for years, and the loneliness, the missing her, was slowly killing him, for he died a thousand deaths with every thought of a new day without her.

"Yes, it is what God said before He made Eve." Boaz's mind whirled with too many thoughts. He could ask Naomi about Ruth. But he was afraid of betraying the only woman he had ever loved. And for that reason, he knew he could never ask.

34

Boaz lifted the heavy stick in both hands and struck the barley against the round stone of the threshing floor again and again. The process was tedious and repetitive, but slowly the kernels loosened from the stalks, the first step before the winnowing, when he could at last remove the barley from the chaff.

He glanced up at the sound of voices. More farmers with bundles on the backs of donkeys or in hand-pulled carts entered the large area. To his right Ezra led the ox that pulled the sledge over the stalks.

"You might try my way one of these days," Ezra called down from above him, smiling. "There is more power in an animal pulling a sledge than that pitiful stick." He laughed, and Boaz just shook his head.

"I have my way, you have yours, my friend." He smiled at the man, surprised that he truly felt the joy a man had when the harvest was brought in. Perhaps life did go on despite one's losses.

Voices of more men circled the stone—men positioning their grain—followed by the rhythmic pounding and stomping of threshing.

"Well, cousin." Melek's voice made him pause. He glanced beside him. "I see you beat us to the threshing floor as usual." Melek entered with Hamul, who wore his perpetual sullen expression.

"It is not a competition, Melek. We simply finished earlier than normal today." He put his weight into flailing the stick against the barley, his almost jovial mood dampened.

Melek pulled a stack of his own barley from the cart and handed it to Hamul. "Don't be idle. I don't have all night."

Boaz stopped mid-swing and studied the boy, but his expression now seemed unreadable. Hamul took up the stick and began the work while Melek stood looking on.

"You might finish more quickly, cousin, if you help your son." Boaz met Melek's gaze. The familiar irritation he always felt in this man's presence caused his jaw to clench.

"Hamul can do the work," Melek said, his voice tense.

Boaz lifted a brow but said nothing. The boy beat the sheaves with a steady rhythm, and Melek watched him like an overseer. Was this Hamul's punishment for what he had done to Hava? The embarrassment he had caused his father?

He pondered the thought as he continued to work on stack after stack of sheaves. Barley heaped high to his left and right, Ezra's mixed with his.

As night waned, the pounding stopped and the workers gathered to eat and drink. Boaz sat near Melek and Hamul, trying to gauge the mood of both men.

"God has blessed you, cousin, with a goodly yield," he said to Melek. "You will have much to share and to feed your large family." He said the words to be polite and attempted a smile as he passed him a clay plate of toasted grain.

"Yes," Melek said, glancing at his son. "God has blessed me." Sarcasm laced his tone.

"And how is your wife?" Boaz asked Hamul, whose countenance had fallen at his father's comment. How quickly words could wound.

Hamul swallowed the grain he was chewing and met Boaz's gaze. "I treat her well, Boaz. I promise I do." He looked at his hands in his lap.

"I am glad to hear it." Boaz had feared the boy would not do right by a girl he had violated in the beginning, even caught himself wondering why the law would put the girl in the home of the very man who had done such a thing.

"She is pregnant," Hamul said softly, drawing Boaz to look at him once more. He saw the look the boy gave his father, saw the longing for him to accept this girl and her child.

Boaz's thoughts circled back to that night when Hava and her father stood in his courtyard, claiming Hamul had done this thing. Only a few weeks had passed. How was it possible?

"So soon?" he asked, looking more at Melek than Hamul. "How would she know so soon?" Adi had never known until at least two moons had passed.

Hamul glanced beyond him, then at his father, then around at the other men, who sat some distance away. At his father's slight nod, Hamul swallowed hard. "I am not sure it is a tale you want to hear." He clasped his hands and again studied them, as though they could speak for him.

"Tell him anyway." Melek crossed his arms, his sudden glare cooling the air.

Hamul cleared his throat. "The child isn't mine," he whispered.

"Hava was waylaid in a different field nearly two months ago. She did not know her attacker and has never seen him since." He paused, wiped sweat from his brow. "I have known Hava all my life—we used to play together as children when our mothers met at the well or the river. I found her crying there a few weeks ago, just before she came to your court."

Boaz stared at his young cousin, his thoughts whirling. "So you told her to name you as her attacker so you could cover her shame."

The young man lifted his chin and gave a slight nod. "She could have been stoned. An unmarried woman carrying a child? I couldn't let that happen to her." Hamul sighed, his gaze moving from Boaz to his father.

"But you did not tell your father."

Hamul shook his head. So this was the reason for Melek's anger.

"You should have told him, gotten his permission, Hamul. You dishonored him by putting him to shame as you did."

Hamul looked at his feet. "I know." He spoke so softly Boaz had to lean forward to hear.

"My grandson will not be rightfully mine." Melek spoke through clenched teeth.

Boaz looked from father to son. So much tension between them. Would he have been in such a battle with his own son had he lived? He shoved aside the ache such thoughts evoked.

"I'm sorry, Father," Hamul said, probably not for the first time, by the look on Melek's face. "I should have told you."

"Of course you should have." Melek's tone carried a hint of hurt. "Do you think I would have turned the girl away when I know you care for her? How cruel do you think me to be?"

Hamul's brows lifted as though the words surprised him. "Her child will not be your grandchild."

"Of course he will," Boaz countered.

"Not by blood." Melek agreed with his son.

Silence descended among them while the conversations of the other men went on in the distance. No wonder the tension had lingered between these men. Boaz understood the hurt on both sides. "I think," he said slowly, breaking the silence, "that you both must accept that Hamul has legally wed Hava and wants to raise her child as his own. That makes her child your family, Melek. It is up to you whether you will accept what your son has done." Boaz saw the slight smile on Hamul's barely bearded face. So young and hopeful and already thinking of others as more important than himself.

"Hamul," Boaz said, leaning across the table, "I owe you an apology. I thought the worst of you when this happened, but now I see that you were doing something none of us understood. I wish you and Hava God's blessing." He paused. "But next time you face something so life-changing, talk to your father. You dishonor him by going behind his back."

Hamul nodded. "Yes, of course."

Melek grunted and looked away. Apparently, it would take some time for him to accept what his son had done—without his approval and to his shame. Despite the truth, which would eventually be made known when the child came too early, the man's pride had been dealt a blow.

Boaz drank deeply from his cup and wondered if he would have felt differently in Melek's place.

Dusk fell as Ruth beat the last of the stalks she had gleaned that afternoon. The last day of barley harvest had arrived, the fields bare. A feeling of celebration hung in the air among the women she worked beside, who rejoiced that the long famine was truly over and God had given them a great harvest. For the next few nights the men would winnow the threshed grain and prepare for the wheat harvest to follow.

Ruth smiled at the thought, her heart grateful for the provision she had found in this new land. She tucked the last of the barley into the basket and glanced at the fading light. A bright moon rose as the sun dipped lower, its glow ablaze on the horizon. She must hurry lest Naomi worry about her. How had the time gotten away from her?

She looked about, seeing a few women still beating the sheaves, and felt a measure of relief that she was not completely alone. Still, she lifted her skirts and half walked, half ran with her burden from the smaller threshing area used by the gleaners toward Bethlehem's open gates.

The distance had never seemed long in the past, but a sense of unease filled her this night. She glanced heavenward at the moon's orb. Her people worshiped the moon on such nights. Was that why she felt a sense of foreboding, even fear? But she was not in Moab, and the streets of Bethlehem had never been anything but safe.

She pulled her cloak tighter against the chill of dusk and breathed a sigh of relief as the gates drew closer. Once inside Bethlehem's stout walls, she slowed her pace. Why on earth had she been so fearful?

She glanced about at the closed merchant shops, saw the lamps glowing in various windows, and rounded a bend toward the section of town where most of the homes stood. The moon hid momentarily behind a cloud, and footsteps sounded behind her. Ruth picked up her pace as male voices drew nearer. Just a little farther around another bend . . .

The voices grew louder, boisterous.

"What do we have here?" a man said, coming up beside her. Or was it a boy? She couldn't quite tell in the darkness.

"It's that foreigner, Naomi's girl," another said.

"The Moabite?" This voice carried a sneer as the three surrounded her, blocking her path. "What made you think we would want a Moabite in Israel?" The young man's breath smelled of wine, and his dark eyes seemed to glow hot.

"I can think of some good uses for her." This from the first man.

"Please," Ruth said loudly, knowing from the raucous nature of Moabite festivals that shouting was better than saying nothing. "Let me pass."

"Let me pass," one mocked her, touching her shoulder. She flinched.

"I don't think you want to face my master Boaz and the town council if you don't move on now." She watched them, her heart thumping. Boaz wasn't her master exactly, for she simply gleaned in his fields, but she knew his name carried weight in this town.

"Boaz isn't here," the drunk one said, his words slurring slightly. He shoved her off balance until she fell into one of the other men.

"Let me go!" This time her words were a near scream. She clutched the basket, fearful of losing a day's work, yet more concerned about what they seemed capable of doing on what she had considered safe streets in a safe town.

"Who goes there?" A man's booming voice came from one of the homes where light glowed through a window.

Ruth glanced in his direction, saw a giant of a man filling the doorway. "Help me!" she cried out, determined to get away from these three, while silently praying that she wasn't leaving one mess for another danger.

The man stepped into the street, his wife behind him. "What is the meaning of this?" His voice bellowed like thunder.

The men scrambled to flee, falling and scurrying like insects avoiding the light of day.

The woman came around her husband to Ruth's side. "Are you all right, my dear?" She touched Ruth's arm, and weak relief coursed through her, draining her.

"Yes, yes. Thank you." She glanced from the woman to the large man.

"Did they hurt you?" the man asked. He leaned closer, peering into her face. "You're Naomi's daughter-in-law, the Moabite."

She nodded. A foreigner. Unaccepted. Unwanted. She could not speak as they gave her a curious look.

"You have done a wonderful thing to come with Naomi in her time of grief and provide for her, young woman. Anyone who shows such devotion is welcome in this town." The man's words brought the sting of tears to Ruth's eyes.

The woman seemed to notice and pulled Ruth into a warm embrace. "Do not let the foolishness of those young men discourage you. If you are ever afraid walking home, you just come right into our courtyard, you understand? We will protect you."

Accepted? The sense of it filled her being. "Thank you." She held the basket tighter. "I must get home to Naomi lest she worry."

The woman looked to her husband. "He will walk with you until you reach her courtyard."

The man nodded. As they began walking, he kept a respectable distance between them until Ruth rounded the bend and fairly flew toward home.

PART 3

Then Naomi her mother-in-law said to her, "My daughter, should I not seek rest for you, that it may be well with you? Is not Boaz our relative, with whose young women you were? See, he is winnowing barley tonight at the threshing floor. Wash therefore and anoint yourself, and put on your cloak and go down to the threshing floor, but do not make yourself known to the man until he has finished eating and drinking. But when he lies down, observe the place where he lies. Then go and uncover his feet and lie down, and he will tell you what to do." And she replied, "All that you say I will do."

Ruth 3:1–5

35

M y daughter, you must not leave the threshing area so late again." Naomi's hands trembled at the news she had pulled from a reluctant Ruth the moment she rushed into the courtyard. They were seated now in the inner room, the door closed and latched, sipping watered wine. "Even in Bethlehem there is sin, and the minds of men rush to evil." She grasped Ruth's hand and squeezed. "You are too important to me to let anything happen to you."

Ruth smiled, but Naomi wondered at the faraway look in her eyes.

"Promise me you will remember." Naomi gently touched Ruth's chin with two fingers, coaxing her to meet her gaze.

"I promise." Ruth released a sigh. "In any case, the barley gleaning has ended. We have some time before I need to go out to the fields again."

Naomi clasped her hands in front of her. "We have plenty of grain stored now, thanks to your hard work. In fact, I think it is time we went to market and used some to barter for other things we need."

Ruth lifted a brow. "What else could we possibly need, Mother? We have everything here except men underfoot." She laughed lightly, but Naomi did not miss the wistful look that passed before her eyes.

"I am sorry, my daughter. I have taken you for granted."

Ruth looked up, eyes wide until her expression changed. She nodded in apparent understanding. "No you haven't, Mother Naomi. I am perfectly content and happy to be here with you rather than in Moab. You and your God are worth far more than anything I might have given up."

Naomi met Ruth's smile, seeing the genuineness in her gaze. "Nevertheless, I will give thought to a husband for you, and soon." She rose slowly, feeling the ache in her knees, wondering why life had gotten so difficult, so painful. "In the meantime," she said, her mind whirling with the many things they would need to change if a husband were to be sought for Ruth, "we will go to the markets in the morning. We will buy spices to add to our oil for a sweet-smelling perfume, and buy wool and a new spindle and distaff, and perhaps we can ask Gilah if she has an extra loom to make you a new robe, and—"

Ruth stood and put both hands on Naomi's bent shoulders. She laughed, a delightful sound. "Let us not get carried away yet. If we barter all of our grain, what will we eat? My robe is perfectly fine." She felt the fabric. "See?"

Did the girl not notice how threadbare it had become? But of course she did. This was Ruth. Always loving. Always giving.

Naomi took Ruth's face between her worn hands. "God blessed me more than I deserved the day He gave me you."

Ruth smiled and kissed Naomi's cheek. "We are doubly blessed."

The next morning, true to her word, Naomi led Ruth through the same streets she had traversed fearfully the night before. What a difference daylight made. They walked, their step light, with Naomi continually glancing her way and smiling. She was planning something, a secret she would not share until she was ready. It was her way, and Ruth loved her for it.

They reached the markets just as they were opening. A caravan from the north had entered Bethlehem's gates, camels draped in colorful wares, merchants already haggling with shop owners.

"Oh, what timing," Naomi exclaimed, as though she had come upon a houseful of gifts. "Perhaps we can find perfume already made and save us the trouble of mixing it ourselves."

Ruth looked at her mother-in-law, felt the sack of barley she carried, and tried not to worry. Naomi was not one to be foolish. She would not spend frivolously.

They ducked under the shop awning of one of Naomi's friends from days gone by, the wife of a shepherd who had rows of fine wool ready to be carded and spun into thread. Ruth touched the wool's softness, noting the different colors, all washed and clean. How long had it been since she had woven a new garment? Not since before Mahlon's death. She glanced at the robe she wore daily to the fields. She had one other, a newer one that she saved for special occasions. She did not need to replace anything yet.

Naomi's robe, on the other hand, was in dire need of replacement, but Ruth knew she would never get Naomi to agree to such a thing as long as they lived on the edge of poverty.

"Did you hear the news about Hamul and Hava?" The merchant's wife leaned close to Naomi, and Ruth could not help but hear. She didn't want to listen where she shouldn't, but she took a quiet step closer just the same.

"What news?" Naomi clearly did not mind the gossip, whether it was true or not.

"Hava is with child!" The woman laughed, slapping her knees.

Naomi frowned. "Already? It has been merely a few weeks since they wed."

"That's the news," the woman said, her tone conspiratorial. She licked her lips like one tasting a sweet morsel. "The child is not Hamul's! Apparently, the whole thing was a ruse so Hamul could marry her to hide her shame. The girl was waylaid months ago, but she didn't know the man. Hamul knew his father would never approve, so they made up the story so he would have no choice." She laughed as though the whole thing was humorous.

"But the poor girl . . ." Memories of the night before, when the same thing could have happened to her, stopped Ruth's words.

Naomi faced Ruth, touched her arm. "Hamul did a brave thing. And nothing is going to happen to you, my daughter."

Ruth merely nodded, though she caught the curious stare of the merchant woman. She released a sigh when other women flooded the tent and Naomi ushered them toward the perfumer's shop.

"Let us see what we can find to make a sweet-smelling oil." She looped her arm through Ruth's as if to reassure her.

"Never mind about Hava and Hamul, my dear. We are here to find a husband for you." Her eyes twinkled. "And Hamul is not the only one who can redeem a woman he loves."

Ruth pondered Naomi's words, trying to make sense of them. How had Hamul redeemed Hava? And what was her mother-in-law thinking now?

The following day Ruth sat in the courtyard with a new spindle and basket of wool while Naomi tossed barley onto the grindstone to begin the grinding for the evening's bread. Naomi's oven had long ago been removed from the court-yard, but a neighbor had willingly shared hers so the widows could bake.

"If you would rather spin, I don't mind grinding." Ruth hated allowing the older woman the harder task, but Naomi had insisted.

"If I wanted to spin I would tell you." Naomi turned the handle on the stone, and Ruth allowed the grating sound to fill the silence.

She'd been trying to gather courage to speak since their visit to the market the day before, but every time the thoughts surfaced, she found reason to hold her tongue.

"I am glad to hear that Hamul is not guilty of such a sin as we first thought," Naomi said, drawing Ruth's thoughts to the very questions that had troubled her. "While I have little use for Melek"—she tsked—"all those wives just to have a son—I will say I had hoped the son would be better than his father. It turns out that perhaps he is." She glanced at Ruth and smiled that knowing smile that had given Ruth cause to toss and wonder in the night.

"What did you mean yesterday," she asked at last, "that Hamul redeemed Hava? He did not buy her back from slavery or sacrifice."

Naomi stopped grinding and looked up. "But he did buy her back from shame. Once word got out of Hava's pregnancy, and she a supposed virgin with no husband . . . the town could have stoned her. It would have been too late to say she was violated since she did not tell anyone in the beginning when it happened. She should have. The men might have found the man who did such a thing. But I suspect Hava feared her father and took a chance on trusting her childhood friend instead." Naomi looked down and began grinding again. "Turns out she made the right choice, I think."

Ruth continued to twirl the spindle and distaff, an action she had done many times in her life, a habit that needed little thought. "So a person can be redeemed from slavery or shame . . ."

"Or poverty." Naomi stopped again, her gaze on Ruth. "Which brings up something I have wanted to say to you, to do for you, for quite some time. I have simply been too selfish, wanting to keep you to myself."

"You could never be selfish."

Naomi waved off the compliment, and Ruth said no more. But Naomi wasn't finished. "My daughter, should I not seek rest for you, that it may be well with you?"

"Rest for me?" She knew now what Naomi was planning to say, for only a husband could give rest and security to a widow—the kind of rest a woman wanted, needed.

"Yes," Naomi said, extending a hand toward Ruth. "You have gleaned now among the young women in Boaz's field for many weeks."

Ruth nodded, her heart skipping a beat as Boaz's image came into her thoughts.

"Is not Boaz our relative?"

Ruth nodded again, her gaze holding Naomi's.

"He is a redeemer, my daughter. He can purchase Elimelech's land and take you as his wife and raise up a son for Mahlon. He can redeem us from poverty and despair."

Ruth heard the urgency in Naomi's voice, saw the sheen of tears in the woman's eyes. Naomi needed her to do this, to allow herself to be part of this redeeming. Just as Hava had needed Hamul to save her, Naomi needed Ruth to save her son's heritage in Israel.

And Ruth would gain a husband in Boaz in the process, a thought that caused her pulse to quicken and the spindle to slowly cease turning.

Naomi continued, interrupting her wild thoughts. "Boaz is winnowing barley tonight at the threshing floor. I want you to wash and anoint yourself, and put on your cloak and go down to the threshing floor, but do not make yourself known to him until he has finished eating and drinking. When he lies down, observe that place. Then go and uncover his feet and lie down, and he will tell you what to do."

"You wish for me to ask him to marry me," she said softly, holding Naomi's gaze.

"Yes." Naomi smiled. "It is a good plan."

"You have given this much thought."

"An old woman has little to do but think."

Ruth chuckled despite her pounding heart. "All that you say I will do."

36

Ruth removed her better robe from a peg on the wall and pulled it over her freshly washed body. The perfumed ointment sat in a small clay jar on a low table. She lifted it, opened the jar, and touched the perfume to her neck, behind her ears, and to her wrists. The scent wafted upward, a pleasing aroma. She inhaled and smiled. How good it felt to be clean.

She capped the jar with a rag plug and left the room where she and Naomi slept, then met Naomi in the larger sitting room. "I am ready," she said, though her hands trembled the slightest bit at what she was about to do. What if Boaz refused her? Her heart tripped at the thought, for she had met no other man as kind in Bethlehem.

"You are beautiful, my daughter." Naomi stepped closer, looking her up and down, at last taking her face in her hands. "The man will surely be taken with you. You wait and see."

Ruth nodded. "I hope so." She hoped so for Naomi's sake, so at least the words were partially true. She glanced through the window at the darkening sky. Would she make it through Bethlehem's streets in peace? A shudder worked through her. "I should go."

Naomi nodded. "Do not be afraid, my daughter. The Lord will be with you. Did He not protect you every moment until now?"

Ruth looked at Naomi, held her gaze. "Yes, He has." And suddenly, she realized the truth of her statement. Adonai had led her to Boaz's fields, where she was safe. The man who lived along the path she took had protected her from those rowdy youths. Could Naomi's God not be trusted with this as well? If she was going to trust Him as Naomi did, must she not trust Him with all?

"Then go in peace," Naomi said, interrupting her thoughts. She touched Ruth's shoulder, gently pushing her toward the door.

Ruth forced her feet forward, took a deep breath, and left the courtyard. She glanced back to wave only once, then hurried through the darkened streets, keeping to the shadows nearest the houses aglow with welcoming light. For the slightest moment she wished for a companion for protection, but she could not give in to her fears or deny that the Lord could be trusted.

But He could be. Couldn't He?

A thousand thoughts filled her mind as she walked quickly toward the gates, then the threshing floor outside the city. She carried no lamp, but the moon was high and bright enough to guide her way. She glanced up at it as the gates grew smaller in the distance.

Oh God, who made the moon and stars, watch over me this night. I trust You. I want to trust You more, but I fear

. . . I have feared much in my lifetime, ever since my father died and Te'oma turned so scheming and violent. Turn my fear into faith, oh Adonai Elohim. Please let me, Your foreign servant, be pleasing in Your sight.

She wondered at the strength of the prayer, so needy, so desperate, coming from the depths of her heart. *Your people shall be my people, and your God my God.* She had vowed it to Naomi the day they left Moab, and the words echoed in her memory, melding with this prayer for the ability to trust. How else was Naomi's God to become hers if she did not trust Him? She had never trusted Chemosh, for she hated his festivals, his demands. But the God of Israel was not like Chemosh. Men like Boaz who trusted in Him were kinder, nobler men than any she had known before.

Surely Boaz would accept her proposal. Surely he would.

She paused, her heart racing with the impact of what she was about to do. To propose marriage to a man? Unheard of even in Moab. And yet here she stood in the shade of a tree, looking down on the wide threshing floor, about to do just that.

What if he didn't accept her? What if he exposed her to all?

She swallowed her fear, reminded herself to trust, and slowly made her way down the hill.

Boaz watched from the sidelines as Ezra, Hamul, and even Melek laughed with the men around them and joined in a song of harvest yield. The winnowing was at last completed, and one glance at the piles of barley made Boaz feel a sense of profound relief. The people would not go hungry this year.

"God has blessed us, would you not agree, my lord?" Ezra, huffing and sweating, walked to Boaz's side and drank water from one of the clay urns that lined the threshing floor. "The famine is at last behind us."

Boaz offered his friend an obligatory smile. "Yes," he said, realizing that despite his losses, he did have much for which to give thanks.

"Praise be to Adonai," Ezra shouted, and the men in the group did the same.

More laughter and singing ensued, and Boaz felt the enthusiasm of the men nudging him. He should give himself over to it, lose himself in the merriment, but grief had taken root these past months, and even now he struggled to shake free of it. *Why, Adonai?* The constant question would not leave, even when he lost himself in work and closed his eyes in sleep. Even when he pondered his slight attraction to the Moabitess.

He stepped away, frustrated with himself for not being able to rise above his need to blame himself—and the Almighty—for not stopping Adi's fall. His stomach churned as he moved toward the place where he would sleep. He had to stop thinking this way. God *had* been good to them at last. Why couldn't he cling to that truth?

He glanced heavenward at the multitude of stars. *Help me.* How small he was in comparison to the One who had stretched out the heavens, who had called the stars by name. Surely Adi was in His presence with their lost children—at peace. He had always believed that when all the suffering was over, he would still live to see God.

Even Naomi seemed to believe it—at least she seemed more at peace than she had when she first entered Bethlehem after all those years away. Surely her losses compared to his. And yet his heart ached so.

Why, Adonai? Help me to see.

His gaze swept the heavens, and he could not stifle a yawn. The work had been backbreaking, and he could feel the twinges in his body from the extra exertion. He needed sleep, not disturbing thoughts.

Help me, Adonai. It is so impossible to understand why . . .

He glanced across the heavens again, then looked about the threshing floor. Movement—was it movement?—caught his eye near his sleeping area. Probably just one of his men. He squinted, but nothing moved now. Exhaustion was playing tricks with his thinking. Exhaustion and grief.

I can't live this way anymore, Adonai. Forgive my anger, if You will. Cleanse me of the bitterness I'm holding against You.

The prayer surprised him, but as he stumbled to the end of the grain heap and rolled out the mat he had waiting in the corner, he felt a strange peace settle around him. Surely Adonai had heard his prayer. He glanced once more at the blinking stars. Awe filled him. Adi *was* at peace, and for the first time in months, he felt the same. Laying his cloak over himself as a covering, he closed his eyes.

Ruth stood in the shadows, listened to the men laugh and sing. Her heart lifted with the sound as she searched and at last found Boaz sitting with Ezra. Her heart beat hard within her chest, and she had to tell herself to pause, to slow her breathing. It would do no good to lie down near the man with her breath coming fast as though she'd run a

great distance. No. She must be calm. Do exactly as Naomi
had instructed.

Oh Adonai, give me courage and strength. Strength because never had she felt her knees weaken so quickly with
just one glance at the man. She watched, willing her thoughts
to take in the moment, to see what most women never saw,
for women did not come to the threshing floor when the
men were winnowing. At least not the kind of women who
wanted to marry a respectable man like Boaz.

Laughter drew her thoughts to the men again, and her
gaze caught Boaz rising from his seat. He stood staring at the
heavens, and she nearly fled when she moved and thought he'd
seen her. Her breath came fast again. *Stay still.* She watched,
waiting, but he did not pursue the movement. He must have
assumed she was one of his men, for a few moments later
he half stumbled—probably from the merriment of the fruit
of the vine—to a mat he laid out near the pile of barley. He
lowered himself to the ground, pulled his cloak to his neck,
and rested his head on some of the grain.

Voices of the other men slowly died away, until the only
sounds were that of crickets and the distant hoot of an owl.
Winged creatures took to the trees, and the night sky and
the moon glowed brighter as she waited.

Time slowed, yet too soon she realized the only sound
besides the insects was that of snoring men. Carefully, she
made her way down the incline toward the large stone floor
and sought the place where Boaz had taken his rest. She stood
over him for the briefest moment, making sure she had seen
correctly, then uncovered his feet and lay down.

She listened to his steady breaths, knowing sleep would
not come to her this night. Breath barely came and she dared

not move, but how would he see her when he awoke, with the moon now hidden by clouds? But surely he would sleep until morning.

She held back a sigh, wishing sleep would come, yet . . . what if she startled him awake? What would she do if he shouted at her and woke the sleeping men?

She waited, aware of his feet so close to her head. She slowly lifted the edge of his cloak to barely cover her shoulder, and she could not help a slight shiver that worked through her from a mixture of nerves and the cool night air.

Then her worst fear was realized—he jerked all of a sudden and turned over. She scooted aside to avoid him kicking her. He sat up, staring. Their gazes held, but in the dark she could barely see the outline of his face. Did he know who she was?

"You are a woman! Who are you?" he said, his voice a low hiss.

"I am Ruth, your servant." Heart pounding, she leaned closer, repeating Naomi's words. "Spread your wings over your servant, for you are a redeemer."

Silence followed her remark. Had he heard her? But of course he had, for her eyes had adjusted to the dark enough to see the furrowed brow and the way he rubbed a hand over his face, as though he was trying to clear his head.

"A redeemer?" he said, as though making sure he had heard her correctly. "I should have realized sooner." His soft smile allowed her to release the breath she had been holding too long. "May you be blessed by the Lord, my daughter. You have made this last kindness greater than the first in that you have not gone after young men, whether poor or rich." He sat up, leaning closer, and glanced about as though fearful of waking the other men. "And now, my daughter, do not fear," he said, his voice hushed. "I will do for you all that you ask, for all my fellow townsmen know that you are a worthy woman." He paused a moment, met her gaze, his own wistful. Was he thinking of the wife he'd lost? Was he truly glad that this duty fell to him?

"Thank you, my lord." She looked at him. "There is Elimelech's land at stake in the redemption. Naomi thought you should know." She waited, her breath holding tight within her again.

He seemed to ponder her words, and she watched him stroke his beard as he had done on other occasions. "It is true that I am a redeemer," he said at last, his gaze suddenly tender. "Yet there is a redeemer nearer than I."

The news fell like a heavy stone to her middle. She had come to hope . . . Why had she hoped?

"He is Elimelech's brother, while I am only a cousin. But do not fear. Remain tonight, and in the morning, if he will redeem you, good—let him do it. But if he is not willing to, then as the Lord lives, I will redeem you. Now, lie down until the morning."

His tone was kind, but the words dealt a blow she had not expected. He waited a moment, looking at her, then lay down as he was. She lay at his feet again, thoughts whirling. By his uneven breathing she doubted he slept either, but they both remained as still as possible.

At last the pale light of predawn crested the eastern ridge, and the threshing floor was bathed in shadows—still too dark to recognize each other. She rose to leave, but his words halted her.

"Let it not be known that a woman came to the threshing floor."

"I will tell no one," she whispered.

He stood. "Bring the garment you are wearing and hold it out."

She pulled the scarf from her head and held the ends like a sack, while he bent to the heap of barley and counted out six measures. She tied the ends into knots, and Boaz helped rest the sack on her head.

"Thank you, my lord," she whispered.

He nodded, and she slipped away back toward the city.

37

Boaz watched Ruth until she disappeared from view. Darkness still shrouded the threshing floor. He stood still, his head tilted, listening. Hearing little movement, just the steady snores of the men, he wiped sweat from his brow. Felt his pulse quicken.

To find a woman—and Ruth, no less!—at his feet in the middle of the night had sent his heart racing so hard he had not slept. He sensed she did not sleep either. Such boldness! Such courage it had taken on her part to enter a man's domain and request marriage.

The thought moved through him with a mixture of dread and awe. He had promised himself he would not marry another. Adi had been his only beloved for so long . . . *Oh Adonai, should I do this?* Was it not showing disloyalty to Adi?

But Ruth . . . hadn't she captured his attention from the moment he caught sight of her in his fields? Her beauty was darker than Adi's, but her grace, her humility, were daily reminders of all Adi had embodied. How was it possible he had found these qualities in a foreign woman?

And now in the dark of night with this vulnerable woman at his feet, he had promised marriage! What was he thinking? Clearly he was not thinking at all, yet he could not imagine Ruth under Melek's roof. Surely if anyone should redeem her, he himself was the logical choice.

Melek had done nothing to redeem Naomi from her poverty from the moment of her return. But now, with the promise of property, the man could find the prospect suitably appealing.

The thought troubled him, reminding him again how much Naomi and Ruth had both lost. Ruth knew sorrow. She would understand about Adi as he understood about Mahlon. Had Adonai saved her for this moment, to bring her to him and fill his lonely house with laughter once more?

He shook himself, pushing the hopes aside. Until he confronted Melek with what was rightfully his first choice, there would be no wedding feast or wife in his house.

Ruth rested one hand on the grain sack atop her head and hurried through the dark streets and through the side door of Bethlehem's larger gates, staying to the shadows as dawn grew brighter in the eastern sky. Neighboring women were just beginning to carry their jugs to the well, while in the distance Ruth could hear the braying of donkeys and the steady turn of the grindstone.

Her heart skipped with every normal sound, heightened in her awareness of *him*. Of what he would say and do today. Of the way he had looked at her.

There is a redeemer nearer than I. Elimelech's brother could only be . . . Melek? She nearly stumbled at the thought of marrying that man. *Oh Adonai, please, no.*

She had seen little to admire in Melek, and he already had three wives. She would mean nothing to him. Just one of many and another mouth to feed, another person to work in his household. Would he expect her to glean in his fields?

A shiver worked through her, and she struggled with the weight of that thought. When she had left Boaz, she could not move quickly enough to keep pace with her pounding heart. But now . . . now she wanted to crumble to the dust and sit in mourning. Why had she ever agreed to this?

If she had known . . . but didn't she know?

Naomi surely knew.

Dawn splayed its pink and yellow fingers to dispel the last vestiges of gray, and Ruth hurried on again. She needed answers. Perhaps Naomi would give them.

She turned onto the lane to Naomi's home and saw her mother-in-law waiting in the courtyard. Naomi rushed toward her and helped her lower the bundle to the stones. She straightened and took Ruth's hand, pulling her into the house.

"How did you fare, my daughter?" Naomi's words were as rushed as Ruth's breath. Had the woman waited all night for the answer? One look into her shadowed eyes and she knew. Naomi had rested little more than Ruth had.

"He told me that there is another redeemer closer than he." She held Naomi's gaze. "Is that redeemer Melek?"

Naomi nodded, her mouth pinched in a slight scowl. "Yes. Elimelech's brother has the first right of redemption."

"Why did you not tell me this?" Ruth could not keep the

worry from her tone. She did not want to marry Melek, but now what choice did she have?

"Do not fear, my daughter. I have seen for some time now the way Boaz looks at you. He will find a way. We must be patient." Naomi patted Ruth's hand as if she had not a care in the world, though by her furrowed brow, Ruth wondered.

"I do not wish to wed Melek," she said softly, her gaze gentle on Naomi's face. "But I will do as you ask." She would do anything for Naomi, to give her a future, a hope.

Naomi touched Ruth's cheek. "Trust, my daughter. Now tell me, what else did Boaz say?"

Ruth drew a breath and nodded. Trust. How simple a word, yet how hard a concept. But she would not let her mother-in-law see her worry any further.

"He gave me these six measures of barley," she said, pointing to the courtyard where they had laid the sack, "for he said to me, 'You must not go back empty-handed to your mother-in-law.'"

Naomi's smile widened, all doubt swept from her lined face. "Wait, my daughter, until you learn how the matter turns out, for he will not rest but will settle the matter today."

Ruth said nothing. Waiting with little to do after a sleepless night would not be easy.

The eastern sky grew brighter with each step as Boaz walked up the hill from the threshing floor and headed toward Bethlehem's gates. He glanced behind him. He could confront Melek here, but no. The proper way was to gather ten elders and have witnesses to the transaction. Otherwise,

Melek could come back and claim he was defrauded. Boaz would not start a marriage that way.

Marriage. Was he ready to let Adi's memories fade enough to make new ones with Ruth? The peace of the night before fell upon him once again. He tested it, searching for his past anger, but found it surprisingly gone. How was that possible?

He lifted his head, saw the sun rising in full brilliance. *May Your will be done.* The prayer left his heart with a sense of rightness. And yet a hint of anxiety remained. What if Melek claimed Ruth for himself?

Please, Adonai . . . No, he would not beg for something that might not be in the Almighty's will. He would wait. Though his pounding heart betrayed the desire to do just that.

Ruth paced the sitting room, twirling the spindle and distaff. The work gave her hands something to occupy them, but her mind would not rest. Why had she come to this land? And why was that question one that still troubled her?

Images of her mother and sister merged with those of Te'oma and Governor Aali. Faces blurred as she thought of Orpah, her lost son. What was her friend doing now? Had she married again?

An ache for the familiar filled her, even as she glimpsed Naomi sitting in the courtyard talking with a neighbor over the stone wall that separated their homes. She was glad Naomi had her life here again. The woman had never felt at home in Moab even after more than eleven years. Though they had tried to observe the Sabbath in the early years of her marriage to Mahlon, in the few years before the men died, the sisters-in-law had stopped caring for the strict adherence to the law and had often gone into the city to purchase things while the men checked on the fields, something Naomi had begged them not to do.

A sigh escaped. How easily her husband had fallen into the grasp of her people and their ways, leaving the teachings of his childhood behind as though they were nothing. What had he possibly found so fascinating about Moab, about Dibon and its violence and sensuality and greed and more?

How many festivals had Naomi missed here in Bethlehem, ones that brought joy instead of sorrow? How Ruth longed to experience the Feast of Weeks, when everyone gathered to offer new grain of the summer wheat harvest to the Lord and rejoice in His provision. Naomi had called it a festival of trust, for it was a time when Israel acknowledged that true provisions came from God alone, not from what their hands could produce on their own. God sent the rain on both those who followed His ways and those who didn't because He loved all that He had created. But Ruth knew too well that not everyone accepted harvest bounty as a gift from God's hand.

She shuddered, weary from a sleepless night yet restless with the waiting. Oh to celebrate the next feast as one who belonged to Israel, a foreigner grafted into the tribe of Judah, walking at Boaz's side.

But with that thought came nagging doubt. She bit her lip. She must stop this worrying! She would know today, Naomi had said. Boaz would not rest until he had an answer for her.

Her pacing grew tiresome in the small space, so she walked through the courtyard and climbed the steps to the roof. Naomi glanced her way and smiled her assurance, but Ruth only nodded. How pinched her face must seem to those look-

290

ing on. How hard it was to trust in Naomi's God . . . *No—my God*. Hadn't she made the vow to worship Adonai Elohim as her God the moment they left Moab? When she had promised Naomi that her God would be Ruth's God as well?

My God.

She reached the top of the steps and glanced toward the city gates. Too far to see anything except the outline of the gates and the walls and people milling below. She walked to the parapet. The spindle slowed and spun to a stop as she searched for his face.

But he was too far away to see. Had he done as he said he would? Was he even now speaking to Melek?

She drew a breath. Let it out. Another.

Do not fear, my daughter.

Trust. She glanced heavenward. *It's hard to trust what I cannot see.*

But in the admission, she felt certain peace wash over her. Was that not what trust meant? To believe with the eyes of the soul, even if the eyes of the body could not see?

She allowed her tense shoulders to relax. She had come with Naomi seeking something else, something better, knowing . . . yes, knowing that Naomi's God was greater than Chemosh.

And hadn't He provided for them through men who obeyed His law? What had she to fear?

Melek's face came into her mind's eye, and for the briefest moment she thought she might feel sick. But she would not allow it. No. If God sent her to live in that man's home, she would find a way to see it as good. For if Naomi's God was as good as her mother-in-law believed, despite all of their losses, she would be thankful—if not for her sake, for Naomi's.

There was a small amount of comfort in that thought.

38

Boaz walked from one end of the gated room to another. Windows and a wide-open door allowed for passersby to see easily into the room where the elders met, and the townspeople could gather to witness transactions happening within. Boaz had chosen this room rather than the more enclosed one closer to the roof meant for private meetings, so he could easily see Melek the moment he entered Bethlehem's gates.

But the sun had already risen halfway in the sky and still the man had not appeared. Did he still sleep at the threshing floor? But that was ridiculous. He undoubtedly saw to his barley, then went home to wash and change his clothes. It could be hours before he showed himself.

Boaz sat down. Glanced at the group of elders who mingled about just outside the room, waiting as he had asked.

One smiled his way. "He will come, my son. Do not fear."

"Shall we send someone to get him for you?" another said.

Boaz stroked his beard, longing to bathe and dress and be

able to go to Ruth and tell her the good news. Would it be good news? Suddenly, he wanted nothing more.

"No. No. I will wait a little longer. He will come." *Please, Adonai, let him come.*

"Look, Boaz. There he is." Another elder spoke from just outside the door.

Boaz jumped up and saw that his cousin was within hearing distance. "Melek," he called. Melek stopped and looked at him. "Turn aside, friend." Boaz motioned him inside. "Sit down here."

Melek cast him a skeptical look but did as Boaz asked. Boaz turned and called the ten elders into the room. He breathed a sigh, relieved when they were all seated.

He faced Melek and drew in a deep breath. He had imagined how to approach this cousin for hours, weighing whether to mention the land first or Ruth first. And now the time had come. Would God grant his desire? *May You do according to Your will, Lord.*

Peace settled again as he gathered his courage. He stood so Melek and the elders could hear him. "Naomi, who has come back from the country of Moab, is selling the parcel of land that belonged to our relative Elimelech."

Melek's brows rose at the comment, the light of interest in his eyes.

"I thought I should bring the matter to your attention and suggest that you buy it in the presence of these seated here and in the presence of the elders of my people. If you will redeem it, do so. But if you will not, tell me, so I will know. For no one has the right to do it except you, and I am next in line."

A slow smile filled Melek's square face. "I will redeem it."

Hadn't he expected as much? Of course Melek would want it. Melek had always wanted the land Elimelech had sold to a neighbor. Boaz had never known him to be satisfied with his own portion.

The urge to breathe deeply filled Boaz, but he held it in check. He smiled as though Melek's answer was a good thing and stood in a relaxed pose, hands at his sides.

Melek stood as if to leave, though they had not finished the legal portion of the transaction.

Boaz held up a hand. "There is more."

Melek sat back down, his thin lips turning downward into a frown.

"The day you buy the field from the hand of Naomi, you also acquire Ruth the Moabite, the widow of Mahlon, in order to perpetuate the name of the dead in his inheritance." Boaz watched the man, saw his eyes move as though a thousand thoughts went through his mind. He would be thinking of his estate, of course. If Ruth bore a son, the land he acquired would not become his at all but would belong to Ruth's son. Hamul would gain nothing more than what his father already owned, and another son could jeopardize even that. And though Boaz knew Melek had struggled with Hamul's disrespect of late, he could never deny the boy anything.

Melek studied his feet a moment, then looked steadily into Boaz's eyes. "Then I cannot redeem it because I might endanger my own estate. You redeem it yourself. I cannot do it." He reached for his sandal, as was the custom of law, and handed it to Boaz. "Buy it yourself," he said as Boaz took the sandal from him.

Relief flooded Boaz. He turned to the elders and to the

men and women who had come to stand at the gate, who had heard every word.

"Today you are witnesses that I have bought from Naomi all the property of Elimelech, Chilion, and Mahlon. I have also acquired Ruth the Moabite, Mahlon's widow, as my wife, in order to maintain the name of the dead with his property, so that his name will not disappear from among his family or from his hometown. Today you are witnesses!"

The elders and the crowd spoke as one. "We are witnesses."

A moment later, one of the elders stood and led the people in the blessing given at the weddings in Israel. "May the Lord make the woman who is coming into your house like Rachel and Leah, who together built up the house of Israel. May you act worthily in Ephrathah and be renowned in Bethlehem, and may your house be like the house of Perez, whom Tamar bore to Judah, because of the offspring that the Lord will give you by this young woman."

The words were a reminder to Boaz of the same blessing they had given to him and Adi so many years ago. He swallowed hard, fighting myriad emotions he could barely identify. He was going to wed again. A woman would live under his roof and, God willing, bear him a son to carry on Mahlon's inheritance. So be it.

Ruth stood at the parapet, heard Naomi's footsteps coming slowly up the ladder to the roof, and then felt her presence at her side. She glanced at her mother-in-law, saw the lines across her brow. So she was worried, despite her assurances.

"Do you think this day will ever end?" Ruth blew out a

breath, the spindle and distaff motionless in her hands. Her shoulders sagged, exhaustion taking its toll.

"We will know soon, my daughter." Naomi pointed toward the gate. "See the crowd that has gathered? So many! The transaction, the decision, is in process, and soon the outcome will be heard in the streets."

Ruth felt her stomach dip. "I had thought . . . that is, I had expected Boaz would come and tell us himself." She held Naomi's gaze. "I didn't expect to hear of my fate from the gossips."

Naomi touched Ruth's arm and drew her away from the parapet. "Boaz will come to tell us as soon as he can," she said, her voice suddenly strong, full of confidence. "Though we may hear it from some of the women first." She shrugged. "It is the nature of living in a town, my girl. With such a crowd at the gate, you can be sure that the news will spread. And quickly." She glanced over her shoulder. "We best go downstairs and wait."

Ruth nodded, too weary to argue. She wanted to stay, to watch the crowd disperse, to see if she could see him coming up the road, eager to tell her all.

But what if the news had not gone the way they both hoped? Her nerves frayed, she followed Naomi down the steps into the sitting room. Quiet descended, and Ruth placed the spindle and distaff into a basket that Boaz had given out of his generosity, along with the cushion where she sat.

She closed her eyes. So weary.

Voices in the courtyard moments later jolted her upright. Naomi was already standing, walking toward the court. Ruth shook herself to clear her head.

"What have you heard?" Naomi's voice was clear through

the open door. Ruth stood slowly and made her way to the threshold, certain she would need its strength to hold her upright.

"Boaz has acquired the land you are selling and Ruth as his wife!" Neta's voice carried a lilt of joy.

Ruth clung to the threshold, watching Neta hug Naomi.

"Isn't it wonderful? Boaz will marry again!"

"And Melek will not," Naomi said wryly. "I am sure you are not disappointed in that." The women exchanged a knowing smile.

"I am not disappointed by that at all. Three wives bring struggle enough. It is especially hard when the third wife gets the greatest respect all because she bore the son." Derision laced her voice.

Ruth felt immense relief wash through her. Her knees weakened, and she feared the sheer weight of this burden now lifted would topple her. How was it possible to feel weak once a burden was no longer there?

Naomi turned toward her, arms outstretched. Ruth stumbled forward and fell into the older woman's arms. "There, there. See, my daughter? Didn't I tell you God would provide? That Boaz would not rest until the thing was settled?" She patted Ruth's back.

"And now it is," Neta said, coming alongside them. She too touched Ruth's back. "May your union be blessed of Adonai."

Ruth straightened, the realization that Boaz would come for her soon rushing through her. "Will he come for me now? Should I do something to prepare?"

Naomi shook her head. "He may come by to tell us, but the wedding will wait. He has announced his intentions, but wheat harvest is upon us. There is no time for celebration until all of the grain is in."

Ruth breathed a sigh. "There is time then."

"Yes, but very little," Neta said, glancing Naomi's way. "She will need new garments, and there is the betrothal ceremony, which must happen by week's end, harvest or not."

Naomi's eyes lit, but Ruth knew only confusion. "Betrothal? But Mahlon came for me in a week and we were wed. Do you mean the feast that followed?"

Naomi shook her head. "No, no. Neta is right. A betrothal is the legal binding of the two of you together. People come bringing gifts, and there is eating and drinking and celebrating. Then the wedding happens up to a year later."

Ruth's eyes grew wide. "A year?" She had not expected that.

"But Boaz will have no need to wait a year, my daughter. He already has a home and can come for you anytime." Naomi looked again to Neta. "Will you help me prepare this place to receive guests? Perhaps Gilah and Liora and some of the older children can be spared to help us fix the broken bricks and whitewash everything."

Neta nodded, her smile wide. "And don't worry about food. I am certain all of the women you have helped in the past will come to your aid now. You can help me to remember and assign treats to each woman willing to bake them."

The women talked fast, their excitement palpable, and Ruth looked from one to the other, caught up in their joy. When they drew a breath, she spoke quickly. "But I thought the transaction at the gate was all the legality we needed for me to belong to Boaz. Why do we also need a betrothal?"

Naomi lifted her hands as if to say she had no answer.

"Just let it be as it should be, my daughter. Yes, today's transaction bound you to Boaz. But the betrothal is part of our tradition. You wouldn't deny an old woman the pleasure of seeing her daughter truly wed, now would you?" She winked, and Ruth laughed.

"Of course not, Mother." She hugged Naomi. "Just tell me what to do," she said. And while the women continued to plan, Ruth's heart sang.

39

Boaz hurried along Bethlehem's streets, half running, half walking until at last his estate came into view. He slowed his steps, though his racing heart longed to rush into his rooms, change his clothes, and hurry to take Ruth from Naomi's house.

But no. He should at least bathe first. He glanced heavenward. It was only midday. He had plenty of time.

Reuven entered the court, and Boaz sat on a bench while a younger servant removed his sandals to wash his feet. Boaz stayed him with his hand and addressed Reuven. "Have the servants draw a bath for me. I am sweaty and dirty from winnowing all night."

Reuven quickly dispatched the younger servant to do Boaz's bidding. "I take it all went well?" he asked, looking Boaz up and down. "I expected you when Ezra brought the carts full of grain."

Boaz nodded. "I expected the same, but there has been a change in plans." He went on to tell Reuven all that had happened with Ruth and Melek and that Ruth would be coming home to be his wife.

"When?" Reuven rubbed a veined hand over the back of his neck, and his intelligent eyes seemed to be calculating all the things the household would need to do for Ruth's coming.

"I had thought to go get her now." Boaz looked at his servant's raised brow. "After I wash and dress for the occasion, of course."

Reuven cleared his throat. "My lord, do you not think it wise to give the young woman time to prepare as well, time to make new garments and whatever it is a woman does to make herself ready?"

He hadn't thought of that. She had seemed ready enough at the threshing floor. But he pushed that thought aside lest he turn crimson with embarrassment.

"There are traditions to go along with a marriage, my lord—the betrothal, the preparation for the bridegroom, the feast. Surely you recall how it was when you and Adi wed. The servants will need a few weeks at least, and then, of course, you have the wheat harvest to attend." Reuven tilted his head in that knowing way he had. "You won't have a moment to spare until the Feast of Weeks is past."

Boaz sank deeper into the bench, his shoulders sagging. "But I was planning to go to her tonight, to tell her the news . . ." He looked beyond Reuven to the roof and the trees that stood tall beyond the wall.

"Then go to her and tell her. But let the rest of the things come as they should."

"But the meeting at the gate already legally tied us as man and wife." He felt the slightest sense of defensiveness rise within him. He suddenly did not want to wait until the end of the wheat harvest and the feast at Shiloh.

"What better place to celebrate your wedding than on the way back from the Feast of Weeks, my lord?" Reuven's words held annoying logic. "The men could follow you from Shiloh to Ruth's house, and your servants could have a feast waiting here."

It was true that only the men were required to appear before the Lord at Shiloh, but often whole families made a celebration of the days together.

"The women and servants could leave a day early to prepare here, while you could delay with the men for a freewill offering, then come to claim your bride." Reuven spoke in a fatherly tone.

"You make much sense, my friend." Boaz hated to admit it. A sigh escaped. "I will still bathe and dress and go to Naomi's house and see if she agrees with you. If she does, we will wait, as you have suggested. If she does not, I will bring Ruth home at week's end. That will give you time enough to make the house ready."

Reuven dipped his head in a single nod. "Whatever you wish, my lord."

Ruth glanced up at the sound of heavy footsteps in their courtyard. She looked at Naomi, who sat spinning the wool they had purchased into workable thread. At Naomi's nod, Ruth stood, set the ball of yarn she had been untangling into a basket, and went to answer the knock on the door.

"Boaz." His presence made her pause, and she had to tell her suddenly racing heart to still. "Won't you come in?" She opened wide the door and ducked behind it, allowing him to greet Naomi. She drew a breath, then another. Had he come for her so soon? But Naomi had said—

"Naomi," he said, bending low to take her hand. "Don't get up on my account."

"Welcome to our home, my son." She smiled. "Please sit while Ruth draws some water for us."

Ruth hurried to the adjoining room, grateful for the short reprieve. Naomi must have noticed her flushed face and wide eyes. She hurried past the man before he could sit and stopped in the cooking area to retrieve the flask of water keeping cool in a hole in the ground. She pulled two clay cups from the shelf and poured the water. Her hands shook so badly she nearly spilled it. What was wrong with her? She had been less anxious at the threshing floor, which was far more dangerous and bold an action!

She breathed in and out slowly until at last she could manage a smile, then carried the water to Boaz and Naomi. His hand slightly brushed hers as he took the cup from her.

"Thank you." His smile warmed her straight to her toes. She nodded.

"But you did not pour any for yourself."

"I could only carry the two. I will get some now." She hurried from the room before he did something completely outlandish like serve her! She found a chipped cup, one that she could fill at least halfway with water, and then replaced the flask and carried it to the sitting room. She settled in the seat opposite him, nearer Naomi.

"I came," he said, looking directly into her eyes, "to tell you that all is well. Melek has declined his redemption rights, and I have legally declared that I will redeem you and your husband's property." He glanced at Naomi. "To raise up a son to carry on your husband's name."

Naomi beamed, and Ruth nearly laughed at the delight in her eyes. They had done the right thing. And look how well God had answered!

A feeling she had never known before filled her at the sight of him, at the gentle kindness of his words. Was this love?

"I had hoped to take you to my home this night—both of you—to give you a place to live that is fitting for what you deserve." He smiled, his look reminding her of an uncertain boy. "But my servant informed me that there must be a betrothal and a wedding feast, and we have the wheat harvest and the Feast of Weeks upon us."

"This is true," Naomi said, nodding. "And we will need time to prepare new garments for Ruth to bring to your home, new bedding, and a wedding robe if there is enough time to weave it."

"Oh, Mother, I can wear the robe I have." Ruth didn't want to sound disagreeable, but she couldn't imagine asking Naomi to go to so much work on her behalf. Besides, the two of them could never finish in a few weeks, especially if she was out gleaning. "I won't have time after gleaning to do—"

Boaz held up a hand. "You will do no more gleaning." His tone was kind but firm. "My sisters will be happy to help you prepare, and I will provide whatever you need—wool, a new loom, servants—everything that will help you be ready. Harvest should last about three to four weeks. Then we will travel to Shiloh for the festival and return to the wedding feast. Can you be ready in a month?"

Naomi spoke before she could. "We can. But we must hold the betrothal by this week's end."

Boaz nodded, while Ruth's head spun. So much of this was new to her. The customs in Moab were similar in some ways but not all.

"Good. Then it is settled." Boaz rose to leave. "At week's end we will have the betrothal ceremony here. I will send servants to help you prepare the house, the food, everything, and we will plan it the day before the Sabbath."

"But you will be working the fields." Ruth looked at him. He couldn't very well leave the harvest, though she supposed Ezra could handle things in his stead.

"We will stop early that day. The workers will want to attend the betrothal." He smiled and took her hand, pulling her to her feet. "Legally, I could kiss you," he said, bending close to her ear. "But I will wait." He touched her cheek lightly, his look intimate. He wanted her, and in that moment she knew she wanted him like no other.

"Yes," she said, her words a whisper.

He smiled again, then slowly released her and left.

The week came to an end too quickly. "I'm not yet ready, Mother Naomi." Ruth pointed to the loom where she had been weaving a new robe at the insistence of Naomi, with goods provided by Boaz. Even with help from several women, she still had to sew the sleeves and finish the belt.

"You will be ready by this evening, my daughter." Naomi came to the corner where light shone best in the windows, now whitewashed along with the walls and patched in all the places where cracks had been. She bent down to see the work.

"I will summon one of the servant girls to finish for you,

for it is time we take you to the river for your ritual purification." She smiled at Ruth's raised brow.

"I thought we did that before the wedding itself, not the betrothal." So many details still crowded Ruth's mind. Though she had been up before dawn, how could she possibly be ready by early afternoon?

"Both times, my daughter." Naomi went to the cooking area where Boaz's sisters were baking and supervising a household of young women to prepare sweet treats and more food than Ruth had seen in years. Not since her marriage to Mahlon.

Mahlon. His name slipped into her thoughts unbidden. She had not considered him as often as she had those first weeks, not since Boaz had taken the uppermost part of her thoughts. Would she compare marriage to Boaz with what marriage had been with Mahlon? Any son she conceived would be Mahlon's heir, so she could not simply put him out of her mind.

A sigh escaped her as Naomi returned with a middle-aged woman experienced in weaving. "Let me," the woman said to Ruth. "You go now with Naomi and make yourself ready."

Ruth stood reluctantly. She had hoped to complete most of the work herself. She had wanted to present the robe as a gift to Boaz, herself dressed in fine clothing to match the fine robes he was sure to wear. Would he wear the same garments he wore to his first wedding?

The thought skirted the edges of her mind as she followed Naomi into the sleeping chamber to retrieve the linens and fresh tunic and ointments and hyssop branch she would need to fully cleanse herself.

"You understand why we do this, do you not, my daughter?" Naomi glanced at her as they wove through town and out toward a private area of a branch of the Jordan River.

Ruth nodded. "I think so. A bride should make herself ready and not come to her husband with the dirt of the week seeped into her skin."

Naomi walked on in silence a moment before saying anything in response. "In part, that is true. But the real reason for the ritual cleansing is to show the bride's purity. She is to cleanse herself and pray that Adonai cleanses her sins in the process. It is not the same as giving a sin offering to the priests, but it is still an important way to prepare our hearts for what is to come."

What is to come? The words made her pause. What did she expect to come of her marriage to Boaz? Did she expect companionship? Did she hope he would love her as everyone said he'd loved Adi? Would God give them children?

She glanced at Naomi as they reached the river's edge. They were secluded here, and the water was not so deep or swift as to cause her to be whisked downriver toward the Dead Sea.

"Are you ready, my daughter?" Naomi set the things Ruth would need for cleansing on the ground to hold open a wide towel for Ruth's privacy.

"I suppose I will never be more ready than I am now." She removed her clothes and stepped into the cold water, shivering. This was simply a ritual she was expected to perform. To prepare to meet Boaz and formally become bound to him.

But as she dunked her head beneath the flowing waters and scrubbed the dirt from her skin with the hyssop branch, she thought of Moab. Of the men in her life—Te'oma and her father and Mahlon—who had failed her either by living to please themselves or by dying and leaving her. How could she put herself through this again, only to risk another loss?

She dunked a second time, then watched the soap bubbles float past her, taking her dirt with them. Taking her sin as well?

Adonai? Will Boaz accept me as none other has? Will he love me?

The sudden desire to know she was truly loved like she had never been before ached in the pit of her soul. She didn't just want to marry the kinsman redeemer for Naomi's sake. She wanted to marry him for her own. She longed to feel redeemed from all that had come before, from all of her misguided dreams, from everything that made her Moabite, to cling to the God of Israel alone.

Your God shall be my God. Yes. That was what she longed for.

And what she hoped Boaz could show her through true and lasting love—what a man who loved his God could be like.

She rose from the water after the third time down and shook the droplets from her hair, laughter bubbling within her.

"Whatever is so humorous?" Naomi asked, her smile wide. "There is joy in your smile, my girl."

"There is joy in my heart, Mother. And when Boaz comes, I will be ready."

40

Ruth sat in Naomi's sitting room surrounded by ten young virgins—nieces of Naomi's and some of the young daughters of the merchants in the city. Flowers from the field were woven through her veil, and she sat with a sheaf of wheat in her lap. She hid a smile at that last little addition. She had asked one of the men who had come to prepare the room to send to Ezra for the sheaf but not to tell Boaz. It was a promise, and she would grant it to him soon.

Voices of the young girls moved around her, but she did not speak to them, did not know them well enough, and in fact felt a little awkward that virgins were chosen to attend her when she was a widow, not a virgin herself.

"It is the way we do things," Naomi had said. "Never fear, my daughter. Just sit and wait for him."

Ruth glanced up at the crowd forming in the room. Waiting— she was used to that. She had waited all of her life—for her father to return from war, which never happened. For Te'oma to be a truly kind man, which also never happened. For Mahlon to become the husband she thought he would be, but he never did.

She shook her head slightly and closed her eyes. None of her dreams had ever come to the place where she could say she was satisfied with their outcome.

A sigh escaped, and she looked up at the sound of male voices. Boaz's laughter came to her from the courtyard, accompanied by the voices of other men. Was that Ezra? And Melek? She knew so few men in the town it was hard to tell.

Through her veil she glimpsed Naomi coming her way. "He is here, my daughter," she whispered, her voice barely containing her excitement. When had she seen Naomi so jubilant?

Memory failed her, for her mother-in-law had always seemed somber, even when she smiled. Was it due to the fact that they had met in Moab? Naomi was definitely happier in Israel.

As are you, she thought, surprised by the admission. How was it possible that a Moabite felt more at home in this land? But it was true. Their God, her God, had made it so.

The male voices drew closer, and she heard Boaz speak to Naomi. "I have the parchment with the marriage agreement here, my mother," he said without preamble. "If it pleases you, I will read it to you." Of course, Naomi could not read the words. This was something Elimelech would have handled for her if Ruth had been a true daughter.

"I trust you, my son," Naomi said, smiling into his tanned face. He had washed and dressed in his finest robes. The men behind him carried gifts—a wooden chest for her linens, fabric already woven to be sewn into garments, a bag of gold for Naomi to purchase whatever Ruth might need, goblets and a flask of choice wine from Boaz's vineyards. The gifts kept coming until Ruth could not count the number at her feet.

She looked into the face of the man she had already come to love, the man she longed to share her life with, and smiled. "Thank you," she said softly.

He bent close but spoke so all could hear. "Behold, you are consecrated unto me from this day forward." He held out his hand and she placed her smaller one in it. She stood and walked with him to the place where the ketubah sat and watched as he put his seal on the bottom. Naomi then took Elimelech's seal, which she had kept, placed it in the wax, and affixed his seal to the contract as well.

"And now we are bound forever and in truth," Boaz said, looking into her face, smiling into her eyes.

"Yes," she said, longing to speak more but not knowing what to say. A moment later she remembered the sheaf. She lifted it to him and placed it in his hands.

He turned it over and gave her a curious look.

"We will wed after the harvest of wheat is secured." She smiled gently and touched his arm. "The sheaf is a promise between us. When the Feast of Weeks is past and our God has been given the thanks due Him for the harvest, we will be man and wife." She touched the sheaf. "This is of your firstfruits."

His smile lingered as he looked from the sheaf to her. He bent low until she could feel his breath on her face. And then he kissed her cheek with the most tender of kisses, near the edge of her mouth. A chaste kiss, though she could tell by the look he gave her that he wanted so much more.

"Until harvest ends," he said, drawing back, his breath heavy. "It isn't so very long to wait."

"No. Not very long." She touched his cheek, wanting instead to take the turban from his head and touch his beard, his hair, and pull him into her arms. But this was not the time or the place with so many people looking on, waiting for the feasting to begin.

"Soon, beloved." He took her hand and squeezed it, and she knew in that moment she had captured far more than his kindness. She had captured his love, and she could not wait to share it.

Boaz awoke before dawn the day after the Sabbath and dressed quickly before Reuven even had a chance to set out his clothes. He smiled into the bronze mirror, more pleased with himself than he should be for a man who had to be coaxed by the woman herself to get him to wed. Memories of the threshing floor, of Ruth's boldness, washed over him, carrying with them deep gratitude. She was so beautiful. She could have chosen any of the younger men, some of whom had surely shown interest. He'd seen the way they looked at her.

He examined himself more closely, saw the strands of gray lining his temples. He was older than Mahlon had been, and Ruth younger. But she had looked into his eyes without hesitance, with what he could almost interpret as longing. For him?

His heart beat faster at the thought. Soon. She would come to his home and become his wife. His step lightened as he moved from his bedchamber to the main sitting room, where his cook set food before him. He sipped from the freshly drawn water and downed some barley porridge with dates. He paused on the second bite. This porridge had been one Adi had created exactly to his liking, and the cook had followed it ever since.

He set the flatbread down, uncertainty filling him. How could he eat food Adi had created for him only weeks before he would take another wife? Was he doing the right thing?

Doubt assailed him, broken only by the sound of Reuven's footsteps.

"Is something wrong, my lord? I thought you were anxious to get to the fields this morning." The old servant rubbed his beard and probably wished to rub his eyes as well.

Boaz looked at this faithful man and felt a twinge of sadness. Reuven had aged, more than he realized. He should lighten his duties and allow him a place of rest these final years.

"My lord?"

Boaz shook himself. "Wrong, yes. No. That is . . ." He paused again and motioned for Reuven to sit near him. "May I ask you something, Reuven?"

"Anything, my lord. I am here to serve you. And your new wife very soon." His smile lit his eyes, and suddenly Boaz was not certain he should ask the question.

He glanced beyond Reuven a moment, debating, then met the man's gaze. "Am I doing the right thing, Reuven?" he said, lowering his voice, leaning closer. "That is, am I doing a disservice to Adi's memory to marry so soon?"

Reuven shook his head. "You are keeping the law to care for a widow who needs redeeming. That should honor Adi's memory, my lord, not dishonor it."

He nodded, his thoughts too full to speak. He picked up the flatbread instead and finished his meal. He would allow Ruth to make the porridge her way if she wanted to. Together they would carve out a new future.

Ruth and Naomi sat with Gilah and Liora and Neta in Naomi's sitting room, weaving and spinning and sewing the garments Ruth would take with her to the marriage.

"You will need to make blankets and swaddling cloths and clothing for the child when he comes," Gilah said, as though certain such a thing would happen.

"And Boaz is a man of great honor and power in Bethlehem, a prince," Liora added. "You will need tunics and robes and belts and sandals." She blew a puff of air. "So much to be done!"

"And not nearly enough time." Naomi smiled. "But with your help and the money Boaz gave us, we can purchase the items we don't have time to make." She looked at Ruth. "I will take you to the sandal maker's shop tomorrow, and we will see if there are some earrings and jewels. Every bride should wear jewels."

The conversation went on around Ruth while she focused her attention on the robe she had nearly finished stitching. The bone needle went in and out to form the sleeves. The fabric, rich with reds and blues and yellows and a few threads of black, nearly took her breath. A merchant from Syria had carried it with him to market, and Boaz had purchased it the moment he saw it still hanging in the weaver's shop. Could she make it into a suitable wedding robe? he'd asked.

She assured him she could. She couldn't help smiling at the way he had looked at her with such approval in his eyes.

"I think this fabric is perfect for an infant. What do you think, Ruth?" Neta held up the softest length of white wool Ruth had ever seen. She set her sewing aside a moment and walked across the room to touch the piece, hold it to her face.

"It's beautiful and smells wonderful." She handed it reluctantly back to Neta and returned to her duties, but she could not stop the small frown she felt crease her brow. "But what if I am unable to bear a child?"

Her question silenced all conversation in the room, until at last Naomi came and sat beside her. "You have no need to fear such a thing, my daughter. Our God is the God of miracles. You remember the stories I've told you of Sarah and Rebekah."

"And don't forget Rachel!" Gilah said. "Even Adi took years." She clamped her mouth shut at the mention of Boaz's first wife. "But you will not have any of the trouble she had." Her face flushed with the words.

"It's all right. I know women die in childbirth. I know women can be barren." Ruth looked into the faces of these dear women. "I guess we will just trust our God for the outcome." Could she trust Him with this? She had once considered offering Adonai Elohim a sacrifice to procure a child with Mahlon, but that was back before she truly believed in Him. Was it proper to ask for a child of her Creator now?

The women nodded. "Yes. Trust," Gilah said. "And we will all pray and say blessings over you at your wedding. You just wait and see. You will be carrying Boaz's son in no time." She stopped abruptly again and glanced at Naomi. "Forgive me. Mahlon's heir."

Naomi shook her head. "No need to apologize, my friend. The child will bear Boaz's name and carry Mahlon's inheritance. He can be both, can he not?"

The women nodded and laughed, and Ruth breathed deeply in a contented sigh. A child. In ten years with Mahlon she had never experienced even one pregnancy. But now . . . Her cheeks heated. Now she desperately wanted to bear Boaz's son. Pray God that she could.

41

Boaz wiped the sweat from his brow as he passed almond and apricot trees green with fruit and grapevines blooming nearby on the way to the wheat fields. In the many years of drought, these trees and vines had shriveled until there were no apricots or almonds or grapes for refreshing wine.

He glanced heavenward. *Thank You, Adonai. Your grace has blessed our land once again.* He couldn't wait to bring the last of the harvest in and head to Shiloh with his sacrifices and share the moment with Ruth. Though they would not officially be man and wife in the truest sense, they were man and wife in the legal sense, and he would take her and Naomi with him to celebrate the Feast of Weeks. It was one of his favorites.

He looked up to see Ezra walking toward him.

"We are on the last few rows of wheat," Ezra told him, motioning to what remained of the standing grain. "And just in time, for the fiftieth day from Passover is nearly upon us."

"You've been counting the days, my friend?"

Ezra shrugged. "It is a joyous feast, is it not, my lord? And more so this year, I daresay."

"I daresay you are probably right." Boaz laughed, surprising himself at the lightness of his heart. "But yes, it is a harvest of joy this year especially. A reminder after the long drought of new birth, of the seed's resurrection at last from its death when we planted it."

"Resurrection." Ezra said the word with sudden reverence. "Do you think it is only the seeds that die and are reborn to new life?" He held Boaz's gaze, his brow furrowed as if in deep thought.

Boaz looked out at the wheat field where the female servants still gleaned behind his reapers, though Ruth was no longer among them. Those gleanings that had led him to Ruth had begun from such tiny seeds, but every farmer knew that a seed had to die to sprout into sustaining food for life. Were the bodies of men and women like those seeds?

"I mean, we are born and we die. I have never seen a single person in my family or among my friends come back again." Ezra leaned closer. "And in my uncle's case, that's not a bad thing." He smacked his leg and laughed.

Boaz smiled. Ezra was good for him. He kept him from becoming too sober and, in the past, too morose. "I think," he said after a lengthy pause, "that the ancients believed they would see God in their own flesh. How could that happen if our bodies remained only in the grave?"

"So we are celebrating the future of resurrection when we celebrate the Feast of Weeks." It wasn't a question, but by his raised brow, Boaz knew Ezra meant it as one to be answered.

"Like the birth and growth and gathering in of the wheat,

yes." Boaz ran a hand over his beard, the thought comforting. "I'm not sure what it means, my friend, but I suspect our God does, and someday our children's children will understand it better than we do today."

His children. Despite all his past losses, he somehow knew one day his words would prove true.

"Are you ready to go, my daughter?" Naomi stood at the threshold of the bedchamber, her robe tied and her belt fitted with a water skin and a bag of parched grain, ready for the trip to Shiloh.

"Almost. Is he here yet?" Ruth stood, her palms moist from more than the summer's heat. Boaz was coming to take them to the festival, and after it ended she would enter his home as his wife.

Wife. She had said the word so many times it slipped unbidden into her thoughts, and yet her nerves were still frayed with anticipation and . . . and what? Would she make him a good wife? Would he be all that she imagined he would be?

"I hear footsteps and the sound of men speaking. I think he is entering the courtyard. Hurry, my daughter." Naomi left her to welcome the men, while Ruth glanced at her reflection in the bronze mirror Boaz had given her. She was becoming much too vain, worrying what he would think of her appearance.

He seemed to like you well enough in poor rags and with disheveled hair. He would accept her dressed as his sisters suggested, wouldn't he?

She tucked the pouch with her own water flask and grain into her belt and walked out to meet the men.

"There you are," Boaz said, his smile warming her. He offered his hand and she slipped hers into it, comforted by his reassuring squeeze. "The Feast of Weeks is like nothing you would have known in Moab. It is a time of joy and thanksgiving, of harvest, and even a time to remember the giving of the law." He glanced into her eyes, his own bright with an inner glow.

"Are there no sacrifices then?" She met his gaze, hoping he didn't see the worried look in her eyes.

He searched her face, understanding dawning in his gaze. "Yes, we do sacrifice two lambs as part of the feast, which we later share in a communal meal. Two loaves of bread made with yeast are waved by the priests in offering to the Lord."

"And that is all? Just an offering of food?" She gave him a puzzled look.

He studied her a moment. "This is a harvest festival, beloved. Thanksgiving to our God for His provision for us, though if we choose, we can give a freewill offering—an animal sacrifice in gratitude to our God."

"So no child or poor man is offered?" Naomi had assured her, but somehow she needed to hear it from him.

"Never," he said softly. "To offer a human sacrifice to our God would be an abomination to Him." He stroked her palm in another reassuring gesture. "You never have to fear the things here that you feared in Moab, Ruth. Our God is the true God, and He is to be feared and obeyed, but not like the gods of the nations around us. He does not ask our obedience to punish us but to preserve us. He always seeks what is best for those He loves."

Ruth walked with him in silence for several moments, while others from Bethlehem joined the throng and proceeded through the gates. Sheep bleated and donkeys brayed and children ran laughing ahead of their parents. Women chattered and men led carts of grain and other gifts to give at Shiloh to the priests as an offering to Yahweh.

She sidled slightly closer to Boaz, though the action felt rather bold on her part. But legally they were man and wife, and she needed him to hear her above the crowd.

"Does God accept me?" She looked into Boaz's face as she spoke, standing on tiptoe to reach his ear, blushing with the question.

Boaz stopped, catching her when she nearly tripped at his abruptness. He turned her to face him, while Naomi and the others in their group continued past them. He touched her cheek. "How I wish I could reassure you—our God is the one who commands us to love the sojourner because we were sojourners in Egypt. God does not ask us to do for others what He has not already done for us. His steadfast love has been upon us for generations—and that includes you because you have chosen to live among us, to make our God your God."

Tears filled her eyes, and he caught the drops with his thumbs. "So even though I'm a Moabite . . ."

He placed a finger over her lips. "It matters not at all, beloved. You belong to Israel now, a branch grafted into the vine of Abraham, Isaac, and Jacob. Our people are your people."

She laughed amidst tears that would not stop. "As I promised to Naomi not so many months ago."

"And Adonai has heard you." He bent low, his face so close she could smell the scent of the spices he had rubbed into his skin.

"I am glad," she whispered, wishing in that moment, not caring who saw them, that he would kiss her.

As if he could read her very thoughts, he did. The thrill of his touch sent tingles rushing through her, and even when he pulled away, the heady feeling lingered.

Shiloh came into view two days later. Two days of camping with the men and women of Bethlehem and other Israelite cities along the way. The air was jubilant, laughter abundant, and Ruth found herself so caught up in the joy that she wondered for the briefest moment how Mahlon could have preferred Moab's festivals to this.

As they approached the tabernacle on the last day, Ruth looked on in awe at the tent of which Moses himself had commanded the design and construction. The large bronze altar stood just beyond the screen of the gate to the court, taking in her whole vision.

"It's so big," she said to Naomi. Boaz had gone ahead with Ezra and his men to prepare the lambs for sacrifice and to present the bread to the priests.

"Yes. Many lambs have been sacrificed on this altar," Naomi said, her voice uncharacteristically sober. "At least since the time of Moses, and when our people wandered in the wilderness." She glanced at Ruth. "Before the tabernacle, our forefathers Abraham, Isaac, and Jacob built stone altars. There were no priests or golden and bronze utensils." She waved her hand in an arc toward the entire tented complex. "None of this existed before we left Egypt."

Ruth looked out over the grounds. A curtained fence stood sentinel in a large rectangle around a smaller tented enclosure— the tent of meeting where the Ark of the Covenant stood enshrined behind a curtain none of them could see or visit.

Naomi pointed to the very structure. "Only the priests can enter the tabernacle and keep the golden lampstand and incense burning and replace the bread of the presence before the Lord. And only the high priest can enter the Holy of Holies once a year."

Ruth squinted, trying better to see, but the curtain over the tabernacle was made of dark goat's hair, impossible to see through. "What is the Holy of Holies?"

"The place where the Ark of the Lord rests inside the tent of meeting. The high priest enters on the Day of Atonement to offer sacrifices for our sins and his own. It is our most sacred holy day."

Ruth nodded, though understanding still seemed to slip through her grasp. "He does this every year?"

Naomi took Ruth's hand and led her closer to the fence, away from some of the other women. "Yes, my daughter. For we sin against the Lord in ways we don't always realize. None of us can keep every commandment every day every year. We break the laws, especially the one that tells us not to covet what another person possesses."

"If the law is so impossible to keep, then why was it given?" The gods of her people had rules and traditions to keep, but most of them were outward, not so probing as to affect a person's inner thoughts and desires.

"To show us that our God is perfect and we are not. But our God has made a way for us to find peace with Him through the blood of the sacrificial lambs. It is a great mercy, my child, for He could just decide we are not worth forgiving or saving. For that matter, He could have left us as slaves in Egypt."

Ruth looked from Naomi to the bronze altar where the priests had begun to offer sacrifices. Closer to the tabernacle, priests held two large loaves of bread and waved them high overhead. The wave offering Boaz had told her about.

"Are the lambs offered for our sins this time?" Ruth looked at Naomi once more.

Naomi shook her head. "This time they are offered as thanksgiving for all God has done for us—to bless our God—and then we share the meat from the lambs with everyone." She smiled and took Ruth's hand. "And there will be singing and dancing and—oh, you just have to wait and see!"

Ruth looked around at the entire group, grateful all over again that Naomi's God—her Adonai—had called her out to join this people. To rejoice in this festival. To understand one more small piece of the mystery of God's intentions. Of His heart.

42

THREE DAYS LATER

Ruth sat once again in Naomi's sitting room dressed in her finest clothes, her veil wrapping her in secretive quiet. The ten virgins had split into two groups and stood waiting in the courtyard. One group had lit their lamps and stood on either side of the walk leading to the house, while the others waited with torches to touch their wicks the moment Boaz stepped into the light.

Ruth sat surrounded by lamps, the whole house illumined as though this was the place where they would feast, but they were simply waiting. Waiting for the bridegroom to claim his bride.

Her heart fluttered at the thought. She tilted her head, straining to listen, but all she could hear were the sounds of female chatter in the courtyard and the low thrum of voices from the women in the cooking room. Not even Naomi joined her here. She waited alone in her veils and jewels and anticipation, longing to hear his voice, to see a glimpse of him coming up the walk.

"He's coming!" one of the virgins called toward the house.

Through the open door she could see the five other virgins hurry to touch the flame to their wicks to set their lamps aglow, then set the torches back in the stands at the edge of the courtyard.

Male voices and boisterous laughter drew closer, until at last Boaz stood at the threshold. "I have prepared a place for you," he said, stepping into the room. He took her hand and pulled her to stand before him. "Come with me, for it is time."

She smiled, though he could barely see beneath her veil, and clasped his calloused fingers. The women emerged from the cooking room and hurried after them, joining the ten virgins and the men who had accompanied Boaz until they were leading a great crowd through the streets of Bethlehem.

At a bend in the road, Boaz stopped. A young donkey's colt stood tied to a post, draped in colorful linens. Boaz lifted Ruth with ease and set her on the donkey's back, then took the reins and led her forward.

Torches danced and spread dappled light over the stone streets, and people stepped into their courtyards to wave and shout well wishes to the happy couple. Ruth watched it all, her eyes taking it in with wonder. The crowd seemed to grow in size behind them, and when Boaz glanced back to look into her face, his smile melted her insides.

Her heart beat faster when at last Boaz's estate came into sight. She glimpsed servants waiting, and the house was lit with so many torches and lamps that it seemed daytime instead of midnight.

Boaz lifted her from the donkey, and a servant took the animal away while he carried her in his arms to a large tent standing in his courtyard. The scent of his spikenard wafted to her, mingling with the heady feeling of his arms about her. Too soon, he placed her on her feet and took her hand in his. They stood beneath a canopy as a town elder came and stood before them.

"May the Lord make the woman who is coming into your house like Rachel and Leah, who together built up the house of Israel. May you act worthily in Ephrathah and be renowned in Bethlehem, and may your house be like the house of Perez, whom Tamar bore to Judah, because of the offspring that the Lord will give you by this young woman."

A cheer followed the blessing, and Boaz took Ruth in his arms and twirled her in a circle, then wrapped his cloak about her shoulders.

"You are now truly consecrated to me," he said, his voice low, hoarse with emotion.

She nodded, too filled with her own emotion to speak. But she could not stop smiling.

The feasting lasted long into the night, with singers and entertainers and dancers and food and wine flowing in abundance. Women with children had gone home a short time ago, and men lay sprawled on the court, either filled with too much wine or tired from so much feasting.

Boaz approached Ruth where she sat with Naomi in one of the inner rooms, where she had received guests until the crowd had thinned. He knelt before her, looked deeply into her eyes, then took her hand. "It's time, beloved."

Naomi stood to leave, but Boaz stayed her with a look. "Mother Naomi, you will stay in the room I have prepared for you. As I indicated from the beginning, you will live with us now." He smiled at Naomi's pleased expression.

"Thank you, my son." She nodded at them both as a servant appeared and led her down a winding hall.

"Your home is large," Ruth said, her palm growing moist beneath the warmth of his hand. "Thank you for doing that for her. I am most grateful."

He pulled her to her feet. "There was never any question." He led her quietly down a different hall to a large bedchamber, obviously masculine. Had he removed all signs of Adi's former presence? Or would she sleep apart from him in rooms of her own?

He closed the door and came to stand before her. "This room needs your feminine touch, my love." He undid the clasp that held her veil and let it fall to her feet, then one by one removed the combs from her dark, flowing hair. A sigh escaped him. "How long I have wanted to see the full length of this." He sifted several strands through his fingers, then let them fall to her waist as he touched her face. "You are most beautiful." He smoothed the short hairs that clung to her temples.

"Thank you, my lord." She felt her breath hitch as he undid the belt at her waist and took the artfully decorated robe from her shoulders. She stood waiting, exhaustion and excitement mingling within her.

He bent closer. His lips skimmed hers ever so slightly as his arms came around her, pulling her close until she felt the beat of his heart against her chest. His kiss deepened, slowly at first, as if uncertain. Did he think of his first wife while he held her? But she shoved the thought aside as his kiss captured her with such hunger it took her breath.

She wrapped both arms about his neck, pulled the turban from his head, and returned the kiss, running her fingers through his hair. He laughed as she fumbled with his robe, his hands resting on hers, causing her to still.

"Let me."

She blushed at the way he held her with a look, but a moment later he swooped her into his arms and carried her to the bed that seemed to occupy one whole side of the room.

"Now you are truly my bride," he whispered, his kiss trailing her ear, her cheeks, her lips.

"And you are my kinsman redeemer." She smiled as she spoke, but the look he gave her made her pause, as though he had forgotten the initial reason they had come to this place. "And beloved husband," she added to reassure him. "I have always wanted it so." She drew closer, kissing him.

His joyous chuckle filled the room, and his love carried her on eagle's wings.

FIVE MONTHS LATER

Naomi sat in a corner of Boaz's plush sitting room, sorting threads of various colors for Ruth to weave into a new robe for Boaz. They were working in secret as best they could when he left the house for the fields. But more than once he had returned home to surprise them, and they had either scrambled to hide the work or acted as though Ruth was planning to sell her weaving to the merchants. Boaz had merely nodded as though he was only half listening.

"Do you think he suspects?" Ruth asked, looking up from the loom. "I need the black thread next," she added, smiling. "This will be the finest robe I've ever made." She glanced at Naomi, her cheeks coloring as though she thought she had spoken out of turn. "That is, it is the best I can do."

"There is no reason not to be proud of your work, my daughter. I have never seen Boaz wear anything finer than what you are weaving now." Naomi leaned into the cushion and watched Ruth work for a moment. Boaz and Ruth had been wed for five months now, and still Ruth said nothing about a babe. Was it possible her daughter-in-law was barren after all?

Oh Adonai, have mercy.

How often she had prayed the prayer, and yet she could not deny that God was good. Had He not seen her through sorrow upon sorrow? Surely He would bless Boaz and Ruth's union.

"Is something wrong, Mother?" Ruth glanced up again from the work.

Naomi shook herself and returned to sorting the threads. "No, no. Nothing is wrong."

Ruth paused until Naomi looked at her. "Something *is* wrong or you would not look at me so." She smiled. "Tell me, please."

"It is just an old woman feeling foolish, that is all." How could Naomi ask the girl such a question? If Ruth was pregnant, she would have told her.

"Feeling foolish about what?" Ruth had a way of prodding her that could sometimes be rather annoying. But Naomi smiled at her just the same.

"I had hoped . . . that is . . . it has been five months, and I wondered . . ." She stopped, feeling like the words were coming out all wrong. How was it possible that sometimes she could speak well and other times she twisted everything upside down?

Ruth laughed. "You are wondering if God has yet blessed us with a child."

Naomi nodded and looked away, embarrassed at her own nosiness. "Forgive me. I know you will tell me when the time is right."

"You will be the first to know . . . even before Boaz."

Naomi lifted her head and met Ruth's suddenly sober gaze. They studied each other in silence.

"I do not know for sure," Ruth said softly. "It has only been a month and I will need another to confirm, so you must not tell him. He will only worry." A smile touched the corners of her mouth with the secret of knowing, and Naomi did not miss the added glow in her dark eyes.

"I will tell no one," she said, returning to her threads. "But as soon as you finish that robe for Boaz, you must start making more cloths and coverings for the babe." She glanced up and gave Ruth a conspiratorial wink. Both of them looked about the room, and Naomi breathed a relieved sigh to find it empty of servants. She must take more care when to speak of these things.

Ruth was right. Boaz would worry. He had lost too many children. He would fear the same with Ruth no matter how much the circumstances differed, no matter how often others reassured him. For who but God knew the outcome of such things?

Please, have mercy, Adonai.

Naomi sensed she would be repeating the prayer for many months to come.

HESHVAN (OCTOBER)

A week passed with a heightened awareness between Naomi and Ruth, and Ruth sensed a closeness with her mother-in-law she had not known before. They walked about Boaz's estate shortly after he left for the fields.

"A few more weeks and we should know," Ruth said when they had passed the gardens and walked beneath the trees lining the walls that protected Bethlehem from invaders. "Do you think two months is enough time? Should I wait three or four before I tell him?"

She reached for Naomi's arm and tucked it beneath hers. The uneven roots protruding from the ground could make a person unsteady, though she would never suggest to Naomi that she could not handle such terrain. She stopped when they reached the end of Boaz's estate and met Naomi's gaze.

"It is a good question, my daughter. I do not know a good answer for you, though. The man has lost so much . . ." She looked beyond her, and Ruth sensed memories had taken her back to all that she had also lost. At last Naomi looked her way again. "I think you should tell him early. He will want to know, and if he fears, we will encourage him. Is not God in this? We will trust Him that all will be well."

A noise coming from the front of the house, a servant calling Naomi's name, stopped Ruth's reply. The servant traveled the length of the house.

"I'm here," Naomi called as the two of them walked toward the inner courtyard.

The servant hurried to a stop and caught his breath. "Melek's wife Neta begs that you come. His grandchild is even now about to be born."

Ruth and Naomi exchanged a glance. "Hava?"

The servant nodded. "Melek has sent a donkey. Neta said for you to hurry."

"I will go with you," Ruth said, following quickly behind.

Naomi shook her head. "You must not run, my daughter. Ride or walk, but if you come, come slowly."

Ruth met her gaze and nodded, knowing. Naomi accepted Ruth's nod, climbed onto the donkey, and let Melek's servant lead her away.

43

Boaz stood at the edge of his fields, wondering where the year had gone. How was it possible that only a few months ago Ruth had gleaned among the harvesters, and now his men walked among the plowed ground, bags tied to their waists, tossing grain among the furrows all over again to await another harvest? He glanced heavenward. The skies spoke heavily of coming rain, and Boaz could smell it on the wind. The winter rains would feed the seed, and the barley and wheat would grow and flourish, another fulfillment of God's provision, His promise.

He walked on, examining each row, catching Ezra's eye across the field. The man nodded his acknowledgment that all was well. Good. The barley would soon be in and the wheat would follow. He smiled. Perhaps by the time the next harvest came around, Ruth might have an announcement of firstfruits of her own.

Would she? The thought both stirred and troubled him. They had been together for five months and she had said nothing. Perhaps she would be as Adi had been and wait years. Hadn't she been wed to Mahlon for ten with no child? What if she were unable to bear?

He walked on, half frustrated with himself for actually thinking such a thing might be good. For if the truth were known, if he could admit it to her, he feared losing her, had come to love her, truly love her. If he lost her . . .

He let the thought die away, vaguely aware of someone shouting in the distance. He turned and saw a man running toward him. His heart jumped in his chest. Had something happened to her? To Naomi?

He hurried to meet the runner and told his breathing to slow as he recognized Hamul. But at the look of terror in his eyes, Boaz's heart picked up its pace again.

"Hamul. What is it?" He reached the young man's side and placed one arm about him. "Tell me."

"Hava." Hamul bent, placed both hands on his knees. "She is in labor with our child." He looked up at Boaz, his eyes showing stark terror. "What if something happens to her?"

Boaz squeezed Hamul's shoulder, and together they began walking the length of his fields. "This is not a time for a man to go anywhere near the birthing chamber, my son." Though Hamul was his cousin, their age difference made the familiar endearment seem right. "You don't need to hear Hava's cries, for you do not know what she is truly feeling. It will only strike fear in you, as I can see it already has."

"But Father is there. He thinks me a coward to flee."

Boaz clenched his jaw. Melek had a thing or two to learn in dealing with his son. But how did he know whether he would do any better as a father? Melek had been doting at first, then he grew so strict the boy could do little. It was no wonder Hamul had turned to making his own decisions where Hava was concerned.

"I can assure you, your father did not attend the births of you or your sisters. And you can be sure he is at the city gate or somewhere far enough from Hava's chambers to drown out her screams." He patted Hamul's back. "When did they send you from her side?"

He laughed at the chagrined look in Hamul's eyes. "How did you know they sent me away?" He gnawed his lower lip.

Boaz smiled. "Because they did the same to me. Women don't like men hovering." He led them along the rest of the rows where the workers had already tossed the grain into the furrows and covered the ground with the tap of a foot. "Now come. Let's both get our minds on the new crop and we'll check on the women later."

Hamul nodded, though by the look he gave Boaz he wasn't convinced that Boaz knew what he was talking about.

"One more push, Hava. I can see the full head of hair, and the shoulders are almost through." Naomi bent her knees before Hava while Neta rubbed the girl's shoulders where she sat on the birthing stool.

Ruth stood to the side, waiting with heated water, while Melek's other wives busied themselves with the bloodied sheets and keeping the room warm. Too warm for Ruth's sake. She wiped sweat from her brow, feeling almost faint. And sick. The scents of sweat and blood and too many women in the same room nearly overwhelmed her.

Hava groaned and pushed, and at last the baby's cry filled the room. Women laughed and cried, "It's a girl!" And Hava wept. But Ruth clung to the table where the bowl of water stood warming and felt the room spinning.

"I don't feel so good." She wondered if her words could be heard above the din, and she struggled to keep herself standing.

Moments later she faintly heard someone shout, "She's going down!" And the blackness beckoned as her knees crumpled beneath her.

"Ruth!" Naomi turned and saw her daughter-in-law fall into a heap behind her. "Someone hurry and help us." She handed the infant to Neta to tend while she raced to Ruth's side. "My daughter." She felt her forehead. "She is too warm. Chana, come and help me lift her out of here."

Chana and Elke both joined her, and together the three of them lifted Ruth up and carried her into the cooler courtyard. Elke ran to get cushions and gave orders to the servants for help.

Naomi placed a cool cloth on Ruth's face and undid the warm robe she wore. "You should have shed this before entering the birthing room." She tsked, angry with herself for not thinking to tell Ruth what to do. The girl had never been in such a situation before except for Orpah's son's birth, and there were fewer women then. And of course, Ruth had not been pregnant. But now . . .

"Send for Boaz," Naomi ordered Chana as if she were a servant, but Melek's first wife did not seem put off by her concern. "And Hamul," she added, remembering that the babe, though a girl, would need her father's blessing. But would Melek bless the child of a man who was not his son?

He could sell her or send her away when she was old enough. As patriarch of his family, he held that power over Hamul, despite what Hamul had done to protect Hava.

The thoughts troubled her as she heard Chana hurry off, sending servants to find all of the men, Melek included.

"My daughter, please wake up." She undid the belt at Ruth's waist and placed another cool cloth over her brow. Her hair was damp, her veil left in one of the rooms in the house when they had entered.

Please, Adonai, I can't lose her too.

Ruth stirred slowly, her eyes blinking open. "What happened?" She tried to sit up, but Naomi placed a hand to her chest. "Don't get up too fast. You fainted, and we dare not let that happen again."

Ruth's brow knit in puzzlement. "I remember feeling sick." She pressed a hand to her middle. "And did Hava have a girl?"

Naomi nodded. "Yes, yes. She did." Her smile grew wide as she looked on this beautiful woman she called daughter. "And you, my dear girl, are most definitely with child."

"But . . ."

"All the signs point to it, Ruth. I should never have allowed you into the birthing room. The first few months tend to bring on the sickness of morn."

"But it is nearly evening."

Naomi shrugged. "Sometimes the sickness comes on in the evenings. Trust me, I know of what I speak."

Ruth looked at her, eyes wide. Moments later the sound of running, pounding feet drew near. She glanced beyond Naomi as Boaz burst into the courtyard ahead of Hamul and Melek. While the other men rushed into the house, Boaz knelt at Ruth's side.

"They said you were hurt." His breath came fast as he took her hand. Naomi backed away, leaving them space.

"No, not hurt," Ruth said, her gaze meeting his. Such love was evident in that one look it made Naomi's heart ache. This was a good thing. A blessing. Despite all of the heartache, Ruth's marriage to Boaz was good.

"Then what?" His brows rose, and he glanced from Ruth to Naomi and back again. "Tell me what is wrong, for they did not tell me to hurry for no reason."

"She fainted," Naomi said. "But not to worry, my son. She was simply feeling a little sick in a room that was too warm."

His puzzled look did not leave when he searched Ruth's face. "Beloved?"

"I believe I am with child," she said softly. "Mother Naomi says I have all the signs. I became sick and fainted because of the babe." She touched the place under her heart where the child grew in secret.

Boaz sat back, wonder in his gaze. "But . . ." A frown creased his brow. "But you fell. Is the babe . . . ?"

"The babe is fine, and your wife is fine, my lord," Naomi said, coming behind him and placing a hand on his shoulder. "Now take your wife home and make sure she rests. In a few days she will be as normal as she has always been."

Boaz looked at Naomi but a moment. His attention was for Ruth alone. Gently, as though he carried a vessel that could easily break, he lifted her into his arms and began the walk toward home.

Naomi watched them leave, her heart full. In her mind's eye she looked back, saw the day Mahlon was born, almost sensed the first small flutter of his body growing within her. What love she had known! But in the ensuing years, the wasted years in Moab, she was certain nothing good or lovely would ever enter her life again. Not after so much loss.

The noise from the household drifted to her, drawing her back to the present. She turned and moved toward the birthing chamber, but stopped at the sight of Melek standing at a window in the sitting room. Hamul was nowhere to be seen. She walked to him, this brother of Elimelech, the one who could have claimed Ruth if he had chosen to do so. How glad she was that he had refused. She had never gotten along well with Melek, always thought his greed had carried too much influence on Elimelech. But that didn't mean she should be unkind to him now.

She approached cautiously, gauging his mood. "A blessed day it is, my brother," she said when she was within arm's length. "You have a granddaughter." Would he agree?

He turned, looked into Naomi's eyes. "Hava has a daughter, yes."

"And your son has chosen to accept the child as his own." Naomi's gaze softened as she glimpsed the hint of pain in Melek's eyes.

"I'm grateful it wasn't a boy. At least that is one thing that will not ruin Hamul's inheritance." He looked beyond her, and she stared at him. The comment shouldn't surprise her. He had always cared more about the land and passing it on to a son, though even Moses had allowed for daughters to inherit where no sons were present.

Naomi sighed, suddenly weary of this brother-in-law who could not see past another's faults. "Will you accept her as your granddaughter then? Will you bless her as the daughter your son loves?"

Melek moved away from Naomi to the other window that

overlooked the courtyard. Voices from the birthing room drifted to them down the hall, and the cry of an infant suddenly pierced the air.

An urgent need to run to them, to help somehow, washed over Naomi, but she waited, saw the way Melek winced at the sound of the child's cries. She stepped closer to him, placed an arm on his shoulder.

"She sounds like every daughter my wives have ever born to me." He looked at her. "Though I suppose all infants cry the same."

Naomi smiled. "Our mothers would probably agree that even we wailed pitifully when we were hungry or wet or in need of our mother's love."

He glanced at her, then looked toward the hall from where the sounds still came. She saw the Adam's apple move in his thick neck, saw his brows knit, and could imagine the anguish going on in his heart and mind. The child had not been conceived in love but in hate. An act of violence against Hava, and yet Hamul had protected her, even going against his father's wishes, which could have caused more problems than it did.

"What will you do, my brother?" Naomi asked, knowing he warred with his own decision.

He did not speak for many moments, but his gaze remained fixed on the hall. And then Hamul emerged from it carrying the squalling, swaddled bundle in his arms. He approached his father, and Naomi stepped back.

"I have come to seek your blessing for my daughter, Father. Will you honor us with your blessing?" He held the child toward Melek, who stood unmoving, arms at his sides.

Hamul waited, tension mounting in the room, as Melek

Redeeming Grace

seemed caught in indecision. Naomi fought the urge to grab the child and thrust her into Melek's arms, like it or not, but she knew the action would not help. She bit back the words she longed to say to force him, to make him see.

But only God could make him see. *Only You, Adonai. Will You give this child a true home as You have done for my Ruth?*

She waited, wondering if the Almighty even concerned Himself with such prayers of an exhausted old woman who needed to go home and tend to her own family.

But as the child's cries quieted, Melek tilted his head slightly to gaze into her face. The child turned her head toward Melek, and if Naomi didn't know better, she almost thought she saw a smile dimple those infant cheeks.

Melek's arms rose slowly, accepting the child from his son's arms. The infant's mouth moved as if looking for sustenance, and Melek chuckled as he held her to his chest. He looked at his son. "You are a better man than I am, my son, for I would have shunned your wife and her child if you had not shown me a better way." He looked down at the child, touched a finger to her cheek.

Naomi's heart squeezed tight and tears threatened.

"And you, little one," he said softly, "may you be blessed of Adonai. May you be wise in the ways of our God and be a blessing to your father's house." He stopped, and she saw the emotion in his expression. How hard it must be for him to set aside his pride, to embrace what was not truly his.

Naomi stepped closer to him, touched his arm. "You have done the right thing," she said, meeting his gaze. They both glanced down at the baby and smiled. "She's beautiful, Melek. One day you will have too many young men seeking her affection, and you will have many more problems to deal with."

Melek laughed softly. "If they dare come too close, they will deal with me." He looked at his son, whose gaze held a mixture of awe and gratitude.

"Thank you, Father." He took the babe from Melek. "She needs to eat." He turned to take her back to Hava.

"What name has Hava given her?" Melek asked, stopping Hamul's gait.

"Geula," he called over his shoulder.

"Redemption," Naomi said, meeting Melek's gaze. Exactly what Boaz had done for Ruth, what Melek had refused but now accepted in this child.

"Yes, redemption." Melek spoke as though to himself, as though the very thought was something new to him. Perhaps it was.

44

SEVEN MONTHS LATER

Boaz tapped his foot and watched as his workers neared the end of harvesting the wheat in this section of Elimelech's field. He probably should have taken a sickle and helped them, but moving from field to field to keep things in order and threshing the wheat at night were becoming harder with the passing of time, though he would never admit it to anyone. Least of all his overseer, who smiled broadly as he approached.

"I had hoped to finish today," he said when Ezra stood next to him.

"The field produced more than we expected." Ezra lifted a brow. "Our God has blessed what was once lost and fallow."

Boaz gave Ezra's words a moment to sink in. "He is the God of renewal, my friend."

"And resurrection." Ezra moved his hands in an arc from the ground to the sky as if trying to express resurrection. They'd discussed the topic many times since that day over a year ago—when Boaz had been too grieved to hope or think clearly. But somehow Ruth and Adonai had turned his life completely around, and he was fairly certain his servants, particularly Ezra, were glad of it.

"Do you want to wait until they finish the work, or go home to your wife? She is due any day now, is she not?"

Boaz nodded.

"I can stay until the men leave." Ezra gave him a knowing look.

"How can you tell this is exactly my desire?" Boaz smiled. Did his expressions show so easily what his heart was feeling? And yet, Ezra knew him well.

"You tap your foot when you grow impatient. Or stroke your beard when you're trying to decide what to say." Ezra shrugged. "Go home. Enjoy time with Ruth before that babe comes and keeps you up at night and you turn back into a bear of a man."

Boaz gave him an affronted look. "I was never a bear."

Ezra huffed. "You should have looked in a mirror."

Boaz rolled his eyes but couldn't stop the smile, and soon both men chuckled. "I was a beast last year at this time, wasn't I?"

Ezra bobbed his head. "A beast. A lion. A bear. Take your pick."

Boaz shook his head. "I don't know how I put up with you." He patted his friend's arm. "I will see you tomorrow."

Ezra waved as Boaz mounted his donkey and rode toward Bethlehem, urging the animal into a faster trot the closer he came. He jumped down and hurried inside the moment he reached the outer court.

"You are home." Ruth trundled toward him, swaying with

the weight of the child. She placed a hand to her back as though it pained her.

"I wanted to spend time with you." He looked her up and down. "All is well?" The ever-present fear, the memories of loss, would not leave.

She nodded and smiled. "Just some slight pain in my lower back. The babe is active today." She held out a hand to him. "Come and see."

He followed her into the sitting room and sat gently beside her. She took his hand and placed it where the babe lay.

He was rewarded with a swift kick. He laughed. "You are right. He moves like his father, who nearly forced the donkey to race the wind the whole way home." He kissed her softly. "Though I am certain he will have the kindness of his mother."

She blushed sweetly beneath his praise, and he loved seeing the shyness creep into her eyes. "He will be blessed to call you Father."

Though they both knew the boy would carry Mahlon's name, her kindness warmed him. "And what if *he* is a *she*?"

"Then *she* will be blessed to call you Abba." She laughed, and the sound of it carried the music of song. She took his hand. "But I am afraid I cannot sit for long, so help me up and let us walk through the house."

He stood and bowed to her. "Yes, my lady."

She playfully patted his arm, and he easily lifted her to her feet. Even nine months with child she was still light, though not as frail as Adi had been.

Adi. How strange it seemed to him that the memory of his beloved no longer brought pain, only longing to one day see her again and introduce her to Ruth . . . if resurrection was anything like he imagined it to be. Somehow he sensed that Adi would be pleased with Ruth, that they would have been friends. And though she might not have chosen to leave this world when she did, if she could see him, he sensed that she would be glad for his choice.

Adonai's choice, he corrected, for he had been too timid to make it himself. Yet God had not allowed him to wallow in his pain.

He took Ruth's hand and tucked it beneath his arm, grateful and a little in awe of what God had done in his heart. They walked through the rooms he had shown her that first week of their marriage.

"Does walking ease the pain in your back?"

She nodded, paused a moment to catch her breath, then released it.

After she had repeated that action several times, he turned her to face him. "Are you in the beginnings of labor, my love?"

She nodded again. "I think so. That is, I have never been in this situation before, but Naomi tells me that this is how it begins."

He glanced around before searching her gaze once more. "Where is Naomi? Should I get her?"

Ruth shook her head. "She is resting, and I am in no danger of giving birth where I stand." She smiled at him. "It helps to walk."

He took her arm again, wanting to believe her. But his heart beat faster with knowing how soon his whole life could change—again.

"Are you afraid, my lord?" They turned toward the inner courtyard where the sun baked the sides of the roof. The stones were hot, and the oven used for baking bread remained warm, even though the fire had been snuffed out long ago.

He wrapped her in his arms, pulling her close to his side. "I dream sometimes," he admitted, not looking at her. "I see my son wrapped in the burial shrouds, and I awake with a jolt, begging God not to let it happen again." His heart thudded so hard he was certain she could hear it in his chest.

"This time will be different," she said softly, stroking the hairs on his arm. "Remember, my lord, that I have also lost those I've loved. And yet God has put me here, with you." She touched his cheek, turning his face to meet her gaze. "Nothing is going to go wrong. Believe, beloved."

Her smile was his undoing. A woman younger than he, who was once a foreigner to his people, was now telling him, a leader in Israel, to believe?

And she had called him *beloved*.

He cupped her face and bent low, kissing her. "You are most blessed of women, my Ruth, my wife, my most beloved." With each kiss, his heart soared that she looked at him with love he had never expected to know again in this life.

The babe kicked between them.

"Already I have competition for your love." He laughed.

"Never competition," she said, laughing with him. "An addition to the blessings."

THE NEXT DAY

Ruth tossed and turned most of the night, praying she would not awaken Boaz, who seemed to be at last sleeping peacefully. The pains that had been minor the day before had increased steadily throughout the night, and before dawn she felt the gush of waters break as she made her way to Naomi's room.

"Mother," she called from the doorway.

Naomi jarred awake, as though she slept on the edge of waiting, and jumped up like a young gazelle despite her aging bones. "Is it time?"

Naomi's scrutinizing look told her the woman would know without a word from her, but Ruth nodded regardless. "My waters just spilled out as I was coming to you. The pains are frequent." She paused on the last word as another contraction seized her. She forced herself not to double over but clenched her middle instead.

Naomi rushed from the room, grabbing towels and a basin and Ruth's arm. "Come." She led Ruth to the room they had set aside for the birthing and settled her among the cushions. "I will check you as soon as I send for help."

She hurried off as Ruth battled another contraction. Servants' voices filtered to her, and lamps were lit. Moments later, Boaz stood wide-eyed at the entrance to the birthing chamber, while Naomi continued to bark orders in the distance.

He came and knelt at her side. "It is time?"

She nodded, gritting her teeth, unable to speak.

"Should I leave?"

She shook her head. "No. Don't go far." She knew he would be happier roaming the hills than hearing her screams, but she also knew he needed to be near, to know she was going to be fine.

Please, Adonai, let all go well.

Naomi burst into the room and stopped short at the sight of him. "The birthing room is no place for a man, my son.

Perhaps go with Reuven and inspect the warehouse for a time. In any case, I need to see how far along she has come."

He stood, and Ruth sensed his uncertainty, his embarrassment. It wasn't a place for men, and yet, had he not been there in the beginning? But he nodded at Naomi and left with only a longing glance Ruth's way.

"Lie back on the cushions and let me see how soon you will need the birthing stool." Naomi's crusty tone told Ruth of the excitement and fear living just beneath the surface. Was not every birth a miracle? And yet every birth involved great risk to the mother.

"Oh my," Naomi said after Ruth complied with her wishes. "The babe is nearly ready to come down. He hasn't crowned just yet, but it will not be long, my daughter."

Ruth breathed in and out, hoping the words were true. Another contraction assaulted her as the noise of servants and the bustle of the women Naomi had sent for descended on Boaz's home.

"How is she? Is the water warmed? Where are the swaddling cloths?" Gilah's questions came quickly, keeping pace with Ruth's racing heart.

"Everything is here, of course." Naomi sounded almost terse, if Ruth judged correctly, but this was a woman's world and Naomi was in her element. When Orpah had given birth, Naomi was not favored to be the main woman at her side, for she had wanted her mother, who took charge the moment she stepped into Naomi's house. But this time Naomi was in charge, and she did not mind letting the other women know it.

Neta checked the water and the fire that warmed it, and Liora fluffed the sheet and pillows where Ruth would nurse the child once he or she was born.

"Water," Ruth said, her voice squeaky from disuse, from holding back the urge to cry out.

Naomi shook her head. "A few sips, my daughter. You should not drink a lot of water during birth." She took the cup and held it slowly to Ruth's parched lips. And pulled it away too soon. But Ruth did not complain, for to do so would do no good.

Another contraction followed, until they were coming in quick succession. Naomi checked her twice more, until at last she declared her fit for the stool.

Neta dragged it from the corner while Gilah stood behind Ruth, holding her up. Liora knelt near Naomi, ready to take the child once Naomi caught him or her on her knees.

"What names have you thought of?" Liora asked, clearly trying to distract Ruth from the pain, but she could not speak past the groaning.

"Never mind that now." Naomi's tone halted all conversation. "She is trying to concentrate. Do not distract her."

The sound of footsteps in the hall made her turn to see Boaz standing at the threshold, his face a mask of misery. But somehow his presence there gave her strength. She bore down, once, twice, until at last the child rushed from her in a wash of blood and water and landed in Naomi's outstretched arms.

"A boy!" came the jubilant cry of all the women.

"Ruth, you have a son!" Naomi beamed, her countenance bright like morning's dawn.

"A son," Ruth said through one final contraction to complete the birthing. Exhaustion filled her as she glanced toward the threshold. Boaz still stood there, his gaze sweeping the room and resting on his son. Their son.

Ruth smiled at him even as Naomi waved him away. "No place for a man," she muttered. "We must clean the babe and you. Then he can see you both."

She handed the child to Liora, who with Neta's help cleaned and wrapped him. Naomi and Gilah tended to Ruth, helping her out of the sweaty tunic and sponging water over her exhausted body. She would be unclean for seven days, Naomi had told her, and then must stay away from holy things for thirty-three days after the birth of a boy. A time for bonding with her son, a time to rest. It seemed that the God of Israel, her God, even cared for a woman in childbirth and made provisions for her to rest from her labor before taking on every task and duty she normally performed.

"There," Naomi said, tucking the babe into her arms at last.

Ruth looked into her mother-in-law's wistful eyes and smiled. "Do you want to hold him longer, Mother?" She handed the child to Naomi. The child who would carry on the line of Naomi's son.

Naomi took the boy and sat beside Ruth, holding him close to her heart. In that moment Boaz returned to the room, apparently unable to stay away, and stopped near Naomi's side.

"Blessed be the Lord," Gilah said to Naomi, "who has not left you this day without a redeemer, and may his name be renowned in Israel!"

"He shall be to you a restorer of life and a nourisher of your old age," Neta agreed, "for your daughter-in-law who loves you, who is more to you than seven sons, has given birth to him."

Ruth looked at her mother-in-law holding her son, and despite the longing to hold him she waited a moment longer and smiled. "You shall be his nurse, Mother."

Tears filled Naomi's eyes as she looked from Ruth to Boaz.

"A son has been born to Naomi," the women in the room all said at once.

"He is the servant of the Lord," Gilah said.

"And a worshiper of Yahweh." Liora spoke with such conviction all eyes turned to her. "He is Obed, for he has been born to redeem this family."

"And all Israel," Boaz said softly.

Ruth looked at him, her brows lifted as she took Obed from Naomi's arms and helped him find her breast. "All Israel, my lord?" He was just a child. A servant, perhaps. A worshiper—she hoped so. But a redeemer of Israel?

"Someday," Boaz said, looking into her eyes, letting his gaze drift down to the beauty of his son, "he will be in the line of the true Redeemer. For he comes from the line of kings, as I come from the line of Judah. Jacob blessed Judah, saying that kings would come from his descendants." He knelt beside her. "You, beloved, are the mother of kings to come."

Of kings? The thought was too unimaginable, too far away to matter, as she nestled her new son against her breast, her heart full. She smiled. Not because of the promise, but because at last Adonai her God and Boaz her beloved had made her a mother.

EPILOGUE

Judah, your brothers shall praise you;
　　your hand shall be on the neck of your enemies;
　　your father's sons shall bow down before you.
Judah is a lion's cub;
　　from the prey, my son, you have gone up.
He stooped down; he crouched as a lion
　　and as a lioness; who dares rouse him?
The scepter shall not depart from Judah,
　　nor the ruler's staff from between his feet,
until tribute comes to him;
　　and to him shall be the obedience of the peoples.

Genesis 49:8–10

Now these are the generations of Perez [son of Judah]: Perez fathered Hezron, Hezron fathered Ram, Ram fathered Amminadab, Amminadab fathered Nahshon, Nahshon fathered Salmon, Salmon fathered Boaz, Boaz fathered Obed, Obed fathered Jesse, and Jesse fathered David.

Ruth 4:18–22

The book of the genealogy of Jesus Christ, the son of David, the son of Abraham.

Abraham was the father of Isaac, and Isaac the father of Jacob, and Jacob the father of Judah and his brothers, and Judah the father of Perez and Zerah by Tamar . . . and Salmon the father of Boaz by Rahab, and Boaz the father of Obed by Ruth, and Obed the father of Jesse, and Jesse the father of David the king.

Matthew 1:1–3, 5–6

NOTE TO THE READER

In researching the timeline for Ruth's story, I came across
two differing points of view. One suggests Ruth's story
came before Deborah's time as judge, during the era of
Moabite oppression of Israel. This timing does allow for a
more acceptable understanding of the genealogy that tells us
Salmon begat Boaz by Rahab, and Boaz begat Obed by Ruth.

The other puts Ruth's story later, nearer the end of the
reign of the judges, which would give Ruth a closer proximity
to David. She is listed as David's great-grandmother. But by
that argument, Rahab is David's great-great-grandmother.
According to what I could find, Rahab lived in approximately
1405 BC, and Ruth's story takes place around 1150 BC. Boaz
was not likely over 250 years old when he met Ruth!

Greater minds than mine can debate this timing issue.
Some suggest that the Jews would often condense a genea-
logical record for the sake of making note of the most important or prominent people in the lineage. This suggests

that "Salmon begat Boaz" could mean that Salmon was an ancestor of Boaz, not necessarily his actual father.

In *The Crimson Cord*, I chose to show Boaz as Rahab's son. It is possible that her actual son born of Salmon had a different name entirely, and that the record in Scripture just skipped a few generations. That possibility does not take away from God's grace to Rahab or the fact that Rahab and Salmon did marry and have a son. The question is whether Boaz was their son or grandson or great-grandson.

For these questions, I admit I have no concrete answers. But I believe God gave us what He needed us to know, and that is the fact that He is a forgiving God, a redeeming God, and a gracious and loving and merciful God. And while He is also the God who judges and holds sovereignty over all, I believe His message in the stories of these women is to show us His great grace.

Whether Rahab birthed Boaz or his ancestor matters little. For both Rahab and Ruth teach us that God included Gentile women who came to faith in the one true God in the lineage of His Son.

So I pray you overlooked the timeline difficulties and enjoyed the story. For the sake of the story, I set Ruth's tale during the middle of Judges, before Deborah's rule. I tend to think that somehow the dates will work themselves out and that maybe Rahab really did birth Boaz and Boaz married Ruth, as it is written.

In His Grace,
Jill Eileen Smith

ACKNOWLEDGMENTS

It's hard to believe that it's been eight years since the release of my first book, *Michal*. And now we are in the middle of my third and fourth series of biblical fiction with *Redeeming Grace*. I've been privileged to continue to work with the same wonderful team at Revell through each one of these books, so I would like to give my thanks to Lonnie Hull DuPont, who first believed in me and always encourages me along the way. To Jessica English, who has a way of editing that always makes me feel good and makes the story better in the process.

To my marketing manager, Michele Misiak, who possesses a wealth of creative ideas. To my publicist and the team who puts together the blog tours, and to those who handle foreign rights—I have books on my shelves that I've written yet can't read. So cool! To Twila Bennett, who oversees more than I can imagine, and Cheryl Van Andel, for letting me watch some of what she does with her amazing covers!

Thanks always to my agent and friend, Wendy Lawton, who prays for her clients and cheers them on.

Super thanks go to my dear friend Jill Stengl, as always, for help with this story.

A special thank-you this time also goes to my pastor, Doug Schmidt, for providing me with information on the biblical feasts. That proved invaluable.

Another special thank-you to my friend Kathy Kroll for the basket idea. These little details make a story so much richer.

Thank you to my readers who wait and pray for me as I write. My prayer team and friends who pray—I really appreciate you.

To my family, immediate and extended—I only wish we lived closer, but I thank God for you and what He still has in store for each of us. Randy—I can't imagine life without you. Jeff, Chris, Molly, and Keaton, Ryan and Carissa—I love you.

Adonai, my Lord, my Savior—may You always be enough. Thank You that You are.

Jill Eileen Smith is the author of the bestselling Wives of King David series and *The Crimson Cord*, as well as the Wives of the Patriarchs, the Daughters of the Promised Land, and the Loves of King Solomon series. Her research has taken her from the Bible to Israel, and she particularly enjoys learning how women lived in biblical times.

When she isn't writing, she loves to spend time with her family and friends, read stories that take her away, ride her bike to the park, snag date nights with her hubby, try out new restaurants, or play with her lovable, "helpful" cat Tiger. Jill lives with her family in southeast Michigan.

Contact Jill through email (jill@jilleileensmith.com), her website (http://www.jilleileensmith.com), Facebook (https://www.facebook.com/jilleileensmith), or Twitter (https://twitter.com/JillEileenSmith). She loves to hear from her readers.

Meet
JILL EILEEN SMITH

at **www.JillEileenSmith.com** to learn
interesting facts and read her blog!

Connect with her on

Jill Eileen Smith

JillEileenSmith

"JILL'S STORYTELLING SKILLS
KEPT ME READING LATE INTO THE NIGHT.
A BEAUTIFUL TALE, BEAUTIFULLY TOLD!"

—LIZ CURTIS HIGGS,
New York Times bestselling author of *Mine Is the Night*

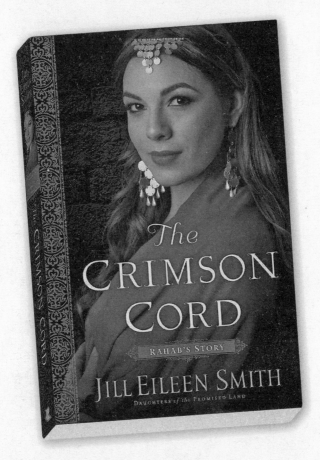

Immerse yourself in a world of dark and dusty streets,
clandestine meetings, and daring escapes as a mysterious biblical figure
claims her full humanity—and a permanent place in your heart.

 Revell
a division of Baker Publishing Group   Available wherever books and ebooks are sold.
www.RevellBooks.com

Canaan has ravaged Israel.
The people are in hiding. All that stands
between surrender and hope is
ONE UNTESTED WOMAN.

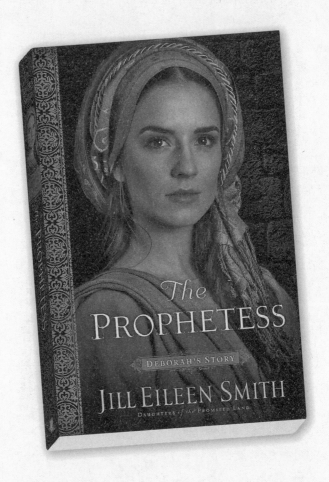

Chosen by God to judge her people, Deborah must find the courage
to save her nation from the armies of Canaan without destroying her family.

Revell
a division of Baker Publishing Group
www.RevellBooks.com

Available wherever books and ebooks are sold.

The Wives of King David series
will transport you back in time

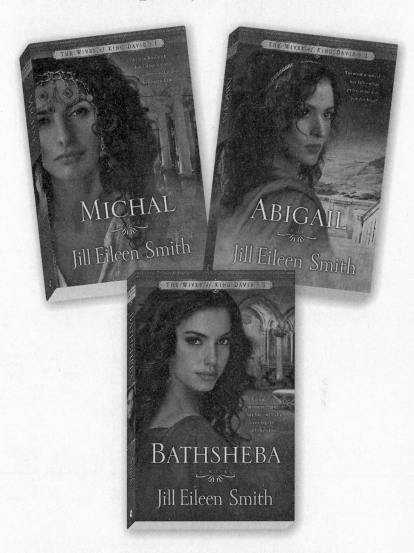

Bestselling author Jill Eileen Smith brings to life the Bible's
most famous stories of passion, betrayal, and redemption.

Revell
a division of Baker Publishing Group
www.RevellBooks.com

Available wherever books and ebooks are sold.

"Rich, biblical drama."

—Lyn Cote, author of *Her Abundant Joy*

Through vivid storytelling and meticulous research, Jill Eileen Smith brings to life the WIVES *of the* PATRIARCHS through these remarkable stories of love, jealousy, and undaunted faith.

Revell
a division of Baker Publishing Group
www.RevellBooks.com

Available wherever books and ebooks are sold. f y

The LOVES of KING SOLOMON

BE SWEPT AWAY with these tales of young love, heartbreaking betrayal, and the power of forgiveness.

Revell
a division of Baker Publishing Group
www.RevellBooks.com

Available wherever ebooks are sold.

Be the First to Hear about Other New Books from REVELL!

Sign up for announcements about new and upcoming titles at

RevellBooks.com/SignUp

Don't miss out on our great reads!

Revell

a division of Baker Publishing Group
www.RevellBooks.com